ROAMING THE DARK

ROAMING THE DARK

STORIES BY
RICHARD MIDDLETON
AND
BARRY PAIN

COACHWHIP PUBLICATIONS
Landisville, Pennsylvania

Roaming the Dark: Stories by Richard Middleton and Barry Pain
Copyright © 2012 Coachwhip Publications
No claim made on public domain material.

Richard Middleton (1882-1911)
Barry Pain (1864-1928)

ISBN 1-61646-118-7
ISBN-13 978-1-61646-118-8

Cover Image: Feline © Cobalt Moon Design

CoachwhipBooks.com

CONTENTS

RICHARD MIDDLETON

BARRY PAIN

RICHARD MIDDLETON

THE GHOST-SHIP

Fairfield is a little village lying near the Portsmouth Road about half-way between London and the sea. Strangers who find it by accident now and then, call it a pretty, old-fashioned place; we who live in it and call it home don't find anything very pretty about it, but we should be sorry to live anywhere else. Our minds have taken the shape of the inn and the church and the green, I suppose. At all events we never feel comfortable out of Fairfield.

Of course the Cockneys, with their vasty houses and noise-ridden streets, can call us rustics if they choose, but for all that Fairfield is a better place to live in than London. Doctor says that when he goes to London his mind is bruised with the weight of the houses, and he was a Cockney born. He had to live there himself when he was a little chap, but he knows better now. You gentle-men may laugh—perhaps some of you come from London way—but it seems to me that a witness like that is worth a gallon of arguments.

Dull? Well, you might find it dull, but I assure you that I've listened to all the London yarns you have spun tonight, and they're absolutely nothing to the things that happen at Fairfield. It's because of our way of thinking and minding our own business. If one of your Londoners were set down on the green of a Saturday night when the ghosts of the lads who died in the war keep tryst with the lasses who lie in the church-yard, he couldn't help being curious and interfering, and then the ghosts would go somewhere where it was quieter. But we just let them come and go and don't make any

9

fuss, and in consequence Fairfield is the ghostiest place in all England. Why, I've seen a headless man sitting on the edge of the well
in broad daylight, and the children playing about his feet as if he
were their father. Take my word for it, spirits know when they are
well off as much as human beings.

Still, I must admit that the thing I'm going to tell you about
was queer even for our part of the world, where three packs of
ghost-hounds hunt regularly during the season, and blacksmith's
great-grandfather is busy all night shoeing the dead gentlemen's
horses. Now that's a thing that wouldn't happen in London, because of their interfering ways, but blacksmith he lies up aloft and
sleeps as quiet as a lamb. Once when he had a bad head he shouted
down to them not to make so much noise, and in the morning he
found an old guinea left on the anvil as an apology. He wears it on
his watch-chain now. But I must get on with my story; if I start
telling you about the queer happenings at Fairfield I'll never stop.

It all came of the great storm in the spring of '97, the year that
we had two great storms. This was the first one, and I remember it
very well, because I found in the morning that it had lifted the
thatch of my pigsty into the widow's garden as clean as a boy's
kite. When I looked over the hedge, widow—Tom Lamport's widow
that was—was prodding for her nasturtiums with a daisy-grubber.
After I had watched her for a little I went down to the "Fox and
Grapes" to tell landlord what she had said to me. Landlord he
laughed, being a married man and at ease with the sex. "Come to
that," he said, "the tempest has blowed something into my field. A
kind of a ship I think it would be."

I was surprised at that until he explained that it was only a
ghost-ship and would do no hurt to the turnips. We argued that it
had been blown up from the sea at Portsmouth, and then we talked
of something else. There were two slates down at the parsonage
and a big tree in Lumley's meadow. It was a rare storm.

I reckon the wind had blown our ghosts all over England. They
were coming back for days afterwards with foundered horses and
as footsore as possible, and they were so glad to get back to Fairfield
that some of them walked up the street crying like little children.

Squire said that his great-grandfather's great-grandfather hadn't looked so dead-beat since the battle of Naseby, and he's an educated man.

What with one thing and another, I should think it was a week before we got straight again, and then one afternoon I met the landlord on the green and he had a worried face. "I wish you'd come and have a look at that ship in my field," he said to me; "it seems to me it's leaning real hard on the turnips. I can't bear thinking what the missus will say when she sees it."

I walked down the lane with him, and sure enough there was a ship in the middle of his field, but such a ship as no man had seen on the water for three hundred years, let alone in the middle of a turnip-field. It was all painted black and covered with carvings, and there was a great bay window in the stern for all the world like the Squire's drawing-room. There was a crowd of little black cannon on deck and looking out of her port-holes, and she was anchored at each end to the hard ground. I have seen the wonders of the world on picture-postcards, but I have never seen anything to equal that.

"She seems very solid for a ghost-ship," I said, seeing the landlord was bothered.

"I should say it's a betwixt and between," he answered, puzzling it over, "but it's going to spoil a matter of fifty turnips, and missus she'll want it moved." We went up to her and touched the side, and it was as hard as a real ship. "Now there's folks in England would call that very curious," he said.

Now I don't know much about ships, but I should think that that ghost-ship weighed a solid two hundred tons, and it seemed to me that she had come to stay, so that I felt sorry for landlord, who was a married man. "All the horses in Fairfield won't move her out of my turnips," he said, frowning at her.

Just then we heard a noise on her deck, and we looked up and saw that a man had come out of her front cabin and was looking down at us very peaceably. He was dressed in a black uniform set out with rusty gold lace, and he had a great cutlass by his side in a brass sheath. "I'm Captain Bartholomew Roberts," he said, in a gentleman's voice, "put in for recruits. I seem to have brought her rather far up the harbour."

"Harbour!" cried landlord; "why, you're fifty miles from the sea."

Captain Roberts didn't turn a hair. "So much as that, is it?" he said coolly. "Well, it's of no consequence."

Landlord was a bit upset at this. "I don't want to be unneighbourly," he said, "but I wish you hadn't brought your ship into my field. You see, my wife sets great store on these turnips."

The captain took a pinch of snuff out of a fine gold box that he pulled out of his pocket, and dusted his fingers with a silk handkerchief in a very genteel fashion. "I'm only here for a few months," he said; "but if a testimony of my esteem would pacify your good lady I should be content," and with the words he loosed a great gold brooch from the neck of his coat and tossed it down to landlord.

Landlord blushed as red as a strawberry. "I'm not denying she's fond of jewellery," he said, "but it's too much for half a sackful of turnips." And indeed it was a handsome brooch.

The captain laughed. "Tut, man," he said, "it's a forced sale, and you deserve a good price. Say no more about it;" and nodding good-day to us, he turned on his heel and went into the cabin. Landlord walked back up the lane like a man with a weight off his mind. "That tempest has blowed me a bit of luck," he said; "the missus will be much pleased with that brooch. It's better than blacksmith's guinea, any day."

Ninety-seven was Jubilee year, the year of the second Jubilee, you remember, and we had great doings at Fairfield, so that we hadn't much time to bother about the ghost-ship though anyhow it isn't our way to meddle in things that don't concern us. Landlord, he saw his tenant once or twice when he was hoeing his turnips and passed the time of day, and landlord's wife wore her new brooch to church every Sunday. But we didn't mix much with the ghosts at any time, all except an idiot lad there was in the village, and he didn't know the difference between a man and a ghost, poor innocent! On Jubilee Day, however, somebody told Captain Roberts why the church bells were ringing, and he hoisted a flag and fired off his guns like a loyal Englishman. 'Tis true the guns were shotted, and one of the round shot knocked a hole in Farmer Johnstone's barn, but nobody thought much of that in such a season of rejoicing.

It wasn't till our celebrations were over that we noticed that anything was wrong in Fairfield. 'Twas shoemaker who told me first about it one morning at the "Fox and Grapes." "You know my great great-uncle?" he said to me.

"You mean Joshua, the quiet lad," I answered, knowing him well.

"Quiet!" said shoemaker indignantly. "Quiet you call him, coming home at three o'clock every morning as drunk as a magistrate and waking up the whole house with his noise."

"Why, it can't be Joshua!" I said, for I knew him for one of the most respectable young ghosts in the village.

"Joshua it is," said shoemaker; "and one of these nights he'll find himself out in the street if he isn't careful."

This kind of talk shocked me, I can tell you, for I don't like to hear a man abusing his own family, and I could hardly believe that a steady youngster like Joshua had taken to drink. But just then in came butcher Aylwin in such a temper that he could hardly drink his beer. "The young puppy! the young puppy!" he kept on saying; and it was some time before shoemaker and I found out that he was talking about his ancestor that fell at Senlac.

"Drink?" said shoemaker hopefully, for we all like company in our misfortunes, and butcher nodded grimly.

"The young noodle," he said, emptying his tankard.

Well, after that I kept my ears open, and it was the same story all over the village. There was hardly a young man among all the ghosts of Fairfield who didn't roll home in the small hours of the morning the worse for liquor. I used to wake up in the night and hear them stumble past my house, singing outrageous songs. The worst of it was that we couldn't keep the scandal to ourselves and the folk at Greenhill began to talk of "sodden Fairfield" and taught their children to sing a song about us:

> "Sodden Fairfield, sodden Fairfield, has no use
> for bread-and-butter,
> Rum for breakfast, rum for dinner, rum for tea,
> and rum for supper!"

We are easy-going in our village, but we didn't like that.

Of course we soon found out where the young fellows went to get the drink, and landlord was terribly cut up that his tenant should have turned out so badly, but his wife wouldn't hear of parting with the brooch, so that he couldn't give the Captain notice to quit. But as time went on, things grew from bad to worse, and at all hours of the day you would see those young reprobates sleeping it off on the village green. Nearly every afternoon a ghost-wagon used to jolt down to the ship with a lading of rum, and though the older ghosts seemed inclined to give the Captain's hospitality the go-by, the youngsters were neither to hold nor to bind.

So one afternoon when I was taking my nap I heard a knock at the door, and there was parson looking very serious, like a man with a job before him that he didn't altogether relish. "I'm going down to talk to the Captain about all this drunkenness in the village, and I want you to come with me," he said straight out.

I can't say that I fancied the visit much, myself, and I tried to hint to parson that as, after all, they were only a lot of ghosts it didn't very much matter.

"Dead or alive, I'm responsible for the good conduct," he said, "and I'm going to do my duty and put a stop to this continued disorder. And you are coming with me, John Simmons." So I went, parson being a persuasive kind of man.

We went down to the ship, and as we approached her I could see the Captain tasting the air on deck. When he saw parson he took off his hat very politely and I can tell you that I was relieved to find that he had a proper respect for the cloth. Parson acknowledged his salute and spoke out stoutly enough. "Sir, I should be glad to have a word with you."

"Come on board, sir; come on board," said the Captain, and I could tell by his voice that he knew why we were there. Parson and

I climbed up an uneasy kind of ladder, and the Captain took us into the great cabin at the back of the ship, where the bay-window was. It was the most wonderful place you ever saw in your life, all full of gold and silver plate, swords with jewelled scabbards, carved oak chairs, and great chests that look as though they were bursting with guineas. Even parson was surprised, and he did not shake his head very hard when the Captain took down some silver cups and poured us out a drink of rum. I tasted mine, and I don't mind saying that it changed my view of things entirely. There was nothing betwixt and between about that rum, and I felt that it was ridiculous to blame the lads for drinking too much of stuff like that. It seemed to fill my veins with honey and fire.

Parson put the case squarely to the Captain, but I didn't listen much to what he said; I was busy sipping my drink and looking through the window at the fishes swimming to and fro over landlord's turnips. Just then it seemed the most natural thing in the world that they should be there, though afterwards, of course, I could see that that proved it was a ghost-ship.

But even then I thought it was queer when I saw a drowned sailor float by in the thin air with his hair and beard all full of bubbles. It was the first time I had seen anything quite like that at Fairfield.

All the time I was regarding the wonders of the deep parson was telling Captain Roberts how there was no peace or rest in the village owing to the curse of drunkenness, and what a bad example the youngsters were setting to the older ghosts. The Captain listened very attentively, and only put in a word now and then about boys being boys and young men sowing their wild oats. But when parson had finished his speech he filled up our silver cups and said to parson, with a flourish, "I should be sorry to cause trouble anywhere where I have been made welcome, and you will be glad to hear that I put to sea tomorrow night. And now you must drink me a prosperous voyage." So we all stood up and drank the toast with honour, and that noble rum was like hot oil in my veins.

After that Captain showed us some of the curiosities he had brought back from foreign parts, and we were greatly amazed, though afterwards I couldn't clearly remember what they were. And then I found myself walking across the turnips with parson, and I was telling him of the glories of the deep that I had seen through the window of the ship. He turned on me severely. "If I were you, John Simmons," he said, "I should go straight home to bed." He has a way of putting things that wouldn't occur to an ordinary man, has parson, and I did as he told me.

Well, next day it came on to blow, and it blew harder and harder, till about eight o'clock at night I heard a noise and looked out into the garden. I dare say you won't believe me, it seems a bit tall even to me, but the wind had lifted the thatch of my pigsty into the widow's garden a second time. I thought I wouldn't wait to hear what widow had to say about it, so I went across the green to the "Fox and Grapes," and the wind was so strong that I danced along on tiptoe like a girl at the fair. When I got to the inn landlord had to help me shut the door; it seemed as though a dozen goats were pushing against it to come in out of the storm.

"It's a powerful tempest," he said, drawing the beer. "I hear there's a chimney down at Dickory End."

"It's a funny thing how these sailors know about the weather," I answered. "When Captain said he was going tonight, I was thinking it would take a capful of wind to carry the ship back to sea, but now here's more than a capful."

"Ah, yes," said landlord, "it's tonight he goes true enough, and, mind you, though he treated me handsome over the rent, I'm not sure it's a loss to the village. I don't hold with gentrice who fetch their drink from London instead of helping local traders to get their living."

"But you haven't got any rum like his," I said, to draw him out.

His neck grew red above his collar, and I was afraid I'd gone too far; but after a while he got his breath with a grunt.

"John Simmons," he said, "if you've come down here this windy night to talk a lot of fool's talk, you've wasted a journey."

Well, of course, then I had to smooth him down with praising his rum, and Heaven forgive me for swearing it was better than Captain's. For the like of that rum no living lips have tasted save mine and parson's. But somehow or other I brought landlord round, and presently we must have a glass of his best to prove its quality.

"Beat that if you can!" he cried, and we both raised our glasses to our mouths, only to stop half-way and look at each other in amaze. For the wind that had been howling outside like an outrageous dog had all of a sudden turned as melodious as the carol-boys of a Christmas Eve.

"Surely that's not my Martha," whispered landlord; Martha being his great-aunt that lived in the loft overhead.

We went to the door, and the wind burst it open so that the handle was driven clean into the plaster of the wall. But we didn't think about that at the time; for over our heads, sailing very comfortably through the windy stars, was the ship that had passed the summer in landlord's field. Her portholes and her bay-window were blazing with lights, and there was a noise of singing and fiddling on her decks. "He's gone," shouted landlord above the storm, "and he's taken half the village with him!" I could only nod in answer, not having lungs like bellows of leather.

In the morning we were able to measure the strength of the storm, and over and above my pigsty there was damage enough wrought in the village to keep us busy. True it is that the children had to break down no branches for the firing that autumn, since the wind had strewn the woods with more than they could carry away. Many of our ghosts were scattered abroad, but this time very few came back, all the young men having sailed with Captain; and not only ghosts, for a poor half-witted lad was missing, and we reckoned that he had stowed himself away or perhaps shipped as cabin-boy, not knowing any better.

What with the lamentations of the ghost-girls and the grumbling of families who had lost an ancestor, the village was upset for a while, and the funny thing was that it was the folk who had complained most of the carryings-on of the youngsters, who made most noise now that they were gone. I hadn't any sympathy with shoemaker or butcher, who ran about saying how much they missed their lads, but it made me grieve to hear the poor bereaved girls calling their lovers by name on the village green at nightfall. It didn't seem fair to me that they should have lost their men a second time, after giving up life in order to join them, as like as not. Still, not even a spirit can be sorry for ever, and after a few months we made up our mind that the folk who had sailed in the ship were never coming back, and we didn't talk about it any more.

And then one day, I dare say it would be a couple of years after, when the whole business was quite forgotten, who should come trapesing along the road from Portsmouth but the daft lad who had gone away with the ship, without waiting till he was dead to become a ghost. You never saw such a boy as that in all your life. He had a great rusty cutlass hanging to a string at his waist, and he was tattooed all over in fine colours, so that even his face looked like a girl's sampler. He had a handkerchief in his hand full of foreign shells and old-fashioned pieces of small money, very curious, and he walked up to the well outside his mother's house and drew himself a drink as if he had been nowhere in particular.

The worst of it was that he had come back as soft-headed as he went, and try as we might we couldn't get anything reasonable out of him. He talked a lot of gibberish about keel-hauling and walking the plank and crimson murders—things which a decent sailor should know nothing about, so that it seemed to me that for all his manners Captain had been more of a pirate than a gentleman mariner. But to draw sense out of that boy was as hard as picking cherries off a crab-tree. One silly tale he had that he kept on drifting back to, and to hear him you would have thought that it was the only thing that happened to him in his life. "We was at anchor," he would say, "off an island called the Basket of Flowers, and the sailors had caught a lot of parrots and we were teaching them to swear. Up and down the decks, up and down the decks, and the language they used was dreadful. Then we looked up and saw the masts of the Spanish ship outside the harbour. Outside the harbour they were, so we threw the parrots into the sea and sailed out to fight. And all the parrots were drownded in the sea and the language they used was dreadful." That's the sort of boy he was, nothing but silly talk of parrots when we asked him about the fighting. And we never had a chance of teaching him better, for two days after he ran away again, and hasn't been seen since.

That's my story, and I assure you that things like that are happening at Fairfield all the time. The ship has never come back, but somehow as people grow older they seem to think that one of these windy nights she'll come sailing in over the hedges with all the lost ghosts on board. Well, when she comes, she'll be welcome. There's one ghost-lass that has never grown tired of waiting for her lad to return. Every night you'll see her out on the green, straining her poor eyes with looking for the mast-lights among the stars. A faithful lass you'd call her, and I'm thinking you'd be right.

Landlord's field wasn't a penny the worse for the visit, but they do say that since then the turnips that have been grown in it have tasted of rum.

THE AMAZING HIEROGLYPHS

I

To inherit property is always in the popular mind a fortunate fate, and to inherit an estate, a very large and valuable estate, with a divine unexpectedness at the pleasantly unsophisticated age of twenty-six, would be for most people, I suppose, a decisive mark of the favour of the gods. Now this had been my lot, yet with the lawyer's papers full of fine unctuous phrases heaped high on the table before me, I could find it in my heart to wish that my Uncle Robert had left me to my little flat and my four hundred a year. Looking thoughtfully about the room, I could see my joyous little collection of water-colours, snuff-boxes and books, each treasure representing a certain restraint in the matter of cab-fares and dinners, and there was no gladness in the thought that with my new income I could buy the whole lot and better a dozen times in a year without being much the poorer for my pains. I felt that in a way Uncle Robert had robbed my emotional treasury, and I re-read the avuncular letter with an impatience which even its genial eccentricity might not wholly destroy.

> *My dear Charles* [he wrote]. *You will probably be very much astonished when you learn, from the infernal thieves whose services our idiotic laws render necessary, that I have left you sole heir to the fortune which my intelligence has enabled me to win from a stupendously foolish world. I am fully aware that nothing is humanly due from an uncle*

to a nephew whose youthful impudence and pretty Oxford accomplishments distinguish him in no way from the thousands of young unemployables with which our educational system endeavours to weary a patient Providence. That foolish boy, your father, accomplished nothing and you, I feel confident, will accomplish nothing. But the best theological and medical authorities having assured me that my possessions will soon be of no use to me, I have decided that they may as well be mal-administered by one of my own name and blood as by charitable organizations. When the thieves have terminated their bickerings, you will possess a considerable sum of money in investments (which you would do well to let alone), my place in Kent and a Square of the best houses in London, the Square that perpetuates my name. That you are in any way competent to take my place, I do not imagine, but you may be pleased to listen to me when I recommend you not to have anything to do with the arch-robbers whose business is the mismanagement of estates. I have always chosen my own tenants and have made a point of looking after the houses in Burton Square myself, even in the smallest details. As a result, I have bequeathed you the finest aggregate of tenants in London, and this, though you may not think it, is not the least part of your inheritance. For the rest you can make a fool of yourself in any way you like but while you manage the houses yourself there is some chance of my money supporting your follies for the term of your life.

Your affectionate uncle,
Robert Barton.

There is a leaking tap at No 4, but a new washer will mend that. On no account buy them a new tap.
R. B.

So it was for this traffic in tenants and their water-taps that I was to sacrifice what Uncle Robert had called my "pretty Oxford accomplishments." While I was reading his letter the vision of Burton Square rose before my eyes, the fruit of a juvenile pilgrimage to that very select neighbourhood. The houses were large, I recalled, and in the very tidy garden in the centre of the Square there was a stately statue of my uncle. It stayed in my recollection as a place dignified even to melancholy, but no doubt it might be profitable in a world which has a sneaking fondness for graveyards. But now that it was mine I would be content with no half impressions and with one last sigh for the joys of my late comparative poverty, I took my hat and set out to view my estate.

II

Within the limits of the postal district curtly named "W" there are a number of Squares more or less resembling Burton Square, places where the unhappy rich may congregate chastely and obtain the minimum amount of esthetic comfort for their money. On the whole, I felt that the dimness of my recollection had done it no injustice. The houses were very large and very solemn, and of that architecture which scoffs at the frivolity of ornament. The grass in the Square garden was as smooth and uninteresting as a carpet, and the buds of the plane-trees might have been nipped off with a razor, so orderly and precise was their growth. Standing by Number 1 and looking round the sombre collection of barracks, I could not help wondering where my uncle had found his tenants. From the exteriors of their houses they might all have been melancholy reproductions of one man. The curtains of Number 1 differed in no wise from those of Number 2, and even in their sun-blinds they were not divided.

How much further I might have carried these speculations I cannot say, for they were cut short by the sudden eruption of a small man with an empurpled countenance and a voice of detestable shrillness from the door of Number 1. From his appearance I should have judged him to be a major from India on the retired list with a liver made mad by pepper and whisky, and there was nothing in the torrent of abuse with which he startled the Square to cause me to correct this conclusion. When, however, I discovered that he was addressing himself to me, I thought it necessary to curb his perfervid eloquence.

"Sir," I said sternly, "there are young children playing in that garden. It would be as well that they should not see you in this unhappy condition."

"Condition!" he shrieked. "What in thunder do you mean?"

"Your anger wrongs me," I replied calmly. "I am far from wishing to condemn the conviviality of one whose hue suggests that he has served his King with distinction in the Empire beyond the seas, but—"

"Nonsense!" he interrupted rudely. "My name in Binyon Long, and I want to know at once what you were doing at the door of my house."

So this was one of my tenants, and a man, moreover, whom I knew by repute. Sir Binyon Long is chairman of the Great Southern Railway and the unofficial head of a certain militant section of the Liberal Party.

"My dear Sir Binyon," I said soothingly, "I am delighted to meet you, even though the circumstances may be unconventional."

"Damn your impudence, sir!" he retorted. "What were you doing at my door?"

"I was looking at it with the just pride of a proprietor," I explained. "My name is Charles Burton, and I'm afraid I'm your new landlord."

"Oh, so you're Robert's scapegrace nephew," he muttered sulkily. "And it's about time you were round here too. You'd better be looking out for a new tenant for this house, I'm thinking."

Resisting a strong but unbusinesslike desire to tell him to go to the devil, I spoke nicely to my tenant.

"Oh, don't say that," I answered. "I'm sure that any little trouble I can put right—I know that Number 4 complains bitterly of his water-taps, but I should feel inclined to give special satisfaction to a tenant like you, Sir Binyon."

For a moment, I really believed that his face was going to burst, the anger made it so red. "Water-taps, little troubles," he bubbled. "Do you think that I'm a man to have little troubles?"

With a snort of rage he seized me by the arm and pointed to the front door of his house.

"Look, you fool! Look at those," he shouted, and put his fingers on some red marks that showed faintly on the white stone pillar by the doorpost. I leant forward to look closely, and, as I did so, I heard Sir Binyon give a sob of despair and turned round to see him shaking like bill-sticker's paste.

"My God! They've changed again," he whispered hoarsely, clutching feebly at my arm. "I shall go mad."

There was something ludicrous in the fear that had supplanted the little man's valorous anger, but he was so genuinely terrified that I stayed my desire to laugh and bent to examine the marks that had inspired his panic. There were about thirty in number and had been neatly made, apparently with red chalk, and enclosed in a ruled square.

"You see!" said Sir Binyon with a touch of his former anger. "You see! Little troubles, oh, my God!"

"My dear Sir Binyon," I replied, "I do not know what these things mean. Certainly they do not appear to be accidental, but it is, above all things, necessary that we should keep calm. Now, a brandy and soda—"

"Come in, man," he said hurriedly. "Come in; it will do you good after your shock."

Under the influence of the spirits my host rapidly recovered his sunset complexion and truculent speech.

"Now, sir," he said, "you are responsible for this. It is your house and it is your duty to see that the matter is cleared up at once."

"Have you no clue, Sir Binyon?"

"Clue!" he stuttered. "Clue! Do you think I'd talk to a boy about the business if I had a clue. But if Seton Randall isn't at the bottom of it, I'll eat one of his dinners."

Now there is probably only one greater railway magnate in England than Sir Binyon Long, and his name is Seton Randall.

"Surely you don't suspect—" I began.

"The man's an unscrupulous blackguard. He's jealous of my brains and my position and he's set one of his filthy Tory secret societies on to me. I tell you he'd make a fortune if I was murdered. Murdered, that's it. What can I do?"

I refilled his glass with brandy and presently he felt better.

"Don't talk of murder," I said soothingly. "After all, secret societies don't usually correspond on their victim's doorposts. Have you seen an expert about the signs?"

"I've had half the British Museum staff down here and they can make nothing of them. And detectives. I had one of those blazing asses hiding here all last week and they never gave a sign, but the moment he's gone . . . I'm going to clear out I tell you."

"Look here, Sir Binyon," I said, rising from my chair. "I shall go into this myself, and if I can't settle it in a week I'll let you off the rest of your lease."

He leant forward quickly.

"Man!" he said. "Will you put that in black and white?"

"I don't think it's necessary," I replied. "I am willing to assume that I am dealing with a gentleman."

It is really a very dreadful thing to see an elderly man become blue in the face, but Sir Binyon said nothing till we were on the doorstep. Then he was pathetic.

"I'm thinking I'm an old man, Mr. Burton," he said, "and I have never a son of my own, but only a daughter, and she's no use in this trouble. Do you think I could have Randall arrested on suspicion?"

"I shouldn't try if I were you," I said. "Trust me to settle this little business."

"If you can—if you can," he muttered morosely, and I left him blinking at the sinister hieroglyphs from the doorstep.

III

I must confess that when I came to consider the question in my flat my confidence in my powers as an amateur detective was rather damped. Putting aside the pompous old man's theories as to Randall and his Tory blackguards, the red symbols were at least peculiar. And the fact that they had ceased when a detective was set to watch the door pointed either to a considerable degree of acuteness on the part of the writer, or to the collusion of some member of Sir Binyon's household. I should have been inclined to dismiss the whole affair as an obscure practical joke, but the care with which the signs had been traced was beyond the patience of the average humorist. One thing at least seemed certain. The marks that perturbed Sir Binyon were made at night, as even in Burton Square, there was too great a traffic of nursemaids and errand boys to permit of their being made in secrecy by day.

So there seemed nothing to do but to endure a midnight vigil, and, after purchasing a revolver and an electric torch to assist me to support my new part, I spent the remaining daylight in a perusal of Gaboriau for inspiration. Already, it seemed, the business of being a conscientious landlord was more fun than I had expected, and I felt grateful to my Uncle Robert for an inheritance that had, after all, romantic possibilities.

Night fell at last and I made my way to Burton Square in a very happy mood. In one pocket I had a real revolver loaded with bullets and in the other the modern equivalent of a dark lantern. One need only have been a boy to see the merit of these things, and I felt that even the stupidest policemen were regarding me with a new suspicion in their steel-grey eyes. I almost wished that I was going to inscribe cabalistic hieroglyphs of sinister import on the door of an enemy myself. It seemed a promising amusement.

My measures were soon taken when I reached the Square. A glance at the door of Number 1 assured me that the morning's inscription had not been altered, and then I scrambled nimbly over the railings and took up my position among the bushes in the Square garden. From my ambush I had a clear view of my door, while no eyes that were not feline might hope to detect me in the shadows in which I stood. And so I began my watch. I suppose for about half-an-hour I continued to find the vigil romantic. Then it smote upon my chilled frame that the bushes were damp and I ventured to light a cigar. At the end of three cigars I had fallen to abusing Sir Binyon and my Uncle Robert with a heartiness which even my enforced silence might not limit. The foot passengers had ceased and the street had fallen silent, save for the occasional cab. Still quarter after quarter struck, and the maker of hieroglyphs gave no sign.

I fancy I must have been nearly asleep when a gleam of light upon the door of Number 1 told my startled mind that I was not the only man in London who had realized the value of electric torches. For a minute the dark stared at me blankly; then the light reappeared and I saw the outline of a man bending over the door-post. It seemed the work of a moment to vault the railings and rush across the road, and yet it gave my quarry time to drop his torch and dash off down the street with a good six yards start. At the time this did not distress me, and second in "the mile" at the 'Varsity sports seemed good enough form to justify my confidence. Yet, as the dark houses leapt by and we ran from one street to another, I found to my surprise that, try as I could, I was unable to lessen the distance between us. And oddly, while my heart was banging against my ribs, I felt that in some way my strange chase recalled a previous incident in my life. Still we pursued our wild career unchecked, and I was in peril of succumbing to stitch when there swam on my throbbing mind the vision of a grey day at Queen's Club, when I had vainly chased Travers of Cambridge home to the tape.

"Travers, Travers!" I yelled. "Stop, you idiot!"

He pulled up short with a grunt of surprise.

"Burton of Trinity. By Jove!" he panted. "And I was wondering how a blessed detective could hold me at the distance."

For a minute or two we stood regarding each other blankly and then we both burst into laughter.

"Well, I'm damned," he said, choking. "Come up to my rooms and have a refresher. I think you need it."

It was not the least strange part of the adventure that all the way to his flat we quarrelled about our respective fitness. But after the second whisky I felt it necessary to become serious.

"Look here, Travers, old man," I said, "I can't have you leaving Egyptian on the walls of my houses and frightening my elderly tenants out of their wits."

His face clouded over.

"I knew you would want to know about it," he said.

"Well, I think—" I began.

"Yes, I know," he interrupted. "After all, perhaps you can help. Tell me, have you ever met that old imbecile's daughter?"

I shook my head.

"Burton, she's the most wonderful girl in all the world; I tell you, if you don't know her you can't possibly imagine how lovely she is. And that pig-headed old fool won't even let her see me," he ended bitterly.

"But why in thunder not?"

"I know I've got a title and lots of money and that sort of thing. But, you know, Burton, that my family's Tory and that old Long is some cranky form of Liberal."

"Politics!" I said sympathetically.

"I tell you I hate them. When I first fell in love with Christine I tried hard to become a Liberal. I listened to their rotten speeches and I read all their beastly papers till my head softened, and yet, I couldn't do it. I suppose it's something in my blood."

"But the hieroglyphs?"

His face lost the melancholy with which his cry had bedecked it.

"Oh, that was rather fun," he said, laughing. "They were love letters, you know. We invented them on the backs of our programmes at balls."

"But why weren't you caught last week?"

"Christine's a very dear girl," he said gratefully. "And when I saw a red lamp in her window I knew that something was up."

"But you nearly did it all in," I commented. "Old Binyon was going to chuck up the sponge and bolt from London."

"I don't know what to do," he answered sadly. "You caught me out right enough over this business. Can't you invent something?"

Thereupon, over many whiskies and sodas, we fell to scheming till the dawn beat through the windows and I thought hopefully of bed.

"I shan't know how to thank you, if it comes off," said Travers as he showed me to a bedroom.

"Man, you'll have the hell of a father-in-law," I said sleepily.

"You wait till you see her," he retorted, and we went to bed.

IV

The scheme, which had appeared promising overnight, seemed more than dubious when we debated it over a late breakfast, but something had to be done and we could not hit on a better idea.

"If he touches me I'll break his neck," said Travers as we made our way to the Square.

"He's an old man and her father," I corrected.

"And a cantankerous madman; but I suppose I mustn't hit him. Burton, if this fails, I'll really have to put friend Seton on to him."

"What a vicious lover you are," I said. "Why don't you murder him yourself?"

"I can't help it," he sighed. "She's—"

When we reached Number 1 I had to beg Travers to cheer up.

"At the worst, you're no worse off than you were before, but be ready to come when I call you."

"My friend will wait for me in the hall," I said to the man who opened the door.

"Very well, sir," he said, and showed me into Sir Binyon's study.

When I saw the old man glowering over his morning paper I was appalled at the magnitude of my task, but I felt that it was best to approach the matter boldly.

"Good morning, Sir Binyon," I said. "I've called to tell you that I've found out about those funny little marks on your door."

I thought for a minute that he was going to have a fit.

"I suppose you are intoxicated," he said at length.

"I should have said that I have discovered their meaning," I replied. "Let me explain. The one like a diseased fish signifies 'Love, your feet are white as the moon on the hilltops,' and the one, more crablike in form, means—"

He stopped me with a roar.

"What the devil do you mean with these infernal idiocies, sir?"

"Perhaps I had better tell you how I discovered these mysteries," I said in a soothing voice, and then I narrated to him with considerable dramatic force how I had waited in the garden, and how Travers—

"Travers! Randall's friend!" The words burst from him with the force of an exploding maroon, and I looked to see him perish then and there in the middle of all the leading Liberal periodicals of the day. But the purple in his face died out to grey, and he allowed me to finish my explanation uninterrupted.

"As I said to Travers," I concluded, "it's not only the dishonesty of your methods, but the fact that they have placed Sir Binyon in rather a ludicrous position. Why, if Seton Randall gets hold of this he'll make him the laughingstock of London."

The old man looked at me grimly for a minute or two. "I suppose you think you're having a game with me," he said.

I disclaimed any such intention.

"All the same, it's true," he added reflectively. "That man Randall is utterly unscrupulous. I suppose you think I ought to let young Travers have her!"

"Lord Travers is rich, young and clever," I said. "You've only got his vile politics against him. And, after all, when he's your son-in-law it ought to be easy enough to make him change them."

"If I ever see him or her!"

"That's where I come in, Sir Binyon. You see, I've got one of my houses to let on the other side of the Square."

He looked at me almost approvingly.

"I can see you're Robert's nephew right enough," he said. "Oh, yes, that's Bob all right."

For a minute he hesitated and I felt as though the universe hung on his next words.

"Oh, I can't be troubled with it any more," he said. "Let him have her and be damned to him."

The words were hardly out of his mouth before I ran to the door.

"Travers," I cried, and stopped abruptly.

There, seated comfortably on the settee in the hall, was Travers talking to one of the most beautiful girls I have ever seen in my life. At the sound of my voice they looked up, and when he saw me standing there with Sir Binyon by my side, Travers caught the significance of the situation and leapt forward with a cry of joy.

"How can I thank you, sir?" he said to Sir Binyon.

Sir Binyon scowled at him ferociously.

"I think you had better thank him," he said, nodding at me sulkily.

"I really do thank you, old boy," said Travers to me in a lower tone.

I looked at Christine Long. She really was very beautiful.

"Upon my word," I said, "I'm beginning to feel sorry that I've done it!"

Lady Travers has a very becoming blush.

THE BOY ERRANT

There are many ways of getting from Brighton to London, and doubtless the philosophical temperament can find merits in all of them, even in what I would venture to assert is the least pleasant method of all of accomplishing that famous journey. For to walk fifty miles at the close of a disastrous expedition in search of the unexpected, in failing boots and without money, is a severe test for amateur pedestrianism, and, when ceaseless rain is added to the normal trials of the road, it needs an extreme optimism to accomplish such a task with an unquenched spirit. Yet physical discomfort is one of those experiences that we soonest forget, and I retain little of that aspect of the journey beyond a sense of monotonous greyness, and the discovery that the weariness of compulsory walking is sufficient to overcome such minor torments as hunger and lack of sleep. When I left Brighton I had not slept or eaten for two days; my feet were blistered; the unexpected had kept unseasonably aloof. When I reached London some twenty-six hours later the condition of my feet was tragic; but hunger and the will to sleep had left me. I only wanted to stop walking.

Nor, I thought at the time, had the accidents of the road justified the whole fond adventure; but, writing now, I am not quite so sure. For from the dimness that is blotting out the mud and weariness of those hopeful, unfortunate days there emerges a very definite impression, and I realise that chance is apt to exact a bigger price for impressions than this. I have eaten and slept since then, and my feet have long recovered from the anger of the Sussex roads;

but the image of Willie—little comrade and fellow Bohemian for a night and half a day—lingers with me pleasantly; and as the details of my fantastic journey grow vaguer and more dream-like, this image becomes, in contrast, more vivid. It will remind me that once I tasted the more bitter wine of vagabond life when all else is forgotten.

It was on a grey hill not far from Brighton that he slipped out from a hedge, and started walking gravely by my side; and, so little accustomed was I to the frank, kindly comradeship of the roads, that instinctively I felt inclined to resent his intrusion on my graceless solitude. But there was something so fragile and, indeed, tender in his little wizened face and wasted body that it hardly needed a glance to make me ashamed of my too-English reticence. When, moreover, in answer to a few questions he blurted out his brief history, I discovered that he was the willing slave of one of those primitive passions that dreamers of the unexpected are bound to admire. His father, he told me, was a foreman in an engineering works, earning six pounds a week, and he had a comfortable home, but . . . the whole helpless spirit of vagabondage lay in his appealing glance. I caught, as it were, a glimpse of that comfortable home—its parlour, its ordered respectability, its unconscious but desolating dullness—and nodded sympathy. Seven times had young Ulysses run away from home; four times he had been taken back by the police, who had been very kind to him; and now, once more, he was limping back of his own accord. His boots were even more pitiful than mine, and he had the loose shambling gait of the genuine tramp; but, with the generosity of a true artist, he consented to overlook the gap that separates the professional from the amateur. He produced bread and cheese from his pocket, and I made pretence to eat as we walked along together.

He had the body of a child of eleven or twelve and the kind, tired eyes of an old man of eighty; but, at a venture, I should say he was about fourteen, and he was one of the vainest and most lovable creatures I have ever met. He would display the artless cleverness that is the common coin of sharp children, and peer at me from the corners of his eyes to detect my admiration; and then, in a breath, he would reveal unconsciously such wisdom as grown men buy with tears. His speech was fragrant with the romance of the road, but it was romance in detail, and not the large, vague romance that deals with dust and stars and the great, restful hills. He had sold newspapers in London and racecards on Epsom Downs. He had lived with those dark folk, the gipsies; he had wandered about the country with fairs and pedlars. He had been bitten by dogs and bullied by righteous country lads; he had been thrashed by farmers for stealing apples and thrashed by the gipsies for failing to steal fowls. Doubtless, often enough, he had been cold and wet and hungry. And yet there it was, running away now from his home, now from some temporary master, he succeeded—dearly enough one would think—in satisfying the rebel in his blood, and even now, with his face set towards his home, he was planning a new venture. Hitherto, his expeditions had been confined to the southern half of England; but he had heard that there were plenty of kind people in the North, and, perhaps, in a few weeks' time— "Yet they don't hit me much at home, either," he reflected, wondering a little, perhaps, at his own restlessness.

Possibly, to the inexpert Bohemian, his most suggestive confession was his own utter weariness of bread and cheese. Anywhere, he told me, he could get more bread and cheese than he could possibly eat; but he greatly preferred bread and butter, which was comparatively scarce. Sometimes a woman would give him a good meal because he was so small, and one or two had wanted to adopt him. "But that's no use to me," he said, boastfully; "I can look after myself, I can."

Indeed, it was hard to say whether he was to be envied or pitied as he shuffled along by my side, bragging of his adventurous existence, that was, in truth, barely to be measured in terms of human hardship, and yet, at the same time, endured with a spirit, a fierce independence, torn as it were from Nature herself, that made me feel that my tame reliance on civilisation was a dwarfing form of cowardice. Yet as night fell he revealed a weakness, childish and touching, but at the same time difficult to reconcile with his manner of living. He, who had slept in a hundred ditches, and divided food with a hundred savage comrades, was afraid of walking in the dark! It was raining steadily, and I had the wild, illogical desire to get back to London that he professed to share, so stopping was out of the question. And so, as I trudged wearily across the night holding his arm in mine, I felt it tremble, and now and again he whispered hoarsely in my ear: "Tighter! hold it tighter!" It was as if night had made him forget all his street-boy tricks and cynicisms, and he had become a child once more.

By the time we reached Crawley he could walk no farther, and so we turned into a field to rest. With the simplicity of habit he flung himself on his back on the wet ground and fell asleep, with the rain beating on his face, as easily and lightly as if his mother had tucked him into bed. I separated my boots from my bursting feet and stayed miserably wakeful. Everyone I had met that day had taken me for a tramp, and I had almost come to believe myself in my mission. But now I realised that I was a fraud; that there were many things I had to forget and even more I had to learn before I could win the friendship of the wide earth and sky. I envied the boy his easy philosophy. We had ragged together about Crawley in search of water and had failed to find it; but the driver of the night mail to Brighton had given the boy some jam sandwiches, and he had immediately forgotten his other need, while I was still thirsty. It is a strange truth that even the profession of tramp demands an apprenticeship.

Day came at last, weeping and miserably grey, and after a while the boy woke up, and pronounced himself willing to continue our journey; but we had not gone far before it was apparent that he had over-estimated his powers. Again and again I had to stop while he rested by the roadside. Presently we came to a grocer's shop, and he produced a secret store of pennies and bought half a loaf of bread and some butter. But I could not eat, even for comradeship; and, while he was taking his breakfast, he admitted that he could walk no farther. The desire to get back to London had taken complete possession of me, and I felt that, if I did not go on, I should never get there at all. So I shook hands with him and left him eating his bread and butter. Some ten minutes later I heard a faint

shout, and, turning round, found him limping along the road behind me. But, when he came up with me, it was only to confess
that he was "done." We shook hands again, and presently I lost
sight of him, a faint black speck sitting by the wayside.

Since I found a comrade so generous and friendly, I feel I did
not venture on the southern roads in vain. I have not seen the boy
since. Perhaps he is threading the Yorkshire Wolds, where the chalk
is white and there are wild pansies; or, perhaps, he lingers still in
his "comfortable home." But I have only to shut my eyes to feel his
thin arm trembling in mine, and to hear his voice in my ear:
"Tighter! hold it tighter!" And to this clear-cut impression the
whole story of those grey wet days has dwindled with the years.

ON THE BRIGHTON ROAD

Slowly the sun had climbed up the hard white downs, till it broke with little of the mysterious ritual of dawn upon a sparkling world of snow. There had been a hard frost during the night, and the birds, who hopped about here and there with scant tolerance of life, left no trace of their passage on the silver pavements. In places the sheltered caverns of the hedges broke the monotony of the whiteness that had fallen upon the coloured earth, and overhead the sky melted from orange to deep blue, from deep blue to a blue so pale that it suggested a thin paper screen rather than illimitable space. Across the level fields there came a cold, silent wind which blew a fine dust of snow from the trees, but hardly stirred the crested hedges. Once above the skyline, the sun seemed to climb more quickly, and as it rose higher it began to give out a heat that blended with the keenness of the wind.

It may have been this strange alternation of heat and cold that disturbed the tramp in his dreams, for he struggled for a moment with the snow that covered him, like a man who finds himself twisted uncomfortably in the bed-clothes, and then sat up with staring, questioning eyes. "Lord! I thought I was in bed," he said to himself as he took in the vacant landscape, "and all the while I was out here." He stretched his limbs, and, rising carefully to his feet, shook the snow off his body. As he did so the wind set him shivering, and he knew that his bed had been warm.

"Come, I feel pretty fit," he thought. "I suppose I am lucky to wake at all in this. Or unlucky—it isn't much of a business to come back to." He looked up and saw the downs shining against the blue, like the Alps on a picture-postcard. "That means another forty miles or so, I suppose," he continued grimly. "Lord knows what I did yesterday. Walked till I was done, and now I'm only about twelve miles from Brighton. Damn the snow, damn Brighton, damn everything!" The sun crept higher and higher, and he started walking patiently along the road with his back turned to the hills.

"Am I glad or sorry that it was only sleep that took me, glad or sorry, glad or sorry?" His thoughts seemed to arrange themselves in a metrical accompaniment to the steady thud of his footsteps, and he hardly sought an answer to his question. It was good enough to walk to.

Presently, when three milestones had loitered past, he overtook a boy who was stooping to light a cigarette. He wore no overcoat, and looked unspeakably fragile against the snow, "Are you on the road, guv'nor?" asked the boy huskily as he passed.

"I think I am," the tramp said.

"Oh! then I'll come a bit of the way with you if you don't walk too fast. It's bit lonesome walking this time of day."

The tramp nodded his head, and the boy started limping along by his side.

"I'm eighteen," he said casually. "I bet you thought I was younger."

"Fifteen, I'd have said."

"You'd have backed a loser. Eighteen last August, and I've been on the road six years. I ran away from home five times when I was a little 'un, and the police took me back each time. Very good to me, the police was. Now I haven't got a home to run away from."

"Nor have I," the tramp said calmly.

"Oh, I can see what you are," the boy panted; "you're a gentleman come down. It's harder for you than for me." The tramp glanced at the limping, feeble figure and lessened his pace.

"I haven't been at it as long as you have," he admitted.

"No, I could tell that by the way you walk. You haven't got tired yet. Perhaps you expect something at the other end?"

The tramp reflected for a moment. "I don't know," he said bitterly, "I'm always expecting things."

"You'll grow out of that;" the boy commented. "It's warmer in London, but it's harder to come by grub. There isn't much in it really."

"Still, there's the chance of meeting somebody there who will understand—"

"Country people are better," the boy interrupted. "Last night I took a lease of a barn for nothing and slept with the cows, and this morning the farmer routed me out and gave me tea and toke because I was so little. Of course, I score there; but in London, soup on the Embankment at night, and all the rest of the time coppers moving you on."

"I dropped by the roadside last night and slept where I fell. It's a wonder I didn't die," the tramp said. The boy looked at him sharply.

"How did you know you didn't?" he said.

"I don't see it," the tramp said, after a pause.

"I tell you," the boy said hoarsely, "people like us can't get away from this sort of thing if we want to. Always hungry and thirsty and dog-tired and walking all the while. And yet if anyone offers me a nice home and work my stomach feels sick. Do I look strong? I know I'm little for my age, but I've been knocking about like this for six years, and do you think I'm not dead? I was drowned bathing at Margate, and I was killed by a gypsy with a spike; he knocked my head and yet I'm walking along here now, walking to London to walk away from it again, because I can't help it. Dead! I tell you we can't get away if we want to."

The boy broke off in a fit of coughing, and the tramp paused while he recovered.

"You'd better borrow my coat for a bit, Tommy," he said, "your cough's pretty bad."

"You go to hell!" the boy said fiercely, puffing at his cigarette; "I'm all right. I was telling you about the road. You haven't got down to it yet, but you'll find out presently. We're all dead, all of us who're on it, and we're all tired, yet somehow we can't leave it. There's nice smells in the summer, dust and hay and the wind smack in your face on a hot day—and it's nice waking up in the wet grass on a fine morning. I don't know, I don't know—" he lurched forward suddenly, and the tramp caught him in his arms.

"I'm sick," the boy whispered—"sick."

The tramp looked up and down the road, but he could see no houses or any sign of help. Yet even as he supported the boy doubtfully in the middle of the road a motor car suddenly flashed in the middle distance, and came smoothly through the snow.

"What's the trouble?" said the driver quietly as he pulled up. "I'm a doctor." He looked at the boy keenly and listened to his strained breathing.

"Pneumonia," he commented. "I'll give him a lift to the infirmary, and you, too, if you like."

The tramp thought of the workhouse and shook his head. "I'd rather walk," he said.

The boy winked faintly as they lifted him into the car.

"I'll meet you beyond Reigate," he murmured to the tramp. "You'll see." And the car vanished along the white road.

All the morning the tramp splashed through the thawing snow, but at midday he begged some bread at a cottage door and crept into a lonely barn to eat it. It was warm in there, and after his meal he fell asleep among the hay. It was dark when he woke, and started trudging once more through the slushy roads.

Two miles beyond Reigate a figure, a fragile figure, slipped out of the darkness to meet him.

"On the road, guv'nor?" said a husky voice. "Then I'll come a bit of the way with you if you don't walk too fast. It's a bit lonesome walking this time of day."

"But the pneumonia!" cried the tramp, aghast.

"I died at Crawley this morning," said the boy.

THE CONJURER

Certainly the audience was restive. In the first place it felt that it had been defrauded, seeing that Cissie Bradford, whose smiling face adorned the bills outside, had failed to appear, and secondly, it considered that the deputy for that famous lady was more than inadequate. To the little man who sweated in the glare of the limelight and juggled desperately with glass balls in a vain effort to steady his nerve it was apparent that his turn was a failure. And as he worked he could have cried with disappointment, for his was a trial performance, and a year's engagement in the Hennings' group of music-halls would have rewarded success. Yet his tricks, things that he had done with the utmost ease a thousand times, had been a succession of blunders, rather mirth-provoking than mystifying to the audience. Presently one of the glass balls fell crashing on the stage, and amidst the jeers of the gallery he turned to his wife, who served as his assistant.

"I've lost my chance," he said, with a sob; "I can't do it!"

"Never mind, dear," she whispered. "There's a nice steak and onions at home for supper."

"It's no use," he said despairingly. "I'll try the disappearing trick and then get off. I'm done here." He turned back to the audience.

"Ladies and gentlemen," he said to the mockers in a wavering voice, "I will now present to you the concluding item of my entertainment. I will cause this lady to disappear under your very eyes, without the aid of any mechanical contrivance or artificial device." This was the merest showman's patter, for, as a matter of fact, it was not a very wonderful illusion. But as he led his wife forward to present her to the audience the conjurer was wondering whether the mishaps that had ruined his chance would meet him even here. If something should go wrong—he felt his wife's hand tremble in his, and he pressed it tightly to reassure her. He must make an effort, an effort of will, and then no mistakes would happen. For a second the lights danced before his eyes, then he pulled himself together. If an earthquake should disturb the curtains and show Molly creeping ignominiously away behind he would still meet his fate like a man. He turned round to conduct his wife to the little alcove from which she should vanish. She was not on the stage!

For a minute he did not guess the greatness of the disaster. Then he realised that the theatre was intensely quiet, and that he would have to explain that the last item of his programme was even more of a fiasco than the rest. Owing to a sudden indisposition—his skin tingled at the thought of the hooting. His tongue rasped upon cracking lips as he braced himself and bowed to the audience.

Then came the applause. Again and again it broke out from all over the house, while the curtain rose and fell, and the conjurer stood on the stage, mute, uncomprehending. What had happened? At first he had thought they were mocking him, but it was impossible to misjudge the nature of the applause. Besides, the stage-manager was allowing him call after call, as if he were a star. When at length the curtain remained down, and the orchestra struck up the opening bars of the next song, he staggered off into the wings as if he were drunk. There he met Mr. James Hennings himself.

"You'll do," said the great man; "that last trick was neat. You ought to polish up the others though. I suppose you don't want to tell me how you did it? Well, well, come in the morning and we'll fix up a contract."

And so, without having said a word, the conjurer found himself hustled off by the Vaudeville Napoleon. Mr. Hennings had something more to say to his manager.

"Bit rum," he said. "Did you see it?"

"Queerest thing we've struck."

"How was it done do you think?"

"Can't imagine. There one minute on his arm, gone the next, no trap, or curtain, or anything."

"Money in it, eh?"

"Biggest hit of the century, I should think."

"I'll go and fix up a contract and get him to sign it tonight. Get on with it." And Mr. James Hennings fled to his office.

Meanwhile the conjurer was wandering in the wings with the drooping heart of a lost child. What had happened? Why was he a success, and why did people stare so oddly, and what had become of his wife? When he asked them the stage hands laughed, and said they had not seen her. Why should they laugh? He wanted her to explain things, and hear their good luck. But she was not in her dressing-room, she was not anywhere. For a moment he felt like crying.

Then, for the second time that night, he pulled himself together. After all, there was no reason to be upset. He ought to feel very pleased about the contract, however it had happened. It seemed that his wife had left the stage in some queer way without being seen. Probably to increase the mystery she had gone straight home in her stage dress, and had succeeded in dodging the stage-door keeper. It was all very strange; but, of course, there must be some simple explanation like that. He would take a cab home and find her there already. There was a steak and onions for supper.

As he drove along in the cab he became convinced that this theory was right. Molly had always been clever, and this time she had certainly succeeded in surprising everybody. At the door of his house he gave the cabman a shilling for himself with a light heart. He could afford it now. He ran up the steps cheerfully and opened the door. The passage was quite dark, and he wondered why his wife hadn't lit the gas.

"Molly!" he cried, "Molly!"

The small, weary-eyed servant came out of the kitchen on a savoury wind of onions.

"Hasn't missus come home with you, sir?" she said.

The conjurer thrust his hand against the wall to steady himself, and the pattern of the wall-paper seemed to burn his finger-tips.

"Not here!" he gasped at the frightened girl. "Then where is she? Where is she?"

"I don't know, sir," she began stuttering; but the conjurer turned quickly and ran out of the house. Of course, his wife must be at the theatre. It was absurd ever to have supposed that she could leave the theatre in her stage dress unnoticed; and now she was probably worrying because he had not waited for her. How foolish he had been.

It was a quarter of an hour before he found a cab, and the theatre was dark and empty when he got back to it. He knocked at the stage door, and the night watchman opened it.

"My wife?" he cried.

"There's no one here now, sir," the man answered respectfully, for he knew that a new star had risen that night.

The conjurer leant against the doorpost faintly.

"Take me up to the dressing-rooms," he said. "I want to see whether she has been there while I was away."

The watchman led the way along the dark passages. "I shouldn't worry if I were you, sir," he said. "She can't have gone far." He did not know anything about it, but he wanted to be sympathetic.

"God knows," the conjurer muttered, "I can't understand this at all."

In the dressing-room Molly's clothes still lay neatly folded as she had left them when they went on the stage that night, and when he saw them his last hope left the conjurer, and a strange thought came into his mind.

"I should like to go down on the stage," he said, "and see if there is anything to tell me of her."

The night watchman looked at the conjurer as if he thought he was mad, but he followed him down to the stage in silence. When he was there the conjurer leaned forward suddenly, and his face was filled with a wistful eagerness.

"Molly!" he called, "Molly!"

But the empty theatre gave him nothing but echoes in reply.

THE COFFIN MERCHANT

London on a November Sunday inspired Eustace Reynolds with a melancholy too insistent to be ignored and too causeless to be enjoyed. The grey sky overhead between the house-tops, the cold wind round every street-corner, the sad faces of the men and women on the pavements, combined to create an atmosphere of ineloquent misery. Eustace was sensitive to impressions, and in spite of a half-conscious effort to remain a dispassionate spectator of the world's melancholy, he felt the chill of the aimless day creeping over his spirit. Why was there no sun, no warmth, no laughter on the earth? What had become of all the children who keep laughter like a mask on the faces of disillusioned men? The wind blew down Southampton Street, and chilled Eustace to a shiver that passed away in a shudder of disgust at the sombre colour of life. A windy Sunday in London before the lamps are lit, tempts a man to believe in the nobility of work.

At the corner by Charing Cross Telegraph Office a man thrust a handbill under his eyes, but he shook his head impatiently. The blueness of the fingers that offered him the paper was alone sufficient to make him disinclined to remove his hands from his pockets even for an instant. But, the man would not be dismissed so lightly.

"Excuse me, sir," he said, following him, "you have not looked to see what my bills are."

"Whatever they are I do not want them."

45

"That's where you are wrong, sir," the man said earnestly. "You will never find life interesting if you do not lie in wait for the unexpected. As a matter of fact, I believe that my bill contains exactly what you do want."

Eustace looked at the man with quick curiosity. His clothes were ragged, and the visible parts of his flesh were blue with cold, but his eyes were bright with intelligence and his speech was that of an educated man. It seemed to Eustace that he was being regarded with a keen expectancy, as though his decision I on the trivial point was of real importance.

"I don't know what you are driving at," he said, "but if it will give you any pleasure I will take one of your bills; though if you argue with all your clients as you have with me, it must take you a long time to get rid of them."

"I only offer them to suitable persons," the man said, folding up one of the handbills while he spoke, "and I'm sure you will not regret taking it," and he slipped the paper into Eustace's hand and walked rapidly away.

Eustace looked after him curiously for a moment, and then opened the paper in his hand. When his eyes comprehended its significance, he gave a low whistle of astonishment. "You will soon be wanting a coffin!" it read. "At 606, Gray's Inn Road, your order will be attended to with civility and despatch. Call and see us!!"

Eustace swung round quickly to look for the man, but he was out of sight. The wind was growing colder, and the lamps were beginning to shine out in the greying streets. Eustace crumpled the paper into his overcoat pocket, and turned homewards.

"How silly!" he said to himself, in conscious amusement. The sound of his footsteps on the pavement rang like an echo to his laugh.

II

Eustace was impressionable but not temperamentally morbid, and he was troubled a little by the fact that the gruesomely bizarre handbill continued to recur to his mind. The thing was so manifestly absurd, he told himself with conviction, that it was not worth a second thought, but this did not prevent him from thinking of it again and again. What manner of undertaker could hope to obtain business by giving away foolish handbills in the street? Really, the whole thing had the air of a brainless practical joke, yet his intellectual fairness forced him to admit that as far as the man who had given him the bill was concerned, brainlessness was out of the question, and joking improbable. There had been depths in those little bright eyes which his glance had not been able to sound, and the man's manner in making him accept the handbill had given the whole transaction a kind of ludicrous significance.

"You will soon be wanting a coffin—!"

Eustace found himself turning the words over and over in his mind. If he had had any near relations he might have construed the thing as an elaborate threat, but he was practically alone in the world, and it seemed to him that he was not likely to want a coffin for anyone but himself.

"Oh damn the thing!" he said impatiently, as he opened the door of his flat, "it isn't worth worrying about. I mustn't let the whim of some mad tradesman get on my nerves. I've got no one to bury, anyhow."

Nevertheless the thing lingered with him all the evening, and when his neighbour the doctor came in for a chat at ten o'clock, Eustace was glad to show him the strange handbill. The doctor, who had experienced the queer magics that are practised to this day on the West Coast of Africa, and who, therefore, had no nerves, was delighted with so striking an example of British commercial enterprise.

"Though, mind you," he added gravely, smoothing the crumpled paper on his knee, "this sort of thing might do a lot of harm if it fell into the hands of a nervous subject. I should be inclined to punch the head of the ass who perpetrated it. Have you turned that address up in the Post Office Directory?"

Eustace shook his head, and rose and fetched the fat red book which makes London an English city. Together they found the Gray's Inn Road, and ran their eyes down to No. 606.

"'Harding, G. J., Coffin Merchant and Undertaker.' Not much information there," muttered the doctor.

"Coffin merchant's a bit unusual, isn't it?" queried Eustace.

"I suppose he manufactures coffins wholesale for the trade. Still, I didn't know they called themselves that. Anyhow, it seems, as though that handbill is a genuine piece of downright foolishness. The idiot ought to be stopped advertising in that way."

"I'll go and see him myself tomorrow," said Eustace bluntly.

"Well, he's given you an invitation," said the doctor, "so it's only polite of you to go. I'll drop in here in the evening to hear what he's like. I expect that you'll find him as mad as a hatter."

"Something like that," said Eustace, "or he wouldn't give handbills to people like me. I have no one to bury except myself."

"No," said the doctor in the hall, "I suppose you haven't. Don't let him measure you for a coffin, Reynolds!"

Eustace laughed.

"We never know," he said sententiously.

III

Next day was one of those gorgeous blue days of which November gives but few, and Eustace was glad to run out to Wimbledon for a game of golf, or rather for two. It was therefore dusk before he made his way to the Gray's Inn Road in search of the unexpected. His attitude towards his errand despite the doctor's laughter and the prosaic entry in the directory, was a little confused. He could not help reflecting that after all the doctor had not seen the man with the little wise eyes, nor could he forget that Mr. G. J. Harding's description of himself as a coffin merchant, to say the least of it, approached the unusual. Yet he felt that it would be intolerable to chop the whole business without finding out what it all meant. On the whole he would have preferred not to have discovered the riddle at all; but having found it, he could not rest without an answer.

No. 606, Gray's Inn Road, was not like an ordinary undertaker's shop. The window was heavily draped with black cloth, but was otherwise unadorned. There were no letters from grateful mourners, no little model coffins, no photographs of marble memorials. Even more surprising was the absence of any name over the shop-door, so that the uninformed stranger could not possibly tell what trade was carried on within, or who was responsible for the management of the business. This uncommercial modesty did not tend to remove Eustace's doubts as to the sanity of Mr. G. J. Harding; but he opened the shop-door which started a large bell swinging noisily, and stepped over the threshold. The shop was hardly more expressive inside than out. A broad counter ran across it, cutting it in two, and in the partial gloom overhead a naked gas-burner whistled a noisy song. Beyond this the shop contained no furniture whatever, and no stock-in-trade except a few planks leaning against the wall in one corner. There was a large ink-stand on the counter. Eustace waited patiently for a minute or two, and then as no one came he began stamping on the floor with his foot. This proved efficacious, for soon he heard the sound of footsteps ascending wooden stairs, the door behind the counter opened and a man came into the shop.

He was dressed quite neatly now, and his hands were no longer blue with cold, but Eustace knew at once that it was the man who had given him the handbill. Nevertheless he looked at Eustace without a sign of recognition.

"What can I do for you, sir?" he asked pleasantly.

Eustace laid the handbill down on the counter.

"I want to know about this," he said. "It strikes me as being in pretty bad taste, and if a nervous person got hold of it, it might be dangerous."

"You think so, sir? Yet our representative," he lingered affectionately on the words, "our representative told you, I believe, that the handbill was only distributed to suitable cases."

"That's where you are wrong," said Eustace sharply, "for I have no one to bury."

"Except yourself," said the coffin merchant suavely.

Eustace looked at him keenly. "I don't see—" he began. But the coffin merchant interrupted him.

"You must know, sir," he said, "that this is no ordinary under-taker's business. We possess information that enables us to defy competition in our special class of trade."

"Information!"

"Well, if you prefer it, you may say intuitions. If our representative handed you that advertisement, it was because he knew you would need it."

"Excuse me," said Eustace, "you appear to be sane, but your words do not convey to me any reasonable significance. You gave me that foolish advertisement yourself, and now you say that you did so because you knew I would need it. I ask you why?"

The coffin merchant shrugged his shoulders. "Ours is a sentimental trade," he said, "I do not know why dead men want coffins, but they do. For my part I would wish to be cremated."

"Dead men?"

"Ah, I was coming to that. You see Mr.—?"

"Reynolds."

"Thank you, my name is Harding—G. J. Harding. You see, Mr. Reynolds, our intuitions are of a very special character, and if we say that you will need a coffin, it is probable that you will need one."

"You mean to say that I—"

"Precisely. In twenty-four hours or less, Mr. Reynolds, you will need our services."

The revelation of the coffin merchant's insanity came to Eustace with a certain relief. For the first time in the interview he had a sense of the dark empty shop and the whistling gas-jet over his head.

"Why, it sounds like a threat, Mr. Harding!" he said gaily.

The coffin merchant looked at him oddly, and produced a printed form from his pocket. "If you would fill this up," he said.

Eustace picked it up off the counter and laughed aloud. It was an order for a hundred-guinea funeral.

"I don't know what your game is," he said, "but this has gone on long enough."

"Perhaps it has, Mr. Reynolds," said the coffin merchant, and he leant across the counter and looked Eustace straight in the face.

For a moment Eustace was amused; then he was suddenly afraid. "I think it's time I—" he began slowly, and then he was silent, his whole will intent on fighting the eyes of the coffin merchant. The song of the gas-jet waned to a point in his ears, and then rose steadily till it was like the beating of the world's heart. The eyes of the coffin merchant grew larger and larger, till they blended in one great circle of fire. Then Eustace picked a pen off the counter and filled in the form.

"Thank you very much, Mr. Reynolds," said the coffin merchant, shaking hands with him politely. "I can promise you every civility and despatch. Good-day, sir."

Outside on the pavement Eustace stood for a while trying to recall exactly what had happened. There was a slight scratch on his hand, and when he automatically touched it with his lips, it made them burn. The lit lamps in the Gray's Inn Road seemed to him a little unsteady, and the passers-by showed a disposition to blunder into him.

"Queer business," he said to himself dimly; "I'd better have a cab."

He reached home in a dream.

It was nearly ten o'clock before the doctor remembered his promise, and went upstairs to Eustace's flat. The outer door was half-open so that he thought he was expected, and he switched on the light in the little hall, and shut the door behind him with the simplicity of habit. But when he swung round from the door he gave a cry of astonishment. Eustace was lying asleep in a chair before him with his face flushed and drooping on his shoulder, and his breath hissing noisily through his parted lips. The doctor looked at him quizzically, "If I did not know you, my young friend," he remarked, "I should say that you were as drunk as a lord."

And he went up to Eustace and shook him by the shoulder; but Eustace did not wake.

"Queer!" the doctor muttered, sniffing at Eustace's lips; "he hasn't been drinking."

THE PASSING OF EDWARD

I found Dorothy sitting sedately on the beach, with a mass of black seaweed twined in her hands and her bare feet sparkling white in the sun. Even in the first glow of recognition I realised that she was paler than she had been the summer before, and yet I cannot blame myself for the tactlessness of my question.

"Where's Edward?" I said; and I looked about the sands for a sailor suit and a little pair of prancing legs.

While I looked Dorothy's eyes watched mine inquiringly, as if she wondered what I might see.

"Edward's dead," she said simply. "He died last year, after you left."

For a moment I could only gaze at the child in silence, and ask myself what reason there was in the thing that had hurt her so. Now that I knew that Edward played with her no more, I could see that there was a shadow upon her face too dark for her years, and that she had lost, to some extent, that exquisite carelessness of poise which makes children so young. Her voice was so calm that I might have thought her forgetful had I not seen an instant of patent pain in her wide eyes.

"I'm sorry," I said at length "very, very, sorry indeed. I had brought down my car to take you for a drive, as I promised."

"Oh! Edward *would* have liked that," she answered thoughtfully; "he was so fond of motors." She swung round suddenly and looked at the sands behind her with staring eyes.

"I thought I heard—" she broke off in confusion.

I, too, had believed for an instant that I had heard something that was not the wind or the distant children or the smooth sea hissing along the beach. During that golden summer which linked me with the dead, Edward had been wont, in moments of elation, to puff up and down the sands, in artistic representation of a nobby, noisy motor-car. But the dead may play no more, and there was nothing there but the sands and the hot sky and Dorothy.

"You had better let me take you for a run, Dorothy," I said. "The man will drive, and we can talk as we go along."

She nodded gravely, and began pulling on her sandy stockings.

"It did not hurt him," she said inconsequently.

The restraint in her voice pained me like a blow.

"Oh, don't, dear, don't!" I cried, "There is nothing to do but forget."

"I have forgotten, quite," she answered, pulling at her shoe-laces with calm fingers. "It was ten months ago."

We walked up to the front, where the car was waiting, and Dorothy settled herself among the cushions with a little sigh of contentment, the human quality of which brought me a certain relief. If only she would laugh or cry! I sat down by her side, but the man waited by the open door.

"What is it?" I asked.

"I'm sorry, sir," he answered, looking about him in confusion, "I thought I saw a young gentleman with you."

He shut the door with a bang, and in a minute we were running through the town. I knew that Dorothy was watching my face with her wounded eyes; but I did not look at her until the green fields leapt up on either side of the white road.

"It is only for a little while that we may not see him," I said; "all this is nothing."

"I have forgotten," she repeated. "I think this is a very nice motor."

I had not previously complained of the motor, but I was wishing then that it would cease its poignant imitation of a little dead boy, a boy who would play no more. By the touch of Dorothy's sleeve against mine I knew that she could hear it too. And the miles flew

by, green and brown and golden, while I wondered what use I might
be in the world, who could not help a child to forget. Possibly there
was another way, I thought.

"Tell me how it happened," I said.

Dorothy looked at me with inscrutable eyes, and spoke in a voice
without emotion.

"He caught a cold, and was very ill in bed. I went in to see him,
and he was all white and faded. I said to him, 'How are you Edward?' and he said, 'I shall get up early in the morning to catch
beetles.' I didn't see him any more."

"Poor little chap!" I murmured.

"I went to the funeral," she continued monotonously, "It was
very rainy, and I threw a little bunch of flowers down into the hole.
There was a whole lot of flowers there; but I think Edward liked
apples better than flowers."

"Did you cry?" I said cruelly.

She paused. "I don't know. I suppose so. It was a long time ago;
I think I have forgotten."

Even while she spoke I heard Edward puffing along the sands:
Edward who had been so fond of apples.

"I cannot stand this any longer," I said aloud. "Let's get out
and walk in the woods for a change."

She agreed, with a depth of comprehension that terrified me;
and the motor pulled up with a jerk at a spot where hardly a post
served to mark where the woods commenced and the wayside grass
stopped. We took one of the dim paths which the rabbits had made
and forced our way through the undergrowth into the peaceful
twilight of the trees.

"You haven't got very sunburnt this year," I said as we walked.

"I don't know why. I've been out on the beach all the days.
Sometimes I've played, too."

I did not ask her what games she had played, or who had been
her play-friend. Yet even there in the quiet woods I knew that Edward was holding her back from me. It is true that, in his boy's
way, he had been fond of me; but I should not have dared to take
her out without him in the days when his live lips had filled the

beach with song, and his small brown body had danced among the surf. Now it seemed that I had been disloyal to him.

And presently we came to a clearing where the leaves of forgotten years lay brown and rotten beneath our feet, and the air was full of the dryness of death.

"Let's be going back. What do you think, Dorothy?" I said.

"I think," she said slowly,—"I think that this would be a very good place to catch beetles."

A wood is full of secret noises, and that is why, I suppose, we heard a pair of small quick feet come with a dance of triumph through the rustling bracken. For a minute we listened deeply, and then Dorothy broke from my side with a piercing call on her lips.

"Oh, Edward, Edward!" she cried; "Edward!"

But the dead may play no more, and presently she came back to me with the tears that are the riches of childhood streaming down her face.

"I can hear him, I can hear him," she sobbed; "but I cannot see him. Never, never again."

And so I led her back to the motor. But in her tears I seemed to find a promise of peace that she had not known before.

Now Edward was no very wonderful little boy; it may be that he was jealous and vain and greedy; yet now, it seemed as he lay in his small grave with the memory of Dorothy's flowers about him, he had wrought this kindness for his sister. Yes, even though we heard no more than the birds in the branches and the wind swaying the scented bracken; even though he had passed with another summer, and the dead and the love of the dead may rise no more from the grave.

THE SOUL OF A POLICEMAN

I

Outside, above the uneasy din of the traffic, the sky was glorious with the far peace of a fine summer evening. Through the upper pane of the station window Police-constable Bennett, who felt that his senses at the moment were abnormally keen, recognised with a sinking heart such reds and yellows as bedecked the best patchwork quilt at home. By contrast the lights of the superintendent's office were subdued, so that within the walls of the police-station sounds seemed of greater importance. Somewhere a drunkard, deprived of his boots, was drumming his criticism of authority on the walls of his cell. From the next room, where the men off duty were amusing themselves, there came a steady clicking of billiard-balls and dominoes, broken now and again by gruff bursts of laughter. And at his very elbow the superintendent was speaking in that suave voice that reminded Bennett of grey velvet.

"You see, Bennett, how matters stand. I have nothing at all against your conduct. You are steady and punctual, and I have no doubt that you are trying to do your duty. But it's very unfortunate that as far as results go you have nothing to show for your efforts. During the last three weeks you have not brought in a charge of any description, and during the same period I find that your colleagues on the beat have been exceptionally busy. I repeat that I do not accuse you of neglecting your duty, but these things tell with the magistrates and convey a general suggestion of slackness."

Bennett looked down at his brightly polished boots. His fingers were sandy and there was soft felt beneath his feet.

"I have been afraid of this for some time, sir," he said, "very much afraid."

The superintendent looked at him questioningly.

"You have nothing to say?" he said.

"I have always tried to do my duty, sir."

"I know, I know. But you must see that a certain number of charges, if not of convictions, is the mark of a smart officer."

"Surely you would not have me arrest innocent persons?"

"That is a most improper observation," said the superintendent severely. "I will say no more to you now. But I hope you will take what I have said as a warning. You must bustle along, Bennett, bustle along."

Outside in the street, Police-constable Bennett was free to reflect on his unpleasant interview. The superintendent was ambitious and therefore pompous; he, himself, was unambitious and therefore modest. Left to himself he might have been content to triumph in the reflection that he had failed to say a number of foolish things, but the welfare of his wife and children bound him, tiresomely enough for a dreamer, tightly to the practical. It was clear that if he did not forthwith produce signs of his efficiency as a promoter of the peace that welfare would be imperilled. Yet he did not condemn the chance that had made him a policeman or even the mischance that brought no guilty persons to his hands. Rather he looked with a gentle curiosity into the faces of the people who passed him, and wondered why he could not detect traces of the generally assumed wickedness of the neighbourhood. These unkempt men and women were thieves and even murderers, it appeared; but to him they shone as happy youths and maidens, joyous victims of love's tyranny.

As he drew near the street in which he lived this sense of universal love quickened in his blood and stirred him strangely. It did not escape his eyes that to the general his uniform was an unfriendly thing. Men and women paused in their animated chattering till he had passed, and even the children faltered in their games to watch him with doubtful eyes. And yet his heart was warm for them; he knew that he wished them well.

Nevertheless, when he saw his house shining in a row of similar houses, he realised that their attitude was wiser than his. If he was to be a success as a breadwinner he must wage a sterner war against these happy, lovable people. It was easy, he had been long enough in the force to know how easy, to get cases. An intolerant manner, a little provocative harshness, and the thing was done. Yet with all his heart he admired the poor for their resentful independence of spirit. To him this had always been the supreme quality of the English character; how could he make use of it to fill English gaols?

He opened the door of his house, with a sigh on his lips. There came forth the merry shouting of his children.

II

Above the telephone wires the stars dipped at anchor in the cloudless sky. Down below, in one of the dark, empty streets, Police-constable Bennett turned the handles of doors and tested the fastenings of windows, with a complete scepticism as to the value of his labours. Gradually, he was coming to see that he was not one of the few who are born to rule—to control—their simple neighbours, ambitious only for breath. Where, if he had possessed this mission, he would have been eager to punish, he now felt no more than a sympathy that charged him with some responsibility for the sins of others. He shared the uneasy conviction of the multitude that human justice, as interpreted by the inspired minority, is more than a little unjust. The very unpopularity with which his uniform endowed him seemed to him to express a severe criticism of the system of which he was an unwilling supporter. He wished these people to regard him as a kind of official friend, to advise and settle differences; yet, shrewder than he, they considered him as an enemy, who lived on their mistakes and the collapse of their social relationships.

There remained his duty to his wife and children, and this rendered the problem infinitely perplexing.

Why should he punish others because of his love for his children; or, again, why should his children suffer for his scruples? Yet it was clear that, unless fortune permitted him to accomplish some notable yet honourable arrest, he would either have to cheat and tyrannise with his colleagues or leave the force. And what employment is available for a discharged policeman?

As he went systematically from house to house the consideration of these things marred the normal progress of his dreams. Conscious as he was of the stars and the great widths of heaven that made the world so small, he nevertheless felt that his love for his family and the wider love that determined his honour were somehow intimately connected with this greatness of the universe rather than with the world of little streets and little motives, and so were not lightly to be put aside. Yet, how can one measure one love against another when all are true?

When the door of Gurneys', the moneylenders, opened to his touch, and drew him abruptly from his speculations, his first emotion was a quick irritation that chance should interfere with his thoughts. But when his lantern showed him that the lock had been tampered with, his annoyance changed to a thrill of hopeful excitement. What if this were the way out? What if fate had granted him compromise, the opportunity of pitting his official virtue against official crime, those shadowy forces in the existence of which he did not believe, but which lay on his life like clouds?

He was not a physical coward, and it seemed quite simple to him to creep quietly through the open door into the silent office without waiting for possible reinforcements. He knew that the safe, which would be the, natural goal of the presumed burglars, was in Mr. Gurney's private office beyond, and while he stood listening intently he seemed to hear dim sounds coming from the direction of that room. For a moment he paused, frowning slightly as a man does when he is trying to catalogue an impression. When he achieved perception, it came oddly mingled with recollections of the little tragedies of his children at home. For some one was crying like a child in the little room where Mr. Gurney brow-beat recalcitrant borrowers. Dangerous burglars do not weep, and Bennett hesitated no longer, but stepped past the open flaps of the counter, and threw open the door of the inner office.

The electric light had been switched on, and at the table there sat a slight young man with his face buried in his hands, crying bitterly. Behind him the safe stood open and empty, and the grate was filled with smouldering embers of burnt paper. Bennett went up to the young man and placed his hand on his shoulder. But the young man wept on and did not move.

Try as he might Bennett could not help relaxing the grip of outraged law, and patting the young man's shoulder soothingly as it rose and fell. He had no fit weapons of roughness and oppression with which to oppose this child-like grief; he could only fight tears with tears.

"Come," he said gently, "you must pull yourself together."

At the sound of his voice the young man gave a great sob and then was silent, shivering a little.

"That's better," said Bennett encouragingly, "much better."

"I have burnt everything," the young man said suddenly, "and now the place is empty. I was nearly sick just now."

Bennett looked at him sympathetically, as one dreamer may look at another, who is sad with action dreamed too often for scatheless accomplishment. "I'm afraid you'll get into serious trouble," he said.

"I know," replied the young man, "but that blackguard Gurney—" His voice rose to a shrill scream and choked him for a moment. Then he went on quietly "But it's all over now. Finished! Done with!"

"I suppose you owed him money?"

The young man nodded. "He lives on fools like me. But he threatened to tell my father, and now I've just about ruined him. Pah! Swine!"

"This won't be much better for your father," said Bennett gravely.

"No, it's worse; but perhaps it will help some of the others. He kept on threatening and I couldn't wait any longer. Can't you see?"

Over the young man's shoulder the stars becked and nodded to Bennett through the blindless window.

"I see," he said; "I see."

"So now you can take me."

Bennett looked doubtfully at the outstretched wrists. "You are only a fool," he said, "a dreaming fool like me, and they will give you years for this. I don't see why they should give a man years for being a fool."

The young man looked up, taken with a sudden hope. "You will let me go?" he said, in astonishment. "I know I was an ass just now. I suppose I was a bit shaken. But you will let me go?"

"I wish to God I had never seen you!" said Bennett simply. "You have your father, and I have a wife and three little children. Who shall judge between us?"

"My father is an old man."

"And my children are little. You had better go before I make up my mind."

Without another word the young man crept out of the room, and Bennett followed him slowly into the street. This gallant criminal whose capture would have been honourable, had dwindled to a hysterical foolish boy; and aided by his own strange impulse this boy had ruined him. The burglary had taken place on his beat; there would be an inquiry; it did not need that to secure his expulsion from the force. Once in the street he looked up hopefully to the heavens; but now the stars seemed unspeakably remote, though as he passed along his beat his wife and his three little children were walking by his side.

III

Bennett had developed mentally without realising the logical result of his development until it smote him with calamity. Of his betrayal of trust as a guardian of property he thought nothing; of the possibility of poverty for his family he thought a great deal—

all the more that his dreamer's mind was little accustomed to gripping the practical. It was strange, he thought, that his final declaration of war against his position should have been a little lacking in dignity. He had not taken the decisive step through any deep compassion of utter poverty bravely borne. His had been no more than trivial pity of a young man's folly; and this was a frail thing on which to make so great a sacrifice. Yet he regretted nothing. His task of moral guardian of men and women had become impossible to him, and sooner or later he must have given it up. And there was also his family. "I must come to some decision," he said to himself firmly.

And then the great scream fell upon his ears and echoed through his brain for ever and ever. It came from the house before which he was standing, and he expected the whole street to wake aghast with the horror of it. But there followed a silence that seemed to emphasise the ugliness of the sound. Far away an engine screamed as if in mocking imitation; and that was all. Bennett had counted up to a hundred and seventy before the door of the house opened, and a man came out on to the steps.

"Oh, constable," he said coolly, "come inside, will you? I have something to show you."

Bennett mounted the steps doubtfully.

"There was a scream," he said.

The man looked at him quickly. "So you heard it," he said. "It was not pretty."

"No, it was not," replied Bennett.

The man led him down the dim passage into the back sitting-room. The body of a man lay on the sofa; it was curled like a dry leaf.

"That is my brother," said the man, with a little emphatic nod; "I have killed him. He was my enemy."

Bennett stared dully at the body, without believing it to be really there.

"Dead!" he said mechanically.

"And anything I say will be used against me in evidence! As if you could compress my hatred into one little lying notebook."

"I don't care a damn about your hatred," said Bennett, with heat. "An hour ago, perhaps, I might have arrested you; now I only find you uninteresting."

The man gave a long, low whistle of surprise.

"A philosopher in uniform," he said, "God! sir, you have my sympathy."

"And you have my pity. You have stolen your ideas from cheap melodrama, and you make tragedy ridiculous. Were I a policeman, I would lock you up with pleasure. Were I a man, I should thrash you joyfully. As it is I can only share your infamy. I too, I suppose, am a murderer."

"You are in a low, nervous state," said the man; "and you are doing me some injustice. It is true that I am a poor murderer; but it appears to me that you are a worse policeman."

"I shall wear the uniform no more from tonight."

"I think you are wise, and I shall mar my philosophy with no more murders. If, indeed, I have killed him; for I assure you that beyond administering the poison to his wretched body I have done nothing. Perhaps he is not dead. Can you hear his heart beating?"

"I can hear the spoons of my children beating on their empty platters!"

"Is it like that with you? Poor devil! Oh, poor, poor devil! Philosophers should have no wives, no children, no homes, and no hearts."

Bennett turned from the man with unspeakable loathing.

"I hate you and such as you!" he cried weakly. "You justify the existence of the police. You make me despise myself because I realise that your crimes are no less mine than yours. I do not ask you to defend the deadness of that thing lying there. I shall stir no finger to have you hanged, for the thought of suicide repels me, and I cannot separate your blood and mine. We are common children of a noble mother, and for our mother's sake I say farewell."

And without waiting for the man's answer he passed from the house to the street.

IV

Haggard and with rebellious limbs, Police-constable Bennett staggered into the superintendent's office in the early morning.

"I have paid careful attention to your advice," he said to the superintendent, "and I have passed across the city in search of crime. In its place I have found but folly—such folly as you have, such folly as I have myself—the common heritage of our blood. It seems that in some way I have bound myself to bring criminals to justice. I have passed across the city, and I have found no man worse than myself. Do what you will with me."

The superintendent cleared his throat.

"There have been too many complaints concerning the conduct of the police," he said; "it is time that an example was made. You will be charged with being drunk and disorderly while on duty."

"I have a wife and three little children," said Bennett softly—"and three pretty little children." And he covered his tired face with his hands.

SHEPHERD'S BOY

The path climbed up and up and threatened to carry me over the highest point of the downs till it faltered before a sudden outcrop of chalk and swerved round the hill on the level. I was grateful for the respite, for I had been walking all day and my knapsack was growing heavy. Above me in the blue pastures of the skies the cloud-sheep were grazing, with the sun on their snowy backs, and all about me the grey sheep of earth were cropping the wild pansies that grew wherever the chalk had won a covering of soil.

Presently I came upon the shepherd standing erect by the path, a tall, spare man with a face that the sun and the wind had robbed of all expression. The dog at his feet looked more intelligent than he. "You've come up from the valley," he said as I passed; "perhaps you'll have seen my boy?"

"I'm sorry, I haven't," I said, pausing.

"Sorrow breaks no bones," he muttered, and strode away with his dog at his heels. It seemed to me that the dog was apologetic for his master's rudeness.

I walked on to the little hill-girt village, where I had made up my mind to pass the night. The man at the village shop said he would put me up, so I took off my knapsack and sat down on a sackful of cattle cake while the bacon was cooking.

"If you came over the hill, you'll have met shepherd," said the man, "and he'll have asked you for his boy."

"Yes, but I hadn't seen him."

The shopman nodded. "There are clever folk who say you can see him, and clever folk who say you can't. The simple ones like you and me, we say nothing, but we don't see him. Shepherd hasn't got no boy."

"What! is it a joke?"

"Well, of course it may be," said the shop-man guardedly, "though I can't say I've heard many people laughing at it yet. You see, shepherd's boy he broke his neck. . . .

"That was in the days before they built the fence above the big chalk-pit that you passed on your left coming down. A dangerous place it used to be for the sheep, so shepherd's boy he used to lie along there to stop them dropping into it, while shepherd's dog he stopped them from going too far. And shepherd he used to come down here and have his glass, for he took it then like you or me. He's blue ribbon now.

"It was one night when the mists were out on the hills, and maybe shepherd had had a glass too much, or maybe he got a bit lost in the smoke. But when he went up there to bring them home, he starts driving them into the pit as straight as could be. Shepherd's boy he hollered out and ran to stop them, but four-and-twenty of them went over, and the lad he went with them. You mayn't believe me, but five of them weren't so much as scratched, though it's a sixty feet drop. Likely they fell soft on top of the others. But shepherd's boy he was done.

"Shepherd he's a bit spotty now, and most times he thinks the boy's still with him. And there are clever folk who'll tell you that they've seen the boy helping shepherd's dog with the sheep. That would be a ghost now, I shouldn't wonder. I've never seen it, but then I'm simple, as you might say.

"But I've had two boys myself, and it seems to me that a boy like that, who didn't eat and didn't get into mischief, and did his work, would be the handiest kind of boy to have about the place."

CHILDREN OF THE MOON

The boy stood at the place where the park trees stopped and the smooth lawns slid away gently to the great house. He was dressed only in a pair of ragged knickerbockers and a gaping buttonless shirt, so that his legs and neck and chest shone silver bare in the moonlight. By day he had a mass of rough golden hair, but now it seemed to brood above his head like a black cloud that made his face deathly white by comparison. On his arms there lay a great heap of gleaming dew-wet roses and lilies, spoil of the park flower-beds. Their cool petals touched his cheek, and filled his nostrils with aching scent. He felt his arms smarting here and there, where the thorns of the roses had torn them in the dark, but these delicate caresses of pain only served to deepen to him the wonder of the night that wrapped him about like a cloak. Behind him there dreamed the black woods, and over his head multitudinous stars quivered and balanced in space; but these things were nothing to him, for far across the lawn that was spread knee-deep, with a web of mist there gleamed for his eager eyes the splendour of a fairy palace. Red and orange and gold, the lights of the fairy revels shone from a hundred windows and filled him with wonder that he should see with wakeful eyes the jewels that he had desired so long in sleep. He could only gaze and gaze until his straining eyes filled with tears, and set the enchanted lights dancing in the dark. On his ears, that heard no more the crying of the night-birds and the quick stir of the rabbits in the brake, there fell the strains of far

67

music. The flowers in his arms seemed to sway to it, and his heart beat to the deep pulse of the night.

So enraptured were his senses that he did not notice the coming of the girl, and she was able to examine him closely before she called to him softly through the moonlight.

"Boy! Boy!"

At the sound of her voice he swung round and looked at her with startled eyes. He saw her excited little face and her white dress.

"Are you a fairy?" he asked hoarsely, for the night-mist was in his voice.

"No," she said, "I'm a little girl. You're a wood-boy, I suppose?"

He stayed silent, regarding her with a puzzled face. Who was this little white creature with the tender voice that had slipped so suddenly out of the night?

"As a matter of fact," the girl continued, "I've come out to have a look at the fairies. There's a ring down in the wood. You can come with me if you like, wood-boy."

He nodded his head silently, for he was afraid to speak to her, and set off through the wood by her side, still clasping the flowers to his breast.

"What were you looking at when I found you?" she asked.

"The palace—the fairy palace," the boy muttered.

"The palace?" the girl repeated. "Why, that's not a palace; that's where I live."

The boy looked at her with new awe; if she were a fairy— But the girl had noticed that his feet made no sound beside her shoes.

"Don't the thorns prick your feet, wood-boy?" she asked; but the boy said nothing, and they were both silent for a while, the girl looking about her keenly as she walked, and the boy watching her face. Presently they came to a wide pool where a little tinkling fountain threw bubbles to the hidden fish.

"Can you swim?" she said to the boy.

He shook his head.

"It's a pity," said the girl; "we might have had a bathe. It would be rather fun in the dark, but it's pretty deep there. We'd better get on to the fairy ring."

The moon had flung queer shadows across the glade in which the ring lay, and when they stood on the edge listening intently the wood seemed to speak to them with a hundred voices.

"You can take hold of my hand, if you like," said the girl, in a whisper.

The boy dropped his flowers about his white feet and felt for the girl's hand in the dark. Soon it lay in his own, a warm live thing, that stirred a little with excitement.

"I'm not afraid," the girl said; and so they waited.

The man came upon them suddenly from among the silver birches. He had a knapsack on his back and his hair was as long as a tramp's. At sight of him the girl almost screamed, and her hand trembled in the boy's. Some instinct made him hold it tighter.

"What do you want?" he muttered, in his hoarse voice.

The man was no less astonished than the children.

"What on earth are you doing here?" he cried. His voice was mild and reassuring, and the girl answered him promptly.

"I came out to look for fairies."

"Oh, that's right enough," commented the man; "and you," he said, turning to the boy, "are you after fairies, too? Oh, I see; picking flowers. Do you mean to sell them?"

The boy shook his head.

"For my sister," he said, and stopped abruptly.

"Is your sister fond of flowers?"

"Yes; she's dead."

The man looked at him gravely.

"That's a phrase," he said, "and phrases are the devil. Who told you that dead people like flowers?"

"They always have them," said the boy, blushing for shame of his pretty thought.

"And what are *you* looking for?" the girl interrupted.

The man made a mocking grimace, and glanced around the glade as if he were afraid of being overheard.

"Dreams," he said bluntly.

The girl pondered this for a moment.

"And your knapsack?" she began.

"Yes," said the man, "it's full of them."

The children looked at the knapsack with interest, the girl's fingers tingling to undo the straps of it.

"What are they like?" she asked.

The man gave a short laugh.

"Very like yours and his, I expect; when you grow older, young woman, you'll find there's really only one dream possible for a sensible person. But you don't want to hear about my troubles. This is more in your line!" He put his hand in his pocket and pulled out a flageolet, which he put to his lips.

"Listen!" he said.

To the girl it seemed as though the little tune had leapt from the pipe, and was dancing round the ring like a real fairy, while echo came tripping through the trees to join it. The boy gaped and said nothing.

At last, when the fairy was beginning to falter and echo was quite out of breath, the man took the flageolet from his lips.

"Well," he said, with a smile.

"Thank you very much," said the girl politely. "I think that was very nice indeed. Oh, boy!" she broke off, "you're hurting my hand!"

The boy's eyes were shining strangely, and he was waving his arms in dismay.

"All the wasted moonlight!" he cried; "the grass is quite wet with it."

The girl turned to him in surprise.

"Why, boy, you've found your voice."

"After that," said the man gravely, as he put his flageolet back in his pocket, "I think I will show you the inside of my knapsack."

The girl bent down eagerly, while he loosened the straps, but gave a cry of disappointment when she saw the contents.

"Pictures!" she said.

"Pictures," echoed the man drily,—"pictures of dreams. I don't know how you're going to see them. Perhaps the moon will do her best."

The girl looked at them nicely, and passed them on one by one to the boy. Presently she made a discovery.

"Oh, boy!" she cried, "your tears are spoiling all the pictures."

"I'm sorry," said the boy huskily; "I can't help it."

"I know," the man said quickly; "it doesn't matter a bit. I expect you've seen these pictures before."

"I know them all," said the boy, "but I have never seen them."

The man frowned.

"It's the devil," he said to himself, "when boys speak English." He turned suddenly to the girl, who was puzzling over the boy's tears. "It's time you went back to bed," he said; "there won't be any fairies tonight. It's too cold for them."

The girl yawned.

"I shall get into a row when I get back if they've found it out. I don't care."

"The moon is fading," said the boy suddenly; "there are no more shadows."

"We will see you through the wood," the man continued, "and say good-night."

He put his pictures back in his knapsack and then walked silently through the murmuring wood. At the edge of the wood the girl stopped.

"You are a wood-boy," she said to the boy, "and you mustn't come any farther. You can give me a kiss if you like."

The boy did not move, but stayed regarding her awkwardly.

"I think you are a very silly boy," said the girl, with a toss of her head, and she stalked away proudly into the mist.

"Why didn't you kiss her?" asked the man.

"Her lips would burn me," said the boy.

The man and the boy walked slowly across the park.

"Now, boy," said the man, "since civilisation has gone to bed the time has come for you to hear your destiny."

"I am only a poor boy," the boy replied simply. "I don't think I have any destiny."

"Paradox," said the man, "is meant to conceal the insincerity of the aged, not to express the simplicity of youth. But I wander. You have made phrases tonight."

"What are phrases?"

"What are dreams? What are roses? What, in fine, is the moon? Boy, I take you for a moon-child. You hold her pale flowers in your arms, her white beams have caressed your limbs, you prefer the kisses of her cool lips to those of that earth-child; all this is very well. But, above all, you have the music of her great silence; above all, you have her tears. When I played to you on my pipe you recognised the voice of your mother. When I showed you my pictures you recalled the tales with which she hushed you to sleep. And so I knew that you were her son and my little brother."

"The moon has always been my friend," said the boy; "but I did not know that she was my mother."

"Perhaps your sister knows it; the happy dead are glad to seek her for a mother; that is why they are so fond of white flowers."

"We have a mother at home. She works very hard for us."

"But it is your mother among the clouds who makes your life beautiful, and the beauty of your life is the measure of your days."

While the boy reflected on these things they had reached the gates of the park, and they stole past the silent lodge on to the high road. A man was waiting there in the shadows, and when he saw the boy's companion he rushed out and seized him by the arm.

"So I've got you," he said; "I don't think I'll let you go again in a hurry."

The son of the moon gave a queer little laugh.

"Why, it's Taylor!" he said pleasantly; "but, Taylor, you know you're making a great mistake."

"Very possibly," said the keeper, with a laugh.

"You see this boy here, Taylor; I assure you he is much madder than I am."

Taylor looked at the boy kindly.

"Time you were in bed, Tommy," he said.

"Taylor," said the man earnestly, "this boy has made three phrases. If you don't lock him up he will certainly become a poet. He will set your precious world of sanity ablaze with the fire of his mother, the moon. Your palaces will totter, Taylor, and your kingdoms become as dust. I have warned you."

"That's right, sir; and now you must come with me."

"Boy," said the man generously, "keep your liberty. By grace of Providence, all men in authority are fools. We shall meet again under the light of the moon."

With dreamy eyes the boy watched the departure of his companion. He had become almost invisible along the road when, miraculously as it seemed, the light of the moon broke through the trees by the wayside and lit up his figure. For a moment it fell upon his head like a halo, and touched the knapsack of dreams with glory. Then all was lost in the blackness of night.

As he turned homeward the boy felt a cold wind upon his cheek. It was the first breath of dawn.

A HUNGERFORD INTERLUDE

Bradford stood on Charing Cross foot-bridge and gazed stead-fastly into the water, a pleasant enough occupation, and infinitely preferable to the odour of the onions which were being cooked for his supper at his lodgings.

While he was thus engaged he became aware of a man who was pacing nervously up and down the wooden planking, as a timid passenger might pace the deck of a ship. Now those who use this deplorable bridge do so in a steady business-like fashion, cover-ing the ground rapidly, with minds intent on catching trains or, if incorrigibly lazy, stopping frankly like Bradford to look, after a common human weakness, over the edge.

But this one did neither, and Bradford turned round to look at this unconventional monster, who neither was honestly idle nor went about his business.

The stranger was not one of those men of strongly-marked features whom novelists love to describe; just an ordinary-looking member of the caste of pointed beards. And now you know him very well.

After a few more turns up and down he approached Bradford and asked, "How long do you propose to remain here?"

"Why?" said Bradford, naturally enough.

The man hesitated a little before replying. "You see," he said timidly, "the fact is I wish to jump over the edge."

"Oh!" said Bradford, and after a pause, "What for?"

The timidity of the stranger increased until Bradford found it quite painful to see. He stuttered and mouthed a long harangue without Bradford being able to catch anything except the two words "My wife." Then he stopped.

"Your wife," said Bradford encouragingly, but the stranger read another meaning in his voice.

"Oh no," he cried with passion. "It is not that. Heaven forbid. She—she—my wife says, in fact, well." He wandered in a confused tangle of words.

"Well?" said Bradford patiently.

"My wife says I have broken her heart and so"—with a pain-pitiful reminiscence of the Surrey Theatre—"and so I must die!"

Bradford suppressed a primitive desire to laugh and tried to grapple with the unreality of the scene. "Your wife says that," he said feebly.

The man shook with impatience. "She says that I have broken her heart, and so I say I must die."

Bradford meditated. The man was so timid and in a way so matter-of-fact. He talked of suicide as one talks of duty, half-heartedly, but nevertheless as a thing to be done. Still, he might be joking. "Are you serious?" he asked.

The man shook his head. "I know," he said with the sigh of an unsuccessful artist. "I know that my manner is sadly lacking in conviction. But really you know it does sound so silly to talk of death and that sort of thing even when one has quite made up one's mind."

That was just how Bradford was feeling himself. "It does indeed," he said frankly. "But will not your wife relent?"

"My wife is a queen of women," said the other proudly. "It is I who have repented. I have broken her heart. I must die."

Bradford thought vaguely of the police, but how could he betray this timid trust? Then he had an idea. "You know," he cried, "the worst of it is I can swim!"

"Well?" said the man.

"I should have to rescue you for the sake of my own respect, and in the effort I might be drowned. That," he said, finding the stranger's style infectious, "that would be unjust."

The would-be suicide looked melancholy.

"What a nuisance," he said at last. "Still," more hopefully, "you might turn your back for a minute, you know."

"No," said Bradford firmly. "It won't do. If you do it at all now you will ruin my whole life. I will think I might have stopped you."

The stranger sighed, "I suppose you are right."

"Yes," said Bradford, warming to his part. "I am very sorry to hinder you in any way, but you see you shouldn't have told me."

"What a nuisance," repeated the man.

"You can go back and no one will be any the wiser," Bradford suggested.

"I—I wrote a letter," said the other, troubled, "to my wife you know. Penitence. Brute. Set her free. Watery grave." He relapsed into vague mutterings.

Bradford whistled his perplexity. "By Jove," he murmured, "you have put your foot in it."

"Yes," said the stranger, pleased with Bradford's sympathy and the complete blackness of his own outlook, "I think I have."

Then ensued a silence which lasted until Bradford's brow ached with the ornamental frown which he thought betrayed the proper amount of sympathetic interest in the other's worries. Then arrived Fate in the shape of a large and excited woman, who gave expression to unrestrained relief when she beheld the stranger.

"Kate!" cried the latter, with nothing now of the melodramatic in his voice.

And then and there before Bradford's eyes they embraced heartily.

The woman remembered first.

"Come away," she cried. "And don't be silly."

And the man followed her humbly enough without saying anything to Bradford in farewell. That one watched them go and wondered if he was really awake.

"How absurd!" he murmured, and tried to laugh. But somehow he couldn't.

THE CLERK

He was a paper-cuffed clerk, old and weary and forty-five years of age, and he left his office at quarter past four like a man who has been too long in prison and cares not whether he goes or stays.

But he passed down along Cheapside and Fleet Street and the Strand and on and on till he came to the purple mountains stained by a mad sun of crushed whortleberries.

There he stopped and wrung his hands a little and cried to the sun.

"Oh, sun, if you could speak you would join me in my song to my beloved, you would say to me, 'Oh, most miserable, how quiet she is and how cool, there is the softness of new snow on her cheeks!' And I should say, 'Truly there is a magic of old stars wandering in her hair!' Now though you are dumb you are more fortunate than I, for you can smile on her and touch her, but I, I, woe is me, can only pass by trembling—"

And he went on to the garden of dull red walls and peach trees and roses and there was a moon there very lovely.

And he cried to the moon in his bitter sorrow:

"My beautiful is very young as you know, having kissed her in the night, oh fortunate moon, and her lips are like a new bud. But you are as old as the hills and I, I am forty-five. Weep with me a little."

And he passed on to the field of stars, but to these he said nothing, because they were part of her.

Now he was mad, and things happening, it fell that he was at home in his own bedroom, and she whom he loved lay in his bed, wakeful and wondering, but he sat apart in the room.

And outside the window the moon smiled and the sun light-ened the east in his joy, but the stars trembled because they were part of her.

In the house a clock ticked off the seconds in the darkness and sung the hours on a little bell, and the hours were very short; yet the clerk sat there marvelling that he had done this thing—that he had stolen her whom he might not speak to, and that she should rest in his bed.

And his blood that had grown weary of longing for the hills and the song of the glistening sea, and his mind that had known too long the yellow desk and electric fires and faces of unloved com-panions, was stirred by the bitter old desire, not as of old in sor-row to break her, but now in joy to kiss her and make her his.

And he heard her breathing and stirring in her sleep with a rustle of wings, and the tears of fire wove in his eyes and wan-dered down his cheeks.

For he knew how long it had been and how lonely ere yet he had taken the sun and moon for his friends and won her too; for all the old and bitter longing now that she was his, she was no more than a dream. Even her breath that sweetened all the room was only a thing thought of long ago. Even her hair that gleamed won-derfully on the white pillow was only a memory of the sunshine of a boy's spring.

Surely if he touched her she would vanish as had all the others.

She was all he had longed for, all he had desired. His lost ideal. He would not have her perish with the rest, so he sat apart in his chair and watched her with filial wakeful eyes.

And the sun came up over the houses and through the window and, kissing her, made her very sweet. And the birds sang at the panes, and her lips moving a little seemed to echo the song, and when her lips parted they were like the breaking of all the rose-buds.

The clerk drew his chair nearer to the bed and leant forward to listen.

Surely there was a singing not of birds. A voice that was not new singing an old song of the spring.

And then bending forward he felt her cool breath beating on his cheek and wrapping round his face. Roses and thyme and lilies.

And the song swelled in his ears and he knew it for his own. The song he had never been able to sing.

And he saw her lips parting—

It was better to lose her, better to take the risk. If it might be, one kiss—

He stood up with a great cry and fell forward on to the bed, dead.

THE INHERITOR

Arthur Bradford pushed away his plate of tepid bacon and eggs and looked at the letter with swimming eyes. His aunt Geraldine, whom he had only seen as a stern vision that disapproved of his mother, had died intestate, leaving property to the value of over twelve thousand pounds.

And he was the only heir, he, Arthur Bradford, clerk in the employment of the Commonwealth Insurance Co., on a salary of £115 a year.

Over twelve thousand pounds—at four per cent. that would be nearly five hundred a year, perhaps he would get five per cent., he knew people in the City who were wise in such matters, six hundred pounds a year—the bed-sitting-room with the faded, silly furniture grew dim and uncertain to his sight; the white table-cloth seemed to move beneath his fingers; it was all so strange.

Once, three years before, when he had first met Molly, he had applied ambitiously for a vacant post, and had narrowly missed getting it. The salary would have been £150 a year, and it was pleasant to recall the old bitterness, now that he need work no more, now that he was rich.

He walked to the window and opened it with fumbling fingers. The sky was grey and threatened rain, and at any other time the outlook would have depressed him; but today he felt that he had at last inherited London, its streets and shops and horses were in a manner his; he could ride in its carriages if he wished.

He thought of Molly in the little dull shop across the water, the shop that sold penny packets of notepaper and gorgeous penholders and ill-printed classics bound in cloth for eightpence halfpenny, and at the thought he smiled. For they could marry now, they for whom marriage had always been an impracticable ideal, they for whom love had been perforce little but a series of Sunday afternoon walks in the park; they could marry and live where they pleased, even in the green country of which folk wrote in books.

Other men, he reflected, in the face of so great an inheritance would make haste to forget the little shop assistant whom they had loved when they were poor. But that was not his way. No! She should share his fortune and serve at a counter no more. He felt that he was not a mean man.

He looked at his watch and saw that he was too late to be in time at his office; and he did not care. He would send them a cheque for a month's salary in lieu of notice, and he found a certain pleasure in the thought that his sudden resignation at balancing time would inconvenience them. Perhaps they would see that his services were worth more than the paltry sum they had been paying him, perhaps even they would offer him an increase in order to tempt him back. He pictured himself declining with a certain courteous dignity; after all, they were a decent enough lot of fellows, he bore them no ill-will.

The rain still held off, and he found the room close and too small for his new aspirations and put on his hat and coat to go into the streets; he would walk across to the shop in Lambeth and tell Molly of his good luck, of their good luck, rather; that would be the graceful way to put it, and then how glad she would be! Of course he was only doing the decent thing, yet he could not help feeling that there were a good many men who would fail to do it in similar circumstances, for although Molly was a quite exceptional girl, she was not, of course, of the same social rank as—

He checked himself with a certain shame and glanced in the faces of the people who were passing to see if they had detected a thought that seemed to him treacherous; then he laughed aloud at his fear and the thing that had caused it.

Why, he was on his way now to tell her of his good fortune. Over twelve thousand pounds, say, if he invested it carefully, some six hundred and fifty a year; how happy she would be! He was going to tell her immediately, the very hour he had heard of it himself. Surely that was what a good man would do.

Now he would be able to buy her new dresses in place of the old drab blouses and skirts and the soiled aprons. And they would forget that she had ever worn such things and served in a cheap stationer's shop, or if they did recall them it would be with pleasure, because they belonged to a grey past and would come again no more.

How mean the shop was, he thought, as he approached it, and how grey and soiled the street in which it stood. Dirty babes too young for school scrambled in the gutters while their mothers, unkempt and ragged, breathed gin and profanity from the doors of the decaying houses. The few shops with their muddy fronts and unclean windows appeared to be on the verge of failure; the one in which Molly worked might well be, he thought, for who in such a neighbourhood would want notepaper or gaudy penholders or cheap ill-printed copies of Ainsworth's novels?

He stopped before the shop and looked through the window past the sheets of verses by the talented author of "The Fireman's Wedding," and saw that Molly was standing inside behind the counter; so he slipped quietly through the open door to take her by surprise.

She was fixing picture post-cards of the most fatuously vulgar character in melancholy rows by means of paper fasteners, and hanging these rows as they were completed from the long gas bracket that was suspended from the ceiling. The dust from the swinging bracket had made her face dirty, there were smudges on her blouse and on her apron, she did not look so pretty as she did on Sunday afternoon in the park. When she looked up and saw him there was mingled with her surprise that he should come to visit her during office hours, obvious annoyance that he should find her in such an untidy condition; but he had news, wonderful news for her.

"Over twelve thousand pounds, Molly, over twelve thousand pounds!"

When he had finished his story and displayed the letter she burst into tears.

So this was the end of his fine thinking and of his generosity, this was the manner in which she received the news of his good fortune, of their good fortune. Arthur Bradford tapped his fingers on the counter in his annoyance. He did not know that she was crying because her face was dirty and she was drab and old—because the shop was dark and the post-cards vulgar and the boxes on the upper shelves so covered with dust that to move them was torment—because the little boys of the street were wont to run into the shop and mock her across the counter.

Still she cried; Arthur could see two women looking curiously through the window and a third approaching to see what they were looking at, and he saw, as if he were a neutral observer, himself the rich man standing in the dark, low shop pleading desperately with a dirty, ill-dressed girl who received his entreaties with sobs and chokings; he felt a wild anger rise in him that anything should have happened to mar his happiness on such a day of good fortune.

Then the horror overcame him; he saw himself and his business laid before a scornful, grinning crowd, he felt that he had allowed himself to be bound to a world of muss and vulgarity and grimy tears at the moment when fortune had given him wings to rise; he saw love as a thing that choked and sniffled.

The crowd had lapped across the door when he burst out of the shop.

Still the rain held off. Folk passed along the twilit streets with their lips parted as if they were thirsty. There would be no peace until the yellow clouds broke and washed the heavy air.

So this was the end and he was a bad man after all. And yet he felt that he had tried to do the decent thing. Why had she cried and made him look ridiculous? Why had everything been so dusty and grey? It was true that it was not too late to go back, but he knew he would never do it. He was free; and even the thought of the untidy little figure crying as though its heart would break in the dark empty shop would not make him retrace his steps to a grey street and a grey business. Was he not rich? And after all, she—she would forget him and marry someone of her own class. Oh, he was a hound and a blackguard, but still he had meant well. A good many men would have dropped her without telling her of their good luck, but he had told her at once, and now he was free and would forget all about it.

Over twelve thousand pounds. What might he not do?

On his table at home he found another letter from the lawyers. Perhaps they were sending a cheque on account.

As he opened it, the storm burst and the rain dashed against the windowpanes with a muffled roar, like the tapping of many fingers on a counter. So the old woman who had disliked his mother had made a will; there was a matter of twelve thousand pounds for three charities, and he, Arthur Bradford, who had lost Molly, would be a clerk for evermore. He dropped his face in his hands and cried like a child.

THE WRONG TURNING

It was a dark night, and the traveller shuddered as he strode along the white road. On each side of that sorely-made way lay the marshes, waiting for a chance slip to catch the blunderer by the heel and slowly suck him under, when nought but the will-o'-the-wisps would know the manner of his passing.

Had it been light he could have seen the dry land shake and tremble and melt into greasy waters, or muddy banks rise like the heads of great reptiles through the surface of pools, but the darkness hid these horrors, and he could only hear the choking of the falling mud, and the harsh cries of sea-birds far away.

He clutched his bag closer to him and hurried on, keeping carefully to the middle of the road, and looking anxiously ahead at the surface of the way, for fear that a land-slip might have turned the path of safety to a deathtrap. So it was he noticed far ahead amongst the dim stars and marsh flames a light, that burned with a steady glow, and neither flickered nor danced.

The traveller paused in some surprise at the sight. He had been told of no house to be passed on the way, while if it should be the light of a fellow-traveller, that one might well be a thief or worse; and where would lie his safety in so forsaken a spot?

But the light burned quite steadily, and the traveller continued on his way reassured. It was, without doubt, a house. As he drew near, and the light proved to come from an uncurtained window in a squat and miserable dwelling, his doubts recurred. What honest man could endure to live in such a place; and its ill-appearance was hardly redeemed by the sign that hung creaking across the sky—"The House of Woe." Who had ever heard of such a name for an inn as that? He had come to a standstill while he scanned the place, but the name decided him; and with his heart like a lump in his throat he began to steal past the place on tiptoe, praying that they might not keep a dog within.

Thus he crept along by the black wall, and had just come to the end when he pulled himself up with a terrible shock.

The road went no farther, and the black waters lay muttering at his feet.

After the first sensation of panic, he found himself thinking with a curious calmness. Of course, the explanation was simple. He had mistaken the path to the inn for the road he should have followed; and all he had to do was to retrace his steps, and all would be well.

So he set himself again to his tiptoeing, and once more passed the house without disturbing its inmates.

But now a new difficulty presented itself; round the inn the ground was dead white, so that it was hard to tell where the road might be. He struck out at a venture, hesitated, took a step, and felt his leg sink to the knee in a soft mass that closed on it like steel. With a frantic effort he flung his body backwards on to the firm ground, and fought silently with the mud in the darkness. At last he rolled back free, but exhausted, with the air striking his panting lungs with the force of a blow.

After a while he pulled himself up and gazed fearfully around him. Behind lay "The House of Woe," dark and forbidding, while before lay the deadly marshes chuckling at the victim they had failed to keep. He felt he durst not venture towards them again while his leg was yet numb with the force of their grip.

He stepped slowly towards the house with the mud oozing in his torn boot, and as he went he comforted himself as timid men do in lonely places, with the thought of great cities and their carefully regulated police. He could have stayed where he was all night, but he felt himself wrought on by a petulant desire for action, being, in truth, too fearful to remain passively between the known dangers of the marsh and that dark and repellent monster with the luminous eye.

The sound of his knuckles on the door set his heart fluttering again, and he would have given kingdoms for the moment, if only the sound might not have been made. Yet his knock was not answered, and so contradictory is the nature of man that after a few minutes he was banging lustily and impatiently on the door, and swearing to himself at the dilatoriness of those within.

The door opened at last, and a man appeared in the dim passage, who, without listening to the traveller's explanations, stood aside silently to let him pass.

That one hesitated, felt that he had gone too far to retreat, stepped trembling past the man, and heard with a heart of lead the door banged and fastened behind him.

At the end of the passage a slit of light showed the presence of a doorway, and with the man treading closely behind the traveller pushed this open, still with the same dread of something terrible within. But his fear seemed misplaced, the room might indeed have been the living- room of an old inn, with its oak panels, wide fireplace, sides of bacon, and strings of onions pendant from the high ceiling, and a bright enough fire burning on the hearth, with the additional light of the lamp in the window, which he had seen from without.

Seated by the fire was an elderly man engaged in stirring the contents of a pot, while in the further corner, with her back turned to the door, was a woman bending over the bed of a little child. Neither the man nor the woman looked up to see who had entered, and when his conductor, still without a word, motioned him to a chair by the table, the wanderer began to think the whole household was deaf and dumb. To walk into a room in the dead of night drenched with mud and water, and to escape practically unnoticed, was disconcerting, and it hardly reassured him to suspect that he was the object of secret scrutiny on the part of the two men.

But when he looked up sharply he only saw the old man stirring his pot, and the other gazing stolidly at the fire.

Suddenly the girl got up and swung round to the room, and as he saw her face the traveller knew why his feet had wandered to that place, and why he was afraid.

"You, Lucy!" he cried.

"Me, Hubert," she said quietly. And deep silence fell on the room.

He sat like one already dead, white and speechless. Lucy and the men and the sides of bacon danced madly in his vision, and he was afraid they would know he was a coward by the loudness of his breathing, but there was such a weight on his chest that when he sought to close his lips he was nearly choked.

It was the silence that he hated—the silence and the suspense. Why did not something happen? Anything rather than those mute and incurious figures.

"For God's sake," he cried, and the tears welled in his eyes at the sound of his voice, so sad and appealing.

There was a pause, and then suddenly the elder man, Lucy's father it would be, threw back his swart and bearded face in a hoarse cackle of laughter. Again and again he renewed it, his dried lips pulled back from the yellow teeth and the cruel red gums; even so might the Prince of Darkness mock a lost soul.

Lucy had turned back to the child.

Anon the man grew tired of his laughing and fell once more to stirring his broth, tasting it from time to time with his spoon and pursing his lips at the heat.

The cruelty of it. The traveller could endure it no longer. He staggered to his feet and clutched his hat to his head, his bag lying forgotten on the floor.

"I—I think I will go out," he said with an effort, and moved to the door.

The man by the fire spoke at last.

"Put the gentleman on the right way, Lucy," he said, and there was a glint of malice in his voice.

Lucy left the bed and walked to the door. She had not always had that iron face. The wanderer followed her quietly and hopelessly down the passage and out into the night. He had only needed one glance at that grim face to know what was his fate.

As he trod behind her through the greying marshes he heard the waters laughing cruelly each side, and the sound reminded him of the man he had left behind in "The House of Woe." And as he thought of that name he knew many things.

"You liked me once, Lucy," he said, but his words ended in a gasp. With a rapid leap or two the woman had passed to a spot about twenty feet off and he knew not which way to tread.

"Your child. I am its father. You cannot kill me."

Lucy did not seem to hear the words, but she began singing very softly, and with a thrill of horror Hubert recognised the words. It was a love song.

She sang without a tremor, but for the rest it was the same sweet voice that had charmed him so much before, and he had prided himself on his taste in such matters.

He heard her fascinated to the end of her song; and as he listened a wave of something like remorse broke on his self-centred mind.

"You know I meant to come back, Lucy," he cried when she had finished. "It was all a mistake."

She looked at him with hard and steady contempt. "I saw you go that morning," she said.

He bowed his head, for there are some things that even the worst man cannot think about without shame. There was no romance about that flight at dawn, that creeping down the stairs with his boots in his hand, that painful straining to hear if Lucy had wakened, all this had been sordid enough. And she had known all the time and let him go.

There was none of the fierce spirit distracted and led astray in this; he merely felt like a mean man, found out, and for the moment he was genuinely penitent, and so lost to externals that he did not even notice that the reason his feet were of lead was because he was slowly sinking, that the mud had risen above his boots.

"I'm sorry, Lucy," he said humbly.

This was a better way.

"Why did you say you loved me, Hubert?" she said sadly.

"I was a brute."

He was watching Lucy's face when he said this, and a sudden change, suggestive of fear, made him look down. The mud reached nearly to his knees.

For a minute he struggled, trying desperately to withdraw one leg, but he only sank the deeper. At last he desisted, and looked wistfully across at Lucy.

"I'm gone," he said.

Lucy stood irresolute, with her face half-turned away, and her fingers plucking at the front of her gown. "I can't!" she cried suddenly, and came running to his side, her trained eye choosing the spots which she knew to be comparatively safe.

He held out his arms to her, and she took his hands one in each of hers as if she would embrace him, but she made no effort to help him out.

"I'm sinking, Lucy," he said plaintively.

"Yes, Hubert," she said simply.

The mud had passed his waist, and she knew no effort of hers could release him.

"You are cruel," he cried, struggling feebly in the scarcely liquid mass.

Lucy dropped his hands, and placing hers on his shoulders thrust his body back with all her might. His arms flailed desperately in all directions, but the mud was sliding over his chest and over his chin and over his face.

When the surface had ceased to quiver and the bubbles had passed, Lucy drew forth her hands and straightened herself against the dawning sky.

"It was better," she said.

And she turned back to her child.

AND WHO SHALL SAY—?

It was a dull November day, and the windows were heavily curtained, so that the room was very dark. In front of the fire was a large arm-chair, which shut whatever light there might be from the two children, a boy of eleven and a girl about two years younger, who sat on the floor at the back of the room. The boy was the better looking, but the girl had the better face. They were both gazing at the arm-chair with the utmost excitement.

"It's all right. He's asleep," said the boy.

"Oh, do be careful! you'll wake him," whispered the girl.

"Are you afraid?"

"No, why should I be afraid of my father, stupid?"

"I tell you he's not father any more. He's a murderer," the boy said hotly. "He told me, I tell you. He said, 'I have killed your mother, Ray,' and I went and looked, and mother was all red. I simply shouted, and she wouldn't answer. That means she's dead. His hand was all red, too."

"Was it paint?"

"No, of course it wasn't paint. It was blood. And then he came down here and went to sleep."

"Poor father, so tired."

"He's not poor father, he's not father at all; he's a murderer, and it is very wicked of you to call him father," said the boy.

"Father," muttered the girl rebelliously.

"You know the sixth commandment says 'Thou shalt do no murder,' and he has done murder; so he'll go to hell. And you'll go to hell too if you call him father. It's all in the Bible."

The boy ended vaguely, but the little girl was quite overcome by the thought of her badness.

"Oh, I am wicked!" she cried. "And I do so want to go to heaven."

She had a stout and materialistic belief in it as a place of sheeted angels and harps, where it was easy to be good.

"You must do as I tell you, then," he said. "Because I know. I've learnt all about it at school."

"And you never told me," said she reproachfully.

"Ah, there's lots of things I know," he replied, nodding his head.

"What must we do?" said the girl meekly. "Shall I go and ask mother?"

The boy was sick at her obstinacy. "Mother's dead, I tell you; that means she can't hear anything. It's no use talking to her; but I know. You must stop here, and if father wakes you run out of the house and call 'Police!' and I will go now and tell a policeman now."

"And what happens then?" she asked, with round eyes at her brother's wisdom.

"Oh, they come and take him away to prison. And then they put a rope round his neck and hang him like Haman, and he goes to hell."

"Wha-at! Do they kill him?"

"Because he's a murderer. They always do."

"Oh, don't let's tell them! Don't let's tell them!" she screamed.

"Shut up!" said the boy, "or he'll wake up. We must tell them, or we go to hell—both of us."

But his sister did not collapse at this awful threat, as he expected, though the tears were rolling down her face. "Don't let's tell them," she sobbed.

"You're a horrid girl, and you'll go to hell," said the boy, in disgust. But the silence was only broken by her sobbing. "I tell you he killed mother dead. You didn't cry a bit for mother; I did."

"Oh, let's ask mother! Let's ask mother! I know she won't want father to go to hell. Let's ask mother!"

"Mother's dead, and can't hear, you stupid," said the boy. "I keep on telling you. Come up and look."

They were both a little awed in mother's room. It was so quiet, and mother looked so funny. And first the girl shouted, and then the boy, and then they shouted both together, but nothing happened. The echoes made them frightened.

"Perhaps she's asleep," the girl said; so her brother pinched one of mother's hands—the white one, not the red one—but nothing happened, so mother was dead.

"Has she gone to hell?" whispered the girl.

"No! she's gone to heaven, because she's good. Only wicked people go to hell. And now I must go and tell the policeman. Don't you tell father where I've gone if he wakes up, or he'll run away before the policeman comes."

"Why?"

"So as not to go to hell," said the boy, with certainty; and they went downstairs together, the little mind of the girl being much perturbed because she was so wicked. What would mother say to-morrow if she had done wrong?

The boy put on his sailor hat in the hall. "You must go in there and watch," he said, nodding in the direction of the sitting-room. "I shall run all the way."

The door banged, and she heard his steps down the path, and then everything was quiet.

She tiptoed into the room, and sat down on the floor, and looked at the back of the chair in utter distress. She could see her father's elbow projecting on one side, but nothing more. For an instant she hoped that he wasn't there—hoped that he had gone—but then, terrified, she knew that this was a piece of extreme wickedness.

So she lay on the rough carpet, sobbing hopelessly, and seeing real and vicious devils of her brother's imagining in all the corners of the room.

Presently, in her misery, she remembered a packet of acid-drops that lay in her pocket, and drew them forth in a sticky mass, which parted from its paper with regret. So she choked and sucked her sweets at the same time, and found them salt and tasteless.

Ray was gone a long time, and she was a wicked girl who would go to hell if she didn't do what he told her. Those were her prevailing ideas.

And presently there came a third. Ray had said that if her father woke up he would run away, and not go to hell at all. Now if she woke him up—

She knew this was dreadfully naughty; but her mind clung to the idea obstinately. You see, father had always been so fond of mother, and he would not like to be in a different place. Mother wouldn't like it either. She was always so sorry when father did not come home or anything. And hell is a dreadful place, full of things. She half convinced herself, and started up, but then there came an awful thought.

If she did this she would go to hell for ever and ever, and all the others would be in heaven.

She hung there in suspense, sucking her sweet and puzzling it over with knit brows.

How can one be good?

She swung round and looked in the dark corner by the piano; but the Devil was not there.

And then she ran across the room to her father, and shaking his arm, shouted, tremulously—

"Wake up, father! Wake up! The police are coming!"

And when the police came ten minutes later, accompanied by a very proud and virtuous little boy, they heard a small shrill voice crying, despairingly—

"The police, father! The police!"

But father would not wake.

THE BIRD IN THE GARDEN

The room in which the Burchell family lived in Love Street, S.E., was underground and depended for light and air on a grating let into the pavement above.

Uncle John, who was a queer one, had filled the area with green plants and creepers in boxes and tins hanging from the grating, so that the room itself obtained very little light indeed, but there was always a nice bright green place for the people sitting in it to look at. Toby, who had peeped into the areas of other little boys, knew that his was of quite exceptional beauty, and it was with a certain awe that he helped Uncle John to tend the plants in the morning, watering them and taking the pieces of paper and straws that had fallen through the grating from their hair. "It is a great mistake to have straws in ones hair," Uncle John would say gravely; and Toby knew that it was true.

It was in the morning after they had just been watered that the plants looked and smelt best, and when the sun shone through the grating and the diamonds were shining and falling through the forest, Toby would tell the baby about the great bird who would one day come flying through the trees—a bird of all colours, ugly and beautiful, with a harsh sweet voice. "And that will be the end of everything," said Toby, though of course he was only repeating a story his Uncle John had told him.

There were other people in the big, dark room besides Toby and Uncle John and the baby; dark people who flitted to and fro about secret matters, people called father and mother and Mr.

Hearn, who were apt to kick if they found you in their way, and who never laughed except at nights, and then they laughed too loudly.

"They will frighten the bird," thought Toby; but they were kind to Uncle John because he had a pension. Toby slept in a corner on the ground beside the baby, and when father and Mr. Hearn fought at nights he would wake up and watch and shiver; but when this happened it seemed to him that the baby was laughing at him, and he would pinch her to make her stop. One night, when the men were fighting very fiercely and mother had fallen asleep on the table, Uncle John rose from his bed and began singing in a great voice. It was a song Toby knew very well about Trafalgar's Bay, but it frightened the two men a great deal because they thought Uncle John would be too mad to fetch the pension any more. Next day he was quite well, however, and he and Toby found a large green caterpillar in the garden among the plants.

"This is a fact of great importance," said Uncle John, stroking it with a little stick. "It is a sign!"

Toby used to lie awake at nights after that and listen for the bird, but he only heard the clatter of feet on the pavement and the screaming of engines far away.

Later there came a new young woman to live in the cellar—not a dark person, but a person you could see and speak to. She patted Toby on the head; but when she saw the baby she caught it to her breast and cried over it, calling it pretty names.

At first father and Mr. Hearn were both very kind to her, and mother used to sit all day in the corner with burning eyes, but after a time the three used to laugh together at nights as before, and the woman would sit with her wet face and wait for the coming of the bird, with Toby and the baby and Uncle John, who was a queer one.

"All we have to do," Uncle John would say, "is to keep the garden clean and tidy, and to water the plants every morning so that they may be very green." And Toby would go and whisper this to the baby, and she would stare at the ceiling with large, stupid eyes.

There came a time when Toby was very sick, and he lay all day in his corner wondering about wonder. Sometimes the room in which he lay became so small that he was choked for lack of air, sometimes it was so large that he screamed out because he felt lonely. He could not see the dark people then at all, but only Uncle John and the woman, who told him in whispers that her name was "Mummie." She called him Sonny, which is a very pretty name, and when Toby heard it he felt a tickling in his sides which he knew to be gladness. Mummie's face was wet and warm and soft, and she was very fond of kissing. Every morning Uncle John would lift Toby up and show him the garden, and Toby would slip out of his arms and walk among the trees and plants. And the place would grow bigger and bigger until it was all the world, and Toby would lose himself; amongst the tangle of trees and flowers and creepers. He would see butterflies there and tame animals, and the sky was full of birds of all colours, ugly and beautiful; but he knew that none of these was the bird, because their voices were only sweet. Sometimes he showed these wonders to a little boy called Toby, who held his hand and called him Uncle John, sometimes he showed them to his mummie and he himself was Toby; but always when he came back he found himself lying in Uncle John's arms, and, weary from his walk, would fall into a pleasant dreamless sleep.

It seemed to Toby at this time that a veil hung about him which, dim and unreal in itself, served to make all things dim and unreal. He did not know whether he was asleep or awake, so strange was life, so vivid were his dreams. Mummie, Uncle John, the baby, Toby himself came with a flicker of the veil and disappeared vaguely without cause. It would happen that Toby would be speaking to Uncle John, and suddenly he would find himself looking into the large eyes of the baby, turned stupidly towards the ceiling, and again the baby would be Toby himself, a hot, dry little body without legs or arms, that swayed suspended as if by magic a foot above the bed.

Then there was the vision of two small feet that moved a long way off, and Toby would watch them curiously as kittens do their tails, without knowing the cause of their motion. It was all very wonderful and very strange, and day by day the veil grew thicker; there was no need to wake when the sleeptime was so pleasant; there were no dark people to kick you in that dreamy place.

And yet Toby woke—woke to a life and in a place which he had never known before.

He found himself on a heap of rags in a large cellar which depended for its light on a grating let into the pavement of the street above. On the stone floor of the area and swinging from the grating were a few sickly, grimy plants in pots. There must have been a fine sunset up above, for a faint red glow came through the bars and touched the leaves of the plants.

There was a lighted candle standing in a bottle on the table, and the cellar seemed full of people. At the table itself two men and a woman were drinking, though they were already drunk, and beyond in a corner Toby could see the head and shoulders of a tall old man. Beside him there crouched a woman with a faded, pretty face, and between Toby and the rest of the room there stood a box in which lay a baby with large, wakeful eyes.

Toby's body tingled with excitement, for this was a new thing; he had never seen it before, he had never seen anything before.

The voice of the woman at the table rose and fell steadily without a pause; she was abusing the other woman, and the two drunken men were laughing at her and shouting her on; Toby thought the other woman lacked spirit because she stayed crouching on the floor and said nothing.

At last the woman stopped her abuse, and one of the men turned and shouted an order to the woman on the floor. She stood up and came towards him, hesitating; this annoyed the man and he swore at her brutally; when she came near enough he knocked her down with his fist, and all the three burst out laughing.

Toby was so excited that he knelt up in his corner and clapped his hands, but the others did not notice because the old man was up and swaying wildly over the woman. He seemed to be threatening the man who had struck her, and that one was evidently afraid of him, for he rose unsteadily and lifted the chair on which he had been sitting above his head to use as a weapon.

The old man raised his fist and the chair fell heavily on to his wrinkled forehead and he dropped to the ground.

The woman at the table cried out, "The pension!" in her shrill voice, and then they were all quiet, looking.

Then it seemed to Toby that through the forest there came flying, with a harsh sweet voice and a tumult of wings, a bird of all colours, ugly and beautiful, and he knew, though later there might be people to tell him otherwise, that that was the end of everything.

LOVE AT FIRST SIGHT

(A paper found among the effects of that
unhappy madman, the late Stanley Barton)

It was Darling that did it you know, she looked so horrid. Not at first, of course. Oh no, at first she was lovely, but afterwards—oh! it makes me sick and crumbled to think of her.

If I had met Darling before her marriage it might have been all right. I had known Benham for a long time at the club, a big man, and I knew he loved somebody, but I never went down to his place till after his marriage, and then I met Darling.

Of course she was Darling from the beginning. I sat between them at dinner, and I looked at her and laughed, and he laughed too because he was stupid; but she kept quite still and her eyes were afraid of me. And that made me very glad. But he knew nothing.

Afterwards he had to go out for a little, and his big feet were hardly down the passage before I had kissed her. You see, I was quite sure. And she gave a little cry and shrank back into her chair, looking at me with funny eyes.

Of course she knew that she could do nothing—that she was all mine, because it had to be so—that her marriage was all a big mistake, because she had not met me before.

And I stood back laughing a little, because I knew that she wanted me to kiss her again, and it was nicer to know that, than to kiss her.

When her husband came back we had said nothing.

That night I was very troubled, because I did not want to share Darling with anybody, and I had no money to take her away for good. But I thought and thought until I saw things a little clearer, and I remembered a cottage that I had down in Surrey, among the pinewoods, where we could go.

So next morning after breakfast I told her that we should go there for a week, and then kill ourselves, together all the time. And I gave her a kiss and it was all settled.

Next day I borrowed some money from her husband and went back to town, and in the afternoon she came to meet me. I was quite sure.

And so we went down to the pinewoods together, Darling and I, to love.

All the days were very sunny and we would walk in the woods under the branches and love terribly.

And the nights were full of stars, and then I would go and dig our grave, and Darling would sit and watch me. I dug it behind the cottage where it was sand with great pieces of ironstone, and when the spade struck the ironstone it was not nice. But the sand was soft and I dug deep, oh deep! and presently we would lie together at the bottom of the grave, and the stars were a long way off. They would dwindle and dwindle until they went out, and we thought we were dead and grew afraid of the worms. But they did nothing and we got out again and found the stars.

And all day long we loved there in the woods, but at last the week was nearly done, and something went wrong, and Darling began to get white and afraid.

I said it was all right, but Darling was not sure, and cried, oh! she did cry—

But, of course, there was nothing else, for we had no money, and there was Darling's husband and lots of things.

So I said "Come and sit in the grave and we must do it," and Darling put her hands over her face and cried, oh bitterly, but I lead her along, and we both sat in the grave for a long time.

But the sun was so shiny and the birds would not stop their noise, so that I did not want to do it, and Darling cried all the time.

And I looked at Darling and it did seem such a pity, but at last I put the pistol in her hand and told her to kill herself, but her hand shook so that she could not, and I was afraid that she would shoot me first by mistake.

So I said "You are a coward, Darling, why don't you do it"—and there was a bang and I shut my eyes.

And Darling began screaming dreadfully, and when I looked, oh! she was nasty. You see her hand had shaken and she had done it all wrong. Such a mess!

I got out of the grave and she kept on crying to me to finish her, but I could not because she had the pistol.

And then I looked up and I saw her husband striding towards me and he had a big dog-whip in his hand, but I could not see any dog. But he looked over my shoulder and saw Darling, and stood quite still saying "Cover her up. Cover her up."

I said "What have you done with your dog?" but this was only an excuse because I did not want to go near her any more.

He did not hear me though, but he dropped the whip and suddenly burst out laughing. "Damn!" he said, "I'll cover her up if nobody else will," and he got the spade and threw a lot of sand on her so that she was quiet at last, but I could not find his dog anywhere.

But he only laughed when I told him.

THE LUCK OF KEITH-MARTIN

London does not change. Every now and then large authorities or ambitious capitalists hew down streets and squares of houses and build marble hotels and theatres on the sites, and yet their efforts do not alter London, as Londoners know it, in the smallest degree. It stands where it did.

Hugh Ingleby returned from six years' hard work in Malta with a heart steeled against the wounds Time might have dealt to his city. He had thought that at first he would find himself a stranger in a new land; he had feared some aloofness, some coldness born of his long absence.

But as he drove up from the Docks he saw that his fears had been groundless; the dome of St. Pauls, the Monument, Big Ben, all were there; the hansoms and omnibuses still performed miracles of execution in the still narrow streets; the Londoners were still hurrying nowhere in particular with nothing in particular upon their tongues.

The old smells were in his nostrils, the old soots on his cuffs, the old cries in his ears. Even the catchwords sounded familiar. Hugh felt the London spirit creeping into his veins once more; the feeling that he had been there at the beginning and would be there at the end; the knowledge that here and here only was his home.

He wondered whether Keith-Martin, too, had remained unchanged. His brief note of welcome in answer to Hugh's letter announcing his visit had been characteristic of the old Keith-Martin, his friend. And he was still at his old rooms, which was pleasant.

Hugh would see again the great room, originally intended for a studio but changed by Keith-Martin to a place of Bohemian luxury, the luxury that dirty boots and bottled beer and tobacco ash do not spoil.

Would it all be just the same, even to Keith's bed half-hidden in an alcove behind a pair of Oriental curtains, scorched and rent by frequent mishaps?

And could the old days, the old times come back again? It seemed too good to be possible, and yet London had not altered, it was just the same. Dear old London!

He drove to an hotel where he could leave his luggage, feeling the exhilaration and the excitement of a schoolboy back for the Christmas holidays. What a time he would have!

He kept the cab waiting while he took his rooms and refused lunch. He could not wait.

How like Keith it was, he thought, not to meet him at the Docks. Always afraid of appearing sentimental and yet what a welcome he would have!

"Drive fast, cabby!" he cried and they slid along to Chelsea splendidly.

The house had not altered.

"Shall I wait, sir?" said the cabman. Hugh paid him, smiling.

Wait! Why—

He ran upstairs and stopped before the old brass plate, *James Keith-Martin*, to enjoy his suspense.

Then he knocked.

"Who's there?" said a voice, a woman's voice, within. Hugh's heart sank as he gave his name. If Keith had married!

"Come in," said the voice.

He opened the door and went in.

The room was perfectly dark.

"Shut the door, please," said the voice. "My eyes—are very weak."

He shut the door behind him and stood there wondering. He could see absolutely nothing.

"I think there must be some mistake," he said. "I wish to see my old friend, Mr. Keith-Martin; I did not know—"

"Just in front of you there is a chair," said the voice politely. "Please sit down. You will see Keith presently perhaps."

Hugh sat down as directed.

Keith! What did that mean? The voice was the voice of a pretty woman, that much he knew.

"You are an old friend of Keith's are you not, Mr. Ingleby?" she went on.

"I am his oldest friend," said Hugh.

"Ah! That is very nice."

The voice sounded mocking, like the voices heard in a bad dream.

"When do you expect him back?" said Hugh, not liking the silence that then ensued.

The answer surprised him alike by its certainty and its purport.

"Never!"

"I don't understand," he said angrily. "You said I might see him presently."

"Not here, though. You had better go away. Keith will write to you perhaps."

"I do not understand you. I don't know to whom I am speaking."

"Please go away. Keith has gone."

"I don't believe it. Who are you?"

"So chivalrous," murmured the voice.

"Who are you?" repeated Hugh.

The woman at first made no reply, then she said abruptly. "I am Keith's luck."

Hugh was beginning to feel really anxious. Was he sitting in the dark with a mad woman? And Keith—

"Where is Keith?" he asked.

There was again no answer, so he repeated the question.

"Keith is dead. Now please go away."

"I am his oldest friend," said Hugh, "and again I say I do not believe you!"

"Yes, I know," said the voice. "The women tell lies in Malta!"

So she knew all about him.

"Who are you?" he repeated.

"Mary Stuart," said the voice inconsequently. "She killed Darnley."

Carrying on a long conversation in the dark with an unknown woman of doubtful sanity is trying for the nerves.

"Damn you!" cried Hugh. "You are fooling. I'm here to see Keith."

"Those poor Maltese ladies, what they have to put up with!"

"I think you must be mad."

"That's right. Quite mad. Keith will write to you about it. It's very sad. Now please go away."

"I will," said Hugh, getting up, "but first we'll have a little light on the scene." He fumbled for the switch.

"I strongly advise you not to," said the voice dispassionately.

"Cover your eyes if it hurts them," said Hugh.

There was a scornful laugh in the blackness.

Then Hugh found the switch and the room blazed with light.

Before him on the sofa lay the body of Keith-Martin, stabbed to the heart.

Hugh looked at the woman dully, her dress was covered with blood.

"I advised you not to," was all she said.

THE MURDERER

He walked down to the Embankment with the paving-stones like velvet under his feet and he swerved like one running. Yet, still, though he meant to end his life in a few minutes, he avoided the traffic with great care, so that paternal policemen judged him newly from the country. The August sun seemed pitiless in its strength and in his fear and wretchedness he cursed it. Better rain, mist, fog—anything but the reproachful blue of the sky and the dancing glitter of the dust. He wanted sympathy and, instead, Nature triumphed over him and emphasized his failure.

The river was a sparkling tumult of gems where he had pictured a secret immutable surface which should flow darkly over him and his wrongs. In place of a great unspeaking god he found a crowd of dancing, laughing children. Where should he seek peace and forgetfulness? He leaned on the parapet and groaned.

A train thundered by over Hungerford Bridge as if in answer. Of course, that was the way—safer, quicker.

He took a ticket at Charing Cross Station and passed to the end of the platform with a strange numbness in his mind and body as if he were already dead. Yet he walked to the extreme end because there was no-one there to interfere.

Presently the train appeared, making its way slowly across the bridge, and he leapt off the platform and laid his head on the rail. It blistered his cheek because the sun had made it so hot.

Then the earth heaved itself up and thrust and tore him between the wheels of the carriages. . . .

When the train had passed he rose to his feet unsteadily and stared stupidly at the mangled body lying at his feet. There was a shrill singing in his ears which was shortly interrupted by the sound of human voices and he felt his arms caught roughly and imprisoned. Soon he made out the word "murder" angrily spoken and found that he was held by platelayers, who were gesticulating violently and pointing at the body; but he would not speak because though the head had become a crushed horror upon the rail he knew that the body was his. Dimly, he was aware that porters and policemen were crowding from the station and that they were lifting the body tenderly from the rails. Then he fainted.

He came to in the police-station and found that his face and hair were dabbled with water. Presently he was formally charged and warned not to say anything incriminating.

He said only, "It was me," but this he repeated several times. He was trying to convince himself.

Then he was removed to the cells and found himself alone. He lay down and slept deeply and the sun had set and risen before he awoke.

At his trial, and after conviction, he did not speak, he seemed too dazed; but as they led him away he broke his silence. "Can a man die twice?" he inquired reflectively. "Can a man die twice?"

There is no more to chronicle—they were his last recorded words.

THE MAKING OF A MAN

He was a weedy clerkling and he had missed his way to Vauxhall Station in the middle of the night and was now walking timidly through sordid but singularly unfrequented streets. He was afraid he was missing his last train, but, when a stray figure did approach him, he lost his nerve and did not ask the way. He thought it might be a thief. At the same time, he knew that the soaking rain was spoiling his only overcoat and the thought made him miserable. Why had he not gone to Waterloo as Murray had suggested? Why had he omitted to borrow an umbrella? Why were there no policemen? He noticed with relief, however, that as he walked along the houses were improving. They were getting larger and more respectable and he hoped he might be approaching a main street.

Presently he saw a lighted window shining on the first floor of one of these houses, and as he neared it the front-door swung open and displayed a woman, who leant out curiously to peer at him.

Simmonds was relieved when he saw her sex, because he was not afraid of women. He was very young.

"Could you tell me the way to Vauxhall Station, please, miss," he asked, and he raised his hat with a glad consciousness of his good manners.

The woman stared at him in a curiously intense way. "Are you a medical student?" she said earnestly. Simmonds was busy discovering that she was a lady, and handsome, and her question took him aback.

"A medical student?" he repeated stupidly.

"No, I see you're not," she said to herself, and Simmonds saw her brow pucker in her effort to think quickly.

"If I could be of any assistance . . ." he said grandly, like the people in novels.

The lady made up her mind in a flash.

"Oh, if you would," she cried. "I do so want help." And she stood aside in the doorway.

Simmonds hesitated and very nearly ran away, but some instinct, he did not know what, made him obey and he stepped past her into the hall and waited under the gas-burner while she fastened the door behind him. Simmonds was sure she must be a lady because she wore so many rings and her dress was brilliant, though there was a bad stain down the front of it. She, for her part, had turned away from the door and was scrutinizing him as if in doubt, and the silence was almost too prolonged for Simmonds' nerves.

"It is upstairs," she said and swept past him up the staircase, leaving him to follow her if he wished.

Simmonds hesitated again, but it was so bad to turn back after all and say that he was afraid. So he ascended meekly and found her waiting for him on the landing with her hand on the handle of a door. When he approached she opened it, and half pushed, half led him into the room.

"There!" she said. "There!"

Simmonds looked and was deadly sick.

The room was furnished well enough as a sitting-room and lit by a gas-burner that squealed abominably. Just beneath it on the floor was a tin trunk, and as if sitting on the edge perched the body of a man with his throat cut right across. The thing wore no coat or waistcoat, and the white shirt was wringing with fresh blood.

Simmonds thought of it and retched while the woman looked at him curiously.

"What are you going to do?" she asked when he seemed better.

He hardly heard her; he could hear nothing but the singing of the gas over the corpse and the sound troubled him.

"Is he dead?" he whispered.

"Dead," repeated the woman. "Dead!" She approached him with the words, but he shrank away from her. There was blood on her dress.

"You must help me," she said fiercely. "You must! You must! I can't get it into the box. I tried and tried but I couldn't. You must help me to cut it up. You can kiss me. Anything you like afterwards."

He looked at her dully. He had never kissed anybody but his mother and that was a long time ago. It had given him no particular pleasure, he thought. In fact, he had rather disliked it. And now this woman— Of course, at the office he had heard things, coarse things. He had said them himself. But he had never wanted to kiss any woman. And yet—there was something—her lips would be warm. Other people seemed to like it—perhaps?

"Anything you like afterwards," she said automatically, looking at him.

Simmonds felt a faint stirring in his veins, as if he would like to kiss those warm lips, if but to try. He found himself gazing at the body without horror. He thought it might almost be pleasant to hack at those dead limbs with a knife. He felt like cutting something.

"Come!" said the woman, and she showed him half a dozen knives. "You'll do it, won't you—for me?"

She bent forward suddenly and kissed him on the lips.

Why, it was nothing, after all—nothing whatever. And yet in a minute he knew that he would give the world to have that nothing again. The lips had only just touched his for a second: lightly like a flower. How if he had pressed them hard to his? till the blood came, with his arms round her tightly? He looked at her with a new light in his eyes, and she read them rightly.

"Afterwards," she said. "Afterwards."

He seized one of the knives and approached the body.

"It will stain my clothes," he stammered.

"Take them off, then," she said. "God, what a boy it is." For he drew back blushing.

She ran quickly through a curtained doorway into the next room and came back with some clothes which she threw at his feet.

"It doesn't matter spoiling these," she said; "they are not wanted any more." Then, as he still paused, "It's all right, I won't look."

And she turned her back on him while he changed into the dead man's clothes. And of the two, hers was the greater wonder.

When he had finished he took the knife and began at first tamely and then fiercely. Every now and then he looked up and the sight of her lips parted made him tremble. But after a time the horror of those cold pieces of dead flesh overcame his passion and he worked away mechanically but stubbornly without knowing why. He had to finish it quickly, quickly—that was all.

The knives were blunt and he knew no anatomy, so that by the time he had finished and the lid was shut down there came through the cracks of the blind grey streaks of light. He had done his task and he rose to his feet. He had almost forgotten the woman and his clothes and hands and face were all dabbled with dry blood.

He was wondering happily why—something or other—he didn't know what. He was very old.

Across the room through a mist he saw the woman, standing and looking at him oddly. There was something—what was it?

She opened her arms suddenly and cried to him across infinite space: "Come!"

And with the word something seemed to break and a fierce stream of passionate blood swept through his body. That was it. The woman! The woman!

He flung himself across the room with a sob on his lips, caught her in his arms and kissed his boyhood away on her hot face.

WET EYES AND SAD MOUTH

He loosed his hands away from the bruised throat, and took a short step back to look at the thing he had done. It was not a pretty sight, though he had to own to himself that there was something attractive about the face. He found himself wondering what it was. Not the mouth, certainly, with its loathsome droop of passive suffering, that still was there, even though the lips were parted in one last automatic effort to sob in breath to the bursting lungs. Nor could it be the eyes, wide open and protruding, and smudged round the lids with grimy marks of tears. The nose was snub, and the chin was weak.

"Ah! that is it," he said to himself at last. "It is not the picture, it is the frame. It is her hair, the way it clings to the face, the way it plays about her neck. Ah! her neck!"

He looked thoughtfully at the dull blues and blacks on her throat, which looked stringy because the head was thrown back so far.

"I have strong fingers," he said softly, looking at his hands and wondering to find them unstained. "And I did not let go. Yes, I have strong hands."

He felt a little proud of his work. In his life he had missed the triumph of making things, but now, his was the strong joy of having broken something.

"I have crushed you, my dear," he said amiably to the body. "You will not torture me with your wet eyes and your sad mouth any more. You will not smile weakly when I curse you; you will not sob softly to yourself when I strike you. You are dead!"

And pleased with his conceit he struck the face of the corpse a savage blow with his fist.

It was cold and loathsome to the touch, but the bosom did not heave, the eyes did not soften and moisten the dull cheeks with tears, and he was satisfied.

"Dead," he said. "Dead, my dear." And he turned his back contemptuously on the corpse and went across the room to the window.

It was a lovely spring morning with a cloudless sky of blue, and a glorious London sun was climbing up the heavens. Among the trees in the square the birds were singing joyfully, and he could see the white pinafores of children playing on the grass in the gardens. Something of the joy of spring seized the man, bringing with it a mingled feeling of hope and regret.

"Damn!" he cried. "The years I have wasted—utterly wasted. Well, anyhow, I am free now. Free!" And he laughed lightly and happily.

What it meant! No longer bound to a weak woman, but a strong man free. Free to laugh, free to enjoy the spring, free to marry, if he wanted to. But he would not do that, he would—what was the word?—philander, that was it, flower to flower, like a butterfly. His spirit was free, and it was the time of spring.

He looked cheerfully at the body.

"The first thing I shall do is to clear away this—this mess," he said, and he strode back to the bedside.

Yes, it was the hair. There was no doubt about it. It would have been awkward if it had been the mouth or the eyes. The thought made him shudder. But that was all nonsense. It was the hair, certainly.

The way it clung to the face.

And yet—

It was a fine spring morning and he was free, free to do what he wished, the whole world through. The best thing to do would be to get away and leave it all. The rooms were taken in her name. Everything was in her name. That was lucky. Of course, there would be a fuss when she was found, but he would be far away by that time. "Over the hills and far away." He laughed aloud. Far from her eyes and mouth and everything. Oh, but he had forgotten those, anyhow, and she was dead. They would trouble him no more, for it was her hair that had caught him. And now he was free.

He opened his Gladstone bag on the floor by the bedside, and began putting his things in neatly. His packing was one of the little things he was proud of, and as he bustled about the room he sang a song, a nursery rhyme, that the spring had given back to his memory. Oh, he would be young again. It was the spring and a jolly day.

Presently he remembered his pyjamas which were on the pillow under her head. He lifted it not unkindly and drew them out.

"What pretty hair!" he said, and found with a shock that he was not looking at her hair. He dropped her head hastily and took refuge in his packing. There was room for his brown shoes here. Oh, and there was a collar on the floor in the corner and his sponge. It would not do to forget them. He cast a glance round the room to make sure that he had not overlooked anything, but all his things seemed to be safely packed. His glance finally fell back on the corpse.

"Poor thing!" he said with a contemptuous pity. "So dead and it is springtime. She cannot hear it," and he paused to listen to the birds, and the children singing together out in the square. Presently he found himself saying absently:

"I wonder whether dead people always have wet eyes," and he flung himself viciously on his knees, and fastened the bag.

He got up from the ground with his spirits a little dashed, and put on his overcoat, looking angrily at the body.

"If you haunt me—!" he cried, shaking his fist at it.

But in a minute he knew this was folly, because it was her hair, and he had forgotten.

So he lit a cigarette and picking up his bag and hat, he stepped firmly to the door.

"Good-bye, my dear!" he said scornfully over his shoulder with his hand on the handle of the door.

"Good-bye, my—dear."

And a minute later he walked out of the house, as one who is free.

Certainly, he had forgotten.

THE LAST ADVENTURE

George Austin Faningford was a young man with a temperament and a handsome income. The former served to make him attractive to all save the very sedate, the latter, which the foresight
of a shrewd father had caused to be paid quarterly, enabled him to
allow his joyous nature full play, so that he took life as young po-
ets take opium, in a series of magnificent quarterly carouses. The
length of these periodical expressions of his youth was determined
by fortune; sometimes when he was unlucky his money would last
for a weary two months; once a gorgeous thirty-six hours sufficed
to land him in a Brighton lodging-house, penniless and with no
more clothes than those on his back. One feature, however, of these
temperamental effervescences was common to them all. Always at
their termination he would wake up like a man who had been
dreaming a pleasant dream and could not quite remember what it
was, and this romantic vagueness was only dispelled on the rare
occasions when the troublesome curiosity of the police served to
expose some part of his lurid adventures. In one sense, of course,
his awakenings differed from those of a man who merely wakes
from his sleep; for he often found himself involved in problems of no
little complexity, and in the difficult situation of having to supply
an answer without any knowledge of what the conundrum might be.

On a night of November, three weeks after his quarterly cheque
had been paid into the bankers, George stepped back suddenly,
but without shock, as was his wont, into the material world. He
was a man of nice taste, but he could find little to criticise in the

decorative scheme of the charming room in which he found himself seated. The carpets were silky as the back of a Persian kitten, the curtains and tapestries were of subtly undecided colours, the furniture had that air of fragile discomfort which modern designers appear to have derived from a study of modern morals; in a word, it was a room that no one could live in—a delightful example of the attractively useless. Nor was it displeasing to George, who did not extend his defiance of convention to his clothes, to find that he was wearing evening dress; and though the clothes were not his own, it was reassuring to trace in their delicate lines the cunning hand of Dawson, that dreamer of sartorial masterpieces. And George was regarding the situation with expectant complacency, when the door opened and a woman, beautifully dressed and with a face that was more than worthy of the creation she wore, walked blithely into the room.

"Now, George, dear," she said, "are you ready for supper?"

To a man of his varied experiences there was nothing extraordinary in being addressed in terms of affection by a woman he had never seen before in his normal life. But that he should be invited to sup at an hour usually devoted to dinner, by one who was beyond doubt a member of the world which he himself adorned, appeared to George in the light of a miracle. And it did not escape his notice that beneath her pleasantly frivolous manner the lady was regarding him with a certain keenness as if she too had cause to wonder.

The true art of diplomacy is to proceed, and George hardly allowed himself a pause in which to register his surprise before he rose and assented with the grace that had cost his parents four thousand pounds.

"I don't know what the servants will think," his companion said, prettily, as they passed along the ferny corridor. "I never do know what they think; possibly about sun-spots or the blind Celtic fish."

"My man is the eighteenth European authority on the chemistry of the ancients," said George. "He writes monographs about it and sells my things to pay for having them printed."

"Of course that isn't true."

They laughed together as they entered the supper-room, a vast chamber of the dimensions of a banqueting hall.

"No, I'm afraid it's only conversation," George admitted, while secretly admiring the curves of her throat. "But all the true things have been said so often."

She looked at him oddly. "I wonder whether they have. Some things are true enough, but—" She screwed her lips into a grotesque smile and they sat down at the table in such an offhand way that George felt that he must have supped with her before in his dreams. The meal, though cold, was admirable, and the wines fit for an undergraduate in the first flush of his credit, but there was no sign of the servants who might wonder—what?

"This is an adventure," George said to himself, cheerfully; and then aloud: "I don't know about that, I'm sure"—he wished that he knew her Christian name. "I myself am to some extent a student of the extraordinary, and, if I may say so, I have seen some unusual things and been in some out-of-the-way places. But, really, the possible is soon exhausted and miracles are rare. Ninety-nine out of every hundred of my adventures are mere perversions of the obvious. In tabulating them I have divided them into ten groups—"

"And how many of the Commandments have you broken?" she asked, smiling queerly.

"All but one, I'm afraid," said George, wondering a little at her quickness.

She laughed aloud.

"Why, that's what you told my husband," she said. "You are not up to date."

Here was something to puzzle about, thought George. This pretty problem had a husband and he had told him—and what in thunder did she mean by her last remark?

"By the way, where is your husband now?" he said, casually.

In itself this does not appear a very humorous question, but it certainly had a remarkable effect on the lady.

"Some people would call you grim," she murmured, between her shrill ripples of laughter. "Perhaps you'd like to have him down to sup with us; he's upstairs, you know."

"Well, I don't mind, you know," said George, feeling his way towards an explanation, "so long as I do not lose the pleasure of supping with you."

The lady looked at him with bright lights of excitement in her eyes.

"It would be a thrill, wouldn't it?" she said, rising, "if you'll help me to carry him."

So her husband was an invalid, a madman, or a picture. "I hope it isn't leprosy," George thought to himself. "There's something about this woman—" But he dutifully followed her upstairs.

She stopped outside a door on the first floor, with her hand on the handle.

"Shall I knock?" she said, flippantly.

George nodded, and her little knuckles set a playful echo trotting lightly down the passage like a child released from lessons. Then she opened the door and beckoned him in.

Thirty seconds later he reeled out of the room into the corridor with a white face and his body shaking.

"Good God! What have you done?" he cried.

The woman, who had followed him, was hardly less disturbed.

"Don't say you've got a conscience! Don't say you've repented! You've been splendid up to now."

He glared at her fiercely.

"What do you mean?" he stammered.

She stood looking at him in obvious amazement.

"It's not possible," she muttered to herself, frowning. Then she caught him by the arm and led him up to a mirror which was set upright in the wall. "Look!" she said, watching him.

On the white front of his shirt, just below his tie, George saw the imprint of four red fingers, and as he looked he wavered and sickened, and thought of the dead thing in the room behind him.

"I thought it so bizarre of you to change everything but that," said the woman, in the tone of one who is disappointed.

George pulled himself up and turned his eyes on her pitifully. "What am I to do?" he cried.

"I should think we had better finish our supper."

He followed her down to the supper-room like a child, and like a child he marvelled that the bitterness of his regret should leave the fact unaltered. The woman seated herself and proceeded to eat with a good appetite, blinking at him over the flowers, while he sat miserably fingering his glass.

"You want about a magnum and a bottle," she said, critically. "It's no use wasting any regrets on him. He was really of very little use to me."

"What are you?" he said, suddenly, gulping a glass of wine.

"That's much better," she replied, with a nod of approval. "I? Well, I'm a widow, I suppose."

He looked at her speechlessly.

"You see," she went on, calmly, "melodrama isn't life, nor is it rational for people of education to fall back on crudities when they do have an excuse for self-expression. Now, what is the situation? I wanted my freedom without a bother, and I have got it. You have spent your life in a search for adventures, and here you are. He— no, I'm not as bad as that. I won't say anything about him. But you can go away after supper and call it a dream if you like."

George drank another glass of wine.

"The body!" he said.

"Polymelus!" said the woman, thoughtfully. "I never thought of that. What *does* one do with bodies? I suppose I've got a trunk somewhere, but I never was good at packing, and my maid is one of the new sort, you know, and objects to everything out of the beaten track. I shouldn't be surprised to hear that she was a novelist."

"Oh, I can't! I can't!" cried George. "Say it's a joke! Say it isn't true!"

She shook her head at him reproachfully.

"More of your Lyceum imaginings, George," she said, sadly. "It wouldn't go down at the Court Theatre, you know. As for this business of a murder, if I must use your sentimental terms, I can easily burn down the house, or something. Thompson, my late husband's valet, now, is a very sensible man, and a thousand pounds, or per- haps two—"

George cut short her remarks, and surprised her by uttering a laugh like the bark of a startled collie.

"Do you know what I ought to do?" he queried.

"Nothing," she said, promptly.

"No, it isn't that. I ought to take that pretty neck of yours and choke you. What difference would it make to anyone, to anyone on earth?"

"Well, you're not going to do it or you wouldn't have mentioned it," she said, calmly. "Besides, it would be bathos. Now, if you'll be a good boy and go home and forget all about it, it will save a lot of bother. And I will give you a very sound piece of advice."

"Well?"

"Don't come out adventuring any more. You haven't got the temperament for it. You allow yourself to be turned from the pursuit of your ideals by trivialities. It is so silly."

George looked at her for a few seconds with leaden eyes.

"I think I shall go home," he said. "I suppose you can manage the body; for all I know you may have done this sort of thing a dozen times."

"No, it's the first time," she said. "But there's really no reason to make a fuss. You've only completed your set."

He walked out into the entrance hall, and the woman followed him. When he reached the door he turned round and looked her in the face.

"If I gave myself up for this—" he said.

"I'm afraid I should laugh dreadfully; it would seem so noble of you."

He bit his lip and opened the door.

"This is my last adventure," he said, with a faint note of tragedy in his voice. "Good-night!"

"At any rate, I think I should wear a hat if I were you," the lady remarked, sweetly.

And so at last he went.

"The servants will be back to-morrow, and it is ten o'clock," thought the woman. "I'm going to be pretty busy, it seems; but anyhow, I spoilt his exit." And she went back to finish her supper.

BARRY PAIN

SMEATH

Percy Bellowes was not actually idle, had a good deal of ability, and wished to make money. But at the age of thirty-five he had not made it. He had been articled to a solicitor, and, in his own phrase, had turned it down. He had neglected the regular channels of education which were open to him. He could give a conjuring entertainment for an hour, and though his tricks were stock tricks, they were done in the neat professional manner.

He could play the cornet and the violin, neither of them very well. He could dance a breakdown. He had made himself useful in a touring theatrical company. But he could not spell correctly, and his grammar was not always beyond reproach. He disliked regularity. He could not go to the same office at the same time every morning. He was thriftless, and he had been, but was no longer, intemperate. He was a big man, with smooth black hair, and a heavy moustache, and he had the manners of a bully.

At the age of thirty-five he considered his position. He was at that time travelling the country as a hypnotic entertainer, under the name of Dr. Sanders-Bell. At each of his entertainments he issued a Ten Thousand Pound Challenge, not having at the time ten thousand pence in the world.

He employed confederates, and he had to pay them. It was not a good business at all. His gains in one town were always being swallowed up by his losses in another. His confederates gave him constant trouble.

But though he turned things over for long in his mind, he could see nothing else to take up. There is no money nowadays for a conjurer without originality, an indifferent musician, or passable actor. His hypnotic entertainment would have been no good in London, but it did earn just enough to keep him going in the provinces.

Also, Percy Bellowes had an ordinary human weakness; he liked to be regarded with awe as a man of mystery. Even off the stage he acted his part. He had talked delirious science to agitated land-ladies in cheap lodgings in many towns.

Teston was a small place, and Percy Bellowes thought that he had done very well, after a one-night show, to cover his expenses and put four pounds in his pocket. He remained in the town on the following day, because he wished to see a man who had answered his advertisement for a confederate, "Assistant to a Hypnotic En-tertainer" was the phrase Mr. Bellowes had used for it.

He was stopping at the Victoria Hotel. It was the only hotel in the place, and it was quite bad. But Percy Bellowes was used to that. A long course of touring had habituated him to doubtful eggs and indistinguishable coffee. This morning he faced a singularly repulsive breakfast without quailing. He was even cheerful and conversational with a slatternly maid who waited on him.

"So you saw the show last night," he said.

"Yes, sir, I did. And very wonderful it was. There has never been anything like it in Teston, not in my memory."

"Ah, my dear. Well, you watch this."

He picked up the two boiled eggs which had been placed be-fore him. He hurled one into the air, where it vanished. He swal-lowed the other one whole. He then produced them both from a vase on the mantelpiece.

"Well, I never!" said the maid. "I wonder if there's anything you can't do, sir?"

"Just one or two things," said Mr. Bellowes, sardonically. "By the way, my dear, if a man comes here this morning and asks for me, I want to see him." He consulted a soiled letter which he had taken from his pocket. "The name's Smeath."

Mr. Smeath arrived, in fact, before Bellowes had finished his breakfast, and was told he could come in. He was a man of extraordinary appearance,

He was a dwarf, with a slightly hunched back. His hands were a size too large for him, and were always restless. His expression was one of snarling subservience. At first Bellowes was inclined to reject him, for a confederate should not be a man of unusual appearance and easily recognizable. Then it struck him that, after all, this would be a very weird and impressive figure on the stage.

"Ever do anything of this kind before?" he asked.

"No, sir," said Smeath. "But I've seen it done and can pick it up. I think I could give you satisfaction. You see, it's not very easy for a man like me to find work."

All the time that he was speaking, his hands were busy.

"When you've finished tearing up my newspaper," said Bellowes.

"Sorry, sir," said the man. He pushed the newspaper away from him, but caught up a corner of the tablecloth. It was frayed, and he began to pull threads out of it, quickly and eagerly.

"Ever been hypnotized?" Bellowes asked.

"No, sir," said Smeath, with a cunning smile. "But that doesn't matter, does it? I can act the part all right."

"It matters a devilish lot, as it happens. And you can't act the part all right, either. My assistants are always genuinely hypnotized. I employ them to save time on the stage. After I have hypnotized you a few times, I shall be able to put you into the hypnotic state in a minute or less, and to do it with certainty. I can't depend on chance people from the audience. Many of them cannot be hypnotized at all, and with most of the others it takes far too long. There are exceptional cases—I had one at my show only last night—but I don't often come across them. Come on up with me to my room."

"You want to see if you can hypnotize me?"

"No, I don't. I know I can. I simply want to do it."

Upstairs in the dingy bedroom Bellowes made Smeath sit down. He held the bright lid of a cigarette-tin between Smeath's eyes and slightly above the level of them.

"Look at that," he said. "Keep on looking at it. Keep on!"

In a few minutes Bellowes put the tin down, put his fingers on Smeath's eyes, and closed them. The eyes remained closed. The little hunchback sat tense and rigid.

An hour later, in the coffee-room downstairs, Bellowes made his definite agreement with Smeath.

"You understand?" said Bellowes. "You'll be at the town-hall at Warlow to-morrow night at seven. When I invite people to come up on the platform, you will come up. That's all you've got to do. Got any money?"

"Enough for the present." Smeath began to pull matches from a box on the table. He broke each match into four pieces. "But suppose that tomorrow night you can't do it?"

"There'll never be a day or night I can't do it with you now. That's definite. Now, then, leave those matches alone. I might be wanting one of them directly."

After Smeath's departure, Percy Bellowes sat for a few minutes deep in thought. In that dingy room upstairs he had seen something which he had never seen in his life before, something of which he thought that various uses might be made. He picked up the newspaper, and was pleased to find that Smeath's busy fingers had spared the racing intelligence. Then he sought out the landlord.

"I say," he said, "I've got a fancy to put a few shillings on a horse. Do you know anybody here it would be safe to do it with?"

"Well," said the landlord, "as a matter of fact you can do it with me, if you like. I do a little in that way on the quiet."

"The police don't bother you?"

"No; they're not a very bright lot, the police here. Besides, they're pretty busy just now. We had a murder in Teston the day before you came."

"Who was that?"

"A Miss Samuel, daughter of some very well-to-do people here. They think it was a tramp. See that plantation up on the hill there? That was where they found her—her head all beaten to pulp and her money gone."

"Nice set of blackguards you've got in Teston, I don't think. Well now, about this race to-day."

When Percy Bellowes left the Victoria Hotel on the following morning he was not required to pay a bill. On the contrary, he had a small balance to receive from the landlord.

"Bless you, I don't mind," said the landlord, as he paid him. "Pretty well all my crowd were on the favourite. Queer thing that horse should have fallen."

II

At Warlow the entertainment went very well. When it was over, Bellowes asked Smeath to come round to the hotel. They had the little smoking-room to themselves.

"You remember when I hypnotized you yesterday?"

"Yes, sir. Yes, Mr. Bellowes."

"Do you remember what you did, or said?"

Smeath shook his head.

"I went to sleep, the same as I did to-night. That was all."

"Know anything about horse-racing?"

"Nothing. Never touched it."

"You mean to say you've never seen a horse-race?"

"Never."

"What did you do before you came to me?"

"I had not been in any employment for some time. I was once in business as a bird-fancier. I had bad luck and made no money in it. You ask me a great many questions, sir."

"I do. That's because I've been turning things over in my mind. I want you to put your name to an agreement with me for three years. A pound a week. That's a good offer. A man who's been in business, and failed, ought to appreciate an absolute certainty like that."

"It would be the same kind of work?" Smeath asked.

"Pretty much the same. When I've finished this tour I am thinking of settling down in London. I should employ you there."

"No, thank you, Mr. Bellowes," said Smeath. "I would rather not."

"Oh, all right," said Bellowes. "Make an idiot of yourself, if you like. It doesn't make a pin's-head of difference to me. I can easily find plenty of other men who would grab at it. I thought I was doing you a kindness. As you said yourself, chaps of your build don't find it any too easy to get work."

"I will work for you for six months—possibly a month or two longer than that. But, afterwards, well, I wish to return to the bird-fancying again."

"No, you don't," said Bellowes, savagely "If you can't take my terms, you're not going to make your own. If you won't sign for three years, out you get! You're talking like a fool, too. How can you go back to this rotten business in six months? D'you think you're going to save the capital for it out of a pound a week?"

"I have friends who might help me."

"Who are they?"

"They are—well, they're friends of mine. You will perhaps give me till to-morrow morning to think it over."

"Very well. If you're not here by ten to-morrow morning to go round to the solicitor's office with me, I've finished with you. Now then, I'm going to hypnotize you again."

"What for?"

"Practice. Now then, look at me."

In a few moments Smeath sat with his eyes open, but fixed.

"Tell me what you see?" asked Bellowes.

"Nothing," said Smeath. "I see nothing."

"Yes, you do," said Bellowes. "There are horses with jockeys on them. They are racing. See? They get near the winning-post."

"Yes," said Smeath, dully. "I see them, but it is through a mist and a long way off. Now they're gone."

"Yesterday when I hypnotized you, you saw clearly. You actually described a race which afterwards took place. You gave me the colours. You gave me the names that the crowd shouted. You described how the favourite crossed his legs and fell. Can you do nothing of the kind to-day?"

"No, not to-day. To-day I see other things."

"What?"

"I see a street in London. There is a long row of sandwichmen. My name is on their boards. There are many fashionable people in the street. Expensive shops. Jewellers' shops, picture-galleries. I can see you, too. You have just come into the street."

"Where have I come from?"

"How can I tell? It may be your own house or offices. Your name is on a very small brass plate by the side of the door. You have got a fur coat on, and you are wearing a diamond pin. You get into a car. It is your own car, and you tell the man who opens the door for you to drive to the bank. You look very pleased and prosperous. Now the car starts. That is all. I can see no more."

Bellowes leaned forward and blew lightly on Smeath's eyes. The tenseness of his muscles relaxed. He rubbed his eyes and stood up.

"Do you know what you've been saying?" Bellowes asked.

"I've been saying nothing," said Smeath. "I have been asleep, as you know. You made me go to sleep."

Bellowes looked round the room. His eye fell on an empty cigarette-box, lying in the fender.

"Pick that up, and hold it in your hands," he said.

Smeath looked surprised, but he did as he was told. There was a loose label on the box, and his fingers began to tear it off in small pieces.

"Now then," said Bellowes, "can you tell me anything about the man who had that box, and threw it down there?"

"Of course I can't. How should I be able to do that? It's not possible."

"Very well," said Bellowes. "I'm going to put you to sleep once more."

"I don't like this," whined Smeath. "There's too much of it. It's bad for one's health."

"Nonsense! Look here, Smeath. I want you for three years, don't I? Then I'm not likely to do anything that will injure your health. You'll be all right."

When Bellowes had hypnotized Smeath, he again put the cigarette-box in his hands.

"And now what do you see?" he asked.

"This is quite clear. It is a short, thick-set man who takes the last cigarette out of the box and throws it down. As he smokes it, he walks up and down the room, frowning. He is puzzled about something. He takes out his pocket-book, and as he opens it a card drops to the floor."

"Can you see what's on the card?"

"Yes. It lies face upwards. The name is 'Mr. Vincent.' And in the left-hand corner are the words 'Criminal Investigation Department, Scotland Yard.' Now he closes his note-book."

"What was written in it?"

"I only saw one word—the name 'Samuel' . . . . Now a waiter comes into the room, and the man asks for a time-table."

Once more Bellowes restored Smeath to his normal state.

"That'll do," he said. "That's all for to-night. You can be off now, and think over that offer of mine."

At ten on the following morning Smeath kept his appointment. He said he would sign an agreement for two years only, and that he would want thirty shillings a week.

"What makes you suddenly think you're worth thirty shillings a week?"

"I have no idea at all, but I know you need me very much. I have that feeling."

"It was three years I said, not two. If I pay you thirty shillings a week, you can sign for three years."

"I cannot. I want to get back to my birds. I will sign for thirty shillings a week for two years, or I will go away."

"Oh, very well," growled Bellowes. "You're an obstinate little devil. Have it your own way. I hope to goodness I'm not going to lose money over you. I've never paid more than a pound to an assistant before. By the way, Smeath, were you ever in London?"

"Yes; several times."

"Do you know Piccadilly, or Bond Street, or Regent Street?"

Smeath shook his head.

"I have only passed through in going from one place to another. I know the names of those streets, but I've never been in them."

"Very well," said Bellowes. "Come along with me, and we'll fix up the agreement."

III

About a month later Mr. Bellowes, who had come up to London for the purpose, called at the office of Mr. Tangent's agency in Sussex Street.

"Appointment," said Bellowes, as he handed in his card, and was taken immediately into the inner office. Mr. Tangent, a florid and slightly overdressed man of fifty, rose from his American desk to shake hands with him.

"Well, my dear old boy," said Tangent, "and how are you?"

"Fit," said Bellowes. "Remarkably fit."

"And what can I do for you? I had an inquiry the other day that brought you to my mind. It's not much. A week, with a chance of an engagement if you catch on."

"Thanks, old man, but I don't want it. I've got on to something a bit better. What I want from you is a hundred and fifty pounds."

Tangent laughed genially. "Long time since I've seen so much money as that. Well, well! What's it for? Tell us the story."

"I've had a bit of luck, Tangent. I've got a man booked up to me for the next two years who is simply the most marvellous clairvoyant the world has ever seen."

"Clairvoyants aren't going well," said Tangent. "Most of them don't make enough to pay for their rent and their ads in the Sunday papers. The fact is there are too many of them. I don't care what the line is—palmistry, crystal-gazing, psychometry, or what you like. There's no money in it."

"Let's talk sense. You say there's no money in it? Do you remember when Merion fell, and a ten-to-one chance romped home?"

"Remember it? I've good reason to. I'd backed Merion both ways, and didn't see how I was going to lose."

"Well, I backed the winner. Not being a Crœsus like yourself, I only had five bob on. I backed him, because my clairvoyant saw the whole thing, and described it to me before the race was run."

"Can he do it again?"

"He has not been able to do it again yet. He has seen what happened in the past many times, and he has never been wrong. He is exceptional. He is only clairvoyant when he is hypnotized. In the normal state he sees nothing. He's an ugly little devil, a dwarf, and if I bring him to London he'll make a sensation. What's more, he'll make money. Pots of money. I know the crowd you've been talking about. They're a hit-or-miss lot. They're no good. This is something quite different. We shall have all the Society women paying any fee I like to consult him. There's a fortune in it."

Tangent lit a cigarette, and pushed the box across to Bellowes. "What is it you propose to do?" he asked.

"Rooms in Bond Street. Good furniture. Uniformed servant. Sandwichmen at first. Once the thing gets started, it will go by itself. Any woman who has consulted him once is absolutely bound to tell all her friends. The man's a miracle. I'll tell you another thing I'm going to do. When the next sensational murder turns up, and Scotland Yard can't put their hands on the man who did it, I'm going to turn my chap on to the job. I'll bet all I've got to sixpence that we find the man."

"There was the case of that girl—Esther Samuel."

"Yes, I remember that. But by this time most of the public have forgotten it. A better chance is bound to turn up soon."

"I don't see how you're going to start on a hundred and fifty."

"I'm not, my boy. I've got money of my own that I'm putting into it as well."

"Let's see," said Tangent, picking up a pencil. "What did you say was this man's name and address?"

Bellowes laughed. "Oh, no, you don't," he said. "At present that's my business. Make it your own business as well and you shall be told everything."

"I don't know why you should call it business at all. You ask me to lend you a hundred and fifty. You offer no security. All I've got is your story that you've found a clairvoyant who's really good."

"Very well. If you satisfied yourself that the man was really good, would you lend the money then?"

"On terms, yes. But they'd have to be satisfactory terms."

"They would be. Well, you shall see for yourself. The man's waiting in a cab downstairs."

"You might have said that before."

"Why? Anyhow, I'll go and bring him up now."

It was a chilly morning, and Smeath shivered in a thick overcoat, which he refused to remove. No time was wasted on preliminaries. Bellowes hypnotized him at once.

"Now then, my boy," said Bellowes. "You shall see for yourself. Give me any article which you or someone else has worn, or has frequently handled."

Tangent opened a drawer in his desk, and produced a lady's glove. "That," he said, "was left in my office a week ago. Let's see what he makes out of it."

Bellowes put the glove in Smeath's hands. Smeath began to pull the buttons off it. He dragged and tore at the glove like a wild animal at its prey. Then suddenly he began to speak.

"I see a handsome woman with bright golden hair. I think the hair has been dyed. It has that appearance. She is talking with Mr. What's-his-name in this room. Each is angry with the other. She is accusing him of something. Suddenly—yes—she picks up an ink-bottle and throws it at him. Ink all over the place. He bangs on a little bell, and a man comes in who looks like a clerk. That is all. I cannot see any more."

"Wake him up and send him down to the cab again," said Tangent. "Then we can talk."

"Now," said Bellowes, when they were alone together. "Had he got that right?"

"Absolutely. The woman was Cora Vendall. She wanted a particular berth, and thought I ought to have got it for her. She's fifty-six if she's a day, and not in any way suitable for it. If I had proposed it, the people would simply have laughed at me. She did get into a blind fury with me, and she did throw the ink at me. She's been made to pay for that, and she's been told not to show her powdered nose inside my office again. Your man is remarkable, Bellowes. There can be no two opinions about it. There is certainly money in him."

"You will find the hundred and fifty, then?"

"Yes, I'll do that. Mind, I must have a word to say in the management. The right sort of people will have to be got to see that man. Once that has been done, I do believe you're right, and the thing will go by itself."

"What interest do you want?"

"I don't want interest. What I do is to buy for a hundred and fifty pounds a share in your profits from your agreement with the clairvoyant."

"You shall have it. It's a jolly good thing I'm putting into your way, Tangent. I had never meant to part with a share, and I'd sooner pay you fifteen per cent, on your money. However, if you insist, you can take a sixteenth."

"Rats!" said Mr. Tangent, impolitely. "This is not everybody's business. Step across to the Bank of England, and see how much they'll advance you on it. There are three of us in it. Him and you and me. I'm going to take a third. Do just as you like about it. If I go into it I can make it a certainty. I can get the right people to see the man."

"A third's too much. You must be reasonable, Tangent. I discovered him."

"A man once discovered a gold-mine. He had no means of getting the gold out. He was a thousand miles from anywhere, and he was all alone. He died on the top of his blessed goldmine. However, I'm not arguing. I'm simply telling you. Give me a third, and my cheque and the agreement will be ready this time to-morrow morning. Otherwise, no business."

Mr. Bellowes hesitated, and then gave in.

IV

At six o'clock on a summer evening, in a well-furnished room that overlooked the traffic of Bond Street, Smeath and his employer sat and quarrelled together. Both of them wore new clothes, but Bellowes had the air of prosperity, and Smeath had not.

"It's no good to talk to me," whined Smeath. "I know what I'm saying. Where an essential consideration has been intentionally concealed, an agreement cannot stand. You never told me I was a clairvoyant."

"No," said Bellowes, "I did not. And I don't tell a man what the colour of his hair is, either. Why? Because he knows it already. You knew that you were a clairvoyant."

"I did not. I swear I did not!" said Smeath, raising his voice.

"Now, don't get excited. Don't squeal."

"I'm not squealing. Do you think that if I'd known, I would ever have come to you for a wage like that? We've had fourteen people here to-day. What did they pay?"

"Mind your own business!"

"But it is my own business. And as you wouldn't tell me, I've taken my own steps to find out. Not one of them paid less than a guinea. You had as much as five guineas from some. And here am I with thirty shillings a week. I can get that agreement set aside. I can prove what I'm saying. I had never been hypnotized until I met you."

"Look here," said Bellowes. "Let us get this fixed up once for all. I don't know who's been cramming you up with these fairy-tales about my fees, but I don't get what you think, or anything like it. I get so little, that I don't want to waste any of it on lawyers. Besides, it would do the business no good, and it would do you no good. I should leave you, and then where would you be? Remember that you are not clairvoyant until I make you clairvoyant."

"You think, perhaps, I have not read what the newspapers say about me? I can find a hundred hypnotists very easily. But there is no other man who's clairvoyant as I am."

"And there is no other man who can run a show as I can. Who brought the newspaper men here? Who paid for the advertisements? Who did pretty well everything? However, I'm not going to argue. If you want more money, you can have it. Name your figure. If it is in any way reasonable, you shall have it, on the understanding that this is the last advance you get. If it is unreasonable, you'll get nothing. You can take the thing into the Courts, and I'll fight it. And, mark my words, Smeath. If I do, you may get a surprise. You know nothing at all about hypnotism. You may find

yourself in the witness-box saying things that you did not intend
to say. Now, then, name your figure."

The little man took time to think it over. He rubbed his chin
with his fingers reflectively. He seemed on the point of speaking,
and then stopped. Suddenly he snapped out:

"I want four pounds a week!"

"It's simply bare-faced robbery," said Bellowes. "But you shall
have it. Mind you, you will have to sign another paper to-morrow,
and this time there shall be no doubt about it."

"If you pay me that, I'll sign anything. With four pounds a week
I can keep some very good birds again. But you are right that it is
bare-faced robbery, and I am the man who is being robbed."

There had been many disputes between the two men during
the six weeks that they had been associated. It was by Tangent's
directions that Bellowes acted in the present quarrel.

"It would be better to pay the little devil twenty pounds a week,
and keep him, than to refuse and lose him," said Tangent. "I believe he's right, and that your precious agreement isn't worth the
paper it's written on. Anyhow, I'll get a new agreement ready. Pay
him what he wants, and he'll sign it." '

"Well," said Bellowes, doubtfully, "if you say so you're probably right. But in that case we ought to get an extension of time
out of him."

"No," said Tangent, "the chap's suspicious of you. He hates you.
If you try any sort of monkeying, he'll be off. Besides, with the fees
you're charging, two years will about see it through. There are not
such a vast number of people who can afford the game."

"As things go at present, it looks as though it might last for ever.
You should see the engagement-book. We've got appointments booked
for two months ahead. It isn't only a game you see. It's not just a
pastime for fashionable women. We get men from the Stock Ex-
change, business men of all sorts, racing-men. Yesterday morning
we had the Prime Minister's private secretary. He didn't give his
right name, but Smeath was on to it, and then he admitted it."

"Hot stuff, Smeath. Do you get much out of him in the way of
prophecy? Foretelling the future?"

"Not very often. He has done some wonderful things that way, but more usually he deals with something that is past."

"Why don't you get him to foretell your own future, Percy?"

Bellowes shook his head.

"Not taking any," he said. "He shall have a shot with you if you like."

But Tangent also refused.

Their business had certainly progressed very rapidly. Tangent arranged a report in a newspaper. He communicated with one or two doctors whom he knew to be interested in the subject. He sent a couple of popular actresses to Smeath. He arranged a special séance for a Cabinet Minister, whose principal interest was psychology. After the first week they no longer employed sandwichmen and advertisements. The ball had begun to roll. Everybody who came to Smeath sent somebody else. Everybody in Society was talking about the hideous little dwarf and his marvellous powers. Bellowes was regarded as a showman and a charlatan, but Smeath was clearly the genuine thing.

Despite their mutual dislike, Bellowes and Smeath both lived in the same house—the Bloomsbury lodging-house. It was Bellowes who had insisted on this. He had never felt quite safe about Smeath, and even after the new agreement had been signed he had his suspicions. He was afraid that Smeath would run away. Bellowes occupied fairly good rooms on the first floor. Smeath had one room at the top of the house, but this happened to suit him. Through his windows he could get out on to a flat, leaded roof. There he made friends with the pigeons and sparrows. The maid-servant at the house, who one day saw him out on the roof with the birds all round him, said that it was witchcraft.

"They were 'opping about all over 'im. Sometimes he put one down and called another up. I never saw anything like it in my life before."

She had the hatred of the unusual which is prevalent amongst domestic servants, and gave notice at once. But before the month was up she had grown quite accustomed to seeing Smeath playing with the birds, and the notice was revoked.

V

Bellowes still used for business purposes the name of Sanders-Bell, but he no longer called himself a doctor. He was meeting too many real doctors, and Tangent had advised against it. The room in Bond Street was divided in two by a curtain. The outer part served as a waiting-room, and here, too, Bellowes had his bureau. In the inner part of the room the actual interview between the client and the clairvoyant took place. Their usual hours were only from eleven to one and from two to four, but Bellowes would sometimes arrange for a special interview at an unusual hour and an increased price. On these occasions he always took care to pacify Smeath. Sometimes he gave him money, and sometimes other presents; on one occasion he gave him a big book about birds, with coloured illustrations, and Smeath remained docile and in a good temper for days afterwards.

"Yes," said Bellowes. "You have complained once that I was robbing you. You can't say that now. You have fixed your own salary. If there is the least little bit of extra work to be done, you always get something for it. You are not as grateful as you ought to be, Smeath. Where would you have been without me? What were you doing before you came to me?"

"Nothing. For some weeks I had been very hungry. I make no complaint against you, but when my time's up I shall stay no longer. I go back to the birds again."

"It would be more sensible of you," said Bellowes, "if you banked your money. What did you want to buy that great owl for? He makes the devil of a row at night. We shall have people complaining about it."

"She is a very good friend to me, that owl," said Smeath. "I am teaching her much. She will be valuable."

At this moment there was the sound of a footstep on the stairs, and Smeath stepped behind his curtain.

The man who entered was not at all the type of client that Bellowes generally received. He was a thick-set man of common appearance, and he was unfashionably dressed. He did not look in the least as if he could afford the fee. Bellowes saluted him some-what curtly.

"It is ten minutes to eleven, sir, and our hour for beginning is eleven. However, as you have called, if you like to pay the fee now—two guineas—I will make an appointment for you, but I'm afraid it will have to be in nine weeks' time."

The visitor looked reflective, turning his seedy bowler hat round in his hands.

"Don't think that would do," he said. "Nine weeks—that's a very long time. Couldn't Mr. Smeath see me to-day? Couldn't he make an exception?"

"Only by giving you a special appointment. And for that a very much higher fee is charged."

"How much?" asked the man.

"He could give you ten minutes at one o'clock to-day. But the charge for that would be six guineas. You see, Mr. Smeath is only clairvoyant while in the hypnotic state, and that cannot be repeated indefinitely."

The visitor took an old-fashioned purse from his hip-pocket. He pulled out a five-pound note, a sovereign, and six shillings

"There you are," he said. "Please book me ten minutes with Mr. Smeath at one o'clock to-day."

"Very good," said Bellowes, opening the engagement-book. He looked up, with his pen in his hand. "What name shall I put down?"

"I am Mr. Vincent."

"You'll be careful to be punctual, of course. Mr. Smeath will be ready exactly at one o'clock."

"I shall be here," said the man.

He had no sooner gone than Smeath emerged from behind the curtain again. "What on earth did you do that for?" he asked excitedly.

"Keep your hair on, Smeath. It's all right. I'm going to buy you a big cage for that owl of yours."

"I do not want any cage. My birds are not kept in cages. It is not the extra work that I mind. It is that I cannot do anything for that man. I tell you he is dangerous."

"In what way dangerous?"

"I don't know. He is dangerous to me."

"He looked to me an honest man enough. He had the appearance of a chap up from the country. Probably wants to know what his best girl is doing. I shouldn't worry about it if I were you. Don't stand in the way of business, Smeath. You don't know what the expenses are here. I've got to pay the rent next week, and if I told you what that was, you wouldn't believe it. If you don't want the bird-cage, you shall have something else."

But it was necessary to show Smeath a sovereign, and to present him with it before he would consent. Even then, he did so with great reluctance.

Clients with appointments came in, and the ordinary business of the morning began. Smeath no longer spoke when in the clairvoyant state, for he was often consulted upon matters requiring secrecy, and what he said might have been heard by other clients in waiting. He had a writing-block, and scribbled down on it in pencil what he saw.

At one o'clock precisely Mr. Vincent returned, and was at once brought behind the curtain. Smeath sat there motionless. His eyes were open, but he did not look up at Mr. Vincent.

"Now then, sir," said Bellowes. "What is it you want?"

Mr. Vincent drew from his pocket a comb wrapped in paper. It was of the kind that women wear in their hair, and it had been broken.

"I want him to tell me about the girl who wore this at the time when it was broken."

Bellowes placed the comb in Smeath's hands. Smeath held it for a moment, and then the fingers relaxed, and it dropped to the floor.

Bellowes again placed it in his hand, and this time Smeath flung it from him. But immediately he began to write, Mr. Vincent watching him narrowly as he did so. He wrote with an extraordinary rapidity. Presently Bellowes, who had been standing behind him, and reading what he wrote, asked Mr. Vincent to wait in the outer part of the room. As soon as he was alone with Smeath, he took the writing-block out of his hands, tore the sheet from it, folded it, and put it in his pocket. Then he rejoined Vincent.

"I am extremely sorry, sir," said Bellowes, "that the experiment has failed completely. There is perhaps some kind of antipathy between Mr. Smeath and yourself. These things do occasionally happen. I find that he can tell you nothing at all, and under the circumstances, I should perhaps return your fee."

Vincent did not seem particularly surprised.

"Very well," he said. "I had hardly expected to get what I wanted, but I thought I might as well try. I paid you six guineas, I think. You seem to be treating me fairly, and I have given you a certain amount of trouble. Supposing you return me five of them."

The money was handed over, and Vincent departed. Bellowes went back to Smeath and brought him out of the trance. Smeath shivered.

"Is he here still?"

"No. Gone."

"Was it all right?"

"It was quite all right."

"I'm glad he's gone," said Smeath. "I was horribly afraid of something. Now I can go out and get my lunch, and I have to buy food for the birds too."

"I shouldn't spend too much money on it if I were you," said Bellowes.

Smeath laughed.

"It is not very expensive," he said. "And I have made one extra sovereign. Why not?"

"Because, in future, Smeath, you are going to work for me for much less money—for a pound a week, to be precise."

"I shall not," said Smeath, loudly.

"I told you once before not to squeal. I don't like it. You will do exactly as I say, and for a very good reason. If you don't you will be taken to prison, and you will be tried before a judge, and you will be hanged, Smeath. Hanged for the murder of Esther Samuel in the woods at Teston."

VI

"What makes you say that? How do you know it?" asked Smeath. The fingers of his big hands locked and separated and locked again. His eyes were fixed intently on Bellowes. He looked excited, but not frightened.

"How do I know it?" echoed Bellowes. "I have it here in your own handwriting." He tapped his breast-pocket. "You do not remember what happened when you were hypnotized. I put a broken comb into your hands. It was a comb which the murdered woman had worn. You began to write at once. You've put the rope round your neck, Smeath."

"And that man—the man that I knew to be dangerous?"

"Mr. Vincent? I told him that the experiment had failed, and returned his fee. He knows nothing. So long as you do exactly what I tell you, you are quite safe."

"Who was he, this Vincent?"

Bellowes shrugged his shoulders.

"How should I know? Possibly one of the Samuel family. Possibly a 'tec. If I had given him what he had paid for, we should have had the police in here by now. I have saved your skin for you, Smeath. Don't forget it."

"Will you read it out to me, the thing that I wrote down?"

"No. It tells one everything, except the motive."

"The motive was obvious enough. I was hungry and had no money. I had tramped to Teston and reached there two days too soon. I had nowhere to go, and I lived and slept in the woods. I begged from the girl at first, and if she had given me a few pence she might have been alive now. She was not the least bit afraid of me. Why should she have been? I was small, misshapen, and looked weak. She was tall and strong. As she turned away from me, she said the tramps in the neighbourhood were becoming a nuisance, and she would send the police after me. Even then I only meant to hit her once, but that is a queer thing—you cannot hit a human being once. You see the body lying at your feet, and you have to go on striking and striking. When I knew she must be dead, I flung the stick down. I took nothing but the money, nothing which could be traced. Even the money made me so nervous that I hid most of it—buried it in a place where I could find it again. If the police had found me, there would only have been a few coppers in my possession, and I did not look like a man who could have done it. But they never did find me."

"I see. That was why, when I offered to advance your railway fare, you told me you had money. You had a pair of new boots on when you turned up at Warlow. I remember what an infernal squeaking row they made on the platform. Well, you've done for yourself, Smeath. You've got to work for me on very different terms now."

"No," said Smeath. "That is not so."

"Very good. I'll write my note to Mr. Vincent now. He'll do the rest."

"No you won't, and I'll tell you why. You can destroy me very likely, but if you do, you'll destroy your own livelihood. And you always take very good care for yourself, Mr. Bellowes."

"Destroy my livelihood?" said Bellowes, thumping on the table with his fist. "That's where you make your mistake, you little devil! Because you're useful, you think you're indispensable. You're not. There's a reward of two hundred pounds out for anyone who finds the murderer of Esther Samuel. I'm a born showman. With two hundred pounds capital I can chuck this and start something else that will pay me just as well."

"It looks as if I shall have to give in. Well, there's no help for it. I must get a much cheaper room, of course."

"No, you won't. You'll stop in the same house as me. D'you think I haven't worked it all out? After you've paid your rent, you've a shilling a day for food, and better men have lived on less. I'm not going to give you a chance to bolt. And mark my words, Smeath, if you do bolt, the very moment I find you've gone I give you up. Don't imagine you can get away. There are not many men of your build. The police would have you for a certainty within twenty-four hours."

"Then I become a slave; I can do nothing. There were other birds that I meant to buy. And in time I could have started a business again. That must all go."

"Quite so. That must all go. In fact, before a fortnight is out I expect you'll sell that big white owl of yours. You'll grudge him his keep."

"It is a she-owl, and I shall not let her go. She can do things that would surprise you."

"Can she?" said Bellowes. "It might be rather effective if you brought her down here. She would impress clients."

"I shall not. I keep her for myself!"

"Don't talk like a fool! You are forgetting that I hold you between my thumb and finger. If I tell you to wring that bird's neck you will have to do it."

Smeath rose to his feet in fury.

"Where's my hat?" he said. "Give me my hat!"

Bellowes stood in front of the door.

"What's the matter with you? Where are you off to?"

"Checkmate for you, Mr. Bellowes. I am going now to give myself up. Where is your two hundred pounds reward, eh? Where is the money that you make out of the clairvoyant?"

"Sit down, and don't talk in that silly way. I never told you to kill the bird. I was only speaking in your interests when I said I doubted if you could afford to keep it. As a matter of fact, I don't care a pin's head about it either way. If you set so much store by it, keep it by all means."

"In that case," said Smeath, "I will go on working for you, and on the terms that you have said."

"That's all right; and now you can go out to lunch. Remember that you have to be back at two o'clock. If you are not here by ten minutes past two, I shall send the police to look for you."

"I shall be here, Mr. Bellowes."

Every Saturday morning at half-past nine Tangent called on Bellowes in Bond Street, to look over the books and to collect his share of the profits. Tangent had no great faith in Mr. Bellowes. Smeath was never allowed to be present on these occasions.

On the Saturday after Mr. Vincent's visit, Tangent was well pleased with the results.

"Mind you," he said, "the little dwarf isn't doing so badly out of it either. He gets his regular four pounds a week. This week I see he's had one pound ten in cash for extra work, and you're charging twelve-and-six for a present to him. What was the present?"

"Oh, a bird of sorts. The little beggar's simply mad about birds. That did more good than if I'd given him the actual cash."

"Oh, I'm not grumbling, Bellowes," said Tangent, surveying with complacency the diamond ring on his ringer. "If, by giving him a trifle extra now and then, you can keep his goodwill, it's quite worth our while to do it. No man will work for nothing, and I suppose he finds this clairvoyance game rather exhausting. Not over and above good for the health, eh?"

"He says it's exhausting. He seems to me well enough."

When Tangent had gone Bellowes smiled. To swindle Tangent was a real pleasure to him, even apart from the profit he made for himself. He remembered the terms which Tangent had forced him to accept for the provision of capital for the enterprise.

The introduction of a large white owl into the Bloomsbury lodging-house could have but one effect. The maid-servant gave notice at once on general principles. It was Smeath this time who persuaded her to remain.

"You must not be afraid of the white owl," he said. "Owls are wise birds. She knows who my friends are, and who my enemies are. You are my friend, and she will never hurt you. She will let you feed her and stroke her feathers. They are very, very soft, the feathers of an owl."

In a week's time Jane was neglecting her work to play with the white owl out on the leads.

VII

For several weeks no change took place. Smeath did his work with patience and docility. He addressed Mr. Bellowes with respect. He made very little objection to private engagements. As a munificent reward, on two occasions Bellowes took him out to luncheon, and once presented him with some Sunday tickets for the Zoo, which he himself did not want. Every Saturday Tangent inspected, with satisfaction, some purely fantastic accounts. Bellowes was specially careful that Smeath and Tangent should never meet, lest the discrepancy between the statements in the books and the actual facts should be discovered.

And then business began to fall off. There was no excessive drop, but the previous standard was not quite maintained. That astute showman, Mr. Bellowes, decided that something would have to be done. Some new feature would have to be introduced, to set people talking again.

"Smeath," he said one day, "didn't you tell me something once about a white owl?"

"Yes," said Smeath, "I have one."

"It does tricks, don't it?"

"It does a few things," said Smeath, grudgingly. "You do not want it. You said that you would leave me my owl."

"You needn't get into a stew about it, and do for goodness' sake keep those great hands of yours still. They get on my nerves. Nobody wants to take your blessed owl away from you. The only thing that I was wondering about was whether it might not be worth while to keep the bird here, instead of at your lodgings."

"No, sir! No, Mr. Bellowes! It is in my leisure time that I want my owl."

"Well, I was talking to Mr. Tangent about it, and he thought it was a good idea; in fact, he said I ought to have done it before. We must think about it. I have been pretty easy with you, Smeath."

"Also, I've worked very hard for you."

"You've done what you were told, and of late you've given me no trouble. You might let Tangent and myself have a look at the bird, anyhow. It would be effective, you know—the dwarf clairvoyant and the great white owl on the back of his chair. Tangent spoke of a poster. I'll tell him to give us a call in Bloomsbury on Sunday morning."

"I do not want my owl to be taken away. It lives there on the leads outside my window. Here it would be unhappy. How could I leave it here all night alone?"

"Don't be unreasonable, Smeath. You will see more of the bird then than you do now."

"No," said Smeath. "The greater part of the time when I'm here I'm like a dead man, and know nothing."

Bellowes had quite realized that this was the point on which Smeath would have to be handled carefully.

"Look here," he said, "I wouldn't do anything to hurt the bird. At any rate, let Mr. Tangent and myself see it. Let us see if it can really do the things that that girl Jane jabbers so much about. If Tangent and I think it would be an asset to the show, I am prepared to go quite beyond our agreement. I'll give you two or three shillings for yourself, Smeath. You can give yourself a treat. You've not been having many treats lately; in fact, you look just about half starved."

It was true. The little dwarf had grown very thin. His eyes seemed to have got bigger and brighter. There was a look in them now which would have made Bellowes suspicious if he had noticed it.

"Jane," said Smeath, as he met her on the stairs that night, "they are coming on Sunday morning to see my owl."

"Then they'll see miracles," said Jane, with confidence.

"And they're going to take it away."

"If that bird goes, I goes!"

Smeath burst into a peal of mirthless laughter.

Mr. Tangent arrived in a taxi-cab at the Bloomsbury lodgings at eleven on the following Sunday morning. He was in a bad temper, and swore and grumbled profusely.

"So I've got to turn out on Sunday morning and work seven days a week, just because you're such a damn bad showman, Bellowes? You've let the thing down. The books on Saturday were perfectly awful."

"I'm not a bad showman, and it's not my fault. The weather's been against us, for one thing. And, besides, no novelty lasts forever. We must put something else into it to buck it up, and we must get that poster out."

"That means more expense. I don't see why we should keep on paying Smeath four pounds a week if business is falling off. And as for that rotten old owl of his, I'm no great believer in it. It will look all right on the poster, but it will do no good in your Bond Street rooms. I know those tricks. The bird picks out cards from a pack, or shams dead, or some other nursery foolery. Stale, my boy, hopelessly stale."

"According to what I hear, the bird does none of those things. It's a new line."

"Is it? I'll bet a dollar it ain't. However, tell Smeath to bring it down, and let's get it over."

"Smeath won't bring it down. We shall have to go up to it. He makes a great favour of showing it to us at all. And, if you will take my tip, you'll say nothing to Smeath beyond a good-morning. I can tell you he wants devilish careful handling about this bird of his. If you interfere, you'll spoil it. All you've got to do, if you think it at all remarkable, is to say to me that it might possibly do. I shall understand. Now then, come along up!"

"All those stairs!" groaned Tangent. He was a heavy and plethoric man. When they reached Smeath's room he stood for a minute, panting.

The room was ordinarily dingy enough. It was a fine morning, and the sun streamed in through the window. On the leads outside they could see the great white owl perched on the bough of a tree which had been fixed there. Smeath, with his hat off, stood beside it, and seemed to be talking to it.

Around his feet were a flock of pigeons and sparrows. He nodded to the two men, and then gave one wave of his hands. The pigeons and sparrows flew off and left him alone with the white owl.

"Funny sight!" grunted Tangent. "Devilish funny sight!"

Smeath opened the window, and called into the room:

"Good-morning, gentlemen! Will you come out?"

"Don't much like it," said Tangent. "I've no head for this kind of thing."

"Oh, you're all right!" said Bellowes. "You needn't go anywhere near the edge."

He placed a chair for him, and Tangent climbed out on to the roof, followed by Bellowes.

"I will leave you to look at the bird by yourselves, gentlemen," said Smeath, and stepped down into the room.

"Then who's going to make the bird do its tricks?" asked Tangent. "It's a fine-looking beggar, anyhow. Seems about half asleep. Tame enough." He passed his jewelled hand over the snowy plumage on the bird's breast. "There's a feather-bed for you," he said, laughing.

The bird opened its eyes, and leaped straight into the face of Bellowes. Its plumage half stifled him, its sharp claws tore his eyes. He screamed for help.

Tangent, in horror, had flung himself down flat on the leads, covering his face. Within the room Smeath stood with folded arms, watching the scene with the utmost calmness.

Bellowes tore at the bird with his hands, but step by step it forced him back. There came one final scream from him, and then two seconds of silence, and then the thud as his body struck the stones below. Up above, the white owl flew swiftly away.

The dwarf rubbed his hands and laughed. And then, changing his expression to one of extreme dismay, went to the help of the prostrate Tangent.

BURDON'S TOMB

The Earthquake

Mrs. Langley and her companion, Miss Gilderay, both thought rather well of Mr. Agravine. It was their first visit to Egypt, and Mr. Agravine's greater experience had been of use to them. He was quiet and without presumption, an elderly man with tired and rather magnetic eyes. "He has a story, of course," said Miss Gilderay.

"We all have," said Mrs. Langley; "and we never tell them."

Miss Gilderay blushed. She was plain, kindly, sincere, and thirty-five. Mrs. Langley was five years older and looked five years younger. She was not beautiful, but everybody said she had nice eyes and a pretty figure.

"I am glad he is coming on the *Rameses*," said Mrs. Langley. "He is useful. He has done it all before, and he knows more than the dragomans. Of course, Mr. Castle is useful too. A frightful nuisance, though."

"Oh, frightful!" Miss Gilderay assented. "Still, one feels sorry for him."

In the lounge of the hotel after dinner that night Mr. Agravine spoke to them about Sir Felix Burdon's tomb. The tomb was thus spoken of by careless people in Cairo and Luxor, but Sir Felix had merely been its excavator, and the work of excavation was not yet quite complete. It was the tomb of a high priest who had died

152

in Thebes twelve hundred years before Christ was born. It was of considerable size and importance, and its mural paintings were interesting and well-preserved. Mr. Agravine wished particularly to see this tomb, and said he should try if anything could be arranged through the dragoman on the boat. He was describing some interesting points about this tomb when young Mr. Castle came up and joined the group. He was always doing that, and sometimes he was a nuisance. He was a young man of twenty-eight, travelling by himself and paying a good deal for excess luggage. He was possessed of many and elaborate clothes. Chance propinquity at the hotel dinner had introduced Mr. Agravine, and Mr. Agravine had in turn presented Mr. Castle. This had been at Mr. Castle's request, for he had very nearly decided to fall in love with Mrs. Langley. She was just enough interested in him to flirt with him, and only just. To-night she sent him away at once. "Go and find out the name of that very beautiful girl with the red hair."

The girl with the red hair was travelling with two elderly ladies, who were set in a totally different key from her. The old ladies were Victorian. The girl looked as if she had walked straight out of a German fairy tale.

Mr. Castle did not know his way about at all. At the end of the evening he had not got the required information. He came back to Mrs. Langley, and, though she laughed, she sent him away again. She was definitely not going to speak to him any more until he could tell her what she wanted to know.

Chance gave it to him next morning. He happened to see the girl come out of her room, and he noted the number. He had only to look now at the numbers in the hall and see what name was attached. He went to Mrs. Langley in triumph. "I've got it," he said. "She is Miss Averil."

"Who is?"

"The red-haired girl that you wanted to know about. She is travelling with two sisters—Miss Bryans. They are probably her aunts."

"I don't think I care," said Mrs. Langley. "It was really her first name that I wanted to know."

The subject turned up again on the first day of their departure from Cairo on the *Rameses*. Miss Averil and her two aunts happened also to be going on to Assouan on the *Rameses*, and Mrs. Langley, in a comparatively short space of time, had taught Miss Bryan an entirely new patience. As she walked the deck that evening after dinner with Mr. Castle by her side she said, "What an idiot you are, if you do not mind my saying so. You never found out that girl's name at all. I give two minutes to it, and find out everything myself."

"And what is her first name?" asked Mr. Castle, patiently.

"Well, you ought to know. You ought to be able to deduce it from looking at her."

"Yseult?" suggested the young man.

"Oh, goodness, no. Her name is Zoe. Don't you think that's right?"

"No," said Mr. Castle. "Zoe is a maid of Athens, very nearly as black as the ace of spades."

"Rubbish! Anyhow, Zoe Averil is not a maid of Athens. She is a maid of Oxford. And what Oxford has done to deserve it I don't know. Her aunts are highly cultivated and belong to a Browning society. Now, why don't you find out interesting things and tell them to me? You never seem to know anything."

She sent him to fetch French coffee for her, and when he brought it decided that she would take Turkish coffee that night. Really, she did not treat him very well. Her manner with Mr. Agravine was quite different.

On the day that they arrived at Luxor Mr. Agravine told them that there was quite a chance that they would be able to see Burdon's tomb. The dragoman of the boat had been Sir Felix Burdon's dragoman during his first season in Egypt. He had assisted him since in some trouble that Sir Felix had had with his labourers. It was quite possible that he would be able to arrange it.

The dragoman did arrange it. Chance favoured him. Sir Felix was waiting for some heavy timbers, and meanwhile the work of excavation had ceased. He cursed the dragoman sincerely. He said most insulting and improbable things about the dragoman's ancestry. He told him that if he ever suggested such a thing again he would break his head with a stick; but none the less he permitted him to bring up his gang from the *Rameses* on the following day. They were not, of course, to enter the two chambers of the tomb which Sir Felix used as his living-room and stores.

The party from the *Rameses*, about thirty in number, crossed the river from Luxor and rode five miles. They halted and dismounted at the top of the long slope which led down to the tomb.

Led by the dragoman, the procession of tourists passed down the sandy slope into the darkness, under a crest piled with great rocks. Then came the burning of magnesium wire and the dragoman's lecture—a little sketchy, because he did not know the tomb—on the paintings and inscriptions. He was most impressive. "This tomb never been shown before, ladies and gentlemen. Special permit. No other dragomans can show it."

He scooped up two inquiring Germans, who would have made a dash for that part of the tomb which they had been particularly requested not to enter, and shepherded his party out into the open again—all but five of them.

Just as these five were leaving, they found themselves confronted by a man in grey flannel trousers and an old Norfolk jacket of brown canvas. He reminded Mrs. Langley at once of Don Quixote. He began to speak to them about what they had seen, and he spoke with evident knowledge and authority.

Miss Gilderay whispered a word to Mrs. Langley, and Mrs. Langley said, "I suppose so," and turned to the stranger:—

"You are Sir Felix Burden, are you not?"

"Yes, that's my name."

"I asked you because we wanted so much to thank you for letting us come in here. It's too interesting for words. I hope we haven't been interrupting your work?"

"Not at all," said Sir Felix. "We don't start digging again till to-morrow. I was just waiting for some stuff to come up from Luxor. I shall be living here for the next two months, you know."

"Living here?" said Miss Gilderay. "Actually in this tomb?"

"Why not? In here or in a tent just outside. I make myself very comfortable, and it saves the bother of going backwards and forwards."

"It seems wonderful. I supposed that you lived on the *Lotus*. We saw it just above Luxor."

"Last year I used the dahabeeyah a good deal, and I am meaning to dine and sleep there to-night; but the *Lotus* leaves to-morrow for Assouan, taking some friends of mine who are to go on to the Second Cataract."

As he spoke he glanced over the party. Mr. Castle carried Mrs. Langley's camera and fly-whisk. Mrs. Langley looked charming and Miss Gilderay earnest, and a pretty girl with red hair was talking to Mr. Agravine on one side.

"I tell you what," said Sir Felix, cheerfully; "there's a very interesting bit of painting in that second chamber on the left there, and I think your dragoman missed it. I should really like to show you that. I will get candles."

"It's very, very kind of you," said Mrs. Langley. "But won't they be waiting for us?"

"Oh, I hope so. Your dragoman knows that you are speaking with me, and therefore he must wait. We shan't keep them five minutes."

He dived away into the darkness as he spoke, and returned with a box of candles.

As they were lighting their candles it chanced that he heard Mr. Agravine's name mentioned.

"I wonder," said Sir Felix, "are you Mr. Agravine, the collector, the great authority on Corot?"

"A great authority on nothing, I'm afraid. But I've been a collector of pictures all my life, to my sorrow."

"But why to your sorrow?"

"A long story, and I should be ashamed to tell it."

"When we get back to the boat," said Miss Gilderay, as she lighted her candle, "the rest will be very jealous of us."

"What on earth for?" asked Sir Felix, laughing.

"Because we have special privileges. The others have only had a dragoman; we get the real explorer."

"Can't understand jealousy," said Sir Felix, "even if it's anything of importance."

"Why not?" Mrs. Langley asked.

Sir Felix shrugged his shoulders.

"To the ancient Egyptian," he said, "death was the only important thing that happened to him in his life. Once one gets that point of view one ceases to be jealous."

"But it's rather amazing that you should have that point of view," said Miss Gilderay.

"Oh, well, explanations are long and tiresome things. Now, then, here is the thing I wanted to show you. Hold your candles up very high, please. That's right. It's really an astonishingly modern idea, considering the date at which it was painted. You see that figure—"

He never finished that sentence. The floor of the chamber seemed to sway upwards. They staggered against one another. Miss Gilderay caught at a sliding surface of wall, and fell to the ground grotesquely. There was a sharp hissing sound, followed by a roar like a cannonade, that drowned their exclamations. Then came a heavy thud—thud, as of some titanic hammer beating down soft earth. And then all was still. Sir Felix alone still held his lighted candle in his hand. The other candles had fallen and gone out.

Sir Felix helped Miss Gilderay to her feet again, and assured himself that nobody was hurt. They found and relit their candles.

"But what on earth was it? What terrible thing has happened?" cried Miss Gilderay.

"It appeared to me," said Mr. Agravine, "like a shock of earthquake. It was as if a mountain had come down on us."

"That is probably what has happened. If you don't mind waiting a moment, I'll go and see what I can find out. I'll be back as soon as I can."

It seemed a long time before he returned. They spoke together in awed tones, speculating on the chances. When Sir Felix came back to them, he saw white, grave faces, but no sign of panic. He hesitated. He had practically to pronounce a death-sentence on these five people and on himself. And then Mrs. Langley spoke.

"You have bad news, I see," said Mrs. Langley. "But we have expected it. The entrance to the tomb is blocked?"

"That is so," said Sir Felix. "It is bad for me, because I brought you back here. The rest of your party are safe outside. However, we must see if we can work a way out. I have a pick and a couple of shovels here."

"Can't we do anything too?" asked Miss Gilderay.

"Nothing at the moment, I think. Make yourselves as comfortable as you can there."

He pointed to the chamber which had been furnished as his own living-room.

The men returned to the entrance-hall, stripped to the waist, and began their labour. It was absolutely ineffective, and Sir Felix had known from the first that it would be ineffective. But everything had to be tried. The sand and rubble fell in on them, and they could make no way. At last they gave it up.

"Will you call the ladies who were with you?" said Sir Felix. "They had better know."

II

The Confession of Sir Felix Burdon and of Mr. Castle

Deck-chairs had been found for the three women. Agravine and Castle sat on the ground, their backs to the wall. Sir Felix remained standing. There were plenty of candles and the hall was brightly lit.

"Tell us now," said Mrs. Langley, "what the chances are."

"We will look at the best side first," said Sir Felix. "We are five miles from Luxor, and Luxor is on the rail. The tools and the men needed for an attempt at rescue ought to be available and to be here within a very few hours. You're with Thomas Cook & Son, and they won't lose anybody if they can help it, and they are pretty potent people in Egypt. The natives will probably be scared, and may be reluctant to come to work here. But baksheesh and the hide-whip are good arguments. I think we will take it for granted that everything that can be done to save us will most certainly be done."

"I see," said Zoe Averil, "that you think it will be of no use."

"I do, but I may be wrong. I am guided by the sounds we heard and by my knowledge of the conformation of the ground round here. I believe that we're buried too deep for them to reach us in less than a week's work. You must remember that they will probably find it difficult at first even to determine the point at which they shall dig. I've been talking it over with Mr. Agravine, and we don't think that the air here will last more than three or four days. So now you see what I've done."

"You must not say that again," said Mrs. Langley. "Nobody here would be mad enough to hold you in any way responsible. Besides, we've talked it over—Miss Gilderay, Zoe Averil and myself—and we also had come to the conclusion that there was very little hope. As it happens, we three, more, perhaps, than most women, can take this quietly and wait for death without making any fuss."

"Yes," said Zoe. "I see you're looking at me, and I know I've been crying. But that was because of my people, and not for myself at all. So far as I myself am concerned—I'll tell you a secret—I'm glad."

"How horrible!" said Agravine.

And then they began to discuss together the best arrangements that could be made for the three days left to them. On one point they were unanimous. Those days were to be made as easy as possible. The candles that lit them, and the flame of the spirit stove, would burn up air. But the tomb was to remain lit, and they would eat and drink, though to-morrow they would die. And when there were signs that the last moments were approaching they would not prolong the period of headache and malaise and nausea. Sir Felix had a charcoal stove, which he used for cooking on in the open. If this were lit all would soon be over.

There was not the slightest fear of any suffering from hunger or thirst. The chamber which Sir Felix used for his store-room had already been filled for the season, and even a modified luxury would be possible. The women claimed for themselves the slight household work that there would be to do. Sir Felix used paper plates and dishes that would not need to be washed, and when used could be thrown, with all other refuse, down the deep shaft at the farther end of the tomb. At night the men would camp in the entrance-hall, on deck-chairs. The women would fare a little more easily, dividing such bedding as there was among them in the room at the other end of the tomb. The big tank had been filled, and there was bottled water for drinking besides. The only thing that seemed likely to distress them was the waiting, the actual waiting for three days before death came.

At present they did not feel this at all. The earthquake shock had thrown them into something approaching stupor. Now came the reaction. They were excited, and talked eagerly. There was much to be done. The floor of the big hall had to be sprinkled with water, that the dust might not bother them. A table and seats had to be improvised, and a meal prepared. Young Castle, under direction, opened tins. Miss Gilderay busied herself at the spirit stove. Mr. Agravine and Sir Felix were occupied with a little rough carpentry. There was much activity and good temper. There was even laughter at minor mishaps. It was an astounding and fantastic picnic in the very face of death.

Presently Mrs. Langley came up to Sir Felix.

"Zoe—Miss Averil—and I have found among your stores a big package of native costumes—women's costumes. May we use them?"

"Of course you may. But please ask permission for nothing again. All that is here is common property. It belongs to all of us. I was commissioned by a lady in England to get those dresses for her. And the commission bored me terribly. Now I feel grateful to that lady."

An hour later they all met at dinner. The materials of the repast had mostly come out of tins, but Miss Gilderay had been very clever. The champagne was excellent, though two of the men were compelled to drink from tea-cups. Mr. Castle's voice began to be heard rather frequently. There was a faintly triumphant note in it, and it was not entirely due to champagne. The propinquity of Mrs. Langley affected him.

At the end of the repast Mr. Castle opened a gold cigarette-case and presented it to Mrs. Langley. She did not appear to see it, taking no notice of it. Selecting a cigarette himself, he took from his pocket a gold matchbox. All his waistcoat-pocket furniture was of pure gold, and silver was nothing accounted.

"Wait one moment, Mr. Castle," said Sir Felix. "What do you think about it, Agravine? It's not as if we could open the windows and make the whole thing fresh again to-morrow."

"By Jove! I hadn't thought of that," said Castle, and returned the cigarette to his case.

"Well," said Agravine, "our principle was that we were to make it as easy for ourselves as possible. This hall is fairly lofty as compared with the smaller chambers. Suppose we permit each person one cigarette after dinner to-night, and then see what it is like to-morrow morning? I imagine we shan't notice it, but, if we do, we can set one of the smaller chambers of the tomb apart as a smoking-room, hanging something over the entrance."

"Good!" said Sir Felix, "I think you are right." He produced his own cigarette-case, and Mrs. Langley and Miss Gilderay both took cigarettes from it. Zoe Averil did not smoke.

There was a little buzz of conversation, and then a sudden silence. And into the silence broke the clear, silvery voice of Zoe Averil.

"I want to ask you something, Sir Felix. You look rather anxious, and I don't understand anxiety when the end is so certain. What is it you are afraid of for us?"

"I'll tell you frankly. I'm afraid of reaction. I have got no words to say how splendid I think you three women have been. You all seem without fear. But we have many hours before us yet. There will be little or nothing to do. Here we shall be in prison together glaring at one another. If our cheerfulness broke down, if we ceased to be good-tempered, if we got to long for the end—well, it's possible."

"Tell us your story, Sir Felix," said Mrs. Langley.

"My story? What do you mean?"

"The story of yourself."

"I've never yet told it. I'd never meant to tell it at all. Yet, now that I come to think about it, I don't know that it wouldn't ease my mind to make a confession before I died. You will none of you think very well of me when you've heard it, and so I must make one condition. There is not to be one word of comment."

To this all agreed.

"I am at present thirty-eight years of age. When I was a boy of fourteen, early one summer morning I wrecked the whole of my life. It is in consequence of what I did, or failed to do, then that I succeeded to the baronetcy—if that is worth anything—and became a rich man, and have never since had one moment of complete happiness. What I've got to tell you is that I was a coward. Even now, in similar circumstances, I think I might be a coward again. There are people who have no fear. There are people who are brave enough for the ordinary things of life, but have one special fear which overmasters them. I believe there are many such, and I was one of them. With some men the overmastering horror is connected with fire. They live in dread of it. They never go to an hotel or a house for the first time without looking from their windows to find what they would do in case of fire. The thing haunts them. My case was different. I was supposed to be a particularly courageous and high-spirited boy, but I also was haunted—by the dread of drowning. I was afraid of the water. As a child, when I first saw the sea I screamed with terror. As I got older and went to school I had to get over this to some extent. I managed, with the greatest agony to myself and with the strictest concealment of my real feelings, to learn to swim. In the summer holidays I bathed every morning with my elder brother in the river before breakfast. I used to pretend that I loved it. And yet every day it was all I could do to get myself to go in. There, can't you guess the rest of it? No, don't speak."

He took a sip of champagne, and continued his story.

On the morning in question Adrian, his elder brother, who was an expert swimmer, had remained long in the water after Felix had left it. Suddenly Adrian was attacked by cramp and cried for help.

"I was unable to move," said Sir Felix. "I stood there on the bank half-dressed, looking at him, and I was actually unable to move. I could not make myself do it. I pictured him dragging me down into the green water. I also began to call loudly for help. I told myself that when he was insensible, and it would be safe for me to tackle him, I would go in and rescue, but it was not till I heard steps and became afraid of being found on the bank that I managed to fall into the water. I never reached my brother. Fear had taken all the power from my muscles. I could not swim at all. I went down at once. When we were taken out by the men who came in answer to my call, he was dead and I was insensible. I recovered, told a lying story, and let people praise my heroism. Can you wonder that the recollection of that morning has haunted me all my life? I, who hate cowardice and lies and selfish brutality, have to look upon myself as a coward, a liar, and a murderer. Since then I have done everything I could, short of actual suicide, to end it. In South Africa the Boer bullets and the enteric took better men and left me free. Here in Egypt I found a fascination. Here also lived people who all their lives through had looked forward to their death. Excavation, too, has its risks, or can be made to have them. I have shirked none of them. I have even invented them. And all the time I have had to put a good face on things before the world. I dared not let people know what I really was. I joined in sports, I laughed at jokes, I pretended to be interested in all manner of things. It is a relief unspeakable to me that from this moment, for the few hours that will elapse before I die, I need pretend no longer. I have shown myself as I am."

There was complete silence when he finished speaking. It had been agreed that there was to be no word of comment. Then openly, across the table, Mrs. Langley stretched out her hand to him, and he held it for a moment. Miss Gilderay, rising, with Zoe Averil close to her, began to clear away things. Mr. Agravine, helping them, sought and found an occasion to say something absolutely commonplace.

Suddenly Mr. Castle brought his hand down on the table.

"Wait a minute," he said. "If you don't mind, I mean. If I don't do it now, I never shall."

"What is it, Mr. Castle?" asked Mr. Agravine.

"My name's not Castle, but that's no matter. It's the only name you'll ever know me by. I've got a story to tell—a true story. The night's young, and in any case we shall be getting a long sleep soon."

"Don't get excited about it, Mr. Castle," said Mrs. Langley, quietly. "We are quite willing to hear you."

Those who had risen from their places sat down again, and the young man began.

"I suppose I ought to blame myself alone for what I am going to tell you, but I don't. I blame my father more than myself. He's a solicitor in Lincoln's Inn Fields. I dare say you'd know the name if I gave it. I have been on bad terms with him all my life. All my life he has kept me short of liberty and short of money. He forced me to take, or to pretend to take, his views in religion and politics and everything. It was only by hypocrisy that I could make life with him tolerable. He insisted upon it that I should follow his profession, although he knew that I hated it. I don't care now whether I'm laughed at or not, and I'll tell you what I wanted to be. I wanted to be an actor. He would not hear of that, of course. He'd given me a good education, public school and Oxford, and I was to go into his office. I hated it, but I did what I was told. I went through my articles, I passed all necessary examinations. I became admitted as a solicitor, and then, for years, I did the work of managing clerk for him for about half a managing clerk's salary. At twenty-seven I had very little more freedom than I had at seventeen. I was not allowed a latch-key. I had to give an account of everything that I did and almost everything that I thought. It would have been just if I had been taken into partnership, but my father would not hear of that. I was to inherit the business when he died, and until then I might wait. So it went on. Month after month of formal and uninteresting routine. Month after month of snubs and checks. If ever a man hated his father, I hated mine. Well, he'd screwed down the safety-valve, and after that it was his own look-out. What happened was inevitable."

He paused a moment, irresolute.

"Go on," said Mrs. Langley.

"Oh, I'm not going to shirk it. One day last July my father handed me the firm's cheque for nine hundred pounds. I was to cash it and go on to the office of another solicitor to complete a purchase on behalf of a client. It was the kind of thing I had often done before. As you know, of course, payment is generally made in Bank of England notes. Until the moment when I had that cheque in my hands I had formed no plan at all. I had had a specially exasperating week with my old father, and was determined that something would have to be done. As I slipped that cheque into my pocket I decided what it should be. I got cash for the cheque, taking the greater part of it in small notes and twenty pounds in gold. I was very well known at the bank. If I had asked for the whole of it in gold I doubt if it would have aroused any suspicion. Then I got into a cab and drove round to one or two shops and bought a dressing-case and some other things. The change had begun already. My father did not permit me to take cabs when a 'bus would serve, or a 'bus when it was an easy walk, though he never went anywhere except in a cab himself. I knew that the last place in which they would look for me would be in the neighbourhood of Lincoln's Inn Fields, and so I went to a small hotel in Holborn. For two or three days I lay low and watched the papers carefully morning and evening, expecting to find some account of my disappearance. There was never a word about it, and then I knew that I was quite safe. My father had not taken the view that I had been abducted by thieves, but that I myself was a thief. To save his name and the name of his firm he would be quite willing to pay that nine hundred out of his own pocket. I laughed at the thought of that. It occurred to me, however, that he would probably have put private detectives on to me, and for some weeks I was careful, going out only at night in closed cabs. It was dull, because I knew nobody. I still watched the papers, and still found no allusion to myself. I had expected a veiled notice in the agony column of the *Times*, but there was nothing. The old man had evidently determined to cut me off altogether. At last, one night, more because I was sick of the solitude than because I thought it was safe, I crossed over to

Calais by the night boat. I remained in Paris for a few weeks, and then started off on a kind of walking tour. I made a good many acquaintances and I thoroughly enjoyed myself. I never had the slightest qualm of conscience, and I am not sure that I have any now. I said to myself that I had not stolen the nine hundred pounds, I had merely drawn my back pay. I got plenty of amusement, and incidentally I improved my French. On my return to Paris I happened to be in Cook's office one day and heard a man inquiring about Egypt. It was now November. My walking tour had cost me very little, and I still had plenty of money left. That is how I came here. There is my story, and you can think what you like."

"Thank you for telling us," said Mrs. Langley. "It is better to make no other comment."

"I notice," said Mr. Castle, bitterly, "that you do not give me your hand."

"I do not," said Mrs. Langley.

"You can treat me as a leper if you like."

"Nor do I do that."

Miss Gilderay broke in hastily. "But what did you mean to do when the money was all gone?"

"I was willing to do anything, except to arise and go to my father. If I had found an opportunity I should have taken it. If I had found none I should probably have committed suicide. Burdon's tomb has spared me my pains."

And from that time onward Mr. Castle began to give trouble.

III

The Confession of Miss Gilderay and of Mrs. Langley

The night seemed interminable. Sir Felix Burdon, an old campaigner, slept well enough in his deck-chair, but all the others were restless. In the passage one candle burned. Its flame, absolutely motionless in the still and yellow air, was like a piece of burnished metal. At the farther end of the tomb, in the chambers where the women slept, low voices could be heard at intervals all through the first hours of night.

At five in the morning all was still. Mr. Agravine, who had tried a thousand positions, had found one in which he was able to sleep. Castle, who had stretched himself at full length on the sandy floor, lay with his face on one arm, breathing heavily.

Suddenly Castle sprang to his feet.

"I want to get out of this," he shouted wildly. "I'm not going to die like a rat in a trap. Let me out. I've got money to spend, I tell you. I must get out."

Sir Felix Burdon, awakened by the noise, sprang to his feet. He was rather angry.

"Hold your row," he said. "D'you want to wake everybody? If you start that screaming again, I'll gag you."

Castle collapsed. He sat on the floor, with his head in his hands, rocking to and fro. "Give me a drink and I'll keep quiet," he said. "If I can't get out, give me a drink."

"Oh, go and get what you want," said Sir Felix, contemptuously.

Agravine, who had lighted his candle, watched the scene with grave and dispassionate eyes.

Castle went off to the stores. They could hear him moving about there. Presently he returned with a cup and a bottle of whisky. His exceedingly elaborate knife contained a corkscrew amongst other implements, and he drew the cork.

"Why don't you all join me?" he asked. "Best thing you can do."

The other men refused, as briefly as possible. Castle poured the whisky into the cup and began sipping it.

"This is doing me good," he said. "I was suffering from chill. That is what it was. Might happen to anybody. This is the finest thing on earth, taken medicinally."

Nobody paid any attention to him. For half an hour he went on sipping steadily, then he drove the cork into the bottle with one blow of his fist, and flung himself at full length on the sand again. A moment later he was snoring. Sir Felix and Mr. Agravine were both awake now. They glanced at him and their eyes met.

"Yes," said Agravine. "I'm afraid he's a skunk. He was all right in the hotel and all right on the boat. But this experience has tried him a little too high. What ought we to do?"

Sir Felix shrugged his shoulders. "I don't see that we can do anything. It's only a short time now, anyhow. I don't know if it's my fancy, but the air here seems to me to be worse and closer already. If he wants to die like a hog, he must. Of course, if he gets noisy, we shall have to take some measures, but as long as the stuff makes him sleep—well, he's best asleep."

And then for a while they dozed fitfully. At seven o'clock they could hear sounds of movement at the farther end of the tomb, and then Zoe Averil appeared at the entrance of the hall. She wore a long native robe of dark blue.

"We're making some tea," she said. "Shall I bring you some?"

"That would be very kind of you," said Sir Felix. "I hope you've slept."

"I slept very well indeed. I had a little room all by myself. But I think the other two did not sleep so well. Miss Gilderay looks very tired and worn out."

Miss Gilderay and Mrs. Langley brought in the tea, but waited only for a moment and then went back to their own quarters. Hot tea, a wash in cold water, and a change of clothing refreshed the two men. They sat up and talked in low voices, while Castle still lay and snored.

"An experience like this," said Agravine, "makes one realize what an absolutely fantastic and foolish thing property is. One begins to wonder why one ever attached any importance to it. As you know, I simply gave up my life to the acquisition of one form of property—beautiful things—pictures. How absolutely absurd! Nothing of it is any good to me now, and I cannot take it along with me. Here in this small, imprisoned society for a few hours we lose the sense of property altogether. I am wearing one of your shirts, Sir Felix. It doesn't seem to me to matter in the least whose shirt it is. I really hardly thanked you. Community of goods becomes quite easy when one knows that one will soon be dead. And," he added sardonically, "becomes still easier when one man in the society finds all the goods, and the rest simply do the communing."

Sir Felix laughed. He pointed with his foot to the prostrate Castle. "Shall we wake the beggar," he said, "and let him clean himself up a bit?"

"No," said Agravine. "The longer he sleeps, the better his nerves will be when he wakes."

An hour later Castle awoke of his own accord. He certainly did seem very much better. He was ashamed of himself and apologetic.

"Afraid I kicked up rather a row last night. Sorry. I suppose my nerves gave way. I shall be all right now that I have had a sleep."

"Oh, yes," said Sir Felix, kindly. "You'll be all right. You've missed some very good tea by your slumbers. I dare say they'll make some more for you."

"Thanks," said Castle. "I don't want to trouble them. I'll wait till they join us."

Meanwhile he proceeded with his toilet, and accomplished the rather difficult task of cutting himself with a safety razor. Of his own accord he washed the cups which had been used, and took them and the whisky bottle back to the storeroom. There he found Zoe Averil and Miss Gilderay, and remained talking with them for a little time. Presently the whole party gathered together again round the trestle-table in the entrance-hall of the tomb.

The table was laid just as neatly and carefully as if it had really mattered. The women had seen to that. Zoe Averil still wore the native robe, the other two were in their ordinary clothes.

Castle was quite good-humoured at lunch and very talkative; it was fairly obvious that he was drinking too much. Suddenly Miss Gilderay, who sat next to him, said, in a low voice, "I used to do that, too."

"Do what?"

"I'll tell you." She raised her voice and addressed the others. "I was just saying to Mr. Castle that I, too, have a confession which I might make. It does not seem to be fair that you, Sir Felix, and you, Mr. Castle, should tell the worst of yourselves, and that I should still let you believe the best of me."

"I don't want you to suppose," said Sir Felix, "that there's the slightest compulsion upon you to say even one word. You mustn't feel bound to disclose anything."

"Down here, so near the end, disclosure is really very easy. You see, it does not matter any more. I shall not be mixing with other people. I have not got to pretend that I am almost without fault.

The only thing I am afraid of is that you will laugh at me, or want to laugh at me. I've got no illusions about myself. I know that I am not pretty and never have been pretty. I am elderly, and it must seem absurd for me to speak of romance and love."

"I feel sure," said Mr. Agravine, "that we shall not want to laugh at you. No one ever wants to laugh at anything which is quite genuine."

"Hear, hear," said Castle, rapping noisily on the table.

Miss Gilderay moistened her lips with the tip of her tongue, looked at them unflinchingly, and began to speak.

"My father was the vicar of a London church which was in its way rather celebrated. The music was very good. The ritual was very ornate, and the sermons were very short. My father was a good musician and a very fair man of the world. He understood business thoroughly, and the greater part of his income was derived from careful speculations. There was a stockbroker in his congregation, an old man called Baldwin, who thought very highly of my father—as, indeed, most people did—and he used to advise him. My father was very careful that the world in general should know nothing of these business transactions, but to me he always defended them. He said that there were many calls upon his charity, and that one could only give in proportion to one's income. If he made money in Steel Commons, then he had the more to give away. He reminded me that some of the apostles themselves got their living as fishermen. It did not seem to me the same thing at all, but I did not criticize him. I was too fond of him to be critical.

"I used to help my father a good deal, doing all his secretarial work for him. I would type out his sermon and his instructions to his broker all in the same morning.

"The choir of the church was for the most part paid, and paid by my father out of his own pocket. He said it was almost impossible to get good music except from professionals. But one day he came to me in a state of great delight. He had found a new and admirable singer, a tenor, who was willing to give his services for nothing. 'He's a gentleman,' said my father, and paused. 'Or almost,' he added. I laughed, and told him that I knew that kind.

"When I saw the new tenor—Henderson his name was—I still felt that I knew that kind. He had good looks of rather a common description. His eyes were too small, his face too fat. He was slightly under the average height, I should say. I was quite prepared to take no interest him whatever.

"And then I heard him sing, and forgot the man in the voice. He had a real tenor, and his singing was perfectly true. Somehow it was impossible to hear it without believing that behind that voice there was a beautiful and noble temperament. As a matter of fact, I know now that this is one of the commonest of illusions. Music has its special beauty, which is quite isolated. It does not imply any other beauty of any kind.

"But that was ten years ago. Every Sunday I heard that man sing. I do not think now that I fell in love with the man, but I fell in love with the voice, and began to make inquiries about him, and found nothing very romantic. He was employed in an insurance office and was doing very well. He was unmarried and lived with his two sisters. One Sunday night he had been taking the solo part in the anthem, and I suppose that I was more than usually impressed. At any rate, when I got home I wrote a foolish letter and sent it to him.

"It was my belief that I had not committed myself in any way. I had given no address and put no signature. In case my hand-writing should be recognized I had typed the letter.

"Some weeks later my father thought he should take some notice of this Mr. Henderson, and told me to ask him to dinner. He came, and every minute I liked him less and less. In the drawing-room afterwards he got a chance to speak with me apart.

"'You do all your fathers typing for him, don't you?' he said.

"I assented. I had typed lists and notices for the use of the choir, which, of course, he would have seen.

"'You ought to have a new letter "f" put on that machine,' he said. 'The top of it's got broken off. I notice these little things. I have noticed that broken "f" in everything that you have typed.'

"I did not lose my head. I said it was very likely, that the machine was always open, and that it was my belief that one of the housemaids used it to type her love-letters on. I said that I would have the 'F' key put right, but that I could not make out how on earth he came to have noticed it. This was as good as I could do, but it did not deceive him, and I saw that it had not deceived him. Before the evening was over I hated him far more than I had ever loved him.

"I spent a sleepless night in an agony of humiliation, and next day I was tortured with neuralgia. That was the beginning of it. To relieve the pain of the neuralgia, for the first time in my life I drank wine."

"Look here, Miss Gilderay," said Sir Felix, "we quite understand. You need not tell us the rest of it."

Miss Gilderay smiled mournfully. "I am not going to tell you the whole story. It is quite loathsome. I do not think I could do it. It is the story of endless effort and endless failure. The thing became public at last, and my father had to leave that parish. He died a few months afterwards, and I suppose his death saved me. At any rate, I have been able to do the most difficult thing of all. I am not what I once was, neither am I an abstainer. I drank a glass of wine at lunch just now. I shall drink another at dinner. But don't imagine that I am proud of my victory over myself. I could not be that, knowing as I do at what cost it was bought. Nor can it ever blot out of my mind the shame of so much previous defeat. I have spoken of it with a reason, though."

She looked full at Mr. Castle. "All right, all right," he said impatiently. "All these things have a physiological explanation."

"Yes," said Mr. Agravine. "And what explains the physiology?"

Mr. Castle glared and said nothing. Zoe Averil changed her place and now sat next to Miss Gilderay.

"It always seemed to me a pity," Mr. Agravine continued, "that any convention which is entirely false should be generally accepted. That is the case of the convention that divides people into saints and sinners. There are no saints, and in a sense there are no sinners. We are human beings, defective, but with some goodness. If we could only get that to be recognized, if that were the general opinion of society, society would be all the better for it."

"I've often thought," Sir Felix said, "that the case is very hard of a man who goes to prison once. What happens to him when he comes out? By most people he is not forgiven, and in the other cases forgiveness is patronage. Both are as bad as can be. And yet I don't see what other line is to be taken. To treat crime solely as disease is more amiable than practical."

"I have no panacea," said Mr. Agravine. "I can't make a new heaven and a new earth. But in my time I have often wished I could make a new earth."

"The fact of the case is," said Mrs. Langley, "that one can't make any general rules at all. We can only deal with special cases as they arrive as intelligently and as humanely as possible."

"I see," said Mr. Castle, "that you take a very superior standpoint, Mrs. Langley. You pose as a righteous person, who is to do her best for people like—well, like Miss Gilderay and myself."

"I do not pose at all," said Mrs. Langley. "I was not thinking of how I should judge, but of how I should wish to be judged. If you want to know, I have already made my confession. Miss Gilderay has been a friend of mine for three years past. Last night I told her something that I had never told her or anybody else before. I am not going to tell you any more now, except that some time after my marriage I went through a week of madness. My punishment has been that I have had to be a coward, that I have had to join in the general combination against more than one woman, though I knew that they were little if at all more guilty than myself. You have made me face this shame before you men. Now are you content?"

"You know perfectly well that I had intended nothing of the kind."

He moved away from the table, and sat in the farthest corner of the hall with his back to the others. Presently he took a cigarette from his case and lit it.

"I say," said Sir Felix. "Just put that down, will you, and stick your heel on it."

Mr. Castle scowled, but did as he was told. The others rose and began to clear away the things on the table.

IV

The Confession of Mr. Agravine and the Story of Miss Averil:
And So to a Conclusion

The three women spent most of the afternoon in their own quarters. In the hall Mr. Agravine, with his pocket-knife in his hands, sat and carved a peach stone; he was astonishingly clever at work of that kind. Sir Felix wrote with the writing-block on his knee. If, as seemed likely, their bodies were ultimately dug out, he wished to leave behind him some instructions with reference to his property, and also with reference to the excavation work which he had in hand. Castle did nothing but sit in sulky silence.

At five o'clock Sir Felix looked at his watch. "Agravine," he said, "we've been shut up now for twenty-six hours. What d'you think of it?"

"I think another twenty-two hours will see the end of it. Before that time we shall have to light the charcoal stove and finish quickly. Have you got it ready?"

"Not yet. Come along to the store-room, and I'll show you how the thing works."

Castle followed the two men and stood watching them, his hands in his pockets. Once or twice he asked a brief question. The visit to the storeroom gave him an opportunity to resume possession of the whisky bottle. Before dinner-time he had finished it. The other two men remonstrated with him, but he said gloomily that a man condemned to death had the right to eat and drink what he liked. He refused to join the others at dinner.

In truth dinner had become a farce. Confinement and oppressive air had destroyed the appetite of all of them. Even their conversation was at first quite without animation. But presently Miss Gilderay said:

"Do you know what Zoe Averil has been telling us this afternoon? She says that she hears somebody coming."

"Don't laugh at me," said Zoe Averil. "I'm quite sure."

Sir Felix looked across at Mr. Agravine. Were they all of them going mad, then?

"I don't see the possibility of it," said Sir Felix.

Suddenly from his corner Mr. Castle burst into a loud laugh. "What else did you expect?" he shouted. "It is the high priest come back to see the Christians who have defiled his tomb, and to watch their last agony."

"I think," said Mr. Agravine, "that you would do better to be quiet, Mr. Castle."

Castle growled that in future he would do what he liked.

"The question rather is," said Miss Gilderay, "if we want anybody to come—I mean, if we want to be rescued. I don't think I do particularly. Life does not hold very much for a plain and unmarried woman of my age, and yet—"

"Yes," said Mrs. Langley, "and yet. I know what you mean. Instinct is too strong for us. We thought we were sick of the world, but we would both go back to it if we could."

"I also," said Sir Felix.

"Not me," shouted Castle. "Not me. I would go back alone, but not with the rest of you. You all know too much. One would never be safe. At least, you think you know too much. That story I told you was make-up, to draw you all on. Idiots! Fools!"

Sir Felix stood up. "Get out of this, Mr. Castle. We cannot have you with us."

Castle did not move till Sir Felix was quite near him. Then he rose and lurched out of the hall and down the passage, flinging himself into one of the chambers at the side.

They went back to the point at which he had interrupted them. "Personally," said Mr. Agravine, "I think I should be contented either way. The effect of being buried alive for a few hours has been to show me that the whole of my life has been a mistake. I have been a collector, as you know. True, I have collected beautiful things. That makes no difference. Property has been my master. Property has made me do base and degrading things. Of one thing I am certain. If by any chance Miss Averil were right, and we were rescued, I would change my way of life. My pictures should go to the nation. I would be the slave of property no longer."

"I don't think I quite understand," said Mrs. Langley, "what you mean by that."

"I will tell you. It can hardly be called a confession. It is really too paltry for that. I was hypnotized, fascinated, by the collector's mania, and that drove me into stupidities."

"Still," said Mrs. Langley, "tell us. It will make the time pass."

"I suppose," said Mr. Agravine, "that it is not the love of beautiful things which degrades. I hope not, for I have always had that love. Degradation comes, not from love, but from possession, and that applies to more things than pictures. Until quite recently I was not a wealthy man. All that I could possibly spare was spent in the acquisition of what might be called stagnant capital. The possession of a thousand-pound picture costs a man forty pounds a year, whether he knows it or whether he does not. I was frequently hard pressed for money. I was frequently tortured by being compelled to relinquish some purchase on which I had set my heart.

"Such things do one no good. Again, I have not been a picture-dealer in the accepted sense of the word, but I have often sold one beautiful thing in order to acquire something which I thought more beautiful. I made the greatest profit that I possibly could. I brought commerce very near to a swindle. One instance particularly lingers in my memory. It was a thing which I did quite deliberately, and it now seems to me both cruel and absurd to have done it. A friend of mine told me that he knew an old Frenchman living at Eastbourne who wished to dispose of a picture. He knew nothing of its history, but believed it to be good. He wanted an expert opinion upon it, and I was an expert. To oblige my friend I went down to Eastbourne one Saturday to see this Frenchman—Janvier his name was. Janvier was a bachelor living in a small house, with just sufficient income of his own. In all matters of art I soon found that he was absolutely ignorant, but none the less he had from time to time bought pictures, some twenty of them. He brought out his great prize, the picture which he believed to be good, and I was able to tell him at once whereabouts in the National Gallery he would be able to find the original of which it was rather a poor copy. But among the twenty there was one other picture which I saw at once I should have to buy. I asked him about it. 'It was sold me,' he said-he spoke admirable English—'as being, in all probability, by Corot.'

"I laughed, and told him that a great many pictures were sold in that way, and that if Corot had lived to a hundred years and painted every minute of his time he could not have covered all the canvases that have since been assigned to him. All the same, that picture was a genuine and very fine Corot, and I knew it.

"'I gave ten pounds for it,' said Janvier, 'and I would not take less than twenty.'

"I told him that a hundred per cent, seemed rather a large profit to expect, but after a certain amount of grumbling I wrote him a cheque for twenty and took the picture back to town with me. It is one of the best things in my collection and it is worth a very large sum, and I am heartily ashamed of it."

"But," said Miss Gilderay, "is there, after all, any-thing dishonest about it? If the people who are ignorant try to do business with the people who are expert, has not the expert got the right to profit by it?"

"It ought not to mean that he should buy a fine Corot for twenty pounds. Do you still hear someone coming, Miss Averil? For I assure you that if we are ever released Janvier shall have his picture back."

"Well," said Sir Felix, "we have all told our stories now except Miss Averil. And she is too young to have any story to tell."

"I have done good things and bad things, but nothing very good or very bad," said Zoe.

"And yet," said Sir Felix, "you said you were not sorry that this had happened, and that your life was to come to an end."

"That is true. But it is the future, and not the past, from which I was eager to escape. I will tell you just a little thing, a scrap of family history. My parents died when I was a child, and one of my earliest recollections is that I was rather proud of my hair, because an artist had admired it and had asked to paint me, and that my mother told me not to be proud of it, and that if I knew it would be a cause of grief to me. I did not know. She was speaking of a tradition which had been in our family for six generations. It was only a year ago that in some papers of my father's I came upon the story. From time to time during the last six generations a girl had been born in the Averil family with hair like mine, and in every case she had come to disaster. In most of the cases recorded she had died insane. During their lifetime my father and mother had said nothing of this to me, and I believed that, if my father had not died so suddenly, he would have destroyed those papers, in order to spare me. Ever since I read them I have been haunted. For it is true that I am not quite normal. Every now and then, not at my own wish, and often to no serious purpose, I have had what Mrs. Langley calls that special sense. I have seen things that were happening far away. It's a pity, because I love life."

"And if we are rescued?" said Mr. Agravine.

"What is to be is to be. If I had meant to take my life, I should have done so a year ago. If I am rescued, I shall go back and meet whatever fate has got for me. And I think we shall be rescued, for now I hear far more distinctly the sound of people coming. Listen! Can you not all hear it?"

For a moment all held their breath. There was a tense, deep silence. And then suddenly Mr. Agravine rose and put his ear to the wall.

"It is so," he said. "Come here, Burdon, and listen."

Sir Felix listened for a moment.

"There can be no mistake about it. That is the sound of picks. There are many of them at work. In a few hours now they should get through to us."

"Wouldn't it be a good thing if I went and told Mr. Castle?" said Zoe Averil. "I think it was he who most wanted to get back to the world again."

"No," said Sir Felix. "Don't do that. I will go and tell him myself."

He went, and in a few moments returned. He said nothing until Miss Gilderay questioned him.

"Yes," he said. "I've told him."

"Hasn't that made any difference?" asked Mrs. Langley. "What did he say?"

"He says that the spirit of the high priest is in him, and that this is his tomb. Nothing else. Mad, of course. But he is perfectly quiet. He will probably recover when he gets out of this."

The women had a feeling that their rescuers should find them ready, and that everything should be in order. Helped by Sir Felix and Mr. Agravine, they cleared the table out of the hall altogether. In the chamber where he lay, they could hear Mr. Castle breathing heavily, as though asleep.

About an hour later, as Sir Felix and Mr. Agravine sat listening to the sound of the picks, the women entered. Mrs. Langley was drawing on her gloves and carried her camera. Zoe had changed into her own clothes again. Miss Gilderay had rearranged her hair. They were all quite ready.

"This is good of you," said Sir Felix. "It will be much pleasanter if we five all wait together. There is only another hour or two now. Listen!"

They could hear the blows of the picks. They sat down, and for a time talked a little, wondering who had organized the rescue and how it had been accomplished. And presently, because the air was very heavy and they had been short of sleep the night before, and a great strain had been taken off their minds, they became drowsy.

"I believe I'm going to sleep," said Miss Gilderay, leaning back in her deck-chair,

"I too," said Sir Felix. "Why not? It will help to pass the time of waiting."

Soon they were so soundly asleep that they did not hear the stealthy footsteps from the adjoining chamber.

Silent and barefooted, carrying the glowing charcoal stove in his hands, Castle crept into the store-room. With deep breaths he drew in the poison. He turned to tear down the curtain that filled the entrance to the room, in order that the fumes might spread and all might die together. But before he could reach it he swayed and fell, and lay motionless.

And now the picks broke down into the entrance-hall of the tomb. Through the opening streamed in a glorious sunlight that made the candle flames pale, and fresh, untainted air. And with these came fresh life and fresh courage to face it—for all, save that dead boy lying behind the curtain by the charcoal stove.

THE UNKNOWN GOD

The air of the primitive and remote island was soft and languorous. Its population consisted of a man and woman, brown-skinned, and without any of the blessings of education and religion. This afternoon the population had been bathing, and now lay on the sand in the sun.

"Presently," said the man, "we will go and look at the boat which has drifted ashore."

"Presently," said the girl, lazily. "It is a good boat."

"Very good boat," echoed the man. "It will be useful to us." And immediately he fell asleep.

In a moment or two the girl awakened him. She was in a philosophical humour, and there is not much fun in being philosophical all by yourself.

"Are you happy?" she asked.

"I do not know," said the man. "I have never thought about it."

"Then you are happy," she said with decision. "People who think about it are not. I, for example, am not."

"If we now roused ourselves a little and caught a few fish—"

"No," said the girl, decisively, "I wish to talk."

The man sighed.

"Do you not know what it is to wish to be taken out of yourself, and to become somebody else—to be full of inspiration from the gods? These days and nights that are always the same are becoming a burden to me. I want to be different for a little while."

"It is not possible," said the man. "There are gods undoubt-edly. It was always the opinion of our forefathers that there were gods, but the gods never interfere with us and we cannot get at them. Therefore they do not concern us, and it is much better to catch a few fish."

The girl, looking as if she might burst into tears at any moment, said that she hated fish, and that she hated her island, and that she hated herself.

"I wish to meet with one of the gods," she said. "I wish to talk with someone who is more than mortal. Tell me what the gods look like."

"As to that," said the man, "more than one opinion has been expressed. There are some who say that the gods are like big men, taller than the palm trees, of gigantic strength. There are others who say that the gods cannot be seen, and that it is only by their influence within us that they may be recognized. To talk of things which we do not know is very foolish. If you will not catch fish, let us go and look at the boat."

The woman arose rather sullenly, and followed him.

They found in the boat a tin containing biscuits. They had never seen biscuits before, but a little investigation showed them the use to which they should be put. They bored holes in them and hung them round their necks.

They found, moreover, a large square bottle, containing a colourless fluid. The girl removed the cork, dipped her finger in the fluid, and touched her tongue.

"Of what does it taste?" asked the man, anxiously.

"Of fire and sleep and sin," answered the girl.

"In that case," said the man, "I will go and fetch our drinking-cups."

The drinking-cups were two halves of the shell of a cocoanut, smooth and polished by much use. The man filled them, and they drank in slow sips. A drink which tastes of fire and sleep and sin cannot be taken hastily. As she filled their cups for the second time, the girl observed that she believed there was a god in that bottle.

Next morning the girl awoke and zigzagged from the point where she had fallen down the beach to the sea. She kept her head under water for the longest possible time. Then she rose to the surface and swam slowly and lazily. Presently the man's head shot up by her side. He also had been down below.

"There can be no doubt about it at all," said the girl. "We have found the unknown god, and by his influence within us he may be recognized."

"I do not feel at all good this morning," said the man.

"Nor I," said the girl. "But last night was magnificent. Never have I danced so long and so wildly. Never have I laughed so much."

"I had an impression," said the man, as he swam by her side, "that I was being unusually witty."

"No," said the girl, "I do not think it was that. Everything was amusing. I laughed at the sea, I laughed at the boat, I laughed at the trees. You also laughed."

"I remember it," said the man. "The entire world had suddenly become ridiculous. But this morning I do not feel at all good." He dived under a wave with the girl after him, and presently they lay side by side on the sand.

"It is about this time in the morning," said the girl, "that we generally catch fish for our breakfast, but to-day I do not wish to catch fish for my breakfast, and I think I do not wish to eat anything more as long as I live."

"I have the same feeling," said the man. "Why then should this be if indeed it was a god that we found in the boat?"

"Because," said the girl, "if with great force you pull the bough of a tree in one direction and then let go, it will swing with great force in the other direction. Because last night we were exalted, therefore this morning we are abased. I am willing. I pay the price. Why do you get up? Where are you going?"

"I am going," said the man, "to see if by any chance there is still left in the bottle a little of that drink which tastes of fire and sleep and sin."

"Lie down again," said the girl. "There is not any left. I have looked into the matter myself."

Two days later the man and the girl built up a rough altar of white stones on the beach, and on the top of the altar they placed the bottle in which the god had lived. The perfume of his presence was still there. The man thinks now that the girl spends too much time in the contemplation of it. And what will happen when the missionaries land?

ROSE ROSE

Sefton stepped back from his picture. "Rest now, please," he said.

Miss Rose Rose, his model, threw the striped blanket around her, stepped down from the throne, and crossed the studio. She seated herself on the floor near the big stove. For a few moments Sefton stood motionless, looking critically at his work. Then he laid down his palette and brushes and began to roll a cigarette. He was a man of forty, thick-set, round-faced, with a reddish moustache turned fiercely upwards. He flung himself down in an easy-chair, and smoked in silence till silence seemed ungracious.

"Well," he said, "I've got the place hot enough for you to-day, Miss Rose."

"You 'ave indeed," said Miss Rose.

"I bet it's nearer eighty than seventy."

The cigarette-smoke made a blue haze in the hot, heavy air. He watched it undulating, curving, melting.

As he watched it Miss Rose continued her observations. The trouble with these studios was the draughts. With a strong east wind, same as yesterday, you might have the stove red-hot, and yet never get the place, so to speak, warm. It is possible to talk commonly without talking like a coster, and Miss Rose achieved it. She did not always neglect the aspirate. She never quite substituted the third vowel for the first. She rather enjoyed long words.

She was beautiful from the crown of her head to the sole of her foot; and few models have good feet. Every pose she took was graceful. She was the daughter of a model, and had been herself a model

184

from childhood. In consequence, she knew her work well and did it well. On one occasion, when sitting for the great Merion, she had kept the same pose, without a rest, for three consecutive hours. She was proud of that. Naturally she stood in the first rank among models, was most in demand, and made the most money. Her fault was that she was slightly capricious; you could not absolutely depend upon her. On a wintry morning, when every hour of daylight was precious, she might keep her appointment, she might be an hour or two late, or she might stay away altogether. Merion himself had suffered from her, had sworn never to employ her again, and had gone back to her.

Sefton, as he watched the blue smoke, found that her common accent jarred on him. It even seemed to make it more difficult for him to get the right presentation of the "Aphrodite" that she was helping him to paint. One seemed to demand a poetical and cultured soul in so beautiful a body. Rose Rose was not poetical nor cultured; she was not even business-like and educated.

Half an hour of silent and strenuous work followed. Then Sefton growled that he could not see any longer.

"We'll stop for to-day," he said. Miss Rose Rose retired behind the screen. Sefton opened a window and both ventilators, and rolled another cigarette. The studio became rapidly cooler.

"To-morrow, at nine?" he called out.

"I've got some way to come," came the voice of Miss Rose from behind the screen. "I could be here by a quarter past."

"Right," said Sefton, as he slipped on his coat.

When Rose Rose emerged from the screen she was dressed in a blue serge costume, with a picture-hat. As it was her business in life to be beautiful, she never wore corsets, high heels, nor pointed toes. Such abnegation is rare among models.

"I say, Mr. Sefton," said Rose, "you were to settle at the end of the sittings, but—"

"Oh, you don't want any money, Miss Rose. You're known to be rich."

"Well, what I've got is in the Post Office, and I don't want to touch it. And I've got some shopping I must do before I go home."

Sefton pulled out his sovereign-case hesitatingly.

"This is all very well, you know," he said.

"I know what you are thinking, Mr. Sefton. You think I don't mean to come to-morrow. That's all Mr. Merion, now, isn't it? He's always saying things about me. I'm not going to stick it. I'm going to 'ave it out with 'im."

"He recommended you to me. And I'll tell you what he said, if you won't repeat it. He said that I should be lucky if I got you, and that I'd better chain you to the studio."

"And all because I was once late—with a good reason for it, too. Besides, what's once? I suppose he didn't 'appen to tell you how often he's kept me waiting."

"Well, here you are, Miss Rose. But you'll really be here in time to-morrow, won't you? Otherwise the thing will have got too tacky to work into."

"You needn't worry about that," said Miss Rose, eagerly. "I'll be here, whatever happens, by a quarter past nine. I'll be here if I die first! There, is that good enough for you? Good afternoon, and thank you, Mr. Sefton."

"Good afternoon, Miss Rose. Let me manage that door for you— the key goes a bit stiffly."

Sefton came back to his picture. In spite of Miss Rose's vehement assurances he felt by no means sure of her, but it was difficult for him to refuse any woman anything, and impossible for him to refuse to pay her what he really owed. He scrawled in charcoal some directions to the charwoman who would come in the morning. She was, from his point of view, a prize charwoman—one who could, and did, wash brushes properly, one who understood the stove, and would, when required, refrain from sweeping. He picked up his hat and went out. He walked the short distance from his studio to his bachelor flat, looked over an evening paper as he drank his tea, and then changed his clothes and took a cab to the club for dinner. He played one game of billiards after dinner, and then went home. His picture was very much in his mind. He wanted to be up fairly early in the morning, and he went to bed early.

He was at his studio by half-past eight. The stove was lighted, and he piled more coke on it. His "Aphrodite" seemed to have a somewhat mocking expression. It was a little, technical thing, to be corrected easily. He set his palette and selected his brushes. An attempt to roll a cigarette revealed the fact that his pouch was empty. It still wanted a few minutes to nine. He would have time to go up to the tobacconist at the corner. In case Rose Rose arrived while he was away, he left the studio door open. The tobacconist was also a newsagent, and he bought a morning paper. Rose would probably be twenty minutes late at the least, and this would be something to occupy him.

But on his return he found his model already stepping on to the throne.

"Good-morning, Miss Rose. You're a lady of your word." He hardly heeded the murmur which came to him as a reply. He threw his cigarette into the stove, picked up his palette, and got on excellently. The work was absorbing. For some time he thought of nothing else. There was no relaxing on the part of the model—no sign of fatigue. He had been working for over an hour, when his conscience smote him. "We'll have a rest now, Miss Rose," he said cheerily. At the same moment he felt human fingers drawn lightly across the back of his neck, just above the collar. He turned round with a sudden start. There was nobody there. He turned back again to the throne. Rose Rose had vanished.

With the utmost care and deliberation he put down his palette and brushes. He said in a loud voice, "Where are you, Miss Rose?" For a moment or two silence hung in the hot air of the studio.

He repeated his question and got no answer. Then he stepped behind the screen, and suddenly the most terrible thing in his life happened to him. He knew that his model had never been there at all.

There was only one door out to the back street in which his studio was placed, and that door was now locked. He unlocked it, put on his hat, and went out. For a minute or two he paced the street, but he had got to go back to the studio.

He went back, sat down in the easy-chair, lit a cigarette, and tried for a plausible explanation. Undoubtedly he had been working very hard lately. When he had come back from the tobacconist's to the studio he had been in the state of expectant attention, and he was enough of a psychologist to know that in that state you are especially likely to see what you expect to see. He was not conscious of anything abnormal in himself. He did not feel ill, or even nervous.

Nothing of the kind had ever happened to him before. The more he considered the matter, the more definite became his state. He was thoroughly frightened. With a great effort he pulled himself together and picked up the newspaper. It was certain that he could do no more work for that day, anyhow. An ordinary, commonplace newspaper would restore him. Yes, that was it. He had been too much wrapped up in the picture. He had simply supposed the model to be there.

He was quite unconvinced, of course, and merely trying to convince himself. As an artist, he knew that for the last hour or more he had been getting the most delicate modelling right from the living form before him. But he did his best, and read the newspaper assiduously. He read of tariff, protection, and of a new music-hall star. Then his eye fell on a paragraph headed "Motor Fatalities."

He read that Miss Rose, an artist's model, had been knocked down by a car in the Fulham Road about seven o'clock on the previous evening; that the owner of the car had stopped and taken her to the hospital, and that she had expired within a few minutes of admission.

He rose from his place and opened a large pocket-knife. There was a strong impulse upon him, and he felt it to be a mad impulse, to slash the canvas to rags. He stopped before the picture. The face smiled at him with a sweetness that was scarcely earthly.

He went back to his chair again. "I'm not used to this kind of thing," he said aloud. A board creaked at the far end of the studio. He jumped up with a start of horror. A few minutes later he had left the studio, and locked the door behind him. His common sense was still with him. He ought to go to a specialist. But the picture—

"What's the matter with Sefton?" said Devigne one night at the club after dinner.

"Don't know that anything's the matter with him," said Merion. "He hasn't been here lately."

"I saw him the last time he was here, and he seemed pretty queer. Wanted to let me his studio."

"It's not a bad studio," said Merion, dispassionately.

"He's got rid of it now, anyhow. He's got a studio out at Richmond, and the deuce of a lot of time he must waste getting there and back. Besides, what does he do about models?"

"That's a point I've been wondering about myself," said Merion. "He'd got Rose Rose for his 'Aphrodite,' and it looked as if it might be a pretty good thing when I saw it. But, as you know, she died. She was troublesome in some ways, but, taking her all round, I don't know where to find anybody as good to-day. What's Sefton doing about it?"

"He hasn't got a model at all at present. I know that for a fact, because I asked him."

"Well," said Merion, "he may have got the thing on further than I thought he would in the time. Some chaps can work from memory all right, though I can't do it myself. He's not chucked the picture, I suppose?"

"No; he's not done that. In fact, the picture's his excuse now, if you want him to go anywhere and do anything. But that's not it: the chap's altogether changed. He used to be a genial sort of bounder—bit tyrannical in his manner, perhaps—thought he knew everything. Still, you could talk to him. He was sociable. As a matter of fact, he did know a good deal. Now it's quite different. If you ever do see him—and that's not often—he's got nothing to say to you. He's just going back to his work. That sort of thing."

"You're too imaginative," said Merion. "I never knew a man who varied less than Sefton. Give me his address, will you? I mean his studio. I'll go and look him up one morning. I should like to see how that 'Aphrodite's' getting on. I tell you it was promising; no nonsense about it."

One sunny morning Merion knocked at the door of the studio at Richmond. He heard the sound of footsteps crossing the studio, then Sefton's voice rang out.

"Who's there?"

"Merion. I've travelled miles to see the thing you call a picture."

"I've got a model."

"And what does that matter?" asked Merion.

"Well, I'd be awfully glad if you'd come back in an hour. We'd have lunch together somewhere."

"Right," said Merion, sardonically. "I'll come back in about seven million hours. Wait for me."

He went back to London and his own studio in a state of fury. Sefton had never been a man to pose. He had never put on side about his work. He was always willing to show it to old and intimate friends whose judgment he could trust; and now, when the oldest of his friends had travelled down to Richmond to see him, he was told to come back in an hour, and that they might then lunch together!

"This lets me out," said Merion, savagely.

But he always speaks well of Sefton nowadays. He maintains that Sefton's "Aphrodite" would have been a success anyhow. The suicide made a good deal of talk at the time, and a special attendant was necessary to regulate the crowds round it, when, as directed by his will, the picture was exhibited at the Royal Academy. He was found in his studio many hours after his death; and he had scrawled on a blank canvas, much as he left his directions to his charwoman: "I have finished it, but I can't stand any more."

LOCRIS OF THE TOWER

I

I am by profession an architect. For the last eight years I have practiced in my native town at Stannoke in Gloucestershire, at first in partnership with my father, and after his retirement alone and on my own account. The greater part of my boyhood was spent in Stannoke, and I have early recollections of the family solicitor, William Locris. Twenty years ago I used to see Locris in church every Sunday morning. He sat with his wife, a rather heavy and plethoric woman, in the pew just in front of our own, accompanied by their son, a boy of my own age. Locris cannot have been more than thirty-five then, and his hair had not yet begun to turn grey. He assisted in the collection of the offertory, and throughout the service maintained an air of decent interest. His son sometimes fell asleep in the sermon, and so did I. My father always did, and, I think, made a point of it, but Locris was always wakeful and quietly attentive. He had an office in the High Street and a villa outside the town—rather an abominable modern construction called "The Elms." He must have been fairly well off, for he had all the best of the business in Stannoke, but he was not reputed to be a rich man. He was regular in his attendance at business, and regular in taking walking exercise. He went away at the right time every year for his summer holiday at the seaside. If at that time, or indeed for many years afterwards, I had wished to express the quintessence of the commonplace, I should have described Locris.

I believe he was a fairly good, but not a brilliant, solicitor. He was honest and punctual and painstaking. He always discouraged litigation, and I owe him a debt of gratitude for having prevented my father from embarking on a very expensive and probably fruitless lawsuit.

I was quite a young man when Mrs. Locris died. I remember she was buried rather sumptuously, and that Locris and his son wore deep mourning for the prescribed time. I no longer saw him in church, for I had ceased to go to church, but I often saw him on his way there, carrying a prayer-book in his gloved hands. He wore black kid gloves, the most rancid form of gloves that has yet been devised. On week-days I used to see him on his way to the office with the same loathsome gloves, but with a copy of the *Times* newspaper in place of the prayer-book.

Later, I came upon him two or three times in the course of business. I am inclined to think the man happy who seldom requires the services of a solicitor, and that good fortune was mine. When he had any work to do for me, I always found him able and practical, and his charges were fair enough.

Five years ago, when I was nearly thirty, and Locris must have been quite fifty, he called on me one morning at my office. He gave me a commission that was quite worth having, but it was of an extraordinary character. Looking at him now closely, I saw something in his eyes which seemed rather to belie the dull and even tenor of his life. I accepted the commission without hesitation, because, although the work was of a kind that I had never done before, I knew where I could get good advice. I had only to run up to London and see my old father about it.

II

My father had lived for by far the greater part of his life in a provincial town, but he preferred London. As soon as circumstances made it reasonable for him to retire and to hand over the business to me, he took a flat in Jermyn Street and went to live there. He had many friends in London and was a member of two clubs. He was glad enough to be free of routine work, but he was still interested in his profession, and was always glad to help me where his greater experience was useful.

We lunched together at his club, and then, in a retired corner of the smoking-room, he asked me what the trouble was.

"Well," I said, "I don't know that I should call it trouble. It's rather a nice little commission. But before we start on that I'd like you to tell me all you can about old Locris."

"Old Locris? Oh, damn it, James, he's not so very old. He's younger than I am. I've only known him professionally. We never had any social relations. He's all right, quite a solid man, I should say."

"Yes, I know that. You wouldn't call him romantic?"

"No, not now. There was a story when he was very much younger, before he married. He wanted to marry Sir Luke Mallow's daughter—Grace her name was. She was a pretty girl, with a lot of golden hair, the kind that you read about in storybooks and never see in real life. They didn't think Locris was good enough, and I suppose from a social point of view they were right, though, for that matter, in spite of her beauty, it was not every man who would have married her. I wouldn't myself. The poor girl was short of one finger on her left hand. She smashed it up when she was a kid, and it had to be amputated."

"So she chucked Locris?"

"No. She did not. He and Sir Luke were fighting it out together, and if Sir Luke did not give way, I fancy Locris meant to run away with her. He is an obstinate chap. However, while they were disputing, Grace settled the question for them by dying quite suddenly—diphtheria, I believe. There was a lot of it about at the time. And within a month Locris was married—daughter of a poor parson and very appropriate. So it's Locris who has given you this commission, is it? Well, the money will be all right. He's never spent half his income. It's quite time he had a better house."

"And suppose I told you that Locris had gone mad?"

"Any man may. It's possible. In his case I should think it is extremely unlikely. Has he gone mad then?"

"Well, he says he has not. While he was talking to me he made his scheme seem perfectly reasonable, but if he is not mad, he is at any rate extremely eccentric."

"Oh, come, come," said my father impatiently. "Let's have it. What is it the man wants?"

"Locris has bought land on the east coast not far from Aldeburgh. He wishes to do there what the old Duke of Portland did before him."

"I see. Rooms underground."

"Yes. One biggish room, forty by thirty, and a smaller anteroom communicating with it. From the anteroom is to be a flight of steps up to the surface, and the entrance is to be masked by a small tower with two or three living rooms in it. Do you call that the project of a sane man?"

"If you wanted to do it yourself I should certainly say you were insane. But I do not think so in the case of Locris. It is not unnatural in a man of a certain history who has come to his time of life. After all, there are days that one does not wish to see. Speaking frankly, the idea has occurred to my own mind before now. I have never done it, and never shall do it. But it is by no means without its fascination."

"That is very much the way in which he put it. In a year's time he means to retire and to leave Stannoke. And during that year this house is to be got ready for him."

"Is the construction to be secret?"

"I asked him that. He said he should make no effort at secrecy, as such efforts always attracted too much attention. He says that people will find their own explanation—that he wants an inordinately big wine-cellar, or something of that kind. In any case, before the tower had been built three years, people would have forgotten that there is this big room below it. I gather that he has chosen rather a lonely spot where he won't be troubled by many callers."

"Did he tell you in so many words what his reason was—why he is doing this?"

"No. But he said it was a thing which he had had in his mind for very many years past, and that he was glad now to have the opportunity to carry the idea out. You see, he is quite alone in the world. His wife's dead, and his son's away."

"The son," said my father, meditatively. "What's the boy doing?"

"Professorship of Greek in an Australian university—I forget which. I don't know what they'll make of him out there. He was an appalling prig."

"Yes," said my father. "I remember him. He was very, very Oxford. Well now, it seems to me you've got nothing to do but to go ahead. Excavation's a much easier job now than it was twenty years ago. I can't go into it now, because I've promised to play bridge. But we will dine at my flat and spend the evening over the plans afterwards."

"Oh, thanks very much, dad, that will suit me admirably. Meanwhile, I will go and have a look at the winter show at the Academy. Oh, by the way, on that question of secrecy—he did say that he didn't want the thing talked about in Stannoke, said it would be unpleasant to be bothered with questions, and that clients would regard him as a lunatic and leave him, and that this would have a bad effect on the value of his practice when he came to sell it. I don't think that anybody but myself knows that he means to leave Stannoke. Down in Suffolk, though, there is to be no secret about the excavation."

On my way to the Academy I was greatly surprised to see Locris himself. He was coming out of a shop where they sell ecclesiastical furniture and vestments. He did not see me, but got into a cab and drove off. I wondered what he could be doing in a shop of that description, and reflected that it was quite possible that he intended to make some presentation to his parish church before leaving Stannoke.

III

During the next year I saw a good deal of Mr. Locris. He liked to be consulted about the details of the work which I had in hand, and he was not an unreasonable man; that is to say, he always gave me my own way in the end. His general principle seemed to be to spend as much money as possible on the underground rooms, and as little as possible on the tower, in which I presumed he would generally live. I did not ask him in so many words if there was any special purpose for which he needed these underground rooms. It might of course be an elderly man's weariness—the fact that, as my father put it, there were some days he did not wish to see, and another explanation also occurred to my mind.

I went up to "The Elms" one night to show Locris, at his own request, the estimates I had obtained for carrying out some elaborate metal-work. The servant, who showed me into the drawing-room, told me that Mr. Locris was in the laboratory. When he came in a minute or two later, I spoke to him chaffingly about this, and asked him if it was another new idea.

"Oh, no," said Locris. "Every man must have a hobby. The law is a very interesting profession, but it would interest me very much less if I did nothing else. I have been a student of chemistry for many years past in my leisure time."

"Going to invent a new poison?" I suggested.

"No," he said. "Something new, perhaps, but not a poison. Shall we get to business?"

In some ways Locris was a disappointment to me. He would not fit in at all with my preconceived idea of what a man should be like who builds himself an underground dwelling. I had to consult him about this time with reference to the renewal of the lease of my house. I wanted to get the renewal, and I did not want the rent to be put up. Locris managed it for me, showing tact and intelligence and all good business qualities in the negotiation. It was true that the law interested him. He would break off his examination of drawings of details for his new abode, in order to speak again of that lease. It contained one or two unusual clauses.

But at any rate I had this other possible explanation for his actions. He was keen on chemistry and was expecting to produce some new discovery. Inventors are jealous people. He might perhaps think himself safer if his laboratory were underground.

He showed himself to be a kindly man. This was particularly the case with regard to poor old Simpson, the verger at the church which Locris attended. Simpson was a man of well over sixty, and incapable of doing any hard work. Rheumatism had compelled him to give up the grave-digging many years before. He was an intermittent drunkard. He had long spells of total abstinence, interspersed with brief bursts of intoxication. As a rule he timed his breakdowns very carefully, so that they should not attract the attention of his employers. But on one occasion he had been found drunk in the churchyard, and he had now been guilty of a still more horrid delinquency. He had been found incapacitated by drink in the church itself, and had been promptly dismissed.

Locris was quite angry about it. He kept on repeating that Simpson was an old man and that there was no chance of his getting any other berth, and that it was a shameful thing to allow the one or two days when he had yielded to temptation to counterbalance his many years of faithful and effective service. It was plausible, but it did not prevail. Locris moved heaven and earth to get Simpson kept on, and Locris had a good deal of influence with the vicar. But the thing was too heinous, and the old man was turned out. It was expected, of course, that, as he had no one to support him, he would have to go to the workhouse. But Simpson did not go to the workhouse. He kept on his small cottage and worked in the scrap of garden which belonged to it. When questioned by the philanthropical or the curious, he maintained that he had private means. Most people guessed that Locris was allowing him a small pension.

In due course the work at Mangay near Aldeburgh was completed, and Locris sold his practice to a couple of young solicitors who were in partnership together. It was announced that he was about to leave Stannoke, and the vicar, in one of his sermons, made a very feeling and sympathetic reference to the impending departure. Locris found himself referred to as "one who has set such an excellent example, not only in the rectitude of his professional career and his private life, but also in his regular attendance at divine worship."

At the same time, the vicar did not know everything about Mr. Locris. He met me in the street one day and stopped me. "So sorry," he said, "you are to lose your friend, Mr. Locris. He tells me that he is going to live in the country."

"That is so, I believe."

"But he did not happen in his conversation with me to mention what part of the country."

"Oh," I said, "there's no secret about it, I believe. He's going to live in Suffolk."

I hurried on. Suffolk as a postal address is perhaps somewhat vague, but I do not like curious vicars. If Locris had meant to have told him everything, he would have done so himself.

IV

For three years I never saw Locris and had no news of him. For a provincial architect I was doing fairly well in my profession. I specialized in bungalows and small houses, and had as much work as I could do. My father thought that I should leave Stannoke and come to London, and I was not altogether averse to making the plunge; but still, the local connection meant a good deal to me, and I did not want to lose it. Life at Stannoke went on with its customary placidity. Market-day was the one day in the week when we all of us seemed to be alive. And Sunday was the one day in the week when we all of us seemed to be dead. On the other days we were in a condition of mild lethargy. In such a town very small things make a sensation. Sir Luke Mallow, son of the Sir Luke to whom my father referred, had an old cart-horse stolen from one of his fields. We talked about it for weeks, and our best policeman seemed practically to live on his bicycle. But neither he nor anybody else ever found the horse or the man who had stolen it. Then old Simpson sold his few sticks of furniture to a dealer one day, paid the three weeks' rent he still owed, and started off into the unknown. We talked a good deal about the fate of Simpson too. There were many theories, but alcohol and sudden death had their part in all of them. A week later, a touring company was unwise enough to visit Stannoke, and the sensation caused wiped out all recollections of Simpson.

And then a man, whose brother lived at Stannoke, decided to build himself a bungalow at Aldeburgh. I knew the brother, and I received the commission. I went down to Aldeburgh to spend some days over the business, and it occurred to me that I was within an easy drive of the tower where Locris lived. I managed to hire a dog-cart of sorts, and drove out there one afternoon.

I left my dog-cart at the one little inn in Mangay, and struck across the fields on foot towards the tower. I had mentioned at the inn that I was going to see Mr. Locris, and found that any interest which might have been taken in him, or his unusual dwelling, had entirely subsided.

"Nice old gentleman," said my landlord. "Wish I had his cellars. I could buy my winter coal in the summer then, and save a bit. There's a fine view, they say, from that tower of his. I suppose that's what he built it for."

"Do you see much of him?" I asked.

"Not to say much," the landlord admitted. "Sometimes when he's out for a walk he'll drop in here for a glass of bitter, but he's not been of late. He doesn't enjoy the best of health, they tell me, and—well, we're none of us so young as we were."

The tower had changed very little since I last saw it. As a piece of work I was not very proud of it. I could have made a good thing of it, but Locris had been very skimpy and ignoble about that tower. He would not let me have the materials I wanted. It seemed absurd enough too, when he was burying good black-and-white marble underground.

Greatly to my surprise the door of the tower was opened to me by old Simpson. He had resumed the suit of black broadcloth, with the bootlace neck-tie, which had been his official costume as verger. He must have recognized me, but he gave no sign of it. He waited there like a stone image for me to speak. I asked if Mr. Locris was in.

"He is, sir," said Simpson, severely. "Kindly wait where you are. I'll inquire if he can see you."

He returned in a moment with the announcement that Mr. Locris would be pleased to see me, and showed me into one of the small living-rooms, where Locris sat writing at a cheap American desk. I noticed at once that he had aged very much in these last few years. He was more bent. He seemed to have shrunken.

He rose as I entered, and shook hands with me.

"It is strange that you have come," he said. "I had just written to you."

He showed me a sealed letter addressed to myself, which was lying on the desk, but he did not give it to me.

"The fact of the case is," he said, "that my son being out of England, I have made you the executor of my will. It will give you very little trouble. I hope you will not refuse to act."

I answered, of course, that I was quite willing to undertake the work, and made the usual banal observation that I hoped the time was still far distant for it.

"I should not say that," said Locris. "I am not well. I am far from well. Dr. Hanneford from Aldeburgh is coming up to see me to-morrow morning. However, I do not want to bore you about my health. I should perhaps tell you that by my will I am leaving you my land here."

"You will pardon me," I said, "but I don't think you should do that. I hope you will reconsider it. You have a son, you know, and I believe you have not quarrelled with him."

"I am on perfectly good terms with my son. I have been in communication with him on this very matter. He is quite content that it should be so. You must remember that these three acres represent a very small portion of my property, and that he will have the rest." He paused and looked at me very intently, as if he were trying to read my thoughts. "Are you wondering," he said, "what you will do with a house like this?"

He had guessed my thoughts exactly, but I told him that the idea had not occurred to me.

"I ask," he said, "because you will not have the house. You will have the land, but not the house."

"I don't understand," I said.

"An explanation will be forthcoming. I may give it to you to-day perhaps—to-morrow perhaps—any day. If you have not received the explanation at the time of my death, it will be waiting for you in my writing. You will have the land, and you will not have the house."

At this moment Simpson brought in some very strong and bitter tea, and some untidy bread and butter. These are not things that I love precisely, but I partook of them meekly. I asked the old man if he found Simpson a useful servant.

"Simpson has been invaluable to me. From the domestic point of view he is perhaps the worst servant that ever existed, but that is a matter of comparatively little importance. I am not a very particular man. Almost anything does. Nowadays I live principally on tea, and I fancy it is not very good tea, is it?"

"Since you ask me, it is a very low grade of Indian tea, and I should imagine that the continued consumption of it might have something to do with the ill-health of which you complain. Really, Mr. Locris, I think you ought to get yourself looked after better."

"I have thought so myself," said Locris, sadly, "Something perhaps must be done. But in any case I must keep Simpson, because he is a faithful man and holds his tongue. You see? He goes down below with me, and he comes up with me, and he does what he is told, and no one hears anything about it. I am never bothered."

I could not quite make out to what he was referring. I suppose I looked puzzled.

"Yes," said Locris, suddenly. "Why not? Better perhaps on the whole. You shall have your explanation now. You shall come down with me."

I consented at once. I was human enough to be rather curious as to the use to which he had put these underground rooms.

He rang the bell, and told Simpson to bring the lanterns. They were just ordinary candle lanterns of japanned tin. The spiral staircase which went up to the top of the tower also descended below the surface to the underground rooms. They were not very far down, the roof of them being twenty feet below the surface. We went through the iron gate and down the stairs together. Old Simpson went first with a lantern, and I followed him. Behind me came Locris with the other lantern.

The aspect of the anteroom seemed to show me that my con-
jecture had been right. It was fitted as a laboratory and looked as
if it had been in recent use. Locris waved his hand towards the
shelves and bottles. "What do you know about that kind of thing?"
he asked.

"Nothing," I said. "It is not in my line. Is there anything very
wonderful there?"

"Yes," said Locris, pointing to a bottle which seemed to con-
tain some brown resinous powder. "That stuff in there is very wonderful."

I raised my hand to take it down and have a look at it, and found
my arm struck down at once by old Simpson. Locris could see that
I was angry, and hastened to apologize.

"Sorry," he said. "But Simpson was quite right. He had to do it
in the interests of your safety."

"I don't see how my safety was concerned. It doesn't kill a man
to touch a bottle. Did he think I was going to eat the stuff?"

"No, no," said Locris. "The thing is very simple. You asked me
once if I was inventing a new poison. I told you that I was not. It
would not interest me in the least. And besides, we have plenty of
the old-fashioned poisons which do their work in a perfectly satisfactory manner. What I really have invented is a new explosive.
There is a specimen of it in that bottle. Had you dropped the bottle,
it would have been the end of all of us."

"Cheerful work," I said. "And the big room beyond? Is that a
continuation of the laboratory?"

"Hush!" said Locris, impressively. "It is not. The room beyond
is a tomb—a chapel of the dead. Come, Simpson, give me the keys.
We shall show this gentleman everything."

I picked up one of the lanterns.

"We shall not need that," said Locris. "The chapel is always
lighted."

Simpson was already pulling back the heavy sliding-doors between the two rooms, and I could see the bright light beyond.
Simpson and Locris entered first. Locris went down on his knees
on a faldstool near the door, and Simpson, a grotesque figure, knelt

on a hassock behind him. I myself stood for a moment in the door-way, astonished by the scene which I witnessed.

In the middle of this underground chapel there was erected a high catafalque, draped with gold and white. On the catafalque there lay in her white shroud the body of a young girl. Her hair, astonishingly golden and profuse, was loose about her shoulders. Her hands were clasped on her breast. As I looked at them, I saw what I had expected to see. The first finger of the left hand was missing. The face in profile, as I saw it, was very beautiful, and had not the yellowish waxy look of the face of a corpse. There was a tinge of colour in the cheeks. One could almost have believed that the girl was alive. On either side of the catafalque were three brass candlesticks, eight or nine feet in height. Each of these candlesticks had seven branches. There were thick yellow candles in them, now burning low. The candle flames lit up the red jewels in a high cross that stood behind the head of the girl. A faint scent of incense still lingered in the air. The walls of the room were draped with white and gold, and but for those things which I have mentioned, the room was empty. Locris and the old verger re-mained kneeling in silence for perhaps five minutes, but it seemed to me a very much longer time. Then Locris arose, and both of them stepped backwards from the room, closing the heavy door behind them.

The silence was perfectly terrible. I wanted to speak, in order to break the spell of it, but found nothing to say. At last came the voice of Locris, almost in a whisper.

"Now do you understand?"

"Partly, I think. Let us come upstairs again."

As before each of the two men took a lantern, and I walked be-tween them. Upstairs in the living-room, Simpson began to clear away the strong tea and the untidy bread and butter. I waited until he had gone, and then I turned to Locris. "How is this to end?" I said.

"Quite simple," said old Locris, rubbing his thin hands together. "I shall know when my time has come, and it cannot now be long delayed. I shall go down to the chapel, and old Simpson with me.

It is his own wish that he should not survive me. I shall have nothing to do then, but to start in the anteroom a little piece of clockwork apparatus. It is connected with that explosive which you have seen. In a few minutes, as we are kneeling there, the crash will come. All your good work will be spoiled, my friend. This tower will fall, and the rooms below it will be buried deep. You will have your simple explanation to give. You knew that I was interested in the chemistry of explosives, and that I worked at the subject in those rooms down there. You will say nothing more than this."

"Very well," I said. I was absolutely convinced of the man's insanity, and was wondering what was the best thing to be done.

"You see nothing unnatural in this, I hope," said Locris. "That, you know, is the only woman whom I have loved or can love. Life would have taken me from her, but I could have prevailed over the living. Death was too strong for me. When she died I had no other aim in life but to do what I have done here. For that purpose alone were all my years of work, and all the money that I made. For me there has never existed any other woman."

I ventured to remind him. "But you were married, Mr. Locris."

"Never," he said vehemently, "never! The man who passes as my son is not my son. I married his mother to save her from ruin, but there was in the marriage no more than the ceremony, and she understood that there never would be any more."

There were other questions which I might have asked him, but I thought it better to get away and take the necessary steps as soon as possible. I did not know, for instance, how he had managed to remove the body from the vault in the churchyard at Stannoke, but the strange alliance between him and the old verger might be at the bottom of this. The details of that removal I never did discover. But I learned that the body had been embalmed, and a doctor told me that the method of embalmment adopted would account for that slight tinge of natural colour in the dead girl's face.

I waited impatiently at the inn for my horse to be put in. My nerves were upset, and I left the man who was with me to do the driving.

"Back to the hotel, sir?" he said.

"No. You know where Dr. Hanneford lives? Drive there, and drive as fast as you can."

About two hours later Dr. Hanneford and three other men, of whom I was one, were driving in the direction of the tower. We had got within a little more than a mile of it when we heard the roar of the catastrophe. The horse in the cart shied violently and fell.

"We are too late," said Dr. Hanneford, as he got down to see to the horse.

LINDA

My elder brother, Lorrimer, married ten years ago the daughter of a tenant farmer. I was at that time a boy at school, already interested in the work which has since made me fairly well known, and I took very little interest in Lorrimer or my sister-in-law. From time to time I saw her, of course, when I paid brief visits to their farm in Dorsetshire during the holidays. But I did not greatly enjoy these visits. Lorrimer seemed to me to become daily more morose and taciturn. His wife had the mind of a heavy peasant, deeply interested in her farm and in little else, and only redeemed from the commonplace by her face. I have heard men speak of her as being very beautiful and as being hideous. Already an artist, I saw the point of it all at once: her eyes were not quite human. Sometimes when she was angry with a servant over some trivial piece of neglect, they looked like the eyes of a devil. She was exceedingly superstitious and had little education. Our guardian had the good sense to send me to Paris to complete my art education, and one snowy March I was recalled suddenly from Paris to his death-bed. I was at this time twenty-two years of age, and of course the technical guardianship had ceased. Accounts had been rendered, Lorrimer had taken his share of my father's small fortune and I had taken mine. But we both felt a great regard for this uncle who, during so many years, had been in the place of a father to us. I found Lorrimer at the house when I arrived, and learned then, for the first time, that our uncle had strongly disapproved of his marriage. He spoke of it in the partially conscious moments which preceded his end, and he said some queer things. I heard little, because Lorrimer asked me to go out. After my guardian's death Lorrimer returned to his farm and I to my studies in Paris. A few months later I had a brief letter from Lorrimer announcing the death of his wife. He asked me, and, indeed, urged me not to return to England for her funeral, and he added that she would not be buried in consecrated ground. Of the details of her death he said nothing, and I have heard nothing to this day. That was five years ago, and from that time until this last winter I saw nothing of my brother. Our tastes were widely different—we drifted apart.

During those five years I made great progress and a considerable sum of money. After my first Academy success I never wanted commissions. I had sitters all the year round all the day while the light lasted. I worked very hard, and, possibly, a little too hard. Of my engagement with Lady Adela I will say nothing, except that it came about while I was painting her portrait, and that the engagement was broken off in consequence of the circumstances I am about to relate.

It was then one day last winter that a letter was brought to me in my studio in Tite Street from my brother Lorrimer. He complained slightly of his health, and said that his nerves had gone all wrong. He complained that there were some curious matters on which he wished to take advice, and that he had no one to whom he could speak on those subjects. He urged me to come down and to stay for some time. If there were no room in the farmhouse that suited me for my painting he would have a studio built for me. This was put in his usual formal and business-like language, but there was a brief postscript—"For Heaven's sake come soon!" The letter puzzled me. Lorrimer, as I knew him, had always been a remarkably independent man, reserved, taking no one into his confidence, resenting interference. His manner towards me had been slightly patronizing, and his attitude towards my painting frankly contemptuous. This letter was of a man disturbed, seeking help, ready to make any concessions.

As I have already said, I had been working far too hard, and wanted a rest. During the last year I had made twenty times the sum that I had spent. There was no reason why I should not take a holiday. The country around my brother's place is very beautiful. If I did work there at all, I thought it might amuse me to drop portraits for a while and to take up with my first love—landscape. There had never been any affection between Lorrimer and myself, but neither had there been any quarrel; there was just the steady and unsentimental family tie. I wrote to him briefly that I would come on the following day, and I hoped he had, or could get, some shooting for me. I told him that I should do little or no work, and he need not bother about a studio for me. I added: "Your letter leaves me quite in the dark, and I can't make out what the deuce is the matter with you. Why don't you see a doctor if you're ill?"

It was a tedious journey down. One gets off the main line on to an insignificant local branch. People on the platform stare at the stranger and know when he comes from London. In order to be certain where he is going, they read with great care and no sense of shame the labels on his luggage. There are frowsy little refreshment rooms, tended by frowsy old women, who could never at any period of their past have been barmaids, and you can never get anything that you want. If you turn in despair from these homes of the fly-blown bun and the doubtful milk, to the platforms, you may amuse yourself by noting that the further one gets from civilization, the greater is the importance of the railway porter. Some of them quite resent being sworn at. I got out at the least important station on this unimportant line, and as I gave up my ticket, asked the man if Mr. Estcourt was waiting for me.

"If," said the man slowly, "you mean Mr. Lorrimer Estcourt, of the Dyke Farm, he is outside in his dog-cart."

"What's the sense of talking like that, you fool?" I asked. "Have you got twenty different Estcourts about here?"

"No," he replied gravely, "we have not, and I don't know that we want them."

I explained to him that I was not interested in what he wanted or didn't want, and that he could go to the devil. He mumbled some angry reply as I went out of the station. Lorrimer leant down from the dog-cart and shook hands with me impassively. He is a big man,

with a stern, thin-lipped, clean-shaven face. I noted that his hair
had gone very grey, though at this time he was not more than thirty-
six years of age. He shouted a direction that my luggage was to
come up in the farm cart that stood just behind, bid me rather
impatiently to climb up, and brought his whip sharply across his
mare's shoulder. There was no necessity to have touched her at
all, and, as she happened to be a good one, she resented it. Once
outside the station yard, we went like the wind. So far as driving
was concerned, his nerves seemed to me to be right enough. The
road got worse and worse, and the cart jolted and swayed.

"Steady, you idiot!" I shouted to him. "I don't want my neck
broken."

"All right," he said. He pulled the mare in, spoke to her and
quieted her. Then he turned to me. "If this makes you nervous," he
said, "I'd better turn round and drive you back. A man who is
easily frightened wouldn't be of much use to me at Dyke Farm
just now."

"When a man drives like a fool, I suppose it's always a consola-
tion to call the man a funk who tells him so. You can go on to your
farm, and I'll promise you one thing—when I am frightened I will
tell you."

He became more civil at once. He said that was better. As for
the driving, he had merely amused himself by trying to take a rise
out of a Londoner. His house was six miles from the station, and
for the rest of the way we chatted amicably enough. He told me
that he was his own bailiff and his own housekeeper—managed the
farm like a man and the house like a woman. He said that hard
work suited him.

"You must find it pretty lonely," I said.

"I do," he answered. "Lately I have been wishing that I could
find it still lonelier."

"Look here," I said, "do you mind telling me plainly what on
earth is the matter?"

"You shall see for yourself," he said.

The farmhouse had begun by being a couple of cottages and two
or three considerable additions had been made to it at different

times; consequently, the internal architecture was somewhat puzzling. The hall and two of the living rooms were fairly large, but the rooms upstairs were small and detestably arranged. Often one room opened into another and sometimes into two or three others. The floor was of different heights, and one was always going up or down a step or two. Three staircases in different parts of the house led from the ground floor to the upper storey. The old moss-grown tiles of the roof were pleasing, and the whole place was rather a picturesque jumble. But we only stopped in the house for the time of a whisky-and-soda. Lorrimer took me round the garden almost immediately. It was a walled garden and good as only an old garden can be. Lorrimer was fond of it. His spirits seemed to improve, and at the moment I could find nothing abnormal in him. The farm cart, with my luggage, lumbered slowly up, and presently a gong inside the house rang loudly.

"Ah!" said Lorrimer, pulling out his watch, "time to dress. I'll show you your room if you like."

My room consisted really of two rooms, opening into one another. They seemed comfortable enough, and there were beautiful views from the windows of both of them. Lorrimer left me, and I began, in a leisurely way, to dress for dinner. As I was dressing I heard a queer little laugh coming apparently from one of the upper rooms, in the passage. I took little notice of it at first; I supposed it was due to one of the neat and rosy-cheeked maids who were busy about the house. Then I heard it again, and this time it puzzled me. I knew that laugh, knew it perfectly well, but could not place it. Then, suddenly, it came to me. It was exactly like the laugh of my sister-in-law who had died in this house. It struck me as a queer coincidence.

Naturally enough, I blundered on coming downstairs and first opened the door of the dining-room.

I noticed that the table was laid for three people, and supposed that Lorrimer had asked some neighbour to meet me, possibly a man over whose land I was to shoot. One of the maids directed me to the drawing-room, and I went in. At one end of the room a log fire flickered and hissed, and the smell of the wood was pleasant.

The room was lit by two large ground-glass lamps, relics of my dead sister-in-law's execrable taste. I had at once the feeling that I was not alone in the room, and almost instantly a girl who had been kneeling on the rug in front of the fire got up and came towards me with hands outstretched.

Her age seemed to be about sixteen or seventeen. She had red hair, perhaps the most perfect red that I have ever seen. Her face was beautiful. Her eyes were large and grey, but there was something queer about those eyes. I noticed it immediately. She was dressed in the simplest manner in white. As she came towards me she gave that little laugh which I had heard upstairs. And then I knew what was strange in her eyes. They also at moments did not look quite human.

"You look surprised," she said. "Did not Mr. Estcourt tell you that I should be here? I am Linda, you know." Linda was the name of my dead sister-in-law. The name, the laugh, the eyes—all suggested that this was the daughter of Linda Estcourt. But this was a girl of sixteen or seventeen, and my brother's marriage had taken place only nine years before. Besides, she spoke of him as "Mr. Estcourt." I was making some amiable and some more or less confused reply when Lorrimer entered.

"Ah!" he said. "I see you have already made Miss Marston's acquaintance. I had hoped to be in time to introduce you."

We began to chat about my journey down, the beauty of the country, all sorts of commonplace things. I was struck greatly by her air, at once mysterious and contemptuous. It irritated, and yet it fascinated me. At dinner she said laughingly that it would really be rather confusing now; there would be two Mr. Estcourts—Mr. Lorrimer Estcourt and Mr. Hubert Estcourt. She would have to think of some way of making a distinction.

"I think," she said, turning to my brother, "I shall go on calling you Mr. Estcourt, and I shall call your brother Hubert."

I said that I should be greatly flattered, and her grey eyes showed me that I had no need to be. From this time onward she called me Hubert, as though she had known me and despised me all my life. I noticed that two or three times at dinner she seemed to fall into fits of abstraction, in which she was hardly conscious that one had spoken to her; and I noticed, moreover, that these fits of abstraction irritated my brother immensely. She rose at the end of dinner, and said she would see if the billiard-room was lit up. We could come and smoke in there as soon as we liked. I gave a sigh of relief as I closed the door behind her.

"At last!" I said. "Now, then, Lorrimer, perhaps you will tell me who this Miss Marston is?"

"Tell me who you think she is—no, don't. She is my dead wife's younger sister, younger by many years. Her father took the name of Marston shortly before his death. I am her guardian. My wife's dying words were occupied entirely with this sister, about whom she told me much that would seem to you strange beyond belief; and at the time she gave me injunctions, wrested promises from me which, under certain conditions, I shall have to carry out. The conditions may arise; I think they will. I don't mind saying that I'm afraid they will."

"Why does she bear her sister's name? Why does she address you as 'Mr. Estcourt'? And why do you address her as 'Miss Marston,' when she introduces herself to me simply as 'Linda'?"

"Her mother had three daughters. The eldest was called Linda. When she died, the second, who was my wife, took that name. When my wife died the name descended to the third of them. There has always been a Linda in the family. The rest is simply Miss Marston's own whim. She has several."

"Who chaperons her here?" I asked.

He smiled. "That question is typical of you. She is little more than a child, and she has an almost excessively respectable governess living here to look after her. Only I can't be bothered with the governess at dinner quite every night. Does that satisfy you?"

"No; well, perhaps yes. I suppose so."

"It may make your rigid mind a little easier if I tell you—and it is the truth—that if I had my own way I would turn Miss Marston out of this house to-morrow, and that I would never set eyes on her again; that I have a horror of her, and she has a contempt of me."

"And of most other people, I fancy. Well, anyhow, what's the trouble?"

"I haven't the time to tell you a long story now; she will be waiting for us. Besides, you would merely laugh at me. You have not yet seen for yourself. What would you say if I told you of a compact made years and years ago with some power of evil, and that this girl was concerned in the fulfilment of it?"

"What should I say? Very little. I should get a couple of doctors to sign you up at once."

"Naturally. You would think me mad. Well, wait here for a few weeks, and see what you make of things. In the meantime, come along to the billiard-room."

The billiard-room was an addition that Lorrimer himself had made to the house. We found Linda crouched on the rug in front of the blazing fire; I soon found that this was a favourite attitude with her. Her coffee cup was balanced on her knees. Her eyes stared into the flames. She did not seem to notice our entrance.

"Miss Marston," said my brother. There was a shade of annoyance in his voice. She looked up at him with a disdainful smile. "Do you care to give Hubert a game?" he asked.

"Not yet. I want to watch a game first. You two play, and I'll mark."

"What am I to give you, Lorrimer?" I asked. "Thirty?" He was not even a moderate player. I had always been able to give him at least that.

"You had better play even," said Linda. "And I think you will be beaten, Hubert."

I looked at Lorrimer in astonishment. "Very well, Miss Marston," he said, as he took down his cue. I could only suppose that during the last few years his play had improved considerably. And even then I did not see why Linda had interfered. How on earth could she know what my game was like?

"This is your evening," I said to Lorrimer after his first outrageous fluke.

"It would seem so," he answered, and fluked again. And this went on. His game had not improved; he did the wrong things and did them badly, and they turned out all right. Now and again I heard Linda's brief laugh, and looked up at her. Her eyes seemed to have power to coax a lagging ball into a pocket; one had a curious feeling that she was controlling the game. I did my best with all the luck dead against me. It was a close finish, but I was beaten, as Linda said I should be.

Linda would not play. She said she was tired, and suddenly she looked tired. The light went out of her eyes. She lit a cigarette, and went back to her place on the rug before the fire. Lorrimer talked about his farm with me. The quiet of the place seemed almost ghastly to a man who was used to London. Presently Linda got up to go to bed. "Good-night, Mr. Estcourt," she said, as she shook hands with my brother. Then she turned to me: "Good-night, Hubert. You shouldn't quarrel with ticket-collectors about nothing. It's silly, isn't it?" She kissed me on the cheek, and ran off laughing. She left me astounded by her words and insulted by her kiss.

Lorrimer turned out the lights over the billiard-table, and we sat down again by the fire.

"What did you think of that game?" he asked.

"It was remarkable."

"Nothing more?"

"I never saw a game like it before. But there was nothing impossible about it."

"Very well. And did you have a row with that ticket-collector?"

"Not a row exactly. He annoyed me, and I may have called him a fool. I suppose you overheard and told her about it."

"I could not have overheard. I was outside the station buildings and you were on the further platform."

"Yes, that's true. It's a queer coincidence."

"I tried that, too, at first—the belief that things were remarkable, but not impossible, and that queer coincidences happen. Personally I can't keep it up any more."

"Look here," I said. "We may as well go to the point at once. Why do you want me here? Why did you send for me?"

"Suppose I said that I wanted you to marry Miss Marston?"

"I thought that at the time of my engagement with Adela I wrote and gave you the news."

"You did. The artistic temperament does sometimes do a brilliant business thing for itself. Lady Adela Marys—"

"We won't discuss her."

"Then suppose we discuss you. You are half in love with Linda already."

"Very well," I said, "let us carry the supposition a little further. Suppose that I or anybody else was entirely in love with her, what on earth would be the use? The one thing that one can feel absolutely certain about in her is that she has an amused contempt for the rest of her species, male and female. It's not affected, it's perfectly genuine. Even if I wished to marry her, she would not look at me."

"Really?" said Lorrimer, with a sneer. "She seemed fond enough of you when she said goodnight."

"That," I said meditatively, "was the cleverest kiss that ever was kissed. It finished what the interchange of Christian names began. It settled the situation exactly—that I was the fool of a brother, and she the good-natured, though contemptuous sister."

"You needn't look at it like that. It is important, exceedingly important that she should be married."

"Marry her yourself—it won't be legal in this country, but it will in others, and I don't know that it matters."

"No, I don't know that it matters. On the day I wrote to you I did ask her to be my wife. She replied that it was disagreeable to have to speak of such things, and that they need not be allowed to come to the surface again, but that, as a matter of fact, *au fond* we hated one another. It was true. I do hate her. What I do for her is for my dead wife's sake, for the promises I made, and, perhaps, a little for common humanity. There are others who would marry her. The man whose pheasants you will be shooting next week would give his soul for her cheerfully, and it's no use. Very likely it will be of no use in your case."

"What was the story that you had not time to tell me after dinner?"

The door opened, and a servant brought in the decanters and soda-water and arranged them on the table by Lorrimer's side. He did not speak until the servant had gone out of the room, and then he seemed to be talking almost more to himself than to me.

"At night, when one wakes up in the small hours, after a bad dream or hearing some sudden noise in the house, one believes things of which one is a little ashamed next morning."

He paused, and then leant forward, addressing me directly. "Look here; I'll say it in a few words. You won't believe it, and that doesn't matter a tinker's curse to me. You'll believe it a little later if you stop here. Generations ago, in the time of the witches, a woman who was to have been burned as a witch escaped miraculously from the hands of the officers. It was said that she had a compact with the devil; that at some future time he should take a living maiden of her line. Death and marriage are the two ways of safety for any woman of that family. The compact has not yet been carried out, and Linda is the last of the line. She bears the signs of which my wife told me. One by one I watch them coming out in her. Her power over inanimate objects, her mysterious knowledge of things which have happened elsewhere, the terror which all animals have of her. A year or two ago she was always about the farm on the best of terms with every dog and horse in the place. Now they will not let her come near them. Well, it is my business to save Linda. I have given my promise. I wish her to be married. If that is not possible, and the moment arrives, I must kill her."

"Why talk like a fool?" I said. "Come and live in London for a week. It strikes me that both Linda and yourself might perhaps be benefited by being put into the hands of a specialist. In any case, don't tell these fairy stories to a sane man like myself."

"Very well," he said, getting up. "I must be going to bed. I am out on the farm before six every morning, and I shall probably have breakfasted before you are up. Miss Marston and Mrs. Dennison— that's her old governess—breakfast at nine. You can join them if you like, or breakfast by yourself later."

Long after my brother had gone to bed I sat in the billiard-room thinking the thing over, angry with myself, and, indeed, ashamed, that I could not disbelieve quite as certainly as I wished. At breakfast next morning I asked Linda to sit to me for her portrait, and she consented. We found a room with a good light. Mrs. Dennison remained with us during the sitting.

This went on for days. The portrait was a failure. I have the best of the several attempts that I made still. The painting's all right. But the likeness is not there; there is something missing in the eyes. I saw a great deal of Linda, and I came at last to this conclusion, that I had no explanation whatever of the powers which she undoubtedly possessed. I also learned that she herself was well acquainted with the story of her house. She alluded to the fact that neither of her sisters was buried in consecrated ground; no woman of her family would ever be.

"And you?" I asked.

"I am not sure that I shall be buried at all. To me strange things will happen."

I had letters occasionally from Lady Adela. I was glad to see that she was getting tired of the whole thing. My conduct had not been so calculating and ignoble as Lorrimer had supposed. She was a very beautiful woman. It was easy enough to suppose that one was in love with her—until one happened to fall in love. I determined to go to London to see Lady Adela, and to give her the chance, which I was sure she wanted, to throw me over. I promised Lorrimer that I would only be away for one night. Lady Adela missed her appointment with me at her mother's house, and left a note of excuse. Something serious had happened, I believe, with regard to a dress that she was to wear that night. But, really, I do not remember what her excuse was. I went back to my rooms in Tite Street, and there I found a telegram from Mrs. Dennison. It told me in plain language, and with due regard to the fact that each word cost a halfpenny, that my brother, in a fit of madness, had murdered Linda Marston and taken his own life. I got back to my brother's farm late that night.

The evidence at the inquest was simple enough. Linda had three rooms, opening into one another, the one furthest from the passage being her bedroom. At the time of the murder Mrs. Dennison was in the second room, reading, and Linda was playing the piano in the room which opened into the passage. Mrs. Dennison heard the music stop suddenly. Linda was whimsical in her playing, as in everything else. There was a pause, during which the governess was absorbed in her book. Then she heard in the next room Lorrimer say distinctly: "It is all right, Linda. I have come to save you." This was followed by three shots in succession. Mrs. Dennison rushed in and found the two lying dead. She was greatly affected at the inquest, and as few questions as possible were put to her.

Some time afterwards Mrs. Dennison told me a thing which she did not mention at the inquest. Shortly after the music had stopped, and before Lorrimer entered the room, she had heard another voice, as though someone were speaking with Linda. This third voice, and Linda's own, were in low tones, and no words could be heard. I thought this over, and I remembered that Lorrimer fired three times, and that the third bullet was found in another part of the room.

Lady Adela was certainly quite right to give me up, which she did in a most tactful and sympathetic letter.

THE DIARY OF A GOD

During the week there had been several thunderstorms. It was after the last of these, on a cool Saturday evening, that he was found at the top of the hill by a shepherd. His speech was incoherent and disconnected; he gave his name correctly, but could or would add no account of himself. He was wet through, and sat there pulling a sprig of heather to pieces. The shepherd afterwards said that he had great difficulty in persuading him to come down, and that he talked much nonsense. In the path at the foot of the hill he was recognised by some people from the farmhouse where he was lodging, and was taken back there. They had, indeed, gone out to look for him. He was subsequently removed to an asylum, and died insane a few months later.

Two years afterwards, when the furniture of the farmhouse came to be sold by auction, there was found in a little cupboard in the bedroom which he had occupied an ordinary penny exercise-book. This was partly filled, in a beautiful and very regular handwriting, with what seems to have been something in the nature of a diary, and the following are extracts from it:

June 1st.—It is absolutely essential to be quiet. I am beginning life again, and in quite a different way, and on quite a different scale, and I cannot make the break suddenly. I must have a pause of a few weeks in between the two different lives. I saw the advertisement of the lodgings in this farmhouse in an evening paper that somebody had left at the restaurant. That was when I was trying to make the change abruptly, and I may as well make a note of what happened.

After attending the funeral (which seemed to me an act of hypocrisy, as I hardly knew the man, but it was expected of me), I came back to my Charlotte Street rooms and had tea. I slept well that night. Then next morning I went to the office at the usual hour, in my best clothes, and with a deep band still on my hat. I went to Mr. Toller's room and knocked. He said, "Come in," and after I had entered: "Can I do anything for you? What do you want?"

Then I explained to him that I wished to leave at once. He said: "This seems sudden, after thirty years' service."

"Yes," I replied. "I have served you faithfully for thirty years, but things have changed, and I have now three hundred a year of my own. I will pay something in lieu of notice, if you like, but I cannot go on being a clerk any more. I hope, Mr. Toller, you will not think that I speak with any impertinence to yourself, or any immodesty, but I am really in the position of a private gentleman."

He looked at me curiously, and as he did not say anything I repeated:

"I think I am in the position of a private gentleman."

In the end he let me go, and said very politely he was sorry to lose me. I said good-bye to the other clerks, even to those who had sometimes laughed at what they imagined to be my peculiarities. I gave the better of the two office-boys a small present in money.

I went back to the Charlotte Street rooms, but there was nothing to do there. There were figures going on in my head, and my fingers seemed to be running up and down columns. I had a stupid idea that I should be in trouble if Mr. Toller were to come in and catch me like that. I went out and had a capital lunch, and then I went to the theatre. I took a stall right in the front row, and sat there all by myself. Then I had a cab to the restaurant. It was too soon for dinner, so I ordered a whisky-and-soda, and smoked a few cigarettes. The man at the table next me left the evening paper in which I saw the advertisement of these farmhouse lodgings. I read the whole of the paper, but I have forgotten it all except that advertisement, and I could say it by heart now—all about bracing air and perfect quiet and the rest of it. For dinner I had a bottle of champagne. The waiter handed me a list, and asked which I would prefer. I waved the list away and said:

"Give me the best."

He smiled. He kept on smiling all through dinner until the end; then he looked serious. He kept getting more serious. Then he brought two other men to look at me. They spoke to me, but I did not want to talk. I think I fell asleep. I found myself in my rooms in Charlotte Street next morning, and my landlady gave me notice because, she said, I had come home beastly drunk. Then that advertisement flashed into my mind about the bracing air. I said:

"I should have given you notice in any case; this is not a suitable place for a gentleman."

June 3rd.—I am rather sorry that I wrote down the above. It seems so degrading. However, it was merely an act of ignorance and carelessness on my part, and, besides, I am writing solely for myself. To myself I may own freely that I made a mistake, that I was not used to the wine, and that I had not fully gauged what the effects would be. The incident is disgusting, but I simply put it behind me, and think no more about it. I pay here two pounds ten shillings a week for my two rooms and board. I take my meals, of course, by myself in the sitting-room. It would be rather cheaper if I took them with the family, but I do not care about that. After all, what is two pounds ten shillings a week? Roughly speaking, a hundred and thirty pounds a year.

June 17th.—I have made no entry in my diary for some days. For a certain period I have had no heart for that or for anything else. I had told the people here that I was a private gentleman (which is strictly true), and that I was engaged in literary pursuits. By the latter I meant to imply no more than that I am fond of reading, and that it is my intention to jot down from time to time my sensations and experiences in the new life which has burst upon me. At the same time I have been greatly depressed. Why, I can hardly explain. I have been furious with myself. Sitting in my own sitting-room, with a gold-tipped cigarette between my fingers, I have been possessed (even though I recognised it as an absurdity) by a feeling that if Mr. Toller were to come in suddenly I should get up and apologize. But the thing which depressed me most was the open country. I have read, of course, those penny stories about the poor little ragged boys who never see the green leaf in their lives, and I always thought them exaggerated. So they are exaggerated: there are the Embankment Gardens with the Press Band playing; there are parks; there are Sunday-school treats. All these little ragged boys see the green leaf, and to say they do not is an exaggeration—I am afraid a wilful exaggeration. But to see the open country is quite a different thing. Yesterday was a fine day, and I was out all day in a place called Wensley Dale. On one spot where I stood I could see for miles all round. There was not a single house, or tree, or human being in sight. There was just myself on the top of a moor; the bigness of it gave me a regular scare. I suppose I had got used to walls: I had got used to feeling that if I went straight ahead without stopping I should knock against something. That somehow made me feel safe. Out on that great moor—just as if I were the last man left alive in the world—I do not feel safe. I find the track and get home again, and I tremble like a half-drowned kitten until I see a wall again, or somebody with a surly face who does not answer civilly when I speak to him. All these feelings will wear off, no doubt, and I shall be able to enter upon the new phase of my existence without any discomfort. But I was quite right to take a few months' quiet retirement. One must get used to things gradually. It was the same with the champagne—to which, by the way, I had not meant to allude any further.

June 20th.—It is remarkable what a fascination these very large moors have for me. It is not exactly fear any more—indeed, it must be the reverse. I do not care to be anywhere else. Instead of making this a mere pause between two different existences, I shall continue it. To that I have quite made up my mind. When I am out there in a place where I cannot see any trees, or houses, or living things, I am the last person left alive in the world. I am a kind of a god. There is nobody to think anything at all about me, and it does not matter if my clothes are not right, or if I drop an "h"—which I

rarely do except when speaking very quickly. I never knew what
real independence was before. There have been too many houses
around, and too many people looking on. It seems to me now such
a common and despicable thing to live among people, and to have
one's character and one's ways altered by what they are going to
think. I know now that when I ordered that bottle of champagne I
did it far more to please the waiter and to make him think well of
me than to please myself. I pity the kind of creature that I was
then, but I had not known the open country at that time. It is a
grand education. If Toller were to come in now I should say, "Go
away. Go back to your bricks and mortar, and account-books, and
swell friends, and white waistcoats, and rubbish of that kind. You
cannot possibly understand me, and your presence irritates me. If
you do not go at once I will have the dog let loose upon you." By
the way, that was a curious thing which happened the other day. I
feed the dog, a mastiff, regularly, and it goes out with me. We had
walked some way, and had reached that spot where a man becomes
the last man alive in the world. Suddenly the dog began to howl,
and ran off home with its tail between its legs, as if it were frightened of something. What was it that the dog had seen and I had
not seen? A ghost? In broad daylight? Well, if the dead come back
they might walk here without contamination. A few sheep, a sweep
of heather, a gray sky, but nothing that a living man planted or
built. They could be alone here. If it were not that it would seem a
kind of blasphemy, I would buy a piece of land in the very middle
of the loneliest moor and build myself a cottage there.

June 23rd.—I received a letter to-day from Julia. Of course she
does not understand the change which has taken place in me. She
writes as she always used to write, and I find it very hard to remember and realize that I liked it once, and was glad when I got a
letter from her. That was before I got into the habit of going into
empty places alone. The old clerking, account-book life has become
too small to care about. The swell life of the private gentleman to
which I looked forward, is also not worth considering. As for Julia,
I was to have married her; I used to kiss her. She wrote to say that

she thought a great deal of me; she still writes. I don't want her. I don't want anything. I have become the last man alive in the world. I shall leave this farmhouse very soon. The people are all right, but they are people, and therefore insufferable. I can no longer live or breathe in a place where I see people, or trees which people have planted, or houses which people have built. It is an ugly word— people.

July 7th.—I was wrong in saying that I was the last man alive in the world. I believe I am dead. I know now why the mastiff howled and ran away. The whole moor is full of them; one sees them after a time when one has got used to the open country—or perhaps it is because one is dead. Now I see them by moonlight and sunlight, and I am not frightened at all. I think I must be dead, because there seems to be a line ruled straight through my life, and the things which happened on the further side of the line are not real. I look over this diary, and see some references to a Mr. Toller, and to some champagne, and coming into money. I cannot for the life of me think what it is all about. I suppose the incidents described really happened, unless I was mad when I wrote about them. I suppose that I am not dead, since I can write in a book, and eat food, and walk, and sleep and wake again. But since I see them now—these people that fill up the lonely places—I must be quite different to ordinary human beings. If I am not dead, then what am I? To-day I came across an old letter signed "Julia Jarvis"; the envelope was addressed to me. I wonder who on earth she was?

July 9th.—A man in a frock-coat came to see me, and talked about my best interest. He wanted me, so far as I could gather, to come away with him somewhere. He said I was all right, or, at any rate, would become all right, with a little care. He would not go away until I said that I would kill him. Then the woman at the farmhouse came up with a white face, and I said I would kill her too. I positively cannot endure people. I am something apart, something different. I am not alive, and I am not dead. I cannot imagine what I am.

July 16th.—I have settled the whole thing to my complete satisfaction. I can without doubt believe the evidence of my own senses. I have seen, and I have heard. I know now that I am a god. I had almost thought before that this might be. What was the matter was that I was too diffident: I had no self-confidence; I had never heard before of any man, even a clerk in an old-established firm, who had become a god. I therefore supposed it was impossible until it was distinctly proved to be. I had often made up my mind to go to that range of hills that lies to the north. They are purple when one sees them far off. At nearer view they are gray, then they become green, then one sees a silver network over the green. The silver network is made by streams descending in the sunlight. I climbed the hill slowly; the air was still, and the heat was terrible. Even the water which I drank from the running stream seemed flat and warm. As I climbed, the storm broke. I took but little notice of it, for the dead that I had met below on the moor had told me that lightning could not touch me. At the top of the hill I turned, and saw the storm raging beneath my feet. It is the greatest of mercies that I went there, for that is where the other gods gather, at such times as the lightning plays between them and the earth, and the black thunder-clouds, hanging low, shut them out from the sight of men.

Some of the gods were rather like the big pictures that I have seen on the hoardings, advertising plays at the theatre, or some food which is supposed to give great strength and muscular development. They were handsome in face, and without any expression. They never seemed to be angry or pleased, or hurt. They sat there in great long rows, resting, with the storm imaging in between them and the earth. One of them was a woman. I spoke to her, and she told me that she was older than this earth; yet she had the face of a young girl, and her eyes were like eyes that I have seen before somewhere. I cannot think where I saw the eyes like those of the goddess, but perhaps it was in that part of my life which is forgotten and ruled off with a line. It gave one the greatest and most majestic feelings to stand there with the gods, and to know that one was a god one's self, and that lightning did not hurt one, and that one would live for ever.

July 18th.—This afternoon the storm returned, and I hurried to the meeting-place, but it is far away to the hills, and though I climbed as quickly as I could the storm was almost passed, and they had gone.

August 1st.—I was told in my sleep that to-morrow I was to go back to the hill again, and that once more the gods would be there, and that the storm would gather round us, and would shut us from profane sight, and the steely lightnings would blind any eye that tried to look upon us. For this reason I have refused now to eat or drink anything; I am a god and have no need of such things. It is strange that now when I see all real things so clearly and easily— the ghosts of the dead that walk across the moors in the sunlight and the concourse of the gods on the hill-top above the storm— men and women with whom I once moved before I became a god are no more to me than so many black shadows. I scarcely know one from the other, only that the presence of a black shadow any- where near me makes me angry, and I desire to kill it. That will pass away; it is probably some faint relic of the thing that I once was in the other side of my life on the other side of the line which has been ruled across it. Seeing that I am a god it is not natural that I can feel anger or joy any more. Already all feeling of joy has gone from me, for to-morrow, so I was told in my sleep, I am to be betrothed to the beautiful goddess that is older than the world, and yet looks like a young girl, and she is to give me a sprig of heather as a token and—

It was on the evening of August 1 he was found.

THE MOON-SLAVE

The Princess Viola had, even in her childhood, an inevitable submission to the dance; a rhythmical madness in her blood answered hotly to the dance music, swaying her, as the wind sways trees, to movements of perfect sympathy and grace.

For the rest, she had her beauty and her long hair, that reached to her knees, and was thought lovable; but she was never very fervent and vivid unless she was dancing; at other times there almost seemed to be a touch of lethargy upon her. Now, when she was sixteen years old, she was betrothed to the Prince Hugo. With others the betrothal was merely a question of state. With her it was merely a question of obedience to the wishes of authority; it had been arranged; Hugo was *comme ci, comme ça*—no god in her eyes; it did not matter. But with Hugo it was quite different—he loved her.

The betrothal was celebrated by a banquet, and afterwards by a dance in the great hall of the palace. From this dance the Princess soon made her escape, quite discontented, and went to the furthest part of the palace gardens, where she could no longer hear the music calling her.

"They are all right," she said to herself as she thought of the men she had left, "but they cannot dance. Mechanically they are all right; they have learned it and don't make childish mistakes; but they are only one-two-three machines. They haven't the inspiration of dancing. It is so different when I dance alone."

She wandered on until she reached an old forsaken maze. It had been planned by a former king. All round it was a high crumbling wall with foxgloves growing on it. The maze itself had all its paths bordered with high opaque hedges; in the very centre was a circular open space with tall pine-trees growing round it. Many years ago the clue to the maze had been lost; it was but rarely now that anyone entered it. Its gravel paths were green with weeds, and in some places the hedges, spreading beyond their borders, had made the way almost impassable.

For a moment or two Viola stood peering in at the gate—a narrow gate with curiously twisted bars of wrought iron surmounted by a heraldic device. Then the whim seized her to enter the maze and try to find the space in the centre. She opened the gate and went in.

Outside everything was uncannily visible in the light of the full moon, but here in the dark shaded alleys the night was conscious of itself. She soon forgot her purpose, and wandered about quite aimlessly, sometimes forcing her way where the brambles had flung a laced barrier across her path, and a dragging mass of convolvulus struck wet and cool upon her cheek. As chance would have it she suddenly found herself standing under the tall pines, and looking at the open space that formed the goal of the maze. She was pleased that she had got there. Here the ground was carpeted with sand, fine and, as it seemed, beaten hard. From the summer night sky immediately above, the moonlight, unobstructed here, streamed straight down upon the scene.

Viola began to think about dancing. Over the dry, smooth sand her little satin shoes moved easily, stepping and gliding, circling and stepping, as she hummed the tune to which they moved. In the centre of the space she paused, looked at the wall of dark trees all round, at the shining stretches of silvery sand and at the moon above.

"My beautiful, moonlit, lonely, old dancing-room, why did I never find you before?" she cried; "but," she added, "you need music—there must be music here."

In her fantastic mood she stretched her soft, clasped hands upwards towards the moon.

"Sweet moon," she said in a kind of mock prayer, "make your white light come down in music into my dancing-room here, and I will dance most deliciously for you to see." She flung her head backward and let her hands fall; her eyes were half closed, and her mouth was a kissing mouth. "Ah! sweet moon," she whispered, "do this for me, and I will be your slave; I will be what you will."

Quite suddenly the air was filled with the sound of a grand invisible orchestra. Viola did not stop to wonder. To the music of a slow saraband she swayed and postured. In the music there was the regular beat of small drums and a perpetual drone. The air seemed to be filled with the perfume of some bitter spice. Viola could fancy almost that she saw a smouldering camp-fire and heard far off the roar of some desolate wild beast. She let her long hair fall, raising the heavy strands of it in either hand as she moved slowly to the laden music. Slowly her body swayed with drowsy grace, slowly her satin shoes slid over the silver sand.

The music ceased with a clash of cymbals. Viola rubbed her eyes. She fastened her hair up carefully again. Suddenly she looked up, almost imperiously.

"Music! more music!" she cried.

Once more the music came. This time it was a dance of caprice, pelting along over the violin-strings, leaping, laughing, wanton. Again an illusion seemed to cross her eyes. An old king was watching her, a king with the sordid history of the exhaustion of pleasure written on his flaccid face. A hook-nosed courtier by his side settled the ruffles at his wrists and mumbled, "Ravissant! Quel malheur que la vieillesse!" It was a strange illusion. Faster and faster she sped to the music, stepping, spinning, pirouetting; the dance was light as thistle-down, fierce as fire, smooth as a rapid stream.

The moment that the music ceased Viola became horribly afraid. She turned and fled away from the moonlit space, through the trees, down the dark alleys of the maze, not heeding in the least which turn she took, and yet she found herself soon at the outside iron gate. From thence she ran through the palace garden, hardly ever pausing to take breath, until she reached the palace itself. In the eastern sky the first signs of dawn were showing; in the palace the festivities were drawing to an end. As she stood alone in the outer hall Prince Hugo came towards her.

"Where have you been, Viola?" he said sternly. "What have you been doing?"

She stamped her little foot.

"I will not be questioned," she replied angrily.

"I have some right to question," he said.

She laughed a little.

"For the first time in my life," she said, "I have been dancing."

He turned away in hopeless silence.

The months passed away. Slowly a great fear came over Viola, a fear that would hardly ever leave her. For every month at the full moon, whether she would or no, she found herself driven to the maze, through its mysterious walks into that strange dancing-room. And when she was there the music began once more, and once more she danced most deliciously for the moon to see. The second time that this happened she had merely thought that it was a recurrence of her own whim, and that the music was but a trick that the imagination had chosen to repeat. The third time frightened her, and she knew that the force that sways the tides had strange power over her. The fear grew as the year fell, for each month the music went on for a longer time—each month some of the pleasure had gone from the dance. On bitter nights in winter the moon called her and she came, when the breath was vapour, and the trees that circled her dancing-room were black bare skeletons, and the frost was cruel. She dared not tell anyone, and yet it was with difficulty that she kept her secret. Somehow chance seemed to favour her, and she always found a way to return from her midnight dance to her own room without being observed. Each month the summons seemed to be more imperious and urgent. Once when she was alone on her knees before the lighted altar in the private chapel of the palace she suddenly felt that the words of the familiar Latin prayer had gone from her memory. She rose to her feet, she sobbed bitterly, but the call had come and she could not resist it. She passed out of the chapel and down the palace-gardens. How madly she danced that night!

She was to be married in the spring. She began to be more gentle with Hugo now. She had a blind hope that when they were married she might be able to tell him about it, and he might be able to protect her, for she had always known him to be fearless. She could not love him, but she tried to be good to him. One day he mentioned to her that he had tried to find his way to the centre of the maze, and had failed. She smiled faintly. If only she could fail! But she never did.

On the night before the wedding day she had gone to bed and slept peacefully, thinking with her last waking moments of Hugo. Overhead the full moon came up the sky. Quite suddenly Viola was wakened with the impulse to fly to the dancing-room. It seemed to bid her hasten with breathless speed. She flung a cloak around her, slipped her naked feet into her dancing-shoes, and hurried forth. No one saw her or heard her—on the marble staircase of the palace, on down the terraces of the garden, she ran as fast as she could. A thorn-plant caught in her cloak, but she sped on, tearing it free; a sharp stone cut through the satin of one shoe, and her foot was wounded and bleeding, but she sped on. As the pebble that is flung from the cliff must fall until it reaches the sea, as the white ghost-moth must come in from cool hedges and scented darkness to a burning death in the lamp by which you sit so late—so Viola had no choice. The moon called her. The moon drew her to that circle of hard, bright sand and the pitiless music.

It was brilliant, rapid music tonight. Viola threw off her cloak and danced. As she did so, she saw that a shadow lay over a fragment of the moon's edge. It was the night of a total eclipse. She heeded it not. The intoxication of the dance was on her. She was all in white; even her face was pale in the moonlight. Every movement was full of poetry and grace.

The music would not stop. She had grown deathly weary. It seemed to her that she had been dancing for hours, and the shadow had nearly covered the moon's face, so that it was almost dark. She could hardly see the trees around her. She went on dancing, stepping, spinning, pirouetting, held by the merciless music.

It stopped at last, just when the shadow had quite covered the moon's face, and all was dark. But it stopped only for a moment, and then began again. This time it was a slow, passionate waltz. It was useless to resist; she began to dance once more. As she did so she uttered a sudden shrill scream of horror, for in the dead darkness a hot hand had caught her own and whirled her round, *and she was no longer dancing alone.*

The search for the missing Princess lasted during the whole of the following day. In the evening Prince Hugo, his face anxious and firmly set, passed in his search the iron gate of the maze, and noticed on the stones beside it the stain of a drop of blood. Within the gate was another stain. He followed this clue, which had been left by Viola's wounded foot, until he reached that open space in the centre that had served Viola for her dancing-room. It was quite empty. He noticed that the sand round the edges was all worn down, as though someone had danced there, round and round, for a long time. But no separate footprint was distinguishable there. Just outside this track, however, he saw two footprints clearly defined close together: one was the print of a tiny satin shoe; the other was the print of a large naked foot—a cloven foot.

THE GREEN LIGHT

The man looked down at the figure of the woman on the couch. The little silver clock on the mantelpiece began to chime; he could not bear the sound of it. He flew at the clock like a madman, and dashed it on the ground, and stamped on it. Then he drew down the blind, and opened the door and listened; there was no one on the staircase. Silence seemed now as intolerable to him as sound had been a moment before. He tried to whistle, but his lips were too dry and made only a ridiculous hissing sound. Closing the door behind him, he ran down the staircase and out into the street. The woman on the couch never moved or spoke. It was late in the afternoon; the light from the low sun penetrated the green blind and took from it a horrible colour that seemed to tint the face of the woman on the couch. Flies came out of the dark corners of the room, sulkily busy, crawling and buzzing. One very little fly passed backwards and forwards over the woman's white ringed hand; it moved rapidly, a black speck.

Outside in the street, the man stepped from the pavement into the roadway; a cabman shouted and swore at him, and someone dragged him back by the arm, and told him roughly to look where he was going. He stood still for a minute, and rubbed his forehead with his hand. This would not do. The critical moment had come, the moment when, above all things, it was necessary that his nerve should be perfect and his thoughts clear; and now, when he tried to think, a picture came before the thought and filled his mind— the picture of the white face with the green light upon it. And his

heart was beating too fast, and, it seemed to him, almost audibly.
He began to feel his pulse, counting the strokes out loud as he stood
on the kerb; then he was conscious that two or three boys and loafers were standing in a little group watching him and laughing at
him. One of the loafers handed him his hat; it had fallen off when
he dodged back on to the pavement, and he had not noticed it. He
took the hat, and felt for some coins to give the man. He found a
half-crown and a halfpenny; he held them in his hand, and stared
at them, and forgot why he had wanted them. Then he suddenly
remembered and gave them. There was a loud yell of laughter; the
boys and loafers were running away, and he heard one of them
shouting, "Let the old stinker out a bit too soon, ain't they?" and
another, "Garn! 'E's tight—that's all's wrong with 'im." Again he
told himself that this would not do. He must not think of the past—
the awful past. He must not think of the future—of his schemes for
escape. He must concentrate his thoughts on the present moment,
until he could get to some place where he could be alone. Yes,
Regent's Park would do well, and it was near. He brushed his hat
with his coat-sleeve, put it on, and walked. He thought about the
movement of his feet, and the best way to cross the road, and how
to avoid running into people, and how to behave as other people
in the street behaved. All the things that one generally does unconsciously and automatically required now for their conduct a
distinct mental effort.

As he walked on, his mind seemed to clear a little. He reached
a spot in Regent's Park where he could lie down in the grass with
no one near him, out of sight. "Now," he said to himself, "I need
concentrate my thoughts no longer—I can let them go." In a second he had gone rapidly through the past—the jealousy that had
burned in his heart, and the way that he had quieted himself and
made his scheme, and carried it out slowly. It had been finished
that afternoon, when he had lost control over himself, and—

Through the transparent leaves of the tree near him the sun
came with a greenish glare. He shuddered and turned away, so that
he could not see it.

Yes, he was to escape—he had made all the arrangements for that. He drew from his side-pocket a roll of notes, and counted them, and entered the numbers in his pocket-book. He had changed a cheque for fifty pounds at the bank that morning. The police would find that out, and endeavour to trace him by discovering where the notes with those numbers were changed. That was one of his means of escape. He would see to it that the notes were never changed by himself, or in any town where he had been or was likely to be. He was going to sacrifice those ten bank-notes to put the police on a wrong scent. He had plenty of money ready in gold—in gold that could not be traced—for his own needs. He chuckled to himself. It was brilliant, this scheme for providing a wrong scent, for making the very carefulness and astuteness of the detectives the stumbling-block in their way; and it would be so easy to get the notes changed by others—the dishonesty of ordinary human beings would serve his purpose.

His mood had changed now to one of exultation. He told himself time after time that he was right. The law would condemn him, but morally he was right, and had only punished the woman as she deserved to be punished. Only, he must escape. And—yes—he must not forget.

He looked round. There was still no one near; but his position did not satisfy him. Not a person must see what he was going to do next. He went on, and found a spot near the canal, where he seemed to be out of sight, and more secure from interruption. Then he took from his pocket a little looking-glass and a pair of scissors. Very carefully he cut away his beard and moustache, that hid the thin-lipped, wide mouth, and the small weak chin. He cut as close as he could, and when he had finished he looked like a man who had neglected to shave for a day or two. A barber would shave him now without suspicion. He was satisfied with the operation. The glass showed him a face so changed that it startled him to look at it. He glanced at his watch—it was time to start for the station, where his luggage had been waiting since the day before, if he meant to get shaved on the way there.

He walked a little way, and sat down again. "How well every-thing has been thought out!" he said to himself. All would succeed. With a new name, and in another country, without that drunken, faithless, beautiful woman, he would grow happy again. He had only meant to sit down for a minute or two, but his thoughts rambled and became nonsense, and suddenly he fell into a deep sleep. He had been overtaxed.

An hour passed. The train that he had intended to take steamed out of the station, and still he slept. It grew dusk, and still he slept. When the park-keeper touched him on the shoulder, he half woke, and spoke querulously. Then consciousness came back, and slowly he realized what had happened.

As he walked slowly out of the park, his mind refreshed with sleep, he for the first time realized something else. In the awful moment when he had left the woman, he had broken down, and forgotten everything. The bag of gold was still lying on the table of the room with the green blind. He must go back and get it. It would be horrible to re-enter that room, but it could not be helped. He dared not change the notes himself, and in any case that amount would be insufficient. He must have the gold.

It added, he told himself, slightly to the risk of discovery, but only slightly. His servants had all been sent out and were not to return until half-past nine. No one else could have entered the house. He would find everything as he left it—the gold on the table and the figure of the woman on the couch. He would let himself in with his latch-key. No passer-by would take any notice of so ordi-nary an incident. He had no occasion to hurry now, and he turned into the first barber's shop that he saw. His mind was as alert now as it had been when he first formed his scheme.

"Let me have your best razor," he said; "my skin's tender; in fact, for the last two or three days I haven't been able to shave at all."

He chatted with the barber about horse-racing, and said that he himself had a couple of horses in training. Then he inquired the way to Piccadilly, saying that he was a stranger in London, and seemed to take careful note of the barber's directions.

He walked briskly away from the shop towards his own house. A comfortable-looking, ruddy-faced woman was coming towards him. A shaft of green light from a chemist's shop-window fell full on her face as she passed, and the horror came back upon him. It was with difficulty that he checked himself from crying out. He hurried on, but that hideous light seemed to linger in his eyes and to haunt him.

"Keep quiet!" he kept saying to himself under his breath. "Steady yourself; don't be a fool!"

There was an Italian restaurant near, and he went in and drank a couple of glasses of cognac. Then only was he able to go on.

As he turned the corner where his house came into sight he looked up. All the house was dark but for one great green eye in the centre that looked at him. There were lights in that room.

He stood still close to a lamppost, just touching it to keep his balance. He spoke to himself aloud:

"It's green . . . it's green . . . someone's there!"

A working man passed him, heard him mumbling, looked at him curiously, and went on.

The great green eye stared at him and fascinated him. Then other lights darted about, red lights, white lights. Someone must be going up and down the staircase and passages. Had she got off the couch? Was the dead woman walking? How his head throbbed! There were two nerves that seemed to sound like two consecutive notes on a piano, struck in slow alternation, then quickening to a rapid shake—whirr! whirr! Now the two notes were struck together, a repeated discord, thumped out—clatter! clatter! No, the sound was outside in the street, and it was the sound of people running. There were boys with excited eyes and white faces, and blowsy, laughing women, and a little old ferret-faced man who coughed as he ran. A police-whistle screamed.

In front of the door of the house a black mass grew up, getting quickly bigger and bigger. It was a crowd of people swaying backwards and forwards, kept back by the police.

The police! He was discovered, then. He must get away at once, not wait another moment. Only the green light was looking at him.

"Stop that light!" he called.

No one noticed him. The green light went on glimmering, and drew him nearer. He had to get there. He was on the outskirts of the crowd now.

Why would not the crowd let him pass? Could not they hear that he was being called? He pushed his way, struggling, dragging people on one side. There were angry voices, a hum growing louder and louder. He caught a woman by the neck and flung her aside. She screamed. Someone struck him in the face, and he tried to strike back. Down! He was down on the road. The air was stifling and stinking there. He tried to get up, and was forced back. Ah! now he was up again, his coat torn off his back, muddy, bleeding, fighting, spitting, howling like a madman.

"Damn you! damn you all!"

The crowd was a storm all round him, tossing him here and there. Again and again he was struck.

There was blood streaming over his eyes, and through the blood and mingled with blood he saw the green light looking.

There came a sudden lull. A couple of policemen stood by him, and one of them had him by the arm, and asked him what he was doing. He began to cry, sobbing like a child.

"Take me up there," he said, panting, "where the green light is; it's the dead woman calling."

The policeman stood for a moment hesitating. For a moment the crowd was motionless and silent. Then one of those white-faced boys shrank further back whispering:

"It's the man!"

THE MAGNET

[Subsequent to the inquest on the body of the Rev. Ingram Shallow, who shot himself in the churchyard of St. John's, Ilworthy, Bedfordshire, on the evening of October 14, the following paper was found at his lodgings in the village, and is here published for the first time. It will be remembered that at the inquest the usual verdict of temporary insanity was returned.]

Thursday, October 6.—The world is still ringing with the news of the ghastly accident to the express the night before last. The *Times* has a column and a half. Nothing else is spoken of in the village. Yesterday afternoon I went over on my bicycle to witness the scene of the accident. Of course, the more horrible traces of it had already been removed; the screams of the injured and dying and the sight of mangled bodies, about which we read in the papers, would have been too much for me. The up line was already clear, and it was expected the down line would also be clear in the course of a couple of hours. There was a perfect army of men at work, with every kind of ingenious contrivance for removing the heavy obstacles. All along the embankment fragments of the debris are still strewn. At a distance of at least forty yards from the point where the accident actually happened I found, among some wet grass and fern, a part of one of those plates they have up in the carriages, giving the number that the carriage is intended to carry. I have often noticed, when standing in the station, the appearance of strength which locomotives and carriages on the fast trains always have. Yet here one saw all this strength of no avail. The engine and the carriages were broken up just like a child's toys. I do most sincerely hope and believe that it was nobody in Ilworthy who was responsible for the disaster. Whoever it is, I do trust and pray that he may be discovered, and that he may pay with his own life for the lives of those hundreds his fiendish action has sent, without a moment of warning, into eternity.

Friday, October 7.—The Vicar came back with me to breakfast this morning after the early service. After some talk about the accident, I asked him if he intended to touch upon it on Sunday morning. He said that he would if I thought it necessary, but that his sermon was already written, being one of a series on the Gospels for the day, which he prepared some time ago. I said that undoubtedly the accident was a terrible event, and one which had sunk very deeply into the minds of everybody in Ilworthy. It was an event which might give point and weight to many a lesson, and it had been my view that Christianity was a practical religion, and the priest should, wherever possible, bring it to bear upon the events of the day. At the same time I did not insist; it was not for me to instruct him, the contrary was rather the case. He smiled good-temperedly, and said that since I seemed to be so full of the accident, and had taken such an absorbing interest in it, I could probably preach a better sermon on it myself, and I might use that as my subject for Sunday evening. I thanked him, and said that I would do so. I have spent the whole day over this sermon. I do not, like the Vicar, read my sermons, but I have written this out in full, and shall commit it to memory. I have given what I think is really a somewhat vivid and impressive picture of the great express rushing at headlong speed to ruin; the obstacle just seen by the driver one moment before his engine crashed into it; the sudden darkness of the train through the extinction of the lights; the screams for help; the sight of the dead bodies laid out on the embankment. . . . I have worked myself up so much about this sermon, that I have only to shut my eyes actually to witness the scene myself. I seem to be standing by the obstruction, and to see the long train crashing down upon me when it is too late to do anything. I hope I am not exciting myself too much about it. It is already past ten, and I think I shall have a cup of hot cocoa quietly and go to bed. I notice that one of the illustrated papers in the reading-room has a magnificent full-page illustration of the accident. I have often thought, by the way, of writing a little for the papers myself. I know I have some taste for the work, and I am inclined to think I have some little gift also. The supplement to one's income would be useful.

Sunday, October 9—I have just returned from church, exhausted. I preached over forty minutes, without the least sign of impatience from any of the congregation. No coughing or shuffling of the feet, or anything of the kind. In the vestry afterwards, Mr. Johnson, our senior churchwarden, took me aside, and told me that it was one of the strongest and most impressive addresses he had ever heard delivered from that pulpit. I hope I did not appear to be unduly pleased at this; one must not think of self in these matters, and I strive against it. I was a little surprised that after this special effort of mine the Vicar should have said nothing at all. He is not a small-minded man, and I cannot believe him to be actuated by jealousy. He spoke of the accident again, and said in what seemed to be rather a patronizing way that he was afraid I was letting it prey too much on my mind. I tried to be humble, and I think I can submit to a rebuke when it is deserved. But, really, this is nonsense. I still picture to myself at times the man standing by the obstruction and watching the express coming towards him. But for the awful wickedness of it, it would be, in a way, a magnificent moment. He would have the thought that he, a weak man, could at his will check the rush of a train, hurl it over, twist and break the strong iron as if it were cardboard, and avenge himself on hundreds of people; and then have all the police in the country hunting for him—and in vain. Exhausted though I am, I am afraid that I shall get no sleep to-night until I have been out in the fresh air a little. The church was crowded, and oppressively hot. The whole village is asleep, and no one will be any the wiser. I think I will get on my bicycle and ride down again to the place where the accident happened. It is within a quarter of an hour to midnight, and so Sunday is practically over. Besides, there are many very good men who do not consider that cycling on Sunday is wrong.

Monday, October 10.—To-day I have been beset by a terrible and most extraordinary temptation. I thank God that I have wrestled against it successfully; but the fact that such a temptation could even occur to me appalls me.

Tuesday, October 11.—The Vicar called this morning. He will take both sermons next Sunday. He said that I looked ill, and that he thought I had been overdoing it, and was in want of a holiday. I think he is right. He is really a very kind man. I shall go away next week. Again, all day long, I have been subject to the same diabolical impulse. I was half tempted to speak to the Vicar about it, but shame prevented me. I get but little sleep now at nights, and if I do sleep I am always haunted by the same dream. I see the lights of the express coming nearer and nearer. . . .

Wednesday, October 12.—It is done now. It had to be done, and it was no good to contend against it. I believe that it must have been the will of God that I should do it, for ever since the burden has been lifted from my mind, and I have been quite myself again. Late last night, or rather very early this morning, finding myself unable to sleep, I got up and went out. I did not take my bicycle. I ran all the way to that point on the line that I have always been thinking about. There is a stack of heavy sleepers there. It is at the bottom of a deep cutting, and you can see the train coming for some distance. I knew by the tables that I had not much time to spare. I had got six of the heavy sleepers across the rails, when I thought I heard it coming, but I was mistaken. I dragged on another, and then I heard the roar; there was no mistake about it. I could see the lights flashing as I saw them in my dream. I am ashamed that I had not the strength of mind to wait until the last moment. I tried to, but I could not. I ran away up the embankment and crossed some fields. I saw some men coming and hid behind a hedge. I knew that detectives were about. I lay there panting, and was afraid they would hear me, but they passed on. I got back to my lodgings while it was still dark; nobody had heard me go out, and nobody heard me come back. That is all right.

Since writing the above I have been to the Wednesday evening service. The Vicar was to deliver an address. At the last moment I felt that I wished to preach on this awful accident and the lessons it must have for every one of us. I crossed over to the Vicar and asked permission to preach. He refused. I warned him that I intended to preach, and that if he attempted to occupy the pulpit he would do so at his peril. Then I suddenly seemed to see the matter in a different light and apologized to him. However, I wish very much to address the village on the subject, and as I am not allowed to preach in church I shall call a public meeting on the recreation-ground. I must remember to get arrangements made as to the printing and posting of bills to-morrow.

THE CASE OF VINCENT PYRWHIT

The death of Vincent Pyrwhit, J.P., of Ellerdon House, Ellerdon, in the county of Buckingham, would in the ordinary way have received no more attention than the death of any other simple country gentleman. The circumstances of his death, however, though now long since forgotten, were sensational, and attracted some notice at the time. It was one of those cases which is easily forgotten within a year, except just in the locality where it occurred. The most sensational circumstances of the case never came before the public at all. I give them here simply and plainly. The psychical people may make what they like of them.

Pyrwhit himself was a very ordinary country gentleman, a good fellow, but in no way brilliant. He was devoted to his wife, who was some fifteen years younger than himself, and remarkably beautiful. She was quite a good woman, but she had her faults. She was fond of admiration, and she was an abominable flirt. She misled men very cleverly, and was then sincerely angry with them for having been misled. Her husband never troubled his head about these flirtations, being assured quite rightly that she was a good woman. He was not jealous; she, on the other hand, was possessed of a jealousy amounting almost to insanity. This might have caused trouble if he had ever provided her with the slightest basis on which her jealousy could work, but he never did. With the exception of his wife, women bored him. I believe she did once or twice try to make a scene for some preposterous reason which was no reason at all; but nothing serious came of it, and there was never a real quarrel between them.

On the death of his wife, after a prolonged illness, Pyrwhit wrote and asked me to come down to Ellerdon for the funeral, and to remain at least a few days with him. He would be quite alone, and I was his oldest friend. I hate attending funerals, but I *was* his oldest friend, and I was, moreover, a distant relation of his wife. I had no choice and I went down.

There were many visitors in the house for the funeral, which took place in the village churchyard, but they left immediately afterwards. The air of heavy gloom which had hung over the house seemed to lift a little. The servants (servants are always very emotional) continued to break dawn at intervals, noticeably Pyrwhit's man, Williams, but Pyrwhit himself was self-possessed. He spoke of his wife with great affection and regret, but still he could speak of her and not unsteadily. At dinner he also spoke of one or two other subjects, of politics and of his duties as a magistrate, and of course he made the requisite fuss about his gratitude to me for coming down to Ellerdon at that time. After dinner we sat in the library, a room well and expensively furnished, but without the least attempt at taste. There were a few oil paintings on the walls, a presentation portrait of himself, and a landscape or two—all more or less bad, as far as I remember. He had eaten next to nothing at dinner, but he had drunk a good deal; the wine, however, did not seem to have the least effect upon him. I had got the conversation definitely off the subject of his wife when I made a blunder. I noticed an Erichsen's extension standing on his writing-table. I said:

"I didn't know that telephones had penetrated into the villages yet."

"Yes," he said, "I believe they are common enough now. I had that one fitted up during my wife's illness to communicate with her bedroom on the floor above us on the other side of the house."

At that moment the bell of the telephone rang sharply.

We both looked at each other. I said with the stupid affectation of calmness one always puts on when one is a little bit frightened:

"Probably a servant in that room wishes to speak to you."

He got up, walked over to the machine, and swung the green cord towards me. The end of it was loose.

"I had it disconnected this morning," he said; "also the door of that room is locked, and no one can possibly be in it."

He had turned the colour of gray blotting-paper; so probably had I.

The bell rang again—a prolonged, rattling ring.

"Are you going to answer it?" I said.

"I am not," he answered firmly.

"Then," I said, "I shall answer it myself. It is some stupid trick, a joke not in the best of taste, for which you will probably have to sack one or other of your domestics."

"My servants," he answered, "would not have done that. Besides, don't you see it is impossible? The instrument is disconnected."

"The bell rang all the same. I shall try it."

I picked up the receiver.

"Are you there?" I called.

The voice which answered me was unmistakably the rather high staccato voice of Mrs. Pyrwhit.

"I want you," it said, "to tell my husband that he will be with me to-morrow."

I still listened. Nothing more was said.

I repeated, "Are you there?" and still there was no answer.

I turned to Pyrwhit.

"There is no one there," I said.

"Possibly there is thunder in the air affecting the bell in some mysterious way. There must be some simple explanation, and I'll find it all out to-morrow."

He went to bed early that night. All the following day I was with him. We rode together, and I expected an accident every minute, but none happened. All the evening I expected him to turn suddenly faint and ill, but that also did not happen. When at about ten o'clock he excused himself and said goodnight I felt distinctly relieved. He went up to his room and rang for Williams.

The rest is, of course, well known. The servant's reason had broken down, possibly the immediate cause being the death of Mrs. Pyrwhit. On entering his master's room, without the least hesitation, he raised a loaded revolver which he carried in his hand, and shot Pyrwhit through the heart. I behave the case is mentioned in some of the textbooks on homicidal mania.

THE BOTTOM OF THE GULF

Three hundred and sixty-two years before Christ a chasm opened in the Roman Forum, and the soothsayers declared that it would never close until the most precious treasure of Rome had been thrown into it. It is said that a youth named Mettus (or Mettius) Curtius appeared on horseback in full armour, and before a very fair audience, exclaiming that Rome had no dearer possession than arms and courage, leaped down into the gulf, which thereupon closed over him. This incident, like most of the legendary history of Rome, has been subjected to severe criticism. Those who too hastily disbelieve in it will reconsider their opinion on reading the account, not previously published, of what took place at the bottom of the gulf.

Curtius and the horse fell in the order in which they had started, with the horse underneath. After a few minutes' rapid passage the horse stopped falling somewhat suddenly, broke most of itself, and died. Curtius, who, though a little shaken, was uninjured, sat up on his dead horse and looked round to see if he could discover the nearest way back. As he looked upward he saw the top edges of the cavern close together, and the daylight shut out. But a curious greenish light still lingered in the cavern in which he found himself, and from one of its recesses came a voice which startled Mettus considerably. It said interrogatively:

"Did you hurt yourself?"

"Not much," replied Curtius. "I didn't know there was anybody down here. You quite startled me. Do come out and let me see you."

"No, thanks," said the voice. "Did you really believe that you would die when you jumped down the gulf?"

"Certainly I did."

The voice laughed, a mean little snigger.

"So you will, too. You'll die of suffocation, slowly, when the air in this cavern is exhausted."

"Then we'd better get to work at once," said Curtius. "I have an excellent sword here and a couple of daggers. I put them on for the occasion. I didn't fall so far as I expected, and if we both of us work hard we shall be able to cut our way out."

"Thanks," said the voice, "but I'm not going to do any work. I'm not of the same kind as yourself. I don't need the air of the outer world. In fact, I don't think much of the outer world, even its best specimens. That's why I live down here. You've got to die. Sorry, but there's no help for it. I've set my trap, and I caught you, and if you're the best specimen they can provide on top, my low opinion of them is confirmed."

"What do you mean by the 'trap'?" asked Curtius.

"Well, it was I who caused the chasm to open, knowing the kind of tomfool thing your soothsayers would remark about it. I sat here wondering what I should get. Shouldn't have been surprised at a brace of vestal virgins. They would have exclaimed, "Purity and devotion," instead of "Courage and arms," amid loud applause, of course. Or it might have been an elderly matron, with a good old tag that Rome held nothing more precious than the tender love of her mothers. It might have been a soothsayer, it might have been anything. As it is, it's you, and I think very little of you. Arms? Of what use do you think all those tin-pot arrangements which you have hung about you are likely to be? Courage? Why, man alive! you've got no courage at all."

"I have," said Curtius stolidly; "I fully expected to die, and I was willing to die."

"Just for one moment," said the voice, "when you had got all that mob of howling fools around applauding you. Applause is an intoxicant, and you got drunk on it. Now you are sober again, and you don't want to die at all. The man who can die alone, slowly and terribly, is courageous. But you've got no more courage in you than a piece of chewed string. You're as white as chalk."

"That's the effect of the green light," interposed Curtius.

"Rubbish!" replied the voice, "green light doesn't make a man shake all over, does it?"

"That's just the shock from the fall," said Curtius. "But I can't stop here arguing with you; I'm off to explore the cavern. There must be a way out somewhere."

"There isn't," said the voice; "but you can explore."

"I can't die like a rat in a trap," said Curtius, whimpering.

And off he went on his exploration. He looked in at the recess from which the voice had proceeded and found nothing. The cave was enormous. For many hours he tramped on and on, and never through one tiny chink in the roof did he see the light of day. Exhausted and ravenous, at last he flung himself down on the floor of the cave, and almost immediately the voice, which had been silent all this time, began again. First of all came that faint, mean little snigger; then it said:

"Hungry?"

"Worn out with hunger," sobbed Curtius; "I'm thirsty, too. My mouth is so parched that I can hardly speak, and there doesn't seem to be one drop of moisture in this damned cavern."

"There isn't," said the voice, "nor one crumb of food either, with the exception of your horse, and I don't think you will be able to find that again. You can try back if you like. Now I come to think of it, you won't die of suffocation, but of starvation. Cuts my entertainment rather shorter than I had hoped, but I must put up with that."

"I can't die like this," sobbed Curtius.

"Courage and arms," replied the voice, "are the things which Rome holds most precious. Go on, my boy; you'll last some time yet."

Then Curtius drew his sword, and went to look for the proprietor of the voice in order to slay him. But he didn't find him. He resumed his explorations.

In a few hours he was too weak to walk any further. He fell into a kind of doze, and when he woke again his arms had been taken from him.

"Where is my sword?" he exclaimed.

"I've got it," replied the voice, this time from the roof of the cavern; "what do you want it for?"

"Want to kill myself," said Curtius.

"If I give you your sword, will you own that you were merely a drunken theatrical impostor?"

"Yes."

"And that you are a coward, and are dying the death of a coward?"

"Yes."

The sword clattered down from the roof on to the floor of the cavern at the feet of the hero.

He picked it up and set his teeth.

THE END OF A SHOW

It was a little village in the extreme north of Yorkshire, three miles from a railway-station on a small branch line. It was not a progressive village; it just kept still and respected itself. The hills lay all round it, and seemed to shut it out from the rest of the world. Yet folks were born, and lived, and died, much as in the more important centres; and there were intervals which required to be filled with amusement. Entertainments were given by amateurs from time to time in the schoolroom; sometimes hand-bell ringers or a conjurer would visit the place, but their reception was not always encouraging. "Conjurers is nowt, an' ringers is nowt," said the sad native judiciously; "ar dornt regard 'em." But the native brightened up when in the summer months a few caravans found their way to a piece of waste land adjoining the churchyard. They formed the village fair, and for two days they were a popular resort. But it was understood that the fair had not the glories of old days; it had dwindled. Most things in connection with this village dwindled.

The first day of the fair was drawing to a close. It was half-past ten at night, and at eleven the fair would close until the following morning. This last half-hour was fruitful in business. The steam roundabout was crowded, the proprietor of the peep-show was taking pennies very fast, although not so fast as the proprietor of another, somewhat repulsive, show. A fair number patronized a canvas booth which bore the following inscription:

POPULAR SCIENCE LECTURES.
Admission Free.

252

At one end of this tent was a table covered with red baize; on it were bottles and boxes, a human skull, a retort, a large book, and some bundles of dried herbs. Behind it was the lecturer, an old man, gray and thin, wearing a bright-coloured dressing-gown. He lectured volubly and enthusiastically; his energy and the atmosphere of the tent made him very hot, and occasionally he mopped his forehead.

"I am about to exhibit to you," he said, speaking clearly and correctly, "a secret known to few, and believed to have come originally from those wise men of the East referred to in Holy Writ." Here he filled two test-tubes with water, and placed some bluish-green crystals in one and some yellow crystals in the other. He went on talking, quoting scraps of Latin, telling stories, making local and personal allusions, finally coming back again to his two test-tubes, both of which now contained almost colourless solutions.

He poured them both together into a flat glass vessel, and the mixture at once turned to a deep brownish purple. He threw a fragment of something on to the surface of the mixture, and that fragment at once caught fire. This favourite trick succeeded; the audience were undoubtedly impressed, and before they quite realized by what logical connection the old man had arrived at the subject, he was talking to them about the abdomen. He seemed to know the most unspeakable and intimate things about the abdomen. He had made pills which suited its peculiar needs, which he could and would sell in boxes at sixpence and one shilling, according to size. He sold four boxes at once, and was back in his classical and anecdotal stage, when a woman pressed forward. She was a very poor woman. Could she have a box of these pills at half-price? Her son was bad, very bad. It would be a kindness.

He interrupted her in a dry, distinct voice:

"Woman, I never yet did anyone a kindness, not even myself."

However, a friend pushed some money into her hand, and she bought two boxes.

It was past twelve o'clock now. The flaring lights were out in the little group of caravans on the waste ground. The tired proprietors of the shows were asleep. The gravestones in the churchyard were glimmering white in the bright moonlight. But at the entrance to that little canvas booth the quack doctor sat on one of his boxes, smoking a clay pipe. He had taken off the dressing-gown, and was in his shirt-sleeves; his clothes were black, much worn. His attention was arrested—he thought that he heard the sound of sobbing.

"It's a God-forsaken world," he said aloud. After a second's silence he spoke again. "No, I never did a kindness even to myself, though I thought I did, or I shouldn't have come to this."

He took his pipe from his mouth and spat. Once more he heard that strange wailing sound; this time he arose, and walked in the direction of it.

Yes, that was it. It came from that caravan standing alone where the trees made a dark spot. The caravan was gaudily painted, and there were steps from the door to the ground. He remembered having noticed it once during the day. It was evident that someone inside was in trouble—great trouble. The old man knocked gently at the door.

"Who's there? What's the matter?"

"Nothing," said a broken voice from within.

"Are you a woman?"

There was a fearful laugh.

"Neither man nor woman—a show."

"What do you mean?"

"Go round to the side, and you'll see."

The old man went round, and by the light of two wax matches caught a glimpse of part of the rough painting on the side of the caravan. The matches dropped from his hand. He came back, and sat down on the steps of the caravan.

"You are not like that," he said.

"No, worse. I'm not dressed in pretty clothes, and lying on a crimson velvet couch. I'm half naked, in a corner of this cursed box, and crying because my owner beat me. Now go, or I'll open the door and show myself to you as I am now. It would frighten you; it would haunt your sleep."

"Nothing frightens me. I was a fool once, but I have never been frightened. What right has this owner over you?"

"He is my father," the voice screamed loudly; then there was more weeping; then it spoke again:

"It's awful; I could bear anything now—anything—if I thought it would ever be any better; but it won't. My mind's a woman's and my wants are a woman's, but I am not a woman. I am a show. The brutes stand round me, talk to me, touch me!"

"There's a way out," said the old man quietly, after a pause.

An idea had occurred to him.

"I know—and I daren't take it—I've got a thing here, but I daren't use it."

"You could drink something— something that wouldn't hurt?"

"Yes."

"You are quite alone?"

"Yes; my owner is in the village, at the inn."

"Then wait a minute."

The old man hastened back to the canvas booth, and fumbled about with his chemicals. He murmured something about doing someone a kindness at last. Then he returned to the caravan with a glass of colourless liquid in his hand.

"Open the door and take it," he said.

The door was opened a very little way. A thin hand was thrust out and took the glass eagerly. The door closed, and the voice spoke again.

"It will be easy."

"Yes."

"Good-bye, then. To your health "

The old man heard the glass crash on the wooden floor, then he went back to his seat in front of the booth, and carefully lit another pipe.

"I will not go," he said aloud. "I fear nothing—not even the results of my best action."

He listened attentively.

No sound whatever came from the caravan. All was still. Far away the sky was growing lighter with the dawn of a fine summer day.

THE UNDYING THING

Up and down the oak-panelled dining-hall of Mansteth the master of the house walked restlessly. At formal intervals down the long severe table were placed four silver candlesticks, but the light from these did not serve to illuminate the whole of the surroundings. It just touched the portrait of a fair-haired boy with a sad and wistful expression that hung at one end of the room; it sparkled on the lid of a silver tankard. As Sir Edric passed to and fro it lit up his face and figure. It was a bold and resolute face with a firm chin and passionate, dominant eyes. A bad past was written in the lines of it. And yet every now and then there came over it a strange look of very anxious gentleness that gave it some resemblance to the portrait of the fair-haired boy. Sir Edric paused a moment before the portrait and surveyed it carefully, his strong brown hands locked behind him, his gigantic shoulders thrust a little forward.

"Ah, what I was!" he murmured to himself— "what I was!"

Once more he commenced pacing up and down. The candles, mirrored in the polished wood of the table, had burnt low. For hours Sir Edric had been waiting, listening intently for some sound from the room above or from the broad staircase outside. There had been sounds—the wailing of a woman, a quick abrupt voice, the moving of rapid feet. But for the last hour he had heard nothing. Quite suddenly he stopped and dropped on his knees against the table:

"God, I have never thought of Thee. Thou knowest that—Thou knowest that by my devilish behaviour and cruelty I did veritably murder Alice, my first wife, albeit the physicians did maintain that she died of a decline—a wasting sickness. Thou knowest that all here in Mansteth do hate me, and that rightly. They say, too, that I am mad; but that they say not rightly, seeing that I know how wicked I am. I always knew it, but I never cared until I loved—oh, God, I never cared!"

His fierce eyes opened for a minute, glared round the room, and closed again tightly. He went on:

"God, for myself I ask nothing; I make no bargaining with Thee. Whatsoever punishment Thou givest me to bear I will bear it; whatsoever Thou givest me to do I will do it. Whether Thou killest Eve or whether Thou keepest her in life—and never have I loved but her—I will from this night be good. In due penitence will I receive the holy Sacrament of Thy Body and Blood. And my son, the one child that I had by Alice, I will fetch back again from Challonsea, where I kept him in order that I might not look upon him, and I will be to him a father in deed and very truth. And in all things, so far as in me lieth, I will make restitution and atonement. Whether Thou hearest me or whether Thou hearest me not, these things shall be. And for my prayer, it is but this: of Thy loving kindness, most merciful God, be Thou with Eve and make her happy; and after these great pains and perils of childbirth send her Thy peace. Of Thy loving-kindness, Thy merciful loving-kindness, O God!"

Perhaps the prayer that is offered when the time for praying is over is more terribly pathetic than any other. Yet one might hesitate to say that this prayer was unanswered.

Sir Edric rose to his feet. Once more he paced the room. There was a strange simplicity about him, the simplicity that scorns an incongruity. He felt that his lips and throat were parched and dry. He lifted the heavy silver tankard from the table and raised the lid; there was still a good draught of mulled wine in it with the burnt toast, cut heart-shape, floating on the top.

"To the health of Eve and her child," he said aloud, and drained it to the last drop.

Click, click! As he put the tankard down he heard distinctly two doors opened and shut quickly, one after the other. And then slowly down the stairs came a hesitating step. Sir Edric could bear the suspense no longer. He opened the dining-room door, and the dim light strayed out into the dark hall beyond.

"Dennison," he said, in a low, sharp whisper, "is that you?"

"Yes, yes. I am coming. Sir Edric."

A moment afterwards Dr. Dennison entered the room. He was very pale; perspiration streamed from his forehead; his cravat was disarranged. He was an old man, thin, with the air of proud humility. Sir Edric watched him narrowly.

"Then she is dead," he said, with a quiet that Dr. Dennison had not expected.

"Twenty physicians—a hundred physicians could not have saved her, Sir Edric. She was—" He gave some details of medical interest.

"Dennison," said Sir Edric, still speaking with calm and restraint, "why do you seem thus indisposed and panic-stricken? You are a physician; have you never looked upon the face of death before? The soul of my wife is with God—"

"Yes," murmured Dennison, "a good woman, a perfect, saintly woman."

"And," Sir Edric went on, raising his eyes to the ceiling as though he could see through it, "her body lies in great dignity and beauty upon the bed, and there is no horror in it. Why are you afraid?"

"I do not fear death, Sir Edric."

"But your hands—they are not steady. You are evidently overcome. Does the child live?"

"Yes, it lives."

"Another boy—a brother for young Edric, the child that Alice bore me?"

"There—there is something wrong. I do not know what to do. I want you to come upstairs. And, Sir Edric, I must tell you, you will need your self-command."

"Dennison, the hand of God is heavy upon me; but from this time forth until the day of my death I am submissive to it, and God send that that day may come quickly! I will follow you and I will endure."

He took one of the high silver candlesticks from the table and stepped towards the door. He strode quickly up the staircase. Dr. Dennison following a little way behind him.

As Sir Edric waited at the top of the staircase he heard suddenly from the room before him a low cry. He put down the candlestick on the floor and leaned back against the wall listening. The cry came again, a vibrating monotone ending in a growl.

"Dennison, Dennison!"

His voice choked; he could not go on.

"Yes," said the doctor, "it is in there. I had the two women out of the room, and got it here. No one but myself has seen it. But you must see it, too."

He raised the candle and the two men entered the room—one of the spare bedrooms. On the bed there was something moving under cover of a blanket. Dr. Dennison paused for a moment and then flung the blanket partially back.

They did not remain in the room for more than a few seconds. The moment they got outside, Dr. Dennison began to speak.

"Sir Edric, I would fain suggest somewhat to you. There is no evil, as Sophocles hath it in his 'Antigone,' for which man hath not found a remedy, except it be death, and here—"

Sir Edric interrupted him in a husky voice.

"Downstairs, Dennison. This is too near."

It was, indeed, passing strange. When once the novelty of this—this occurrence had worn off, Dr. Dennison seemed no longer frightened. He was calm, academic, interested in an unusual phenomenon. But Sir Edric, who was said in the village to fear nothing in earth, or heaven, or hell, was obviously much moved.

When they had got back to the dining-room. Sir Edric motioned the doctor to a seat.

"Now, then," he said, "I will hear you. Something must be done—and to-night."

"Exceptional cases," said Dr. Dennison, "demand exceptional remedies. Well, it lies there upstairs and is at our mercy. We can let it live, or, placing one hand over the mouth and nostrils, we can—"

"Stop," said Sir Edric. "This thing has so crushed and humiliated me that I can scarcely think. But I recall that while I waited for you I fell upon my knees and prayed that God would save Eve. And, as I confessed unto Him more than I will ever confess unto man, it seemed to me that it were ignoble to offer a price for His favour. And I said that whatsoever punishment I had to bear, I would bear it; and whatsoever He called upon me to do, I would do it; and I made no conditions."

"Well?"

"Now my punishment is of two kinds. Firstly, my wife, Eve, is dead. And this I bear more easily because I know that now she is numbered with the company of God's saints, and with them her pure spirit finds happier communion than with me; I was not worthy of her. And yet she would call my roughness by gentle, pretty names. She gloried, Dennison, in the mere strength of my body, and in the greatness of my stature. And I am thankful that she never saw this—this shame that has come upon the house. For she was a proud woman, with all her gentleness, even as I was proud and bad until it pleased God this night to break me even to the dust. And for my second punishment, that, too, I must bear. This thing that lies upstairs, I will take and rear; it is bone of my bone and flesh of my flesh; only, if it be possible, I will hide my shame so that no man but you shall know of it."

"This is not possible. You cannot keep a living being in this house unless it be known. Will not these women say, 'Where is the child?'"

Sir Edric stood upright, his powerful hands linked before him, his face working in agony; but he was still resolute.

"Then if it must be known, it shall be known. The fault is mine. If I had but done sooner what Eve asked, this would not have happened. I will bear it."

"Sir Edric, do not be angry with me, for if I did not say this, then I should be but an ill counsellor. And, firstly, do not use the word shame. The ways of nature are past all explaining; if a woman be frail and easily impressed, and other circumstances concur, then in some few rare cases a thing of this sort does happen. If there be shame, it is not upon you but upon nature—to whom one would not lightly impute shame. Yet it is true that common and uninformed people might think that this shame was yours. And herein lies the great trouble—the shame would rest also on her memory."

"Then," said Sir Edric, in a low, unfaltering voice, "this night for the sake of Eve I will break my word, and lose my own soul eternally."

About an hour afterwards Sir Edric and Dr. Dennison left the house together. The doctor carried a stable lantern in his hand. Sir Edric bore in his arms something wrapped in a blanket. They went through the long garden, out into the orchard that skirts the north side of the park, and then across a field to a small dark plantation known as Hal's Planting. In the very heart of Hal's Planting there are some curious caves: access to the innermost chamber of them is exceedingly difficult and dangerous, and only possible to a climber of exceptional skill and courage. As they returned from these caves. Sir Edric no longer carried his burden. The dawn was breaking and the birds began to sing.

"Could not they be quiet just for this morning?" said Sir Edric wearily.

There were but few people who were asked to attend the funeral of Lady Vanquerest and of the baby which, it was said, had only survived her by a few hours. There were but three people who knew that only one body—the body of Lady Vanquerest—was really interred on that occasion. These three were Sir Edric Vanquerest, Dr. Dennison, and a nurse whom it had been found expedient to take into their confidence.

During the next six years Sir Edric lived, almost in solitude, a life of great sanctity, devoting much of his time to the education of the younger Edric, the child that he had by his first wife. In the course of this time some strange stories began to be told and believed in the neighbourhood with reference to Hal's Planting, and the place was generally avoided.

When Sir Edric lay on his deathbed the windows of the chamber were open, and suddenly through them came a low cry. The doctor in attendance hardly regarded it, supposing that it came from one of the owls in the trees outside. But Sir Edric, at the sound of it, rose right up in bed before anyone could stay him, and flinging up his arms cried, "Wolves! wolves! wolves!" Then he fell forward on his face, dead.

And four generations passed away.

II

Towards the latter end of the nineteenth century, John Marsh, who was the oldest man in the village of Mansteth, could be prevailed upon to state what he recollected. His two sons supported him in his old age; he never felt the pinch of poverty, and he always had money in his pocket; but it was a settled principle with him that he would not pay for the pint of beer which he drank occasionally in the parlour of The Stag. Sometimes Farmer Wynthwaite paid for the beer; sometimes it was Mr. Spicer from the post-office; sometimes the landlord of The Stag himself would finance the old man's evening dissipation. In return, John Marsh was prevailed upon to state what he recollected; this he would do with great heartiness and strict impartiality, recalling the intemperance of a former Wynthwaite and the dishonesty of some ancestral Spicer while he drank the beer of their direct descendants. He would tell you, with two tough old fingers crooked round the handle of the pewter that you had provided, how your grandfather was a poor thing, "fit for nowt but to brak steeans by ta rord-side." He was so disrespectful that it was believed that he spoke truth. He was particularly disrespectful when he spoke of that most devilish family, the Vanquerests; and he never tired of recounting the stories that from generation to generation had grown up about them. It would be objected, sometimes, that the present Sir Edric, the last surviving member of the race, was a pleasant-spoken young man, with none of the family wildness and hot temper. It was for no sin of his that Hal's Planting was haunted—a thing which everyone in Mansteth, and many beyond it, most devoutly believed. John Marsh would hear no apology for him, nor for any of his ancestors; he recounted the prophecy that an old mad woman had made of the family before her strange death, and hoped, fervently, that he might live to see it fulfilled.

The third baronet, as has already been told, had lived the latter part of his life, after his second wife's death, in peace and quietness. Of him John Marsh remembered nothing, of course, and could only recall the few fragments of information that had been handed down to him. He had been told that this Sir Edric, who had travelled a good deal, at one time kept wolves, intending to train them to serve as dogs; these wolves were not kept under proper restraint, and became a kind of terror to the neighbourhood. Lady Vanquerest, his second wife, had asked him frequently to destroy these beasts; but Sir Edric, although it was said that he loved his second wife even more than he hated the first, was obstinate when any of his whims were crossed, and put her off with promises. Then one day Lady Vanquerest herself was attacked by the wolves; she was not bitten, but she was badly frightened. That filled Sir Edric with remorse, and, when it was too late, he went out into the yard where the wolves were kept and shot them all. A few months afterwards Lady Vanquerest died in childbirth. It was a queer thing, John Marsh noted, that it was just at this time that Hal's Planting began to get such a bad name. The fourth baronet was, John Marsh considered, the worst of the race; it was to him that the old mad woman had made her prophecy, an incident that Marsh himself had witnessed in his childhood and still vividly remembered.

The baronet, in his old age, had been cast up by his vices on the shores of melancholy; heavy-eyed, gray-haired, bent, he seemed to pass through life as in a dream. Every day he would go out on horseback, always at a walking pace, as though he were following the funeral of his past self. One night he was riding up the village street as this old woman came down it. Her name was Ann Ruthers; she had a kind of reputation in the village, and although all said that she was mad, many of her utterances were remembered, and she was treated with respect. It was growing dark, and the village street was almost empty; but just at the lower end was the usual group of men by the door of The Stag, dimly illuminated by the light that came through the quaint windows of the old inn. They glanced at Sir Edric as he rode slowly past them, taking no notice of their respectful salutes. At the upper end of the street there were two persons. One was Ann Ruthers, a tall, gaunt old woman, her head wrapped in a shawl; the other was John Marsh. He was then a boy of eight, and he was feeling somewhat frightened. He had been on an expedition to a distant and foetid pond, and in the black mud and clay about its borders he had discovered live newts; he had three of them in his pocket, and this was to some extent a joy to him, but his joy was damped by his knowledge that he was coming home much too late, and would probably be chastised in consequence. He was unable to walk fast or to run, because Ann Ruthers was immediately in front of him, and he dared not pass her, especially at night. She walked on until she met Sir Edric, and then, standing still, she called him by name. He pulled in his horse and raised his heavy eyes to look at her. Then in loud clear tones she spoke to him, and John Marsh heard and remembered every word that she said; it was her prophecy of the end of the Vanquerests. Sir Edric never answered a word. When she had finished, he rode on, while she remained standing there, her eyes fixed on the stars above her. John Marsh dared not pass the mad woman; he turned round and walked back, keeping close to Sir Edric's horse. Quite suddenly, without a word of warning, as if in a moment of ungovernable irritation, Sir Edric wheeled his horse round and struck the boy across the face with his switch.

On the following morning John Marsh—or rather, his parents—received a handsome solatium in coin of the realm; but sixty-five years afterwards he had not forgiven that blow, and still spoke of the Vanquerests as a most devilish family, still hoped and prayed that he might see the prophecy fulfilled. He would relate, too, the death of Ann Ruthers, which occurred either later on the night of her prophecy or early on the following day. She would often roam about the country all night, and on this particular night she left the main road to wander over the Vanquerest lands, where trespassers, especially at night, were not welcomed. But no one saw her, and it seemed that she had made her way to a part where no one was likely to see her; for none of the keepers would have entered Hal's Planting by night. Her body was found there at noon on the following day, lying under the tall bracken, dead, but without any mark of violence upon it. It was considered that she had died in a fit. This naturally added to the ill-repute of Hal's Planting. The woman's death caused considerable sensation in the village. Sir Edric sent a messenger to the married sister with whom she had lived, saying that he wished to pay all the funeral expenses. This offer, as John Marsh recalled with satisfaction, was refused.

Of the last two baronets he had but little to tell. The fifth baronet was credited with the family temper, but he conducted himself in a perfectly conventional way, and did not seem in the least to belong to romance. He was a good man of business, and devoted himself to making up, as far as he could, for the very extravagant expenditure of his predecessors. His son, the present Sir Edric, was a fine young fellow and popular in the village. Even John Marsh could find nothing to say against him; other people in the village were interested in him. It was said that he had chosen a wife in London—a Miss Guerdon—and would shortly be back to see that Mansteth Hall was put in proper order for her before his marriage at the close of the season. Modernity kills ghostly romance. It was difficult to associate this modern and handsome Sir Edric, bright and spirited, a good sportsman and a good fellow, with the doom that had been foretold for the Vanquerest family. He himself knew the tradition and laughed at it. He wore clothes made by a London tailor, looked healthy, smiled cheerfully, and, in a vain attempt to shame his own head-keeper, had himself spent a night alone in Hal's Planting. This last was used by Mr. Spicer in argument, who would ask John Marsh what he made of it. John Marsh replied, contemptuously, that it was "nowt." It was not so that the Vanquerest family was to end; but when the thing, whatever it was, that lived in Hal's Planting, left it and came up to the house, to Mansteth Hall itself, then one would see the end of the Vanquerests. So Ann Ruthers had prophesied. Sometimes Mr. Spicer would ask the pertinent question, how did John Marsh know that there really was anything in Hal's Planting? This he asked, less because he disbelieved, than because he wished to draw forth an account of John's personal experiences. These were given in great detail, but they did not amount to very much. One night John Marsh had been taken by business—Sir Edric's keepers would have called the business by hard names—into the neighbourhood of Hal's Planting. He had there been suddenly startled by a cry, and had run away as though he were running for his life. That was all he could tell about the cry—it was the kind of cry to make a man lose his head and run. And then it always happened that John Marsh was urged by his companions to enter Hal's Planting himself, and discover what was there. John pursed his thin lips together, and hinted that that also might be done one of these days. Whereupon Mr. Spicer looked across his pipe to Farmer Wynthwaite, and smiled significantly.

Shortly before Sir Edric's return from London, the attention of Mansteth was once more directed to Hal's Planting, but not by any supernatural occurrence. Quite suddenly, on a calm day, two trees there fell with a crash; there were caves in the centre of the plantation, and it seemed as if the roof of some big chamber in these caves had given way.

They talked it over one night in the parlour of The Stag. There was water in these caves. Farmer Wynthwaite knew it; and he expected a further subsidence. If the whole thing collapsed, what then?

"Ay," said John Marsh. He rose from his chair, and pointed in the direction of the Hall with his thumb. "What then?"

He walked across to the fire, looked at it meditatively for a moment, and then spat in it.

"A trewly wun'ful owd mon," said Farmer Wynthwaite as he watched him.

III

In the smoking-room at Mansteth Hall sat Sir Edric with his friend and intended brother-in-law, Dr. Andrew Guerdon. Both men were on the verge of middle-age; there was hardly a year's difference between them. Yet Guerdon looked much the older man; that was, perhaps, because he wore a short, black beard, while Sir Edric was clean shaven. Guerdon was thought to be an enviable man. His father had made a fortune in the firm of Guerdon, Guerdon and Bird; the old style was still retained at the bank, although there was no longer a Guerdon in the firm. Andrew Guerdon had a handsome allowance from his father, and had also inherited money through his mother. He had taken the degree of Doctor of Medicine; he did not practice, but he was still interested in science, especially in out-of-the-way science. He was unmarried, gifted with perpetually good health, interested in life, popular. His friendship with Sir Edric dated from their college days. It had for some years been almost certain that Sir Edric would marry his friend's sister, Ray Guerdon, although the actual betrothal had only been announced that season.

On a bureau in one corner of the room were spread a couple of plans and various slips of paper. Sir Edric was wrinkling his brows over them, dropping cigar-ash over them, and finally getting angry over them. He pushed back his chair irritably, and turned towards Guerdon.

"Look here, old man!" he said. "I desire to curse the original architect of this house—to curse him in his down-sitting and his uprising."

"Seeing that the original architect has gone to where beyond these voices there is peace, he won't be offended. Neither shall I. But why worry yourself? You've been rooted to that blessed bureau all day, and now, after dinner, when every self-respecting man chucks business, you return to it again—even as a sow returns to her wallowing in the mire."

"Now, my good Andrew, do be reasonable. How on earth can I bring Ray to such a place as this? And it's built with such ingrained malice and vexatiousness that one can't live in it as it is, and can't alter it without having the whole shanty tumble down about one's ears. Look at this plan now. That thing's what they're pleased to call a morning room. If the window had been *here* there would have been an uninterrupted view of open country. So what does this forsaken fool of an architect do? He sticks it *there*, where you see it on the plan, looking straight on to a blank wall with a stable yard on the other side of it. But that's a trifle. Look here again—"

"I won't look any more. This place is all right. It was good enough for your father and mother and several generations before them until you arose to improve the world; it was good enough for you until you started to get married. It's a picturesque place, and if you begin to alter it you'll spoil it." Guerdon looked round the room critically. "Upon my word," he said, "I don't know of any house where I like the smoking-room as well as I like this. It's not too big, and yet it's fairly lofty; it's got those comfortable-looking oak-panelled walls. That's the right kind of fireplace, too, and these corner cupboards are handy."

"Of course this won't *remain* the smoking-room. It has the morning sun, and Ray likes that, so I shall make it into her boudoir. It is a nice room, as you say."

"That's it, Ted, my boy," said Guerdon bitterly; "take a room which is designed by nature and art to be a smoking-room and turn it into a boudoir. Turn it into the very deuce of a boudoir with the morning sun laid on for ever and ever. Waste the twelfth of August by getting married on it. Spend the winter in foreign parts, and write letters that you can breakfast out of doors, just as if you'd created the mildness of the climate yourself. Come back in the spring and spend the London season in the country in order to avoid seeing anybody who wants to see you. That's the way to do it; that's the way to get yourself generally loved and admired!"

"That's chiefly imagination," said Sir Edric. "I'm blest if I can see why I should not make this house fit for Ray to live in."

"It's a queer thing: Ray was a good girl, and you weren't a bad sort yourself. You prepare to go into partnership, and you both straightway turn into despicable lunatics. I'll have a word or two with Ray. But I'm serious about this house. Don't go tinkering it; it's got a character of its own, and you'd better leave it. Turn half Tottenham Court Road and the culture thereof—Heaven help it!— into your town house if you like, but leave this alone."

"Haven't got a town house—yet. Anyway I'm not going to be unsuitable; I'm not going to feel myself at the mercy of a big firm.

I shall supervise the whole thing myself. I shall drive over to
Challonsea to-morrow afternoon and see if I can't find some intelligent and fairly conscientious workmen."

"That's all right; you supervise them and I'll supervise you.
You'll be much too new if I don't look after you. You've got an old
legend, I believe, that the family's coming to a bad end; you must
be consistent with it. As you are bad, be beautiful. By the way, what
do you yourself think of the legend?"

"It's nothing," said Sir Edric, speaking, however, rather seriously. "They say that Hal's Planting is haunted by something that
will not die. Certainly an old woman, who for some godless reason
of her own made her way there by night, was found there dead on
the following morning; but her death could be, and was, accounted
for by natural causes. Certainly, too, I haven't a man in my employ
who'll go there by night now."

"Why not?"

"How should I know? I fancy that a few of the villagers sit booz-
ing at The Stag in the evening, and like to scare themselves by
swopping lies about Hal's Planting. I've done my best to stop it. I
once, as you know, took a rug, a revolver and a flask of whisky and
spent the night there myself. But even that didn't convince them."

"Yes, you told me. By the way, did you hear or see anything?"

Sir Edric hesitated before he answered. Finally he said:

"Look here, old man, I wouldn't tell this to anyone but yourself. I did think that I heard something. About the middle of the
night I was awakened by a cry; I can only say that it was the kind
of cry that frightened me. I sat up, and at that moment I heard
some great, heavy thing go swishing through the bracken behind
me at a great rate. Then all was still; I looked about, but I could
find nothing. At last I argued as I would argue now that a man who
is just awake is only half awake, and that his powers of observation, by hearing or any other sense, are not to be trusted. I even
persuaded myself to go to sleep again, and there was no more dis-
turbance. However, there's a real danger there now. In the heart
of the plantation there are some eaves and a subterranean spring;
lately there has been some slight subsidence there, and the same
sort of thing will happen again in all probability. I wired today to

an expert to come and look at the place; he has replied that he will come on Monday. The legend says that when the thing that lives in Hal's Planting comes up to the Hall the Vanquerests will be ended. If I cut down the trees and then break up the place with a charge of dynamite I shouldn't wonder if I spoiled that legend."

Guerdon smiled.

"I'm inclined to agree with you all through. It's absurd to trust the immediate impressions of a man just awakened; what you heard was probably a stray cow."

"No cow," said Sir Edric impartially. "There's a low wall all round the place—not much of a wall, but too much for a cow."

"Well, something else—some equally obvious explanation. In dealing with such questions, never forget that you're in the nineteenth century. By the way, your man's coming on Monday. That reminds me to-day's Friday, and as an indisputable consequence to-morrow's Saturday, therefore, if you want to find your intelligent workmen it will be of no use to go in the afternoon."

"True," said Sir Edric, "I'll go in the morning." He walked to a tray on a side table and poured a little whisky into a tumbler. "They don't seem to have brought any seltzer water," he remarked in a grumbling voice.

He rang the bell impatiently.

"Now why don't you use those corner cupboards for that kind of thing? If you kept a supply there, it would be handy in case of accidents."

"They're full up already." He opened one of them and showed that it was filled with old account-books and yellow documents tied up in bundles. The servant entered.

"Oh, I say; there isn't any seltzer. Bring it, please."

He turned again to Guerdon. "You might do me a favour when I'm away to-morrow, if there's nothing else that you want to do. I wish you'd look through all these papers for me. They're all old. Possibly some of them ought to go to my solicitor, and I know that a lot of them ought to be destroyed. Some few may be of family interest. It's not the kind of thing that I could ask a stranger or a servant to do for me, and I've so much on hand just now before my marriage—"

"But of course, my dear fellow, I'll do it with pleasure."

"I'm ashamed to give you all this bother. However, you said that you were coming here to help me, and I take you at your word. By the way, I think you'd better not say anything to Ray about the Hal's Planting story."

"I may be some of the things that you take me for, but really I am not a common ass. Of course I shouldn't tell her."

"I'll tell her myself, and I'd sooner do it when I've got the whole thing cleared up. Well, I'm really obliged to you."

"I needn't remind you that I hope to receive as much again. I believe in compensation. Nature always gives it and always requires it. One finds it everywhere, in philology and onwards."

"I could mention omissions."

"They are few, and make a belief in a hereafter to supply them logical."

"Lunatics, for instance?"

"Their delusions are often their compensation. They argue correctly from false premises. A lunatic believing himself to be a millionaire has as much delight as money can give."

"How about deformities or monstrosities?"

"The principle is there, although I don't pretend that the compensation is always adequate. A man who is deprived of one sense generally has another developed with unusual acuteness. As for monstrosities of at all a human type one sees none; the things exhibited in fairs are, almost without exception, frauds. They occur rarely, and one does not know enough about them. A really good text-book on the subject would be interesting. Still, such stories as I have heard would bear out my theory—stories of their superhuman strength and cunning, and of the extraordinary prolongation of life that has been noted, or is said to have been noted, in them. But it is hardly fair to test my principle by exceptional cases. Besides, anyone can prove anything except that anything's worth proving."

"That's a cheerful thing to say. I wouldn't like to swear that I could prove how the Hal's Planting legend started; but I fancy, do you know, that I could make a very good shot at it."

"Well?"

"My great-grandfather kept wolves—I can't say why. Do you remember the portrait of him?—not the one when he was a boy, the other. It hangs on the staircase. There's now a group of wolves in one corner of the picture. I was looking carefully at the picture one day and thought that I detected some over-painting in that corner; indeed, it was done so roughly that a child would have noticed it if the picture had been hung in a better light. I had the over-painting removed by a good man, and underneath there was that group of wolves depicted. Well, one of these wolves must have escaped, got into Hal's Planting, and scared an old woman or two; that would start a story, and human mendacity would do the rest."

"Yes," said Guerdon meditatively, "that doesn't sound improbable. But why did your great-grandfather have the wolves painted out?"

IV

Saturday morning was fine, but very hot and sultry. After breakfast, when Sir Edric had driven off to Challonsea, Andrew Guerdon settled himself in a comfortable chair in the smoking-room. The contents of the corner cupboard were piled up on a table by his side. He lit his pipe and began to go through the papers and put them in order. He had been at work about a quarter of an hour when the butler entered rather abruptly, looking pale and disturbed.

"In Sir Edric's absence, sir, it was thought that I had better come to you for advice. There's been an awful thing happened."

"Well?"

"They've found a corpse in Hal's Planting about half an hour ago. It's the body of an old man, John Marsh, who used to live in the village. He seems to have died in some kind of a fit. They were bringing it here, but I had it taken down to the village where his cottage is. Then I sent to the police and to a doctor."

There was a moment or two's silence before Guerdon answered.

"This is a terrible thing. I don't know of anything else that you could do. Stop; if the police want to see the spot where the body was found, I think that Sir Edric would like them to have every facility."

"Quite so, sir."

"And no one else must be allowed there."

"No, sir. Thank you."

The butler withdrew.

Guerdon arose from his chair and began to pace up and down the room

"What an impressive thing a coincidence is!" he thought to himself. "Last night the whole of the Hal's Planting story seemed to me not worth consideration. But this second death there—it can be only coincidence. What else could it be?"

The question would not leave him. What else could it be? Had that dead man seen something there and died in sheer terror of it? Had Sir Edric really heard something when he spent that night there alone? He returned to his work, but he found that he got on with it but slowly. Every now and then his mind wandered back to the subject of Hal's Planting. His doubts annoyed him. It was unscientific and unmodern of him to feel any perplexity, because a natural and rational explanation was possible; he was annoyed with himself for being perplexed.

After luncheon he strolled round the grounds and smoked a cigar. He noticed that a thick bank of dark, slate-coloured clouds was gathering in the west. The air was very still. In a remote corner of the garden a big heap of weeds was burning; the smoke went up perfectly straight. On the top of the heap light flames danced; they were like the ghosts of flames in the strange light. A few big drops of rain fell. The small shower did not last for five seconds. Guerdon glanced at his watch. Sir Edric would be back in an hour, and he wanted to finish his work with the papers before Sir Edric's return, so he went back into the house once more.

He picked up the first document that came to hand. As he did so, another, smaller, and written on parchment, which had been folded in with it, dropped out. He began to read the parchment; it was written in faded ink, and the parchment itself was yellow and in many places stained. It was the confession of the third baronet—

he could tell that by the date upon it. It told the story of that night when he and Dr. Dennison went together carrying a burden through the long garden out into the orchard that skirts the north side of the park, and then across a field to a small, dark plantation. It told how he made a vow to God and did not keep it. These were the last words of the confession:

"Already upon me has the punishment fallen, and the devil's wolves do seem to hunt me in my sleep nightly. But I know that there is worse to come. The thing that I took to Hal's Planting is dead. Yet will it come back again to the Hall, and then will the Vanquerests be at an end. This writing I have committed to chance, neither showing it nor hiding it, and leaving it to chance if any man shall read it."

Underneath there was a line written in darker ink, and in quite a different handwriting. It was dated fifteen years later, and the initials R.D. were appended to it:

"It is not dead. I do not think that it will ever die."

When Andrew Guerdon had finished reading this document, he looked slowly round the room. The subject had got on his nerves, and he was almost expecting to see something. Then he did his best to pull himself together. The first question he put to himself was this: "Has Ted ever seen this?" Obviously he had not. If he had, he could not have taken the tradition of Hal's Planting so lightly, nor have spoken of it so freely. Besides, he would either have mentioned the document to Guerdon, or he would have kept it carefully concealed. He would not have allowed him to come across it casually in that way. "Ted must never see it," thought Guerdon to himself. He then remembered the pile of weeds he had seen burning in the garden, He put the parchment in his pocket, and hurried out. There was no one about. He spread the parchment on the top of the pile, and waited until it was entirely consumed. Then he went back to the smoking-room; he felt easier now.

"Yes," thought Guerdon, "if Ted had first of all heard of the finding of that body, and then had read that document, I believe that he would have gone mad. Things that come near us affect us deeply."

Guerdon himself was much moved. He clung steadily to reason; he felt himself able to give a natural explanation all through, and yet he was nervous. The net of coincidence had closed in around him; the mention in Sir Edric's confession of the prophecy which had subsequently become traditional in the village alarmed him. And what did that last line mean? He supposed that R.D. must be the initials of Dr. Dennison. What did he mean by saying that the thing was not dead? Did he mean that it had not really been killed, that it had been gifted with some preternatural strength and vitality and had survived, though Sir Edric did not know it? He recalled what he had said about the prolongation of the lives of such things. If it still survived, why had it never been seen? Had it joined to the wild hardiness of the beast a cunning that was human—or more than human? How could it have lived? There was water in the caves, he reflected, and food could have been secured—a wild beast's food. Or did Dr. Dennison mean that though the thing itself was dead, its wraith survived and haunted the place? He wondered how the doctor had found Sir Edric's confession, and why he had written that line at the end of it. As he sat thinking, a low rumble of thunder in the distance startled him. He felt a touch of panic—a sudden impulse to leave Mansteth at once and, if possible, to take Ted with him. Ray could never live there. He went over the whole thing in his mind again and again, at one time calm and argumentative about it, and at another shaken by blind horror.

Sir Edric, on his return from Challonsea a few minutes afterwards, came straight to the smoking-room where Guerdon was. He looked tired and depressed. He began to speak at once:

"You needn't tell me about it—about John Marsh. I heard about it in the village."

"Did you? It's a painful occurrence, although, of course—"

"Stop. Don't go into it. Anything can be explained—I know that."

"I went through those papers and account-books while you were away. Most of them may just as well be destroyed; but there are a few—I put them aside there—which might be kept. There was nothing of any interest."

"Thanks; I'm much obliged to you."

"Oh, and look here, I've got an idea. I've been examining the plans of the house, and I'm coming round to your opinion. There are some alterations which should be made, and yet I'm afraid that they'd make the place look patched and renovated. It wouldn't be a bad thing to know what Ray thought about it."

"That's impossible. The workmen come on Monday, and we can't consult her before then. Besides, I have a general notion what she would like."

"We could catch the night express to town at Challonsea, and—"

Sir Edric rose from his seat angrily and hit the table.

"Good God! don't sit there hunting up excuses to cover my cowardice, and making it easy for me to bolt. What do you suppose the villagers would say, and what would my own servants say, if I ran away to-night? I am a coward—I know it. I'm horribly afraid. But I'm not going to act like a coward if I can help it."

"Now, my dear chap, don't excite yourself. If you are going to care at all—to care as much as the conventional damn—for what people say, you'll have no peace in life. And I don't believe you're afraid. What are you afraid of?"

Sir Edric paced once or twice up and down the room, and then sat down again before replying.

"Look here, Andrew, I'll make a clean breast of it. I've always laughed at the tradition; I forced myself, as it seemed at least, to disprove it by spending a night in Hal's Planting; I took the pains even to make a theory which would account for its origin. All the time I had a sneaking, stifled belief in it. With the help of my reason I crushed that; but now my reason has thrown up the job, and I'm afraid. I'm afraid of the Undying Thing that is in Hal's Planting. I heard it that night. John Marsh saw it last night—they took me to see the body, and the face was awful; and I believe that one day it will come from Hal's Planting—"

"Yes," interrupted Guerdon, "I know. And at present I believe as much. Last night we laughed at the whole thing, and we shall live to laugh at it again, and be ashamed of ourselves for a couple of superstitious old women. I fancy that beliefs are affected by weather—there's thunder in the air."

"No," said Sir Edric, "my belief has come to stay."

"And what are you going to do?"

"I'm going to test it. On Monday I can begin to get to work, and then I'll blow up Hal's Planting with dynamite. After that we shan't need to believe—we shall know. And now let's dismiss the subject. Come down into the billiard-room and have a game. Until Monday I won't think of the thing again."

Long before dinner, Sir Edric's depression seemed to have completely vanished. At dinner he was boisterous and amused. Afterwards he told stories and was interesting.

It was late at night; the terrific storm that was raging outside had awoke Guerdon from sleep. Hopeless of getting to sleep again, he had arisen and dressed, and now sat in the window-seat watching the storm. He had never seen anything like it before; and every now and then the sky seemed to be torn across as if by hands of white fire. Suddenly he heard a tap at his door, and looked round. Sir Edric had already entered; he also had dressed. He spoke in a curious, subdued voice.

"I thought you wouldn't be able to sleep through this. Do you remember that I shut and fastened the dining-room window?"

"Yes, I remember it."

"Well, come in here."

Sir Edric led the way to his room, which was immediately over the dining-room. By leaning out of window they could see that the dining-room window was open wide.

"Burglar," said Guerdon meditatively.

"No," Sir Edric answered, still speaking in a hushed voice. "It is the Undying Thing—it has come for me."

He snatched up the candle, and made towards the staircase; Guerdon caught up the loaded revolver which always lay on the table beside Sir Edric's bed and followed him. Both men ran down the staircase as though there were not another moment to lose. Sir

Edric rushed at the dining-room door, opened it a little, and looked in. Then he turned to Guerdon, who was just behind him.

"Go back to your room," he said authoritatively.

"I won't," said Guerdon. "Why? What is it?"

Suddenly the corners of Sir Edric's mouth shot outward into the hideous grin of terror.

"It's there! It's there!" he gasped.

"Then I come in with you."

"Go back!"

With a sudden movement, Sir Edric thrust Guerdon away from the door, and then, quick as light, darted in, and locked the door behind him.

Guerdon bent down and listened. He heard Sir Edric say in a firm voice:

"Who are you? What are you?"

Then followed a heavy, snorting breathing, a low, vibrating growl, an awful cry, a scuffle.

Then Guerdon flung himself at the door. He kicked at the lock, but it would not give way. At last he fired his revolver at it. Then he managed to force his way into the room. It was perfectly empty. Overhead he could hear footsteps; the noise had awakened the servants; they were standing, tremulous, on the upper landing.

Through the open window access to the garden was easy. Guerdon did not wait to get help; and in all probability none of the servants could have been persuaded to come with him. He climbed out alone, and, as if by some blind impulse, started to run as hard as he could in the direction of Hal's Planting. He knew that Sir Edric would be found there.

But when he got within a hundred yards of the plantation, he stopped. There had been a great flash of lightning, and he saw that it had struck one of the trees. Flames darted about the plantation as the dry bracken caught. Suddenly, in the light of another flash, he saw the whole of the trees fling their heads upwards; then came a deafening crash, and the ground slipped under him, and he was flung forward on his face. The plantation had collapsed, fallen through into the caves beneath it. Guerdon slowly regained his feet; he was surprised to find that he was unhurt. He walked on a few steps, and then fell again; this time he had fainted away.

THE GRAY CAT

I heard this story from Archdeacon M —. I should imagine that it would not be very difficult, by trimming it a little and altering the facts here and there, to make it capable of some simple explanation; but I have preferred to tell it as it was told to me.

After all, there is some explanation possible, even if there is not one definite and simple explanation clearly indicated. It must rest with the reader whether he will prefer to believe that some of the so-called uncivilized races may possess occult powers transcending anything of which the so-called civilized are capable, or whether he will consider that a series of coincidences is sufficient to account for the extraordinary incidents which, in a plain brief way, I am about to relate. It does not seem to me essential to state which view I hold myself, or if I hold neither, and have reasons for not stating a third possible explanation. I must add a word or two with regard to Archdeacon M. At the time of this story he was in his fiftieth year. He was a fine scholar, a man of considerable learning. His religious views were remarkably broad; his enemies said remarkably thin. In his younger days he had been something of an athlete, but owing to age, sedentary habits, and some amount of self-indulgence, he had grown stout, and no longer took exercise in any form. He had no nervous trouble of any kind. His death, from heart disease, took place about three years ago. He told me the story twice, at my request; there was an interval of about six weeks between the two narrations; some of the details were elicited by questions of my own. With this preliminary note, we may proceed to the story.

In January, 1881, Archdeacon M —, who was a great admirer of Tennyson's poetry, came up to London for a few days, chiefly in order to witness the performance of "The Cup," at the Lyceum. He was not present on the first night (Monday, January 3), but on a later night in the same week. At that time, of course, the poet had not received his peerage, nor the actor his knighthood.

On leaving the theatre, less satisfied with the play than with the magnificence of the setting, the Archdeacon found some slight difficulty in getting a cab. He walked a little way down the Strand to find one, when he encountered unexpectedly his old friend, Guy Breddon.

Breddon (that was not his real name) was a man of considerable fortune, a member of the learned societies, and devoted to Central African exploration. He was two or three years younger than the Archdeacon, and a man of tremendous physique.

Breddon was surprised to find the Archdeacon in London, and the Archdeacon was equally surprised to find Breddon in England at all. Breddon carried off the Archdeacon with him to his rooms, and sent a servant in a cab to the Langham to pay the Archdeacon's bill and fetch his luggage. The Archdeacon protested, but faintly, and Breddon would not hear of his hospitality being refused.

Breddon's rooms were an expensive suite immediately over a ruinous upholsterer's in a street off Berkeley Square. There was a private street-door, and from it a private staircase to the first and second floors.

The suite of rooms on the first floor, occupied by Breddon, was entirely shut off from the staircase by a door. The second floor suite, tenanted by an Irish M. P., was similarly shut off, and at that time was unoccupied.

Breddon and the Archdeacon passed through the street-door and up the stairs to the first landing, from whence, by the staircase-door, they entered the flat. Breddon had only recently taken the flat, and the Archdeacon had never been there before. It consisted of a broad L-shaped passage with rooms opening into it. There were many trophies on the walls. Horned heads glared at them; stealthy but stuffed beasts watched them furtively from under tables. There was a perfect arsenal of murderous weapons gleaming brightly under the shaded gaslights.

Breddon's servant prepared supper for them before leaving for the Langham, and soon the two men were discussing Mr. Tennyson, Mr. Irving, and a parody of the "Queen of the May" which had recently appeared in *Punch*, and doing justice to some oysters, a cold pheasant with an excellent salad, and a bottle of '74 Pommery. It was characteristic of the Archdeacon that he remembered exactly the items of the supper, and that Breddon rather neglected the wine.

After supper they passed into the library, where a bright fire was burning. The Archdeacon walked towards the fire, rubbing his plump hands together. As he did so, a portion of the great rug of gray fur on which he was standing seemed to rise up. It was a gray cat of enormous size, larger than any that the Archdeacon had ever seen before, and of the same colour as the rug on which it had been sleeping. It rubbed itself affectionately against the Archdeacon's leg, and purred as he bent down to stroke it.

"What an extraordinary animal!" said the Archdeacon. "I had no idea cats could grow to this size. Its head's queer, too—so much too small for the body."

"Yes," said Breddon, "and his feet are just as much too big."

The gray cat stretched himself voluptuously under the Archdeacon's caressing hand, and the feet could be seen plainly. They were very broad, and the claws, which shot out, seemed unusually powerful and well developed. The beast's coat was short, thick, and wiry.

"Most extraordinary!" the Archdeacon repeated.

He lowered himself into a comfortable chair by the fire. He was still bending over the cat and playing with it when a slight chink made him look up. Breddon was putting something down on the table behind the liquor decanters.

"Any particular breed?" the Archdeacon asked.

"Not that I know of. Freakish, I should say. We found him on board the boat when I left for home—may have come there after mice. He'd have been thrown overboard but for me. I got rather interested in him. Smoke?"

"Oh, thank you."

Outside a cold north wind screamed in quick gusts. Within came the sharp scratch of the match on the ribbed glass as the Archdeacon lit his cigar, the bubble of the rose-water in Breddon's hookah, the soft step of Breddon's man carrying the Archdeacon's luggage into the bedroom at the end of the L-shaped passage, and the constant purring of the big gray cat.

"And what's the cat's name?" the Archdeacon asked.

Breddon laughed.

"Well, if you must have the plain truth, he's called Gray Devil—or, more frequently, Devil *tout court*."

"Really, now, really, you can't expect an Archdeacon to use such abominable language. I shall call him Gray—or perhaps Mr. Gray would be more respectful, seeing the shortness of our acquaintance. Do you object to the smell of smoke, Mr. Gray? The intelligent beast does not object. Probably you've accustomed him to it."

"Well, seeing what his name is he could hardly object to smoke, could he?"

Breddon's servant entered. As the door opened and shut, one heard for a moment the crackle of the newly-lit fire in the room that awaited the Archdeacon. The servant swept up the hearth, and, under Archidiaconal direction, mixed a lengthy brandy-and-soda. He retired with the information that he would not be wanted again that night.

"Did you notice," asked the Archdeacon, "the way Mr. Gray followed your man about? I never saw a more affectionate cat."

"Think so?" said Breddon. "Watch this time."

For the first time he approached the gray cat, and stretched out his hand as if to pet him. In an instant the cat seemed to have gone mad. Its claws shot out, its back hooped, its coat bristled, its tail stood erect; it cursed and spat, and its small green eyes glared. But a close observer would have noticed that all the time it watched not only Breddon, but also that object which had chinked as Breddon had put it down behind the decanters.

The Archdeacon lay back in his chair and laughed heartily.

"What funny creatures they are, and never so funny as when they lose their tempers! Really, Mr. Gray, out of respect to my cloth, you might have refrained from swearing like that. Poor Mr. Gray! Poor puss!"

Breddon resumed his seat with a grim smile. The gray cat slowly subsided, and then thrust its head, as though demanding sympathy, into the fat palm of the Archdeacon's dependent hand.

Suddenly the Archdeacon's eye lighted on the object which the cat had been watching, visible now that the servant had displaced the decanters.

"Goodness me!" he exclaimed, "you've got a revolver there."

"That is so," said Breddon.

"Not loaded, I trust?"

"Oh yes, fully loaded."

"But isn't that very dangerous?"

"Well, no; I'm used to these things, and I'm not careless with them. I should have thought it more dangerous to have introduced Gray Devil to you without it. He's much more powerful than an ordinary cat, and I fancy there's something beside cat in his pedigree. When I bring a stranger to see him I keep the cat covered with the revolver until I see how the land lies. To do the brute justice, he has always been most friendly with everybody except myself. I'm his only antipathy. He'd have gone for me just now but that he's smart enough to be afraid of this."

He tapped the revolver.

"I see," said the Archdeacon seriously, "and can guess how it happened. You scared him one day by firing the revolver for joke; the report frightened him, and he's never forgiven you or forgotten the revolver. Wonderful memory some of these animals have!"

"Yes," said Breddon, "but that guess won't do. I have never, intentionally or by chance, given the 'Devil' any reason for his enmity. So far as I know he has never heard a firearm, and certainly he has never heard one since I made his acquaintance. Somebody may have scared him before, and I'm inclined to think that somebody did, for there can be no doubt that the brute knows all that a cat need know about a revolver, and that he's scared of it.

"The first time we met was almost in darkness. I'd got some cases that I was particular about, and the captain had said I could go down to look after them. Well, this beast suddenly came out of a lump of black and flew at me. I didn't even recognise that it was a cat, because he's so mighty big. I fetched him a clip on the side of the head that knocked him off, and whipped out my iron. He was away in a streak. He knew. And I've had plenty of proof since that he knows. He'd bite me now if he had the chance, but he understands that he hasn't got the chance. I'm often half inclined to take him on plain—shooting barred—and to feel my own hands breaking his damned neck!"

"Really, old man, really!" said the Archdeacon in perfunctory protest, as he rose and mixed himself another drink.

"Sorry to use strong language, but I don't love that cat, you know."

The Archdeacon expressed his surprise that in that case Breddon did not get rid of the brute.

"You come across him on board ship and he flies at you. You save his life, give him board and lodging, and he still hates you so much that he won't let you touch him, and you are no fonder of him than he is of you. Why don't you part company?"

"As for his board, I've rarely known him to eat anything except his own kill. He goes out hunting every night. I keep him simply and solely because I'm afraid of him. As long as I can keep him I know my nerves are all right. If I let my funk of him make any difference—well, I shouldn't be much good in a Central African forest. At first I had some idea of taming him—and, besides, there was a queer coincidence."

He rose and opened the window, and Gray Devil slowly slunk up to it. He paused a few moments on the window-sill and then suddenly sprang and vanished.

"What was the coincidence?"

"What do you think of that?" Breddon handed the Archdeacon a figure of a cat which he had taken from the mantelpiece. It was a little thing about three inches high. In colour, in the small head, enormous feet, and curiously human eyes, it seemed an exact reproduction of Gray Devil.

"A perfect likeness. How did you get it made?"

"I got the likeness before I got the original. A little Jew dealer sold it me the night before I left for England. He thought it was Egyptian, and described it as an idol. Anyhow, it was a niceish piece of jade."

"I always thought jade was bright green."

"It may be—or white—or brown. It varies. I don't think there can be any doubt that this little figure is old, though I doubt if it's Egyptian."

Breddon put it back in its place.

"By the way, that same night the little Jew came to try and buy it back again. He offered me twice what I had given for it. I said he must have found somebody who was pretty keen on it. I asked if it was a collector. The Jew thought not; said it was a coloured gentleman. Well, that finished it. I wasn't going to do anything to oblige a nigger. The Jew pleaded that it was a particularly fine buck-nigger, with mountains of money, who'd been tracking the thing for years, and hinted at all manner of mumbo-jumbo business—to scare me, I suppose. However, I wouldn't listen, and kicked him out. Then came the coincidence. Having bought the likeness, next day I found the living original. Rum, wasn't it?"

At this moment the clock struck, and the Archdeacon recognised with horror that it was very, very much past the time when respectable Archdeacons should be in bed and asleep. He rose and said goodnight, observing that he'd like to hear more about it on the morrow.

This was extremely unfortunate, for it will be seen it is just at this part of the story that one wants full details, and on the morrow it became impossible to elicit them.

Before leaving the library Breddon closed the window, and the Archdeacon asked how "Mr. Gray," as he called him, would get back.

"Very likely he's back already. He's got a special window in the kitchen, made on purpose, just big enough to let him get in and out as he likes."

"But don't other cats get in, too?"

"No," said Breddon. "Other cats avoid Gray Devil."

The Archdeacon found himself unaccountably nervous when he got to his room. He owned to me that he had to satisfy himself that there was no one concealed under the bed or in the wardrobe. However, he got into bed, and after a little while fell into a deep sleep; his fire was burning brightly, and the room was quite light.

Shortly after four he was awakened by a loud scream. Still sleepy, he did not for the moment locate the sound, thinking that it must have come from the street outside. But almost immediately afterwards he heard the report of a revolver fired twice in quick succession, and then, after a short pause, a third time.

The Archdeacon was terribly frightened. He did not know what had happened, and thought of armed burglars. For a time—he did not think it could have been more than a minute—fear held him motionless. Then with an effort he rose, lit the gas, and hurried on his clothes. As he was dressing, he heard a step down the passage and a knock at his door.

He opened it, and found Breddon's servant. The man had put on a blue overcoat over his night-things, and wore slippers. He was shivering with cold and terror.

"Oh, my God, sir!" he exclaimed, "Mr. Breddon's shot himself. Would you come, sir?"

The Archdeacon followed the man to Breddon's bedroom. The smoke still hung thickly in the room. A mirror had been smashed, and lay in fragments on the floor. On the bed, with his back to the Archdeacon, lay Breddon, dead. His right hand still grasped the revolver, and there was a blackened wound behind the right ear.

When the Archdeacon came round to look at the face he turned faint, and the servant took him out into the library and gave him brandy, the glasses and decanters still standing there. Breddon's face certainly had looked very ghastly; it had been scratched, torn and bitten; one eye was gone, and the whole face was covered with blood.

"Do you think it was that brute did it?"

"Sure of it, sir; sprang on his face while he was asleep. I knew it would happen one of these nights. He knew it too; always slept with the revolver by his side. He fired twice at the brute, but couldn't see for the blood. Then he killed himself

It seemed likely enough, with his eyesight gone, horribly mauled, in an agony of pain, possibly believing that he was saving himself from a death still more horrible, Breddon might very well have turned the weapon on himself.

"What do we do now?" the man asked.

"We must get a doctor and fetch the police at once. Come on."

As they turned the corner of the passage, they saw that the door communicating with the staircase was open.

"Did you open that door?" asked the Archdeacon.

"No," said the man, aghast.

"Then who did?"

"Don't know, sir. Looks as if we weren't at the end of this yet."

They passed down the stairs together, and found the street-door also ajar. On the pavement outside lay a policeman slowly recovering consciousness. Breddon's man took the policeman's whistle and blew it. A passing hansom, going back to the mews, slowed up; the cab was sent to fetch a doctor, and communication with the police-station rapidly followed.

The injured policeman told a curious story. He was passing the house when he heard shots fired. Almost immediately afterwards he heard the bolts of the front-door being drawn, and stepped back into the neighbouring doorway. The front-door opened, and a negro emerged clad in a gray tweed suit with a gray overcoat. The police-man jumped out, and without a second's hesitation the black man felled him. "It was all done before you could think," was the policeman's phrase.

"What kind of negro?" asked the Archdeacon.

"A big man—stood over six foot, and black as coal. He never waited to be challenged; the moment he knew that he was seen he hit out."

The policeman was not a very intelligent fellow, and there was little more to be got out of him. He had heard the shots, seen the street-door open and the man in gray appear, and had been felled by a lightning blow before he had time to do anything.

The doctor, a plain, matter-of-fact little man, had no hesita-tion in saying that Breddon was dead, and must have died almost immediately. After the injuries received, respiration and heart-action must have ceased at once. He was explaining something which oozed from the dead man's ear, when the Archdeacon could stand it no longer, and staggered out into the library. There he found Breddon's servant, still in the blue overcoat, explaining to a policeman with a notebook that as far as he knew nothing was missing except a jade image or idol of a cat which formerly stood on the mantelpiece.

The cat known as "Gray Devil" was also missing, and, although a description of it was circulated in the public press, nothing was ever heard of it again. But gray fur was found in the clenched left hand of the dead man.

The inquest resulted in the customary verdict, and brought to light no new facts. But it may be as well to give what the police theory of the case was. According to the police the suicide took place much as Breddon's servant had supposed. Mad with pain and unable to bear the thought of his awful mutilation, Breddon had shot himself.

The story of the jade image, as far as it was known, was told at the inquest. The police held that this image was an idol, that some uncivilized tribe was much perturbed by the theft of it, and was ready to pay an enormously high price for its recovery. The negro was assumed to be aware of this, and to have determined to obtain possession of the idol by fair means or foul. Fair means failing, it was suggested that the negro followed Breddon to England, tracked him out, and on the night in question found some means to conceal himself in Breddon's flat. There it was assumed that he fell asleep, was awakened by the screams and the sound of the firing, and, being scared, caught up the jade image and made off. Realizing that the shots would have been heard outside, and that his departure at that moment would be considered extremely suspicious, he was ready as he opened the street-door to fell the first man that he saw. The temporary unconsciousness of the policeman gave him time to get away.

The theory sounds at first sight like the only possible theory. When the Archdeacon first told me the story, I tried to find out indirectly whether he accepted it. Finding him rather disposed to fence with my hints and suggestions, I put the question to him plainly and bluntly:

"Do you believe in the police theory?"

He hesitated, and then answered with complete frankness:

"No, most emphatically not."

"Why?" I asked; and he went over the evidence with me.

"In the first place, I do not believe that Breddon in the ordinary sense, committed suicide. No amount of physical pain would have made him even think of it. He had unending pluck. He would have taken the facial disfigurement and loss of sight as the chances of war, and would have done the best that could be done by a man with such awful disabilities. One must admit that he fired the fatal shot—the medical evidence on that point is too strong to be gainsaid—but he fired it under circumstances of supernatural horror of which we, thank God! know nothing."

"I'm naturally slow to admit supernatural explanation."

"Well, let's go on. What's this mysterious tribe the police talk about? I want to know where it lives and what its name is. It's wealthy enough to offer a huge reward; it must be of some importance. The negro managed to get in and secrete himself. How? Where? I know the flat, and that theory won't do. We don't even know that it was the negro who took that little image, though I believe it was. Anyhow, how did the negro get away at that hour of the morning absolutely unobserved? Negroes are not so common in London that they can walk about without being noticed; yet not one trace of him was ever found, and equally mysterious is the disappearance of the Gray Cat. It was such an extraordinary brute, and the description of it was so widely circulated that it would have seemed almost certain we should hear of it again. Well, we've not heard."

We discussed the police theory for some little time, and something which he happened to say led me to exclaim:

"Really! Do you mean to say that the Gray Cat actually was the negro?"

"No," he replied, "not exactly that, but something near it. Cats are strange animals, anyhow. I needn't remind you of their connection with certain old religions or with that witchcraft in which even in England to-day some still believe, and not so long ago almost all believed. I have never, by the way, seen a good explanation of the fact that there are people who cannot bear to be in a room with a cat, and are aware of its presence as if by some mysterious extra sense. Let me remind you of the belief which undoubtedly exists both in China and Japan, that evil spirits may enter into certain of the lower animals, the fox and badger especially. Every student of demonology knows about these things."

"But that idea of evil spirits taking possession of cats or foxes is surely a heathen superstition which you cannot hold."

"Well, I have read of the evil spirits that entered into the swine. Think it over, and keep an open mind."

COACHWHIP PUBLICATIONS

COACHWHIPBOOKS.COM

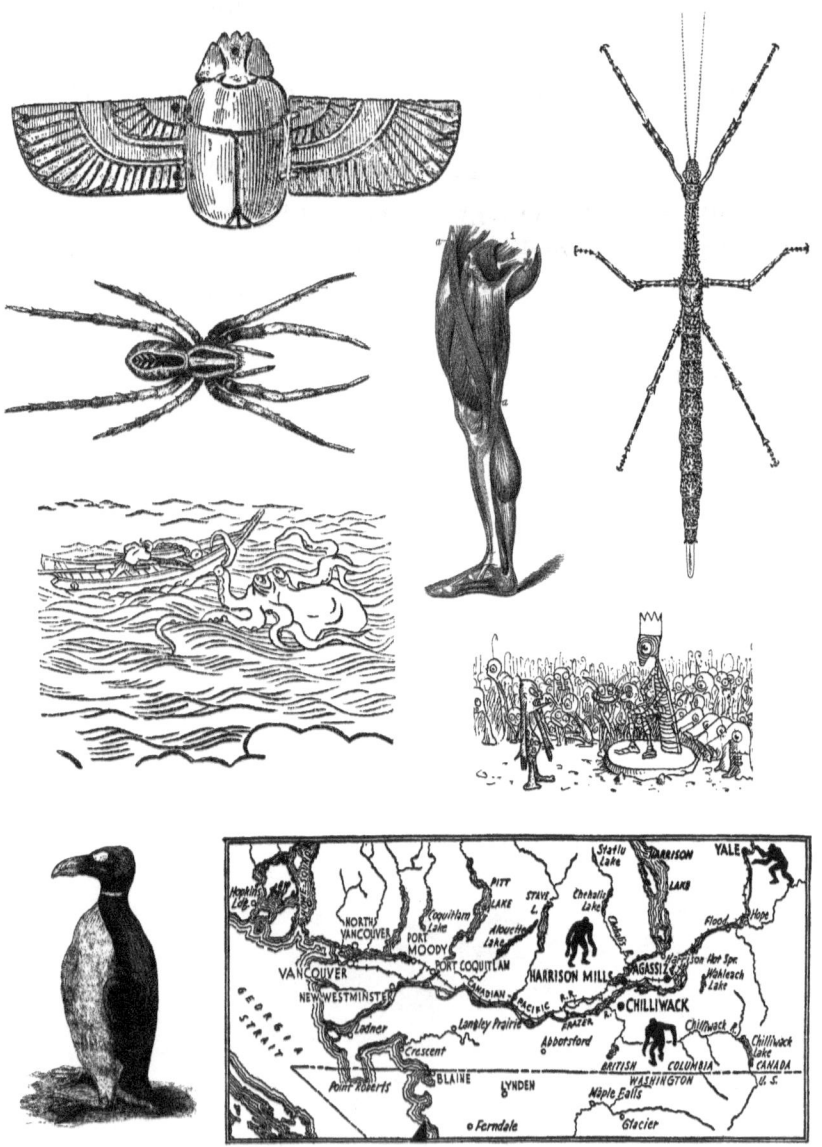

COACHWHIP PUBLICATIONS

COACHWHIPBOOKS.COM

Shadows Gothic and Grotesque
ISBN 1-61646-059-8

ANCIENT
HAUNTS

The Stoneground
Ghost Tales
by E. G. Swain

Tedious Brief Tales
of Granta and Gramarye
by Arthur Gray

Ancient Haunts:
Stoneground Ghost Tales / Tedious Brief Tales
ISBN 1-61646-005-9

STRANGE HAUNTS

STORIES BY
F. MARION CRAWFORD &
H. B. MARRIOTT WATSON

Strange Haunts:
F. Marion Crawford & H. B. Marriott Watson
ISBN 1-61646-091-1

COACHWHIP PUBLICATIONS

ALSO AVAILABLE

DANCING SHADOWS

TALES OF THE SUPERNATURAL
BY BERNARD CAPES

Dancing Shadows:
Tales of the Supernatural by Bernard Capes
ISBN 1-61646-093-8

Days of Doom:
Apocalyptic Visions & Unearthly Nightmares
ISBN 1-61646-110-1

www.ingramcontent.com/pod-product-compliance
Lightning Source LLC
Chambersburg PA
CBHW020947260626
47169CB00006B/1858